PRINCE OF LIES

LUCY LENNOX

LENNOX

romance with humor, heart, and heat

Cover Art: Natasha Snow Designs
Editing: One Love Editing
Proofreading: Victoria Rothenberg
Beta Reading: May Archer, Leslie Copeland, and Jodi Duggan

PRINCE OF LIES

Rowe Prince is many things.
Gorgeous? Yes.
Unintentionally hilarious? Absolutely.
The hottest, sunshiniest virgin to ever set foot in Manhattan? Oh, yeah.

One thing he's not, though, is a reclusive billionaire named Sterling Chase who supposedly founded *my* company. So when the man (literally) stumbles into a charity gala saying precisely that, I do what anyone would: I set out to prove he's a liar.

Except it turns out Rowe's ridiculous falsehoods are surprisingly... enchanting. The heart of gold beneath his borrowed tux makes even a jaded businessman like me start to believe in fairy tales. And there's no faking the heat between us when the man's in my bed.

But when it turns out Rowe's lies conceal a secret that threatens the company I've spent years building, I have to choose: say goodbye to the sweet pretender I'm falling for, or risk everything for a man who just might be... the prince of lies.

ONE

ROWE

"Please don't make me wear the sombrero, dude. The mustache is bad enough."

I gave my cousin a no-nonsense look that I hoped was visible in the dim light of the alley. "The sombrero is mandatory, Joey. I know it's a pain in the ass, but you have to do it right, or Lea will fire me, and I very much need this job. And don't forget, you need to strum the tiny guitar and sing the song after you hand over the food, too. *My name is Burrito Bandito...*"

Joey watched my demonstration in dismay. "I forgot about the song. *Shit.* Do I really have to do the little toe-kick thing?"

"Technically, the toe-kick was my invention," I admitted. I stripped off my Burrito Bandito T-shirt and handed it over, exchanging it for the slightly wrinkled tuxedo shirt Joey pulled out of a shopping bag. "But if you're gonna do a thing, you've gotta commit, you know? And it's increased my tips by twenty percent, so it's worth a little embarrassment."

"Fine," he groaned. "*Fine.* The things I do for you, Rowe Prince."

"And I appreciate them," I assured him fervently. "All of them." I waved a hand in the air, encompassing the sombrero and mustache, the tuxedo in the bag, the dumpster we were crouched behind, and the glittering lights of the Museum of Modern Art beyond. "Letting me crash at your place for weeks, figuring out a way for me to get into this fundraising gala, taking over the rest of my Burrito Bandito shift... I don't know what I'd do without you."

"Yeah, alright, okay," Joey mumbled. He patted my shoulder awkwardly. "I, like, support you and shit. You know that. We don't need to talk about it."

I laughed a little despite my nerve-induced nausea.

"Now, shake a leg and get in there before the whole damn party is over. Here." He snagged a black bow tie from the bag. "Put that on. And you got your ticket, right? 'Cause I only managed to snag *one* from my boss's office before they were mailed out."

"No, I know. It's in my pocket— Uh, wait." I blinked down at the silky fabric of the tie in the dim light. "Joey, are there rabbits embroidered on this tie?"

"You said you needed a tux, so I brought you the magician costume I wear at kids' birthday parties." He beamed proudly. "Pays to have a cousin who works in the catering and event entertainment business, eh?"

"Joey," I moaned. "I'm supposed to look like I belong in there. The goal is to impress Justin Hardy enough to get a meeting so I can pitch him my project. I don't know if frolicking rabbits give off a '*take me seriously*' aesthetic."

"Not everybody cares about aesthetics the way you do, Mr. Second-Hand Bougie." Joey grabbed the fabric from my hands and draped it around my neck. "Your other choice was the tux I wear when I'm dancing at bachelorette parties, and believe me, the shit embroidered on that one would definitely send the wrong message." He knotted the tie around my neck in record time—clearly, he'd worked a *lot* of bachelorette parties—and stood back to admire his work. "Besides, nobody's gonna notice they're rabbits unless they're all up in your personal space. And who are you planning on getting that cozy with at the freakin' Coalition for Children fancypants gala?" He pulled the tuxedo jacket from the bag and held it up so I could slide my arms into the sleeves. "You're gonna be fine if you just chill. And remember, beggars can't be choosers."

I blew out a long, shaky breath. Joey was right. I'd scoured the racks at the local Second Chance Savers but hadn't found a single cast-off tuxedo, and my wallet was so empty I couldn't afford to rent one. His loaner was my only shot at being able to blend in at this event. I just needed to calm down and get on with it.

"So, this ticket..." I pulled the crumpled card stock from my pocket, where I'd tucked it right next to the lucky tattoo on my hip. "Do we know whose it is? The front of the envelope doesn't have a person's name. It only says *Sterling Chase*—which is a company."

"Ironic, huh? Considering Sterling Chase shot you down when you asked them for a pitch meeting? Serves the fuckers right." He grinned slyly. "You'll go in as one of them, then score a meeting with Hardy Development, their biggest competitor. It's... whajamacallit. Poetic justice."

"Is it, though? I mean, yeah, it sucked when Sterling Chase turned me down," I admitted. "I'd thought the Trauma Communication Protocol would be a perfect fit there—"

"Stupid name for your project," Joey scoffed. "I liked the old name better."

So did I.

"*Project Daisy Chain* doesn't sound professional, so I'm trying to come up with a new one." I tugged at my collar. "Gotta appear as professional as possible since I don't have a fancy degree or personal recommendation to make me sound legit. Sterling Chase was only one of the sixteen companies that rejected me without a second look."

"Yeah, but they were the one with the shittiest 'fuck off' letter."

"Well... true."

"What if the invitation was for Sterling Chase, the founder of the company himself? *Heh.* Wouldn't that be killer?" Joey straightened the cuffs of my jacket.

"Uh... no." Low-key panic blossomed in my chest, making breathing tricky. "That would be a *disaster*. Is there even a person named Sterling Chase? I've never seen him mentioned in any articles."

Joey shrugged. "Dude, I'm a cater-waiter. My boss didn't exactly discuss the guest list with me. But I thought I heard somewhere that Sterling Chase was the guy who started the Sterling Chase company. You know, like Justin Hardy started Hardy Development, and Grey Blackwood founded Blackwood Holdings, and Walt Disney created Disney World, and Chef Boyardee invented ravioli?"

I blinked. At least one of those things was factually inaccurate, but that didn't mean Joey was entirely wrong.

Before I'd sent out my meeting request, I'd done some research on Sterling Chase. The company was owned by a bunch of smaller businesses, which was pretty common, fronted by a CEO named Clarissa Comfrey and a head of development named Austin Purcell, and overseen by a five-person board of directors. Their first major deal had been packaging and selling a piece of software with the unassuming name of ETC—Emergency Traffic Control—which Sterling Chase had sold for multiple billions of dollars. As a company, they were committed to diversity and philanthropy. Their headquarters was praised by environmental groups for being a green space. Their projects consistently won awards for technological innovation. Blah, blah, blah.

I hadn't seen a single thing about who'd founded the business, though... and in retrospect, that seemed odd. Was it possible there was a reclusive billionaire out there pulling the strings?

"Why would someone hide their involvement in a hugely successful company, though?" I wondered out loud. "That would be weird. Wouldn't there be *some* reference to the guy on the internet? A picture or a bio—"

"Shit, Rowe, who knows why rich people do the wacky things they do, especially if they're genius types? Maybe Mr. Chase just doesn't want his picture to be public, so he flies under the radar. Maybe he's like Batman. Or the Wizard of Oz."

Huh. "I guess," I said slowly. But if that was the case, then... "Joey," I demanded, high-key panicked now. "You stole me *Sterling Chase's* invitation?"

"Guess so?" Joey appeared utterly unconcerned. "Dude, *chill*. If you've never seen a picture of Sterling Chase, these bozos haven't, either," he said reasonably. "Besides, this shindig is invite-only, and if you've got Sterling's, you know you're not gonna run into the man himself in there."

"Oh, shit." I clutched my stomach. "I'm gonna be sick."

Joey gave my tie a final tweak. "You're not. Just lay low, find Justin Hardy, make your pitch, get your meeting, and leave before anyone realizes who you really are so neither of us gets in trouble." He grabbed my chin firmly. "No freaking out."

I whimpered slightly, and Joey shook his head. "You're *so* freaking out."

I spread my hands helplessly. "It's just... It's hard enough for me to walk in there and pretend to belong among a bunch of rich people. It's another thing if I have to impersonate an actual billionaire. What if someone asks me a question? I'm the worst liar ever, Joey. You know this. Remember your mom's fiftieth birthday? She asked me point-blank if there was going to be a surprise party, and of course I said *no*... then I got so stressed about lying I broke out in hives and ended up in the ER."

"Shit, yeah." Joey winced. "Never knew a person's entire face could swell like that."

"And the summer we all vacationed on the lake, remember how you told me to pretend I couldn't swim so the cute lifeguard would save me... but I got so flustered I *actually* forgot how to swim?"

Joey scratched the back of his neck. "Now that you mention it, that ended in the ER, too, didn't it?"

"Yes! In fact, the Venn diagram of Rowe Prince's Lies and Rowe Prince's Injuries is practically a circle. It ends in misery every time."

"Okay, so don't think of it as lying," Joey said firmly. He smoothed down my curly hair, which was probably getting unruly, thanks to the humidity. "Think of it as... upcycling. Like what you did with that old-as-fuck dresser you got your mom at Goodwill. Underneath, you're still *Rowe* with, like, good bones and shit. But for tonight, you're sanded and painted and with better hardware." He tweaked my tie. "Or go for the fairy-tale thing—you're like Cinderella getting all dressed up for the ball, and I'm your fairy godmother. For tonight, you're not Rowe Prince. You're Sterling Chase, a quirky rich guy. And betcha you'll be more charming than the real Sterling ever could be."

A warm breeze blew trash-scented air across the alley, and it seemed like a heck of a stretch to apply interior design concepts *or* fairy tales to this scenario.

"Rowe," Joey said firmly, "if there's one thing I've learned from working parties and events all these years, it's that when you're hanging with rich folks, you've gotta *own* it. Walk with brass balls. Believe that you belong, and you will. Don't act like you're here begging for a chance—act like you're offering them an opportunity. And definitely don't do that babbling thing you do when you're nervous."

I scowled. I did not babble.

"Most important, remember *why* you're here." His eyes bored into mine. "You've been pouring your blood, sweat, and tears into Project Daisy Chain. You've sacrificed your money and time, the career you could have had... your freakin' dignity." He twirled the sombrero in the air. "And you didn't do all that shit so you could freak out when your goal was in reach." He shook my shoulders lightly. "You said emailing people to ask for a meeting wasn't working. You said you needed to make a personal connection first. Right?"

"Well, yeah—"

"Okay. So you're gonna take that rabbit bow tie and that magician tux, you're gonna go in there, and you're gonna make shit happen. Hear me?"

"Yes." I straightened my shoulders. "I *will*."

"Fuck yeah, you will." Joey grinned suddenly and clapped a hand to my chest, right over the breast pocket of my tuxedo. "And whatever you do, don't pull this pocket square, okay? It's a pain in the ass to get it folded back up again." He shot me a wink, then jammed the sombrero on his head. "Check in later, cuz. I got burritos to deliver."

He wandered off down the alley, humming the Burrito Bandito song under his breath, and I shook my head. As much as Joey bitched and moaned about taking my shift, I knew I could trust him to do a good job at it. We'd grown up several states apart from each other—me in Indiana and him in New York—but our parents had instilled in us a strong work ethic and an even stronger sense of Prince family loyalty. Neither of us would let the other one down, especially if it involved our jobs.

And for all his goofiness, Joey was right. This was it. The chance I'd been waiting for. All the sleepless nights, all the dates I'd missed out on, all the years of research, all the soul-crushing form-letter rejections had led me here. Tonight, I was going to meet the head of Hardy Development in person, explain my idea—and the reason behind it—in a way Justin Hardy couldn't refuse, and convince him to help me make my dream a reality.

My hands were a little clammy, and I couldn't help but notice the tux I wore smelled like cotton candy and corn chips, but I was not going to let that stop me. I checked my breast pocket again for the business cards I'd shoved in there. Sure they were old-fashioned, but I couldn't think of another way to force my contact info on any good funding leads I might get tonight.

Walk confidently. Brass balls. You're Sterling Chase, Quirky Billionaire.

You belong.

I snuck around the pretentious red-carpet area, where photographers were snapping pictures of beautiful people, and made my way through the security area to the check-in table.

"Ticket?" the woman behind the table asked politely. Thankfully, the area around the reception table was so busy she barely noticed how crumpled my ticket was. She quickly exchanged it for a name tag that said Sterling Chase... exactly as Joey had predicted.

Damn it.

For the first time, it occurred to me that appearing with Sterling's name on my name tag might not be the best way to talk to Justin Hardy, his business rival.

"Uhh, actually." I swallowed. "Is there any way to get a name tag with a different name? Like, I dunno, let's say... Rowe?"

"Rowe." The lady blinked at me. "Sir, this ticket is in the name of Sterling Chase. Is it not your ticket?" Her eyes shifted to the security personnel standing nearby.

"I... I..." *What would Sterling Chase do?* I stuck my chin in the air and affected the most obnoxious rich-person accent I could muster. "Of course it's mine, my dear." I smiled winningly. "Yes, indeed! It's just that I like to..." I coughed lightly. "Play pranks on my friends! It's quite common amongst billionaires like myself. Sterling Chase is a notorious prankster. Ask anyone who knows him... er, *me.*"

The woman raised an eyebrow, and I felt a bead of sweat drip down the back of my neck.

"B-but obviously, it's no problem for me to simply... be Sterling Chase. Since I *am* Sterling Chase. So sorry to trouble you." I took my name tag and made a big show of affixing it to my pocket, then gave her a stiff bow. "I bid you good night, lovely lady."

I quickly walked past her, following the crowd dressed in millions of dollars of couture fashion.

Sweet fucking fuck. It was possible that Joey had a point about my nervous babbling.

"Bonjour, Mika, darling!" A woman nearby gave air-kisses to another woman before flashing perfect, bright-white teeth. "How long has it been? *Eons.* I haven't seen you since Joplin's wine tasting in SoHo."

I resisted the urge to rub my damp palms against my thighs, feeling immediately and hopelessly out of place. My magician's tux felt too tight despite being at least a size too big, and I doubted the name on my badge was the fakest thing in the room.

This glittering, champagne-bubble world was not one I'd ever dreamed of navigating, growing up in rural Indiana. In Linden, the richest family around were the Timmonses, who owned the local chicken operation, and Bucky Timmons hadn't put on airs despite his dad always driving a tricked-out Ford F-350 that was never more than three years old. The only things I knew about the ultra-wealthy came from reality TV and the grocery store tabloids my mother sometimes read.

Now here I was in New York City, trying to get my project funded before I ran out of money entirely, which meant connecting with people as disconnected from my reality as aliens from another planet. And, I noted, hardly any of them were wearing *their* name badges.

I ducked behind a "Support the Coalition for Children" sign propped on an easel, took a deep breath, and used my fingernail to remove my name badge—or tried to, anyway. The damn thing snagged on the shiny material of Joey's tux. The harder I tried to pick at it, the more it refused to budge, and I was afraid I'd end up destroying the tux if I kept trying.

My pits were noticeably wet by that point, my forehead damp with perspiration, which meant my curls were probably bouncing all over the place. I needed to find the man I was looking for before I ended up looking like a demented clown and smelling like something worse than Fritos.

I stood on tiptoe so I could peek over the sign to scan the crowd, but I didn't see anyone who looked like Justin Hardy's picture on his website because that would be too easy.

"You're not going to find the handsome billionaire by hiding in the corner, Prince," I grumbled to myself. "Get out there, pretend rich people aren't incredibly intimidating, and get this done." I tugged my tuxedo jacket down, set my shoulders back, and stepped out into the crowd of laughing socialites with an entirely put-upon confidence.

Immediately, someone bumped into me from behind like I was invisible, shoving me into the sign and setting it rocking on its flimsy stand. I grabbed it, terrified, but ended up knocking it off its perch and overbalancing myself at the same time. My foot came down on the sign—the slippery, *slippery* sign—and while my other foot dangled in the air, I sailed several feet across the black marble floor, only stopping when I managed to catch myself on a support pillar and duck into a shadowy alcove behind a potted fern.

"Good. Fucking. *Fuck*," I panic-panted, bending over with my hands on my thighs so I could catch my breath.

Lay low, Joey had said. *Be a quirky billionaire.* I wasn't sure skate-boarding across the shiny floors of the Museum of Modern Art on a charity poster was what he'd had in mind.

Who knew fundraising galas could be so damn dangerous? Who knew one human could be so freaking awkward?

I hadn't injured myself, though, so that was an improvement. I straightened up carefully and assessed the situation. No sprained muscles. No need to call an ambulance. Not even a rip in the tux. Best of all, no one in the crowd on the other side of the plant even seemed to have noticed, so I could still blend in—

"Impressive dismount," the deepest, sexiest voice I'd ever heard said from behind me, laughter lurking in every golden syllable. "But I'm afraid you're going to need to find your own potted plant to hide behind. This one's taken."

TWO

BASH

I was supposed to be climbing Mount Kinabalu this week.

I'd been prepared for some physical discomfort, for long days navigating unfamiliar terrain and communicating in a foreign language, but I relished the challenge and unpredictability of extreme adventures. Climbing icy peaks, diving out of airplanes, and rafting turbulent rivers pared a person's existence down to their most important qualities: intelligence, courage, strength of will. That was what made them fun.

Then I'd made the mistake of answering my mother's phone call.

One brief convo later—"*Sebastian, darling, the Dayne family has donated hundreds of thousands to the Coalition for Children over the years. Your father and I are in the South of France and can't possibly attend, but it wouldn't do for us to snub the organization at their largest annual fundraiser. Can't your trip wait?*"—my expedition to Borneo had somehow morphed into a world-class guilt trip.

Oh, there was still physical discomfort, alright, but in the form of a stuffy tuxedo. And there were communication challenges, too, like explaining (repeatedly) that I wasn't looking for a boyfriend, an amazing new investment opportunity, or to get anyone's kid a job at

Sterling Chase just because I happened to sit on the board of directors. My existence had been pared down to what was most important in *this* world: my bank balance and my connections... and it was the opposite of fun.

In fact, this gala was a fun wasteland, where everything was black and white, cold and flat, and nothing new or exciting ever happened.

As I stood in a small alcove off to the side of the MoMA's elegant reception room, trying to coax my brain cells back to life after a mind-numbing conversation with Constance Baxter-Hicks about her topiary garden, her eligible, gay nephew Patrick, how much Patrick loved topiaries, and how desperately she'd like us to grow topiaries *together*, I decided I'd reached the upper limit of my boredom tolerance. Since I wasn't leaving for Borneo, better to get some rest so I could focus on work in the morning.

I'd only taken a single step for the door when a man sailed across the polished floor directly in front of my hidden alcove, arms wind-milling wildly. His face—snub-nosed and freckled and sort of weirdly... *angelic*—was frozen in terror until he managed to grab a support column like a drowning sailor grabbing a life preserver and swing himself into the shadows directly in front of me, where he landed on his feet.

Well. *This* was different.

"Good. Fucking. *Fuck*," the man said succinctly and a bit breathlessly, bending over at the waist to catch his breath.

I resisted the sudden urge to laugh out loud. For someone who looked like he'd walked out of a Botticelli painting, he had a hell of a mouth on him... and the curve of the ass he was inadvertently displaying in his black pants wasn't bad, either.

"Impressive dismount," I said mildly, startling the angel into jumping nearly a foot. "But I'm afraid you're going to need to find your own potted plant to hide behind. This one's taken."

He gasped and spun toward me, and his face morphed into an expression not unlike a disgruntled kitten—adorable and cranky.

"You saw *nothing*," he informed me with a glare. "Now back off—

uh..." He hesitated as he belatedly looked me up and down, then from shoulder to shoulder. His eyes widened, and he wet his lips, seemingly unconsciously. "...please?"

A knot of anticipation coiled in my gut.

A stray curl chose that precise moment to flop directly in the center of his forehead, and I bit my cheek, torn between amusement and a burning desire to pull the man against me—

Whoa. No. Bad Sebastian.

Clearly, I'd had too much champagne because I did *not* hook up with strangers I met at fundraising galas. In fact, I'd rarely hooked up with anyone at all recently, and for very good reason.

But even knowing all that, I couldn't stop myself from returning the man's up-down look with a slow, appreciative appraisal of my own. Shiny brown curls, doe eyes, plush lips, fair skin. His tux was a size too big, but I could still see hints of the toned body it hid. And for the first time in a while, I felt a pulse of desire and challenge that reminded me a lot of the feeling I got when I prepared to scuba dive into a Mexican cenote or paraglide off a Turkish mountain.

Yes, this evening had definitely gotten considerably more interesting.

Still staring at me, the man swallowed and made a strangled noise, then swallowed some more, like he was experiencing a powerful reaction as well. Either that or going into anaphylactic shock.

"You alright?" I asked, concerned.

"Me? Oh, ha! No. Yes. *No.*" He clapped a hand to his mouth and stared at me in horror, like the words had babbled out against his will.

Curiouser and curiouser.

My lips twitched. "Enlightening. Thank you. Blink twice if whatever you have is life-threatening, three times if it's contagious, Mr...." Belatedly, I glanced down to read his name tag and froze. "Wait. Sterling Chase?" I lifted an eyebrow. "You work there?"

That idea doused the flames of attraction in an instant.

Sterling Chase was *my* company. My baby.

It had begun as a way for me and my four closest friends to market the software we'd come up with our senior year at Yale—the Emergency Traffic Control software—but had grown into a billion-dollar startup incubator that helped other technology developers bring their big ideas to market. It was the place where I spent most of my time and all of my energy.

If this delectable stranger worked for Sterling Chase, that made him utterly off-limits. But... I couldn't imagine how I could have failed to notice this man if he worked for me. He was nothing if not memorable.

Emotions flitted across his expressive face as he wrestled with the answer to what should have been a yes or no question. Fear. Nausea. Determination. He straightened his spine.

"*Work* there?" The man chuckled with excessive enthusiasm. "Ha! Do I *work* at Sterling Chase? No, my good man. No, indeed. I own the company." He tapped his name badge proudly. "I... I *am* Sterling Chase."

I blinked in disbelief. Beneath the freckles that dotted his nose and cheeks like a kaleidoscope of tiny butterflies, a blush of color crept across his face. A kind of nervous, excited, defiant energy rolled off him in waves... and no wonder. This Not-Sterling person was an angel-faced, sexy-as-fuck, lying *liar*. And he wasn't even attempting to be subtle about it.

Despite rumors to the contrary, there was no Sterling Chase. Not a human one anyway. In fact, as only maybe five other people on the planet knew, my friends and I had named the company after their college pets: Silas's iguana, Chase, and Zane's ridiculously hairy, pain-in-the-ass Peruvian guinea pig, Sterling.

But even as I stared at the man, waiting for him to back down or equivocate, Not-Sterling set his jaw, threw his shoulders back so forcefully his shirt buttons would have popped if the garment had fit properly, and attempted to look down his nose at me—no mean feat since I was six foot one, and he was at least six inches shorter.

Logic said I should contact security about this man immediately.

But a fun-starved corner of my brain reminded me that it had been a hell of a long time since I'd been so intrigued by anything—not by a scientific breakthrough, or an extreme adventure, or the men who occasionally warmed my bed. So when that part of me whispered that I should fuck with the man instead, I listened.

"Sterling Chase." I gave him a broad smile. "I must say, you're not at all how I pictured you."

"I bet." He coughed lightly. "I mean... I bet you imagined Sterling Chase was old and crotchety?" He nodded to himself. "And you probably thought since Sterling had more money than god, he'd be all high-and-mighty, too, but no. Sterling Chase is down-to-earth. One might even say... quirky. You know, the sort of billionaire who smells like corn chips on purpose."

Dear god.

I ran a hand over my mouth to hide the smile I couldn't restrain. "And I imagine talking about yourself in the third person is part of the quirkiness?"

"Er." His blush deepened, and he stuck a finger in his collar like his tie was suddenly tight. "Yes. Exactly."

My gaze narrowed on his collar and on the tie that ringed it. I leaned closer for a better look, inhaling the clean, soapy smell of him. "Pardon me, but are those... bunnies? That's very quirky indeed."

He clapped a hand to his throat, hiding his tie, and his face went even redder. "Er. Yes. Well. In fact, they're, ah, *Playboy* bunnies. You know, as in... *Hugh?*" He made it sound like he was name-dropping a close personal friend... who nobody had notified him died years ago. "They're on my socks also. Always match your socks to your tie, my grandfather used to say."

We both simultaneously looked down at his feet, where red-and-green Christmas socks protruded from his oxfords.

"I mean..." he stammered. "I mean, match your *underwear* to your bow tie."

"Your grandfather taught you to match your underwear to your bow tie," I repeated blandly. "How avant-garde. Was he a dancer, perhaps?"

Not-Sterling looked vaguely panicked... then captivatingly confused. But when any sane man would have shut his mouth, this man kept babbling himself into a deeper pit. "Uh. Yes. I believe he did foxtrot from time to time. Before the war."

"Fascinating," I said, shocked to find I meant it, not about his dancing grandfather but about the man himself.

Who *was* this guy with his strange babble, and his lies, and his overwhelming air of innocence?

All I knew was that when he darted a glance around the small space like he was planning his escape, I was determined to keep him talking.

"Well, Sterling." I stuck out a hand for him to shake. "I'm *Bash*. It's lovely to meet you in person at last."

Not-Sterling frowned. "Bash."

"Your new personal assistant, of course. We've been communicating by email for weeks. Don't you remem— Ah!" I wagged a playful finger at him. "I see what's happening here. You're teasing, aren't you?"

My lying angel's eyes went nearly as wide and panicked as when he'd sailed across the floor. "I... yes," he agreed faintly. "Ha! You caught me... Bash. Erm. Lovely to meet you in person."

He put his smaller hand in mine, and I gripped it tightly, my skin tingling at the warmth of him. Not-Sterling's breath caught.

"I must say, I didn't expect to meet you here tonight," I went on without releasing his hand. "You tend to avoid social gatherings. And I thought you were hiking Mount Kinabalu this week."

"Did you?" His eyes darted around the small space like a cornered animal, his voice so strangled I worried he wasn't getting enough oxygen.

"Wasn't that what your last email said?" I blinked at him innocently. "Two weeks in Borneo, during which you'd be out of communication? Did you decide to skip the last portion of the trip? Did something happen?"

He nodded slightly and then squeezed his eyes tightly shut. His pulse fluttered frantically against my fingers. For a moment, I was certain he was going to drop the pretense and confess that he wasn't who he'd claimed to be... but I was wrong.

"Yes, I... I'm afraid I can't talk about the trip, Bash. It's too, ah... too fresh. Too painful." He shook his head sadly. "Another of my quirky billionaire eccentricities. You understand."

Quirky billionaire eccentricities. This was going to be good.

"I'm your assistant, Mr. Chase," I said in a low tone, still holding him in place. "You can tell me anything."

"Oh." He leaned toward me like he was imparting a secret. I couldn't help but lean in also. "You see... I lost my true love on the side of Mount Kinababloo." He sighed gustily. "Poor Bubbles. I really... can't speak of it any more."

I shook my head. This man was a liar—an unrepentant liar—and I should have been—*was*—disgusted. I knew better than anyone on the planet that money attracted con artists, cheats, and opportunists the way nectar attracted bees, and I hated that kind of manipulation.

But Jesus, there was something about this man—maybe how innocently and *poorly* and entertainingly he lied—that got past my defenses. He was doing an impersonation of a rich person that should have been incredibly insulting but somehow managed to be endearing. And he made me want to see what he came up with next.

"How very tragic—" I began when a deep voice behind me called my name.

"Bash?"

I whipped my head around in surprise to find my friend Silas ducking around the potted plant. He froze in place when he saw that I wasn't alone and raised a single dark eyebrow at me when he saw Not-Sterling's hand in mine.

Shit.

I hadn't expected Silas to attend tonight. He wasn't based in New

York, and though he still served on the board of directors at Sterling Chase, he was also a sought-after business strategist who spent most of his time traveling around the world consulting with Fortune 500 companies and governmental agencies. Ordinarily, seeing one of my best friends would have been cause for celebration. At the moment, however, I was tempted to ask him to turn right the fuck around.

Silas was sensible. Calm. Rational. And I wasn't being any of those things at the moment.

"Am I interrupting something?" Silas asked. His voice was mild, but the accompanying look he gave me spoke volumes... most of it in italics with exclamation points.

"Of course not, *Mr. Concannon*." I widened my eyes meaningfully. "I didn't know you were coming tonight. Are you enjoying your evening, sir?"

Silas's head tilted to one side, a very clear *What game are we playing, Sebastian?*

I smiled winningly. *Go with it.*

"Oh, yes, it's been delightful," Silas said at length. "I'm on a mission to make sure every member of the Sterling Chase board of directors in attendance shakes the hand of at least fifty millionaires for networking purposes. I've done my part, but you'd be shocked at how many of them hide away or find themselves otherwise distracted at these events."

I nearly snorted. I'd been the only member of the board in attendance before Silas showed up, which meant Kenji, the personal assistant who ruled our lives, had sent Silas here to make sure I didn't cut out early or hide away.

It was uncomfortable to be known so well.

Silas glanced at Not-Sterling's hand in mine once again. "How's *your* evening, Bash?"

"Unbelievable." *Literally.* "I finally got to meet my boss after being his personal assistant for weeks and weeks." I drew a very reluctant Not-Sterling forward a few feet, presenting him to Silas. "Sterling Chase, this is Silas Concannon. Mr. Concannon, I'm sure you remember Sterling Chase? Since you're on the board of directors at *his* company?"

Silas blinked. He looked at me, then down at Not-Sterling's name tag. At our linked hands, then Not-Sterling's rabbit bow tie and Christmas socks. I could practically see the neurons firing in his brilliant brain as Silas assessed the situation. Then he extended a hand for Not-Sterling to shake. "No, we've never met in person, strangely enough."

Not-Sterling nodded, like the idea of a company's owner never meeting the people who served on his own board of directors didn't faze him in the slightest.

Silas's smile was a sharp-edged thing. "I somehow pictured you with more hair, Sterling."

I coughed to cover my laugh, envisioning the same Peruvian guinea pig Silas was.

Not-Sterling pulled away from me so he could shake Silas's hand, and I stuck my suddenly empty fingers in my pocket before they could reach for him again.

"Yes. Well." Not-Sterling patted his plentiful brown curls, perhaps wondering how much more hair a human head could sustain. "I'm sure there are many incorrect rumors about Sterling Chase out there. I pay them no mind."

"Rumors about... Sterling Chase?" Silas repeated, eyes flicking to me again. "That's an odd way to phrase it."

"Oh, Sterling enjoys talking about Sterling's self in the third person," I explained, deadpan. "It's one of his many, as he likes to call them, 'quirky billionaire eccentricities.'"

Silas blinked. "Well. I suppose I've heard of billionaires doing stranger things..." he said pointedly, and when his eyes met mine, I very clearly heard the words he'd left unsaid: "*...take, for example, the two of us, doing whatever the fuck we're doing right now.*"

"Quite true." Not-Sterling nodded imperiously. "I once heard about a European billionaire who bought a castle for his cat... which seems rather excessive when one ponders that there are people out there who'd just like an upgrade from their cousin's lumpy futon." He cleared his throat, his cheeks turning that addictive shade of pink again. "There's also a chap in Asia, I do believe, who's attempting to clone himself a pet dinosaur."

"Ooof. That won't end well," I murmured, shaking my head. "Has he never seen *Jurassic Park*?"

Not-Sterling chuckled light and low, a sound of startled, honest amusement, and answering heat flared through my body. He turned those big brown eyes up at me... but the instant his gaze met mine, he seemed to recall exactly where he was, who he was talking to, and who he was trying to impersonate. He looked away immediately.

Silas frowned at both of us... but mostly at me.

"Yes, we billionaires are a quirky lot!" Not-Sterling forced a laugh. "You should see us when we get together at our secret billionaire club." He paused. "Um. Not that there *is* a secret billionaire club. Or that I could talk about it if there was." He mimed zipping his lips and locking them tight. "First rule of secret billionaire club, you know?"

Silas nodded slowly, studiously *not* looking at me now.

Not-Sterling's lies were skirting closer to the truth than he knew.

When Silas and I, along with our three best friends, had created the ETC software, we'd been excited at the possibilities of what the software could do for the world and had hoped that selling it would earn us a nice little nest egg—*maybe a couple hundred thousand dollars apiece!*—that we could use as seed money to build our futures.

We'd been incredibly fucking naive.

Fortunately, I'd scored a couple of mentors through my family connections who'd given us solid guidance. Create a company to bring the software to market, they'd said. Don't list your own names as owners; instead, create individual corporations. *Hide, hide, hide.*

At the time, it had seemed ridiculous, expensive, and overly complicated. I'd had to front the money to pay for the lawyers who set it all up since I'd been the one with family money.

But then we'd sold the software for 7.3 billion, and all hell had broken loose.

Even though we'd kept the source of our newfound wealth a secret, money-hungry relatives had still emerged the moment they'd noticed us enjoying the fruits of our labor. Unscrupulous business advisors had wanted a piece of the action. We'd been betrayed by friends, siblings, and romantic partners. And we'd realized that the best way to protect ourselves was to keep new friends in the dark as much as possible.

According to official records, Sterling Chase had created the ETC, and Sterling Chase had profited. The five of us were technically members of Sterling Chase's board, but this wasn't widely known because our company had no shareholders to report to, and we made sure our photos were never posted in articles or on the company website.

I hid my wealth behind inherited family money and kept my involvement in the company mostly behind the scenes. The others—Zane, Silas, Dev, and Landry—distanced themselves from Sterling Chase almost entirely, using their money to pursue their own interests.

And no one outside the five of us—plus Kenji—had a clue just how many zeroes were at the end of our bank balances.

Secret billionaire club indeed.

"Anyway," Not-Sterling babbled on, "when you think about it, Sterling Chase is really only... mildly quirky. Quirk-*lite*. In fact, the quirkiest thing about him—*me*—is that I, uh..." He swallowed hard and lifted his chin a fraction higher, which made his curls bob. "I like my close associates to call me Rowe."

"Rowe," Silas repeated thoughtfully. "Well, that's easy enough to remember, isn't it?" He sent me a quick flick of a glance that said he'd be reporting this information to Kenji within minutes so he could pull images from the security tapes, begin a background check... and possibly schedule me some sort of intervention if I continued conversing with this impostor.

Logically, I knew he was absolutely right. Someone needed to investigate Rowe-Not-Sterling and learn his true motives... but it wouldn't be me because, for the moment, I was thinking with my dick.

"Indeed!" Rowe agreed. "Very easy. One syllable, four little letters. Well!" He clapped his hands together once and attempted a friendly smile. "It's been lovely chatting with you, good sirs," Rowe managed to choke out. "I really must dash. I need to speak to someone about a time-sensitive issue. *Adieu*," he said with a little flourish-bow and a curious British lilt.

He was outrageous. Silly. *Criminal*. Not at all sexy.

So why was I consumed with the desire to lick into his mouth and taste the lies on his lips?

"Perhaps we can help you locate the person you're looking for," I blurted. "Mr. Concannon here knows everyone."

Silas shot me a distinctly unappreciative look.

"Er, yes..." Rowe hesitated. "I don't suppose you know Justin Hardy?"

Hearing the name of Silas's ex-boyfriend was like being doused with cold water. Beside me, Silas's entire body went tense, and I struggled to keep my voice light. "Yes. I'm acquainted with him. One of your company's biggest competitors, isn't he?"

"Oh, *that*." Rowe laughed weakly. "Much ado about nothing. Justin's perfectly lovely. Very friendly. He built his business entirely on his own, you know. A self-made man."

"Is he really?" Silas set his jaw. "Do you do much business with Justin?"

"Not often, no. But I do need to speak to him on a matter of business tonight. I have an idea that will suit Hardy Development perfectly," Rowe said with an eagerness he couldn't hide. "So... could you point me to him?"

Finally, a plausible explanation for why someone would want to masquerade as the head of my company.

Rowe was probably an app developer trying to sell Justin Hardy his revolutionary new game or convince Justin to invest in Rowe's sinking ship of a tech company. Rowe had probably purchased a ticket in Sterling's name or stolen one of the extra spots my company had purchased for our employees, thinking Sterling's name would give him instant credibility.

It wasn't unusual by any means. Just that night, I'd had people I barely knew approach me for investments and job opportunities simply because we happened to be in the same place at the same time. And I'd gotten so tired of being approached by entrepreneurs hoping I'd hear their pitches on behalf of Sterling Chase over the years I'd hired a CEO and a head of development just so I could throw my hands up and pretend I wasn't a decision-maker in my own company.

It shouldn't have been this disappointing to find that Rowe was a schemer like all the rest... but it was.

Stranger still, even knowing he was a liar and a schemer, the idea of him having anything to do with an asshole like Justin Hardy made red flash across my vision.

The silence stretched so long that Silas and Rowe both darted worried glances at me. Finally, Silas answered Rowe's question himself. "I haven't seen him. Bash, have you?"

Given how Justin Hardy had treated Silas, he was unlikely to show his treacherous face anywhere in my vicinity, let alone Silas's.

I merely shook my head. "Not tonight."

"Well." My angelic liar blew out a disappointed breath and set his shoulders like he was off to fight a battle. "Thank you anyway, Bash." He gave me a smile that was small and shy—not at all like his Sterling Chase persona, and all the more appealing for being genuine. "I'm certain we'll be in touch. Toodaloo!"

I let him walk away, sighing as the fern snapped back into place behind him because I knew exactly what was coming in five, four, three—

"*Toodaloo?*" Silas repeated incredulously. "Bash, what the fuck did I just witness?"

"Let it go," I said, more snappily than I'd intended.

Silas was loyal to a fault. Protective and kind. Doggedly determined. And once he'd set his sights on a goal, whether it was improving management practices at a company or buying new underwear, he didn't stop until it was achieved.

But I didn't want to be one of his projects.

"What are you doing in town?" I asked, a casual, not-so-subtle attempt to change the subject. "Big meeting?" I lowered my voice. "Is Landry in trouble again?"

"Probably, but that's not why I'm here. I figured, since I was coming to town in a couple weeks for the Innovation Awards anyway, I'd just come early to see the polo match tomorrow and catch up with Dev."

I stared at him blankly. "Polo match?"

"Honestly, Sebastian." Silas rolled his eyes. "The second half of the charity benefit the company's sponsoring this weekend? Someone should be there representing Sterling Chase—the company, I mean, not your new friend—and technically, Devon will be there since he's coming up to check on some horses stabled there, but..."

"But Dev doesn't do socialization anymore. Right." I rubbed my forehead. "Fuck. I forgot about the polo thing."

"And here I thought personal assistants were supposed to have strong organizational skills," he said blandly.

I shot him a look. "I was supposed to be in Borneo climbing a mountain right now."

"Right. And yet here you are... pretending to be the personal assistant of a fake human being who is trying to do business *with my ex-boyfriend*... why?"

"Because I was bored and he's entertaining?" It wasn't exactly a lie, but honesty compelled me to add, "There was something about him. He got under my skin."

Silas narrowed his eyes. "More like *you* wanted to get under his tuxedo."

"That, too. He's fucking gorgeous. And I haven't hooked up with anyone in... a long while." Against my will, my eyes roamed the crowd over the potted fern, looking for a head of messy curls.

"He's got a cute-and-charming thing going on, yes. But—" Silas's voice hardened, drawing my attention back to him. "—he's a *liar*, Bash. An identity thief. So whatever this fascination is, let it go. Besides, anyone who associates with Justin is bad news."

I sighed. For the billionth time, I cursed myself for ever introducing Justin Hardy to Silas. The second my boarding school classmate had met my best friend, he'd seen Silas as prey. At the time, Silas had been working with me to negotiate a contract between Sterling Chase and a client he'd met through his own private consulting business—a contract worth millions. But Justin hadn't hesitated to poach that client, damaging Silas's reputation in the process.

I didn't give a shit about the lost money in the grand scheme of things, but he'd broken Silas's heart, and that was something I would never forgive.

"I hear you." I clapped Silas on the shoulder. "Just remember, Rowe isn't Justin, okay? There's no reason to believe they're conspiring simply because Rowe mentioned his name. And if he *was* working with Justin, he'd know better than to tip us off."

Silas nodded unhappily.

"But Silas, even if they are in cahoots, it doesn't matter. No one is getting near the company." *Not again.* "I promise."

Silas gave me a look that said I was missing the point entirely. "I'm not worried about the business, Bash. There are other ways you can be hurt."

"Like, he's gonna break my heart?" I snorted. "You remember who you're talking to, right? When was the last time I had a serious relationship?"

Silas opened his mouth, then shut it again because the answer was *never*. I had learned from my friends' mistakes. There was no way to tell who wanted you for you and who wanted you for your wealth and connections. It was easier to stay away from even having to make that determination.

"Exactly. I am married to Sterling Chase—the business, not my new friend." I winked, and Silas snorted. "So stop worrying. I'm not falling for the guy. I'm only having fun."

"Sebastian." Silas blew out a long-suffering breath and muttered, "I'd be less worried if your idea of fun didn't so often align with wild adventures that could nearly kill you." He shook his head and groaned. "You're going to talk to him again, aren't you?"

My gaze had somehow found its way back to the curly head and those big brown eyes, which were now wide with fresh panic at something Constance Baxter-Hicks was saying. I wondered what topiary-related information the woman was imparting that made the man so terrified.

I wondered why the world's worst liar had thought putting on the world's worst-fitting tux (complete with bunny tie), sneaking into an event like this, and pretending to be someone who didn't exist was the best way to advance his business idea.

I wondered if the interest I'd seen flash in those pretty eyes was all part of his act.

I wondered who Rowe really was... and what he really wanted.

And I kinda wanted to hear him lie to me some more.

"Oh, yeah," I agreed, my eyes still fixed on the man who'd crash-landed into my hiding spot, filling the black-and-white evening with glorious color. "In fact, I'm thinking Sterling Chase might enjoy some polo."

THREE

ROWE

I was *so* getting the hang of this lying thing.

Okay, yes, there'd been a hairy moment or ten back there when I'd been sweating rivers into my tuxedo and my blood had rushed away from my brain so fast I'd felt faint. And yeah, I'd let myself get caught up in the moment like I sometimes did, staring a little too long, and laughing a little too loud, and talking way, way too much. But I hadn't accidentally lit myself on fire or randomly blurted out my real name and social security number, and the police hadn't come to escort me out, so all in all, that made this a *win*. Right?

If I'd known before I'd arrived that I'd have to hold a whole-ass conversation with someone who was meant to be my *fake employee*— a twelve-foot-tall, male-model look-alike fake employee, no less, who wore a tux so perfectly fitted it had to be custom-made, who was armed with a snarky smile and a mischievous eyebrow, and whose cologne made my cock stiffen every time the air-conditioning blew a delicious whiff of him in my direction—I might have said it was impossible and called the whole thing off.

But in reality, even though Bash had made me forget my damn name—the real one and the fake one—talking with him had been kind of... fun. Like the roller coasters my twin sister had dragged me on as a kid, where stark terror had yielded to a rush of euphoria because I'd done the impossible and survived.

But you still haven't actually done anything *tonight, Rowe Prince. You came here for a purpose, remember?*

I blew out a breath. *Right.*

I was not at the gala for fun or to get flirty with a personal assistant who probably made more per year than my parents' house was worth. I was here because I needed someone—I didn't care if it was Justin Hardy, or one of his competitors, or the freaking Tooth Fairy, if she had the right resources—to give me a meeting so I could show them Project Daisy Chain. There wasn't a doubt in my mind that if I actually got a chance to pitch someone the project, they'd see how amazing and life-changing it could be. And once they'd committed, once they'd promised to make this dream into a reality, I'd hand over the amateur-level tracking and communication app I'd taught myself to code and the mountains of data on hospital workflows and case studies of healthcare outcomes I'd compiled over the years, and I'd be satisfied to let them take it from there.

Then I'd go back to Linden knowing I'd done my very best—more than I'd ever thought I was capable of—to make shit happen. I'd draw a deep breath for the first time in a decade. And maybe I'd stop missing my sister with every beat of my lonely heart.

"That's not going to happen," a young woman's voice said firmly.

Given the direction of my thoughts, maybe it wasn't surprising that when I wheeled around, I half expected to see Daisy standing there somehow whole and alive, self-assured and sassy as ever... and magically transported from rural Indiana to this glittering room in New York.

But the young woman standing by the buffet table was nothing like my twin. She was blonde and statuesque as a Greek goddess, where my sister had been a ball of mischievous energy even shorter than me. Not to mention, this woman was wearing a dress encrusted with far more sparkles than my sister ever would have tolerated.

"Miranda, darling, I'm only suggesting—" the older woman standing beside her argued.

"That I starve myself while there's a buffet of food right here?" Miranda interrupted around a mouthful of food. "Do the eligible bachelors of New York enjoy women who fall at their feet from low blood sugar?"

It was exactly the sort of thing my sister would have said, and I couldn't hide my smile. Unfortunately, Miranda noticed and immediately pointed in my direction.

"You, there," she said before I could move away. "Do *you* think women should starve themselves at a gala simply to keep up appearances?"

"I, uh... No?"

"No." Miranda tilted her head toward her mother triumphantly. "See?"

"Miranda, must we do this now?" Her mother, whose name badge read Constance Baxter-Hicks, glanced around the room and lowered her voice to a whisper. "I simply reminded you that this season's styles are all quite formfitting and that I want you to be happy—"

"Yes. And I'm telling you prosciutto and brie make me happy." She nodded down at the plate she held, where an absolutely delicious-looking bread-and-cheese thing sat.

My stomach, which had lately subsisted on microwaved oatmeal and free employee burritos, chose that moment to rumble. "*Oooh,*" I said, glancing longingly at the buffet table. I was a man on a mission, yes, but I could pause for prosciutto.

Constance flicked me a disapproving glance, but when she caught sight of my name tag, she straightened like she'd been goosed with a cattle prod. "Sterling Chase?" One immaculate eyebrow rose in disbelief. "*The* Sterling Chase? Of... *Sterling Chase?*" She waved a hand toward one of the signs listing the names of the gala's sponsors.

Ah, shit. This again.

I cleared my throat. "Yes! It is I, Sterling Chase," I agreed magnanimously. "Lovely to meet you, my good woman. Now if you'll excuse me..."

I attempted to dart around her toward the delicacies on the buffet table, but she sidestepped, neatly blocking my path. "Mr. Chase, I'm Constance Baxter-Hicks, and this is my daughter, Miranda. I don't believe we've had the pleasure of meeting."

"Er. No." I found myself sweating again, and now that I'd acknowledged my hunger, my stomach was nearly cramping with the need for food. "That is to say, I rarely mingle in society—"

"Wish *I* could rarely mingle in society," Miranda muttered.

I feinted left in another attempt to get to the food, and once again, Constance blocked me more effectively than any softball player covering home plate.

She wrinkled her nose and gave me an up-down look, from my hair to my borrowed magician's tux, no doubt tallying up the total cost of my ensemble. I fought the urge to curl my toes, like that would somehow hide my cheap shoes from her perusal.

Then I heard Joey's voice in my head. *Brass balls. Belong. Own it. Right. Okay.*

I straightened and returned her appraisal with a superior-ish look of my own, then turned to Miranda. "These events are deadly dull. I, too, prefer something a bit more..." Shit, what was a fancy word for secondhand thrift store? What word had Bash used earlier? "Avant-garde," I said smoothly, gesturing to my ensemble. "It's... one of my billionaire quirks. Why waste money on couture when you can put on any ole thing and pass it off as the next big thing?"

Miranda blinked. She took a deliberate bite of her prosciutto morsel—*dear god, that looks tasty*—and grinned. "I love that." She leaned toward me. "And I fucking hate this dress."

"Mir-*an*-da!" Constance pursed her lips and turned her ire on me. "You're much younger than I thought you'd be, Mr. Chase."

"Oh. Well. The wonders of healthy living, you know." I eyed the array of artery-clogging meats and cheeses over her shoulder with glee.

She narrowed her eyes. "And I hadn't heard that you were such a style connoisseur."

"No? Well. Sterling Chase is a bit of a Renaissance man. If you'll pardon me, please, madam—"

"Sterling!" a way-more-familiar-than-it-should-be voice called.

Shoot. My stomach trembled with excitement, and my dick perked up as Bash appeared at my side. "I got you a drink. Sterling Chase's favorite. Beluga on the rocks."

Oh. Great. We were still doing the third-person-talking thing.

Bash grinned at me, eyes dancing, which made it hard to breathe or swallow, let alone talk. Instead, I looked down at the glass of clear liquid he handed me.

"Right," I managed. "Of course. Many assistants would think Sterling Chase prefers an ice-cold beer, but you know me so well. Sterling Chase appreciates that." I took a sip without thinking, hoping it would calm my nerves, but when the straight vodka hit the back of my throat with a stark burn, I choked.

Bash looked at me in concern.

"Good," I gasped out. "*Hngh.* So tasty."

Bash's eyes went unfocused for a second, which helped neither the breathing situation nor the situation in my pants.

"Constance, you're looking just as ravishing as you were earlier this evening! I see you've met Sterling Chase? Have you been regaling him with tales of your magnificent topiaries?" Bash asked.

"Bash, dear, you and Mr. Chase are... acquainted?" Constance said, more of an accusation than a question.

"Indeed," Bash said easily. "Sometimes it feels like I've known Sterling Chase for as long as he's lived."

"Hmph. Well then, you're in luck. Mr. Chase was just about to enlighten us with his thoughts on *style.*" Constance raised an eyebrow, clearly expecting me to embarrass myself.

I felt my face go hot and fought the need to squirm. "Uh. Well. I think..." I cleared my throat. "That is to say..."

"You don't need to do this," Bash said, bending his head so he was nearly speaking in my ear. His voice was low and steady. Almost soothing... Or at least it would have been if his proximity hadn't made my pulse stutter out *T-A-K-E-M-E-N-O-W* in Morse code. "Sterling Chase doesn't owe anyone his precious opinions, does he?"

My eyes met his, and for a moment, in this sea of fakeness and impostors, it felt like I'd found a friend. An ally. Someone who stood on my side of a huge divide between the people who *had* and the people who *needed*.

The handsomest man in the room—this man who was all mocking eyebrows, and intelligent glances, and plush, kissable lips— was reminding me that I could stand up to someone rich and entitled. And it felt so damn good, so empowering, I found myself rooted to the spot when I should have fled and talking when I should have kept my mouth shut.

"I, uh... I think style is about... honesty?" I blurted, the statement coming out more like a question. I took a deep breath. *Brass balls, brass balls, brass balls.* "Rather than replicating what you see on the runway or on social media and doing what you think is expected of you, take the time to figure out what you actually like. What makes you happy. What makes you feel most comfortable and... *you.*"

"So we should all just wear pajamas in the ballroom, then?" Constance tittered. "How amusing."

"N-no," I protested. Her quick dismissal fired something in my blood. "That's actually the *opposite* of what I'm saying. I'm saying don't be lazy. Don't take the path of least resistance. Don't make excuses about not having the time, or the money, or the skills to make your clothes, or your home, or your dreams what you want them to be. Put in some effort. Acquire the skills. Make it a priority. Take a risk. Question things and know *why* you're doing what you're doing. It's hard and uncomfortable a lot of the time. Sometimes you'll misstep. Sometimes you'll look foolish. Sometimes you'll even *feel* foolish. But you only get one life, and if fear holds you back from living it the way you want, you're wasting it, as my sister used to say. And, uh..."

Thinking of Daisy made my thoughts stumble for a fraction of a second, which was just long enough for me to emerge from whatever fugue state I'd been in. The knowledge of where I was and what I'd been doing—soapboxing in the middle of a ballroom to a bunch of rich socialites, sounding a whole lot more like Rowe Prince than Sterling Chase ever should, while "my" personal assistant stood right there, hearing the whole thing—crashed over me like icy lake water.

Constance stared at me with wide eyes. Miranda gaped like I'd been speaking in tongues. And Bash...

When I finally scraped together the courage to lift my head, I found him staring at me with a kind of laser-beam, crawl-inside-my-brain intensity that made me want to melt into a puddle and tell him all my secrets.

Shit.

Abort mission, abort mission! There was no way I could stick around tonight. Not with Bash around. Not when it was so impossible to think clearly in his presence.

"And. Um. Miranda should wear dresses she likes," I concluded lamely. I desperately wished I had Joey's magician's wand to go with his tux so I could hocus-pocus away all memory of this conversation. "Now, if you'll excuse me, miladies—"

I bowed deeply, then darted around Constance while she was still stupefied by my ridiculous speech. I set my mostly full drink on the buffet table and made a beeline for the exit, praying that Bash wouldn't follow me and, *please, oh please,* that I wouldn't slip on the marble again.

I'd blown my cover, no doubt. Blown it to smithereens. I'd been a hairsbreadth from talking about Daisy, and my love of thrift stores, and fucking *Linden, Indiana*, all of which was as out of place at this party as... well, *me*. Now Joey was going to kill me because I'd wasted this whole opportunity he'd handed me, and I didn't even have time for prosciutto, goddamn it, because I needed to escape before—

"Rowe!"

Mother. Fucker.

"Sorry," I called over my shoulder, finding Bash hot on my heels, damn his excessively long legs. "Must dash. Very busy. I need to—"

"You need to find Justin Hardy," Bash said when I was a mere twenty feet from the exit. "I can help with that, Mr. Chase!"

I stopped in my tracks.

Damn, damn, damn it all. I couldn't turn that down. And he'd called me Mr. Chase, so maybe...

"Here." Bash came up beside me, a bit breathless, and handed me a small plate filled with prosciutto bites. "I grabbed you some of these... *sir.*"

I took the plate, staring up at him blankly, and he shrugged. "You watched Miranda eating them so closely I figured either you were attracted to Miranda..."

I made a startled noise, and Bash smiled warmly.

"—or you were attracted to her prosciutto bites."

I couldn't resist sneaking one in my mouth, and when the salty flavor hit my tongue, I closed my eyes and moaned. "I think I might be a whore for prosciutto bites," I mumbled, telling another truth before I could stop myself.

But when I darted a glance up at him, the look on Bash's face wasn't mocking or disapproving. It was intent. Heated.

"Another of your quirky billionaire eccentricities, *Rowe?*" The low, intimate rumble of his voice reached down into me, and for a second, I wished I hadn't told him my real name. Something about the way he said it—like he knew the actual Rowe Prince—made me think things I had no business thinking. "Thank you. For the food."

"All in a day's work for your intrepid personal assistant." He looked away. "So. Justin Hardy?"

I nodded. "Right. Yes. You said you could help me find him?"

"Yes... and no." Bash's lips twisted as he imparted this devastating news. "He's not here tonight."

"But I thought..." I shook my head, unwilling to believe this. "He always attends charity galas, especially ones that benefit children. I read online that he donated thousands to fund after-school programs.

And there was a picture of him on the *Daily News* talking about a plan to create an endowment..."

Bash's eyes shuttered. "Yes, I'm sure his picture is on *all* the gossip and news sites. The fact remains, he's not here."

"Oh." I tried to hide it, but that single syllable contained a metric ton of heartbreak.

Justin Hardy was my last great hope. The meager savings I'd put aside working extra shifts at Bobby's Tech Barn last winter were nearly gone. My parents were barely making ends meet without my support, and I couldn't keep crashing on Joey's futon, delivering burritos to pay my share of food and utilities for much longer.

I needed to make that meeting happen, damn it. Because if I went back to Linden with nothing to show for my time, how could I ever justify taking a risk like this again?

"But I may have another idea of where you could find him," Bash went on.

"Really?" I demanded, clutching this dangling thread of hope. "What is it? Let's do it!"

Bash's lips quirked. "I wasn't sure if you'd be up for it after what happened with..." He lowered his voice. "Bubbles."

"Who?"

Bash bit his lip. "Bubbles. Your one true love? Who died? On your trip to Mount Kinabalu?"

Oh. Shit.

"Bubbles didn't die," I said firmly. "No, indeed."

"But you said..."

"When I said I lost him, I meant..." I licked my lips. What *had* I meant? "I meant literally lost. Poor chap took a right instead of a left and wandered that mountain for days."

Bash's eyes widened. "And then what?"

"Then he was found, obviously. By a... a villager. Who nursed him back to health. And they fell in love. Got married in a very quiet ceremony." I sucked a bit of brie off the side of my finger. "Very disappointing, naturally, but I'm sure we'll all remain friends in the end."

Bash shook his head. His smile gleamed bright white under the light of the chandelier, beautiful and dangerous and *knowing*. "You amaze me, Sterling Chase," he said, but it sounded like he was saying something different.

Before I could wonder too much about it, though, he cleared his throat and went on. "Well. As long as you're feeling up to it, why not try to find him at the polo match tomorrow out at Hollow Brook? Since it's the second part of this fundraiser, I assume you're still planning on attending."

Polo? The glittering whirl of the gala was already leagues outside my comfort zone. I couldn't imagine attempting to navigate a gathering of people who played sports involving animals that cost more than a car. *But you survived this*, I reminded myself. And if these people had more money than sense, that was their business. Getting one of them to spearhead a project that could literally save lives was mine.

I nodded slowly. "Yes, of course! Polo. Sterling Chase loves polo. Sterling Chase was a polo champion back in high school! And you're saying Justin will be at the match?"

"I wouldn't know," Bash said modestly. "I'm only a personal assistant, of course. But there's a strong chance. And Devon McKay will be there, too. He's..."

"On the Sterling Chase board of directors," I mused, remembering his name from my research on the company. "I mean, uh... *my* board of directors. Though I haven't met him in person yet, either."

Bash nodded before looking away as if searching the crowd. "As you're probably aware, the people on your board have lots of connections, if you're looking for funding from outside the company."

I chewed my lip. I hadn't been looking for an investor, per se, because money alone was not what I needed. I needed someone with experience, with the in-depth knowledge of how businesses worked that I hadn't been able to acquire no matter how hard I tried.

But... maybe money was better than nothing.

"I'll make your usual arrangements for the match, then," Bash went on, turning back to me. "The town car will pick you up at noon, and I'll let your teammates know you're planning to play."

It took me a minute to process what he'd said. "Play? You want me to *play* polo?" My voice rose an octave. "You want me to *ride a horse?*"

Bash grinned. "You're funny, Rowe. Don't worry. You can wear your street clothes, and I'll have your riding gear brought to the stables. There's a nice dressing room there, as I'm sure you're aware."

"Riding gear?" I squeaked. "Like... *horse*-riding gear?"

Bash patted me on the shoulder, a move unexpected enough to nearly send me careening into a server carrying a tray of drinks. "You're such a kidder. I remember you telling me how much you love a good polo match. I'll send the car to your Park Avenue address—it's 740 Park, right?—and after you play, you can tell Devon all about your project, assuming you don't find Justin first."

My mind had stopped processing this after hearing that Sterling Chase lived on Park Avenue. Because of course he would live some-place swanky and so far from Joey's place it'd be nearly impossible to get there if I worked even part of my Burrito Bandito shift.

"W-wait." I gulped. "Will you be there tomorrow?"

"Maybe." Bash shrugged. "I've attended matches in the past. Would you like me to?"

"Yes!" I blurted before he'd finished speaking. Getting through the match without committing a horrible etiquette mistake would be impossible without someone I could trust to guide me. I wasn't sure when the hot fake employee I'd known for thirty minutes had become that someone, but like Joey said, beggars couldn't be choosers. "In fact, I insist that you accompany me. In case I require my assistant."

Fake-Sterling Chase needed all the fucking assistance he could get.

"In that case, of course I will. I'll have the car pick me up first, then."

"Good. Yes. Thank you, my good man."

Bash's lips twitched. "Sleep well, Rowe," he said softly, taking my empty plate before turning and losing himself in the crowd.

Oh my stars and garters. What did I just agree to?

My phone dinged as I made my way toward the exit.

> **JOEY**
>
> Dude, you didn't tell me the rivalry in this fast food delivery game was so fucking intense. So help me, if that Sandwich Shark gets up in my grill with his doo doo doo song one more time...

> **ME**
>
> Can you cover my shift again tomorrow? I will owe you BIG TIME.

> **JOEY**
>
> Yeah, I can do that. Guess that means we're not celebrating yet?

> **ME**
>
> No. Ha. Definitely not.

> **JOEY**
>
> Damn. Well, could be worse, cuz! At least you're not drowning.

I wasn't so sure about that. I'd felt like I was in over my head even before learning I'd need to become a polo expert overnight. And when Bash looked at me, I got a breathless adrenaline rush, like I was in danger and sinking fast.

My supposed personal assistant was seriously magnetic. The kind of man who made me want to empty my pockets and give him everything I had... which was a problem since I had absolutely nothing to give. And if and when the man found out I wasn't actually his mysterious, world-traveling boss, he would not be happy.

If we'd been any other two people, at any other time, I'd have pushed the gorgeous man up against the wall in that tiny, shadowed alcove and kissed the smile off his lips. I'd have caressed the broad shoulders hidden under his tux, and done—

Shit. Considering how little experience I had with guys, I wasn't sure what I'd do, exactly. But I had a laundry list of dirty fantasies, so maybe I'd bring them to life one at a time. Sink to my knees on the hard floor while he kept the hot force of his attention on me the entire ti—

"Good *heavens!*" a woman yelped in a high-pitched voice as I crashed into her, too lost in my fantasy to realize where I was going.

Cold champagne seeped through my shirt, down my pants, and onto the floor, then splashed back onto the frothy skirt of the woman I'd nearly mowed down.

"Oh, god, I'm so sorry," I gasped in horror. That dress probably cost more than I earned at Burrito Bandito in a year.

I pulled the handkerchief from my breast pocket to soak up the liquid... and kept pulling... and pulling. Brightly colored gossamer scarves spilled out, along with the stack of white business cards I'd stuck in there. For a moment, they soared through the air like butterflies, then flitted to the damp ground, where they landed in a soggy heap... along with my dreams of leaving the party without causing another scene.

Several people around me clapped politely.

My face flamed, but I gathered all of the cards and scarves as quickly as I could and sketched another bow, like this had all been a part of my act.

"Sterling Chase bids you all a good night," I announced as I swept out of the room, raced for the building's exit, and made my way to the subway that would bounce me back to Queens.

What had I been saying to Joey earlier about a little embarrassment being worthwhile? I'd lied. Surely there had to be a better, easier way to get this meeting with Justin. Something with fewer lies, less electrically charged lust-haze, less promise of impending disaster.

Or you could live a little, Rowe. My sister's voice in my head was snarky and loving in equal measure, just as she had been in life, and I couldn't help pressing on the tattoo on my hip—the one that I'd gotten for her. *Do the brave, exciting thing. Don't be scared.*

Daisy would have laughed herself breathless over tonight's events, but she'd never get the chance, and that was why I had to live for both of us.

For her sake, I could do anything. *Be* anything.

A burrito deliverer.

An accidental magician.

Even a fucking polo player if I had to be.

"I'm Sterling Chase, Quirky Billionaire," I whispered and willed myself to believe it.

FOUR

BASH

"His name is Thomas Rowe Prince." Kenji clicked a button on his tablet, and Rowe's picture appeared on my office wall screen. "He's twenty-four, from Linden, Indiana, no college degree, no criminal record, pitifully small bank balance, and he's currently working under the table delivering fast food. Sent the full report to your email and the group chat."

I sat back in my leather chair and stared at the DMV photo from several years ago. That was definitely the man I'd met last night. Same enormous, innocent eyes. Same sweet, slightly rounded features. Same brown hair, though the man in the picture kept his ruthlessly tidy.

But there was something different about him, too. Despite the horrible lighting, the person in the photo looked confident and care-free, while the guy I'd met last night had seemed... well, nervous as fuck.

Maybe because he hadn't been attempting to steal someone's identity back then, I thought grimly as I turned away from the photo and sipped my coffee. "Any idea what game he's playing?"

According to Kenji's info, Rowe had no background in app development, no company that needed funding. So what the hell had brought him to the city looking for a meeting with Justin Hardy?

Kenji turned from the wall, set his hands on his lean hips, and regarded me for a long moment. "You mean *besides* the game of impersonating a fictional person, probably in an attempt to ingratiate himself with the people at the gala so he can steal their money?"

I grunted. It was a fair assessment, and it shouldn't have set me on edge as much as it did. "He won't be getting any from me, that's for damn sure."

"Oh, no, you're far too smart for that, sir." Kenji cocked his head to one side, though his shiny hair was too well-groomed to budge. "You're merely spending the afternoon enjoying polo with him."

"First off, the match is for *charity*." I fixed him with a steely glare. "As my assistant loves to remind me, networking and being philanthropic is an important part of my job as a member of Sterling Chase's board of directors."

"I see." Kenji rolled his eyes. "You're associating with the sexy schemer for *philanthropic* purposes. Such a giver."

"And secondly," I went on, ignoring a pulse of *something* at Kenji's description of Rowe, "I'm going because I have a gorgeous mare with a blaze on her nose and three white socks who's been sadly neglected for weeks."

"Ah. You're cavorting with the cute con artist for Starlight's sake."

The weight of my personal assistant's judgment was crushing, but I forced myself to straighten in my seat. "If you have something to say, Kenji, say it."

"*Moi?* I'd never presume to tell my boss his business..."

"Of course not."

"But since you're asking." Kenji plopped into the heavy wooden side chair on the other side of my desk, his tablet on his lap. "What the heck is so special about this guy, Sebastian? If you're looking for a hookup, I could find you a hundred men who aren't liars or users and have a whole lot more in common with you than a guy from a tiny speck of a town who has an annual subscription to *Furniture Refin-*

ishing Quarterly Magazine and recently worked the customer service desk at..." He glanced down at his tablet. "Bobby's Tech Barn."

I picked up a pen from the desk and toyed with it idly, staring at Rowe's picture on the wall screen. I'd wrestled with that very question for hours after I'd finally fallen into bed last night. Why Rowe?

Because he was gorgeous? Because he had a face like an angel and a body that seemed like it would fit perfectly against mine? Well, yes, but Kenji was right; I could find that lots of places.

Because he lied like every word was being wrenched from him, but when he told the truth, he spoke with passion that couldn't possibly be fake? That, too. But not just that, either.

Because he had secrets, and I was insanely curious about them?

Because he was adorably awkward, and I wanted to protect him from anything that could hurt him, including himself?

Because he was fucking with me, and I wanted to rage at him and throttle him?

Because he made me feel wrong-footed and on edge and amused and constantly surprised, but he made me *feel*... and I hadn't realized how dull and emotionless my life had become until he'd practically face-planted in it and shaken it up?

Yes. All of that.

And more besides.

Last night at the gala, my chest had gone tight when Rowe had wished me a good night and walked away. I'd wanted badly to call out to him, to confess that I wasn't actually his personal assistant, and to take him home to my bed. Of course, I hadn't been quite that foolish... but I hadn't been able to stop myself from turning to watch him leave.

I'd witnessed the whole spectacle when he'd walked directly into Mitzy Forman, gasped in apologetic shock, and reached for his pocket square, only to pull out a piece of red silk tied to a piece of yellow silk tied to a piece of green silk. Yards of pocket square and bits of card stock flowed out of his suit, a veritable *flood* of color against the black and white of the room.

Rowe had been horrified. He'd also been charming. I'd laughed my ass off, more amused than any attendee at a society charity gala had a right to be. And when Silas had shepherded me around the room later, forcing me to shake hands with the required number of society notables, I'd knelt and picked up one of the discarded business cards and tucked it away like a knight with a lady's favor.

Kenji and Silas were right. It wasn't like me. Sebastian Dayne did not *do* smitten.

Except, apparently, I did.

"I don't know. There's something about the guy, Kenji," I said at length, because spewing out all the rest would probably make me sound insane.

"That's exactly what Silas told me you'd say." Kenji sounded far more bewildered than I thought was warranted by the situation. "He said you're not acting like yourself, but I didn't really believe it." He followed the direction of my gaze toward the wall screen.

"You tell *Silas* nobody likes a tattletale." I resolutely turned toward my laptop in an attempt to actually focus on work for the first time all morning. "Especially after I let that asshole show me around the gala like a prize steer, shaking hands with a hundred of my mother's millionaire cronies."

Kenji snorted. "She'd be so proud."

I shot him a look that told me exactly how much I cared about that. "For the record, none of last night would have happened if I'd been having fun in Borneo hiking Mount Kinabalu as planned. So, really, isn't my mother the person who deserves your Stern Disapproval Look this morning?"

"If you'd *really* wanted to be climbing that mountain, you wouldn't have caved when she called you." Kenji smirked because we both knew he was right. "You told me yourself the last adventure trip wasn't as fun as you'd hoped. It left you feeling more restless than before."

I cursed past-Bash for telling that truth.

"Still better than a *gala*," I grumbled, taking a folder from him so I could sign the papers inside. "And I have other options. I could go to the house in the Hamptons and hang out by the pool with sexy dilettantes."

"You hate dilettantes."

"I don't need to like them to let them suck my dick," I teased.

"Classy." Kenji rolled his eyes before grabbing the folder back. "So, about this guy—"

Whatever warning Kenji was going to deliver was nothing I hadn't already heard from Silas. Nothing I hadn't already told *myself*.

"Don't you have a family event to get to?" I interrupted.

Kenji pursed his lips. "Yes. I'll be leaving for the airport soon."

"Great. And did you get me a car and driver for this afternoon and take care of those other arrangements I asked you to make?"

"Yes," he sighed. "Though Silas warned me not to give in to your whims."

"You're my PA," I countered. "It's literally your job to give in to my whims. And stop listening to Silas. You know he's been fucked-up since his relationship with Justin ended."

Kenji gave me The Look again. "What Silas had with Justin wasn't a *relationship*. It was a manipulation by a narcissist fuckwad who was only out for his money, and since Silas loves you, he doesn't want to see that happen to you. Can you blame him?"

I blew out a breath and cast my eyes to the ceiling. No, of course I couldn't. And I knew Silas's experience with Justin wasn't unusual, either. Every member of our brotherhood had been targeted by users more than once.

Having this level of wealth had brought each of us incredible opportunities. Zane was pursuing his dream of becoming a professional musician, Dev had his horses, Landry had... an ever-changing harem of men to fuck. But opportunities like that came at a price—a loss of privacy, a loss of innocence, a constant worry about people's motivations when they got too close.

Unlike the others, though, I'd grown up in this world. I'd learned early to invest my time and passion in things I could control, like my business. And aside from the brotherhood, I never let anyone get too close.

Kenji leaned forward. "Wait. Does Dev know you're coming to the stables? Does he know you're not coming alone?"

"Come on." It was my turn to roll my eyes. "Of course he knows. I wouldn't force him to interact with a stranger without warning. And, yes—" I held up a hand. "—before you ask, he lectured me also."

You're playing with fire, Bash, Dev had texted. *Cut the guy loose.* But because he knew me well enough to know that I wouldn't take his warning, he'd also promised to get me a set of riding clothes in Rowe's size, too.

"Good." Kenji bit his lip. "Look, I know technically you and the others are my bosses, and a good personal assistant probably wouldn't comment on his boss's personal life—"

"Wait, really?" I snorted. "Where can I get one of those *good* assistants, just out of curiosity?"

"—but as the guy who manages your online orders of bougie lube and sex toys, and keeps track of Zane's tour dates, and bails fucking Landry out of his messes every week, I feel like I know you guys. For reasons I cannot fathom, I care about you all."

"Jesus." I ran a hand over my face. I sometimes worried that we didn't pay Kenji enough for all he did, but if we paid the man what he was worth, he'd own the company.

"But... not everyone we're attracted to is good for us. And sometimes you don't see the danger until it's too late. Trust me."

I sighed. I loved my friends, Kenji included, but sometimes they were a bunch of mother hens. "Look, I appreciate the concern. But this guy—" I jerked a thumb toward Rowe's picture on the screen. "—can't lie his way out of a paper bag. He's not a danger."

Kenji was the king of long-suffering sighs. "Why must you people always do things the hard way? Fine, then. Proceed at your own risk." He tapped on his tablet. "FYI, I'm adding a line item to the budget for dealing with the fallout of this. Let's call it the Fake Sterling Chase Escape Fund. We can use it to buy champagne when we toast you successfully evading the wiles of a con man... Or, alternatively, buy you a ticket to Central America so you can paraglide into an active volcano to cheer yourself up after it all ends in disaster."

I opened my mouth to retort that I'd need no such thing when I heard a rap on my office door.

"Hey, hey!" Austin Purcell, Sterling Chase's head of development, breezed in, his brown hair sleek and tidy, his smile bright. "Bash, do you have time for a quick chat?"

"Hey, yourself." I gave him a genuine smile and gestured him toward the unoccupied seat in front of my desk. "Come in. Sit."

"Mr. Purcell, Mr. Dayne doesn't have an appointment with you on his calendar." Kenji had dialed his chilly politeness up to a level that would give polar bears frostbite.

Austin shrugged good-naturedly. "Since he was supposed to be out today, I thought maybe his schedule would be open. Figured it wouldn't hurt to ask. But I can come back another time if you're busy."

"Kenji, it's fine," I said, waving a hand. "I've got a few minutes. I planned to call Austin this morning anyway."

Kenji sniffed, plainly displeased when Austin stretched out his long legs in the chair beside him.

I smothered a grin. For all his flawless efficiency, Kenji tended to be fairly easygoing with most people—a requirement, working for my friends and me—but there were a couple of people the man simply never seemed to warm to. Landry was one. Strangely enough, Austin Purcell was another.

He claims he's just passing by when his office is at the other end of the building. He lies in wait for you in your office in the morning, ready to ambush you with overly sweet coffee and enthusiasm. No one should smile with so many teeth. He takes liberties, Sebastian!

Personally, though, I liked Austin a lot. We weren't close outside of work, but he was dedicated to his job as head of development, his team loved him, and Clarissa, our CEO, considered him her right-hand man. When he'd first started, we'd actually clashed a little—

before Austin, I'd been the one taking meetings with potential clients on behalf of Sterling Chase's board of directors, and though I'd been the one to initiate the change, I'd also struggled to give up control, especially to someone I'd seen as needlessly risk-averse.

Then Austin had executed the first of his drive-by "hey, hey" conversations.

Trust me to manage this, Bash, he'd said. *You've done an amazing job during your time as the face of the company. But if you want Sterling Chase to grow, to be famous for anything besides the Emergency Traffic Control launch, we can't simply follow your whims anymore when deciding which projects Sterling Chase will acquire. The more successful our project launches, the bigger our profit—which will keep the company's owners happy—and the better our reputation, which will attract even better projects to us in the future. Projects that deserve your passion and expertise.*

He'd been right. Thanks to his tireless work, I'd scaled back my public involvement in the company and focused my attention on one or two of Sterling Chase's projects each year where I could really dig in, help fledgling entrepreneurs hone their visions, and then bring them to life.

There were times when I almost felt bad that Austin and Clarissa didn't know the truth—that my four mostly silent partners and I were the founders and owners of Sterling Chase and the creators of the ETC program—but telling them would be a decision all five members of our brotherhood would have to make unanimously, and none of the others knew Austin and Clarissa as well as I did.

Instead, I showed Austin my trust and friendship in other ways, like respecting his position as head of development and supporting his projects as much as I could.

"I spoke to Clarissa yesterday," I told him. "She's going to be at least another week in Sierra Leone since the launch of the digital education venture hit another snag."

Austin grimaced. "It's always the ones that seem simple..."

"True story. But—" I let my grin build slowly. "—she wanted to make sure I knew how impressed she was by your work on the MRO project. She said your team's just waiting for clearance from the folks in Legal so you can move into beta testing and that you'd already found a municipality willing to test it for us, too? Fucking amazing." I leaned back in my chair.

Austin's ruddy face went even redder at this praise. "It just hits different when the project you're working on is an invention you came up with yourself. When the patent is going to be in your own name. This one's special to me."

I nodded in total understanding. That had been one of the reasons I'd talked my friends into expanding Sterling Chase as a startup incubator, even after we'd gotten our windfall. I'd seen the importance of a company that would offer support and resources to inventors and entrepreneurs when launching products that would hopefully go on to improve people's lives.

I thought it said a lot about our company when an employee like Austin, who'd been working on his brilliant MRO plan in his free time for years, decided to bring it to Sterling Chase for development.

"And it's gonna net us a tidy profit on this thing once it hits the market. I think there are many avenues we can explore with this, also. Like the insurance component—higher reimbursements for companies with this technology in place, for example. But really, once we open this up to the marketplace, it can be used in many ways. The potential ROI is... *Sorry.*" Austin gave me a sheepish look and shifted in his seat. "I'm getting carried away. First things first—beta testing. Not sure if Clarissa mentioned to you that Upper Valley County in Virginia is the municipality that's willing to test it?" He pulled his phone from his pocket, consulting his notes. "They're going to install the system in all of their vehicles by the end of the week—"

"Did you consider my suggestion about the satellite uplink?"

A shadow of something passed over Austin's face, and his smile turned wry. "Bash. We've talked about this. The kind of uplink you suggested would cost at least five times as much. That means the budget just to test it would be astronomical, and when we tell the buyers what their investment would be to run it? Nobody'd be able to afford it."

It was on the tip of my tongue to say, "Then let's work harder. Let's develop new technology and bring the cost down." But I had to remind myself this was Austin's project, not one of the ones I was personally managing, so I sighed and nodded. I had to remember I was scaling back. That meant trusting Austin to manage things his own way. Letting go still wasn't easy. That was one of the reasons I'd tried distracting myself with adventure travel recently. Maybe I needed an even bigger distraction.

"For a guy with a business degree, you're very idealistic, and I love that about you. But we've gotta be logical since we operate in the real world." Austin's teasing grin was back, taking the sting out of his words, telling me that he didn't begrudge my control-freak tendencies, and encouraging me to smile with him. "Remind me again why a bunch of savvy operators like the folks who founded Sterling installed a bunch of idealists and dreamers onto the board of directors?"

I gave a half chuckle. "Austin, you wouldn't believe me if I told you. But go on. What's the next step, after the system is installed?"

"Right, yeah. So, Legal's getting us final approval before the beta program can go live," he said earnestly. "There are a few i's to dot and t's to cross, but it should be out of our hands late next week, and I'm thinking I'll do a celebratory lunch for the team. Jonas is working on pricing models now, and even though it's a bit premature, I think..."

Austin droned on about cost/income projections, but despite my interest in the project, I found my gaze straying over his head to the picture on the wall screen, my focus stolen by a pair of big brown eyes.

There was nothing logical about my fascination with Rowe Prince. He was a bright blob of technicolor ink that had come out of nowhere and splashed across the orderly canvas of my life. A distraction I couldn't afford. A risk that wouldn't pass any of Austin's cost-benefit analyses.

But looking at his eyes, at the curve of his cheek... I couldn't make myself care.

He couldn't manipulate me when I already knew he was a liar. I wasn't going to fall for his con when I was already on the lookout for it.

And I wanted him, more than I'd wanted anything for a long time.

I wanted him on his back in my bed, his body beneath mine.

I wanted to get in his head, to learn all his secrets.

I wanted to stop his lies with my lips on his.

I wanted *him* to be my distraction.

"Erm. Bash?"

I blinked at Austin. "Yes! God, sorry. I was just thinking over everything you said. It's... a lot."

Kenji, who knew I was lying, gave a strangled cough.

Austin, who didn't, looked confused. He turned to see what I'd been looking at, and his brow furrowed. "Do I know that guy?"

"Doubtful." I stood, then motioned to Kenji, who tapped a few keys on his tablet that made the picture disappear. "I'm running late for my next meeting, Austin, but seriously, awesome job on this project. Let's check in again next week. I'll have Kenji put you on my calendar officially."

Austin grinned and stood, offering me a handshake. "Sounds great," he said. He flashed a smile at Kenji, who looked faintly nauseated, then walked out of the office.

Kenji stood slowly, shaking his head. "Holy ulterior motives, Batman. That man wants to kiss your ass in more ways than one."

"Nah, I don't get that vibe from him. Austin wants to impress me because I'm on the board of directors at the company he works for. He's probably hoping for a fat annual bonus, a nice raise, and a promotion if Clarissa ever leaves."

"You could be right," Kenji grudgingly agreed.

"I am." I lifted an eyebrow significantly. "It's almost as if I'm a decent judge of character, Kenji. Almost like... I know what I'm doing and can handle myself."

Kenji rolled his eyes as he headed for the door. "Keep telling yourself that, sir," he called over his shoulder, a grin in his voice. "But every time you do, I'm upping the budget for the Escape Fund."

"And I'm gonna use it to get myself one of those *good* personal assistants!" I called back, but Kenji pretended not to hear me.

————

I asked Morris, my driver, to arrive at the Park Avenue address twenty minutes early so I could hop in the town car and look like he'd picked me up first. The ruse was a little comical, and I felt ridiculous taking part in it... but the minute Rowe approached from the direction of the nearest subway stop, saw the car idling at the curb, and began limping in an exaggerated fashion, I let out a bark of laughter, caught up in the silliness and the challenge of him all over again.

The poor man looked legitimately terrible, with bags the size of suitcases under his eyes, a face pinched with nerves, and his hair even wilder than the night before, like maybe he'd had to run from the train. But somehow, he'd found himself a perfectly tailored pair of dark jeans and a tweed jacket, so whoever was supplying his costumes had leveled up overnight.

I hopped out of the car and threw on my cheeriest smile.

"Good afternoon, Mr. Chase! Are you ready for—oh no! it looks like you have a hitch in your giddy-up." I held the door open and ushered him in. The scent of coffee and fresh soap wafted off his skin as he took a seat in the deep plush leather seat. "Hopefully nothing that will interfere with your playing today."

He darted a look at me from under his eyelashes and swallowed hard.

"Ah... Actually, Bash, I'm afraid it might. It very well might. Such a disappointment. You know Sterling Chase loves... playing the ponies." He shook a fist at the sky. "Curse you, fate!"

Just like that—*just like that*—any doubts or second thoughts I might have had about whether I was doing the right thing faded away into the pure joy of being in this terrible liar's presence.

"I'm so sorry. What happened?"

"It's rather a long story. You see, after I left the gala, I was, um... I was set upon by ruffians. It was quite upsetting."

I shook my head. "Ruffians," I repeated in a hushed voice. "On the way to your limo? My god. Did they attack you? Did you hurt yourself running away?"

"Run? Why the hell would I run?" he demanded, eyes narrowed in genuine annoyance. Then, like he'd remembered he was supposed to be in character, he straightened in his seat. "No, my good man, I attacked *them*." He nodded once, like he was convincing himself. "I wasn't trained in martial arts for nothing. But I may have injured myself in the fray."

"How devastating. Is it your trick knee, sir?" I leaned toward him to palpate his knee, ignoring the hitch in his breathing when I touched him. "Let's see... it doesn't feel like anything's out of place..."

While I had intended to call his bluff, I hadn't expected my hands to relish the job I'd given them. Rowe's legs were shapely beneath his dark pants. The muscles curved under my touch and bunched as I squeezed them.

I looked up suddenly to meet his eyes before moving my hands down slowly over his calf. "Or is it your ankle?" My voice suddenly sounded rougher.

"I-it was Sally Struthers!" he blurted, yanking his leg away. "I was trying not to offend your delicate sensibilities since I know you're a polo fan, but I can't lie to you, Bash! I don't really have an injury. What really happened was that as I was watching television, a commercial came on the air. This woman spoke so eloquently about how cruel humans can be to our poor animal brethren, and I-I decided then and there that I cannot force that indignity on my poor horse ever again. In fact, I think I'm going vegan." Rowe crossed his arms in front of his chest. "It'll be another of my—"

"—quirky billionaire eccentricities," he and I finished at the same time.

I had to bite my lip to keep from laughing in Rowe's face. Christ, this was fun.

"Being vegan is going to be quite a change for you, Mr. Chase. Does that mean you'll want to cancel your big-game hunting trip for next month? And what will that mean for your Texas cattle ranch?"

Rowe's nose wrinkled in disgust. "Sterling Chase hunts big game?" He blinked. "I mean. I mean... Sterling Chase does *not* hunt big game. No, sir. Not anymore. Cancel the trip immediately and put the cattle up for auction."

I had to bite my tongue against a laugh. Even while bullshitting me, he was pretty damned cute, and part of me wished I had a cattle herd to sell on his behalf.

After pretending to type a note in my phone about selling his fictional ranch, I regarded him for a long moment, watching the afternoon sunlight filtering through the skylight gild his hair while he tried not to squirm under my gaze.

The man was so nervous I could practically feel the molecules in the air around him dancing with it. Yet here he was, in a car heading out of town, still doing his own flawed, adorable impression of a quirky billionaire, despite his nerves. I remembered what he'd told Miranda last night, about how letting fear hold you back was a waste of your life, and I couldn't help feeling a grudging respect for the man.

I blinked and forced myself to look away. That kind of thinking was exactly the shit Silas and Kenji were worried about. I was here for flirtation. For fun. To fuck with the man and then, if he was amenable, to fuck him. To sort the truth from his lies. I immediately resolved to get this interaction back on track.

"You seem a little... tense," I noted, leaning toward him to study his face more closely.

"D-do I?" Rowe leaned back against his seat.

I lowered my voice to a purr. "If you want, I know something that could help with that, Mr. Chase."

His eyes widened.

I leaned in closer... close enough to see the tiny birthmark under his eyebrow and a spot on his cheek he'd missed while shaving. His lips parted, and his breath came out in a shaky, needy sigh that made my blood thrum.

Abruptly, I shifted left and grabbed the coffee cup I'd placed in the holder earlier.

"Coffee!" I said triumphantly. "I grabbed that new flavor you liked so much from your favorite bakery."

He shut his eyes for a moment. "C-coffee. Right. Good." He accepted the cup with a small smile. "You know me and my coffee." He took a large sip and immediately choked. "This is... uh. This is very sweet."

"Just the way you like it. Caramel-fudge-accino with extra pumps and double whip." I beamed. "I made a note of it, per your last email. Oh, speaking of which..." I pretended to consult my phone once again. "I scheduled your colonoscopy for next week, and I took the liberty of changing your full-body wax to this Thursday since you're back in town early."

"You... but..."

"Also, your mother called to set you up on a date with her friend's daughter. A woman named—" I squinted at my phone screen as if attempting to suss out the details. "—Jade, who's a studio art major at NYU, runs fifteen miles a week and practices something called *Reiki*. Sounds fancy. Also, she's not, and I quote, 'out for your money, darling.' Unquote." I looked at him seriously. "Now, I know the situation with Bubbles must be fresh in your mind, sir, but since he's happily married now, I'm sure he'd want nothing more than for you to find love again. So I set that up for Friday." I winked and added in a whisper, "After the wax."

Rowe's eyes had gotten wider with every additional detail before he firmed his jaw. "My mother doesn't know I'm gay," he said gruffly.

"Make an excuse and cancel the date. A-and I don't need a body wax. I don't have any, um... Just cancel it."

Well, then.

He turned to look out the window, staring at the trees that bordered the highway now that we'd escaped the city and were heading west. His hands were clenched together tightly in his lap.

"What can you tell me about the man we're going to see? Have you met Devon before?"

I wanted to reach out and grab Rowe's hands in mine, to tell him not to worry because Dev was one of the sweetest, gentlest humans I knew. But the truth was, Dev was probably not going to be friendly— especially not after hearing from Silas that Rowe was a fraud. And I'd lied last night when I said everyone on the board knew lots of people outside Sterling Chase who'd invest in Rowe's project. These days, Dev made it a point to talk to as few people as possible.

"Yes. I know him well. He's a nice guy. Great at research. Huge animal lover. He studied veterinary medicine in college."

"Oh, that's great." He exhaled in relief. "Looking forward to meeting him."

Some mischievous impulse made me add, "I've also heard him described as *supercute*, and I happen to know he's gay. Maybe the two of you..." For some reason, I couldn't even finish the suggestion. The thought of Rowe hooking up with my friend made my stomach twist in an ugly way.

"Uh, *no*," Rowe said dismissively. "Not interested in hooking up with some rich prick who plays po—uh..." He broke off with a blush and darted a guilty glance in my direction. "I mean, I'm not interested in a romantic connection at this time. Thank you anyway."

I poked the inside of my cheek with my tongue, feeling my temper rise. It shouldn't have stung as badly as it did to hear his opinion of people who had money. After all, his impression of a billionaire was so absurd it was almost insulting, and I highly doubted it was drawn from real life since people with ten-figure net worths weren't thick on the ground in Nowheresville, Indiana. But it was pretty fucking ironic that he was slamming all rich guys as pricks while seeking out a meeting with Justin Hardy, the prickiest prick of all.

Besides, some of us couldn't help being rich. Some of us were born this way.

"Strange that you should have a chip on your shoulder about people with money, Mr. Chase," I bit out, "when you yourself are worth over 2.5 billion dollars."

"I am?" His eyes flared wide. "That is, I... I so rarely count it all up."

I barked out a laugh. "Such a jokester. I didn't get that from your emails. You're very different in person."

"That's me," Rowe said with a weak smile. "A joke a minute."

"Why don't you tell me about this side project that you're hoping to discuss with Mr. Hardy," I suggested. "I can make notes for you, if you'd like."

"Well..." He paled, then took a deep breath and opened his mouth to speak. I sat poised on the edge of my seat, wondering which side of his nature was about to emerge, adorably conniving liar or the passionate, truth-telling angel.

Then the car made a very distinct left turn into the driveway that led to the polo field, and Rowe shut his mouth again.

I clenched my teeth in frustration. "Later, then." I forced a smile.

When Morris opened the door, Rowe peeked outside anxiously, like an alien who'd crash-landed his ship on a distant planet and wasn't quite sure the landscape was hospitable.

I looked out also... and saw nothing but the usual low white buildings of the clubhouse and stables, wide swaths of grass, several horses, and a few clusters of players and spectators casually chatting. Some of them looked pretty boisterous, like they'd already begun celebrating, but none of them looked intimidating or even particularly interesting.

"Out you go, Rowe," I said softly, ushering him ahead of me. As he stood beside the car, I couldn't help adding, "Everything is going to be fine."

I quickly shepherded him toward the stables, hoping not to run into anyone I knew so I could avoid awkward introductions. But we hadn't taken more than a step in that direction when one of the spectators chatting in front of the entrance broke away from his friends and jogged over, pointing a finger at Rowe.

"It's *you!*" He grinned, wide and boozy. "Oh my god. This is amazing."

"M-me?" Rowe stammered. "No."

"Yes! I told my friends I recognized you, and they didn't believe me. They said it was like that time I swore I saw Elton John at my cousin's sweet sixteen. But now that I'm up close, I'm a hundred percent sure." He folded his arms across his pink polo, which was slightly damp in patches, either with sweat or beer. "Sing the song, man."

The panicked look in Rowe's eyes suggested that he was attempting to melt into the lush grass of the polo field. "Song? I'm afraid I don't know what you mean."

The man began strumming a tiny, invisible guitar and launched into song. "My name is Burrito Bandito... and I've come here today to say..." He made a rolling motion with his hand like he expected Rowe to continue.

"No way," Rowe said flatly, unintentionally continuing the rhyme of the song.

He darted a glance at me, horror-struck.

Color bloomed on his cheeks, spreading an answering warmth through my belly.

And before I knew it, I'd burst out laughing once again.

FIVE

ROWE

I freaking hated polo.

I'd figured as much last night while I was reading article after article on polo rules and etiquette while simultaneously watching highlight reels of the "Ten Most Amazing Feats in Polo History"—which, by the way, was a massive oversell since as far as I could tell, they all involved men playing croquet on horseback.

My suspicion had only deepened when we'd pulled up to this polo club with its huge green fields that looked plusher than my mom's living room carpet and made me shudder at the memory of muggy weekend mornings as a teenager pushing a mower around my parents' front yard.

And now, as the mediocre tipper from one of the accounting firms where I delivered serenaded me with the Burrito Bandito song loud enough to draw a crowd, I could one hundred percent confirm that I hated, hated, *hated* polo, and I absolutely should not have come here no matter how badly I wanted to meet Justin or how tempting it was to spend an afternoon with my gorgeous "assistant." My stomach clenched, and the microwave oatmeal I'd eaten for breakfast threatened to make a reappearance.

My accuser's face fell. "You were supposed to say '*olé*,'" he said, aggrieved that I wasn't playing along.

"Uh. P-pardon me?" I stammered, cool as a cucumber trapped in boiling oil. "I don't understand this ritual, I'm afraid."

Polo was worse than the gala. Infinitely worse. Lying about being a mysterious rich guy no one knew had nearly killed me—literally, since I'd almost dived face-first into a potted plant. Lying about belonging at a polo club while *Bash*, the personal assistant sent to tempt me to sexy, sexy hell, stood by choking on laughter was bound to finish the job.

I fixed my face in a grimace of disapproval and hoped it was far enough from my usual friendly smile that my accuser would second-guess himself. But, just my luck, the man was drunk enough to stick to his guns... and get belligerent about it.

"You're the burrito guy! I work at 201 East Sixty-Fifth Street, remember? Dos burrito Mexicanos, extra red sauce? That's me. I didn't know you guys delivered this far out of the city."

My cheeks burned. *Extra red sauce, indeed.*

Bash stopped laughing when he noticed my distress and took a protective step forward. I made a mental note to give him a fake raise as long as I was acting as his fake boss.

"I'm..." I swallowed. "I'm quite confident I don't know what you mean, friend. Sterling Chase does not eat burritos." I kicked my grimace up a notch, and the man cocked his head like a confused puppy.

"Nahhhh. Dude, I know you. Come on. Do the little toe kick." He leaned around me and grabbed my arm before Bash could intervene.

Bash instantly bristled with anger, growing taller and broader right in front of me. His eyes narrowed like he was shooting laser beams at my accuser's hand, and the anger coming off him made the air tremble.

Under other circumstances, it might have felt nice to have someone—especially a funny, kind, Bash-like someone—sticking up for me in this crowd of rich folks. But in that moment, I envisioned Bash throwing a punch to defend his "boss" and getting kicked out, or arrested, or even injured if this dude managed to land a blow before Bash destroyed him. I couldn't let any of that happen.

Of all the mortifying ways I'd envisioned this charade ending, I'd never imagined it would be with a command performance of the Burrito Bandito song on a polo field to avert a fistfight. Massive oversight on my part.

"Bernard Hennicker," an imperious, feminine voice said. "For heaven's sake, stop accosting Sterling Chase! Remove your hand from his person this instant."

All heads in the vicinity, including mine, turned to watch the blonde tornado bearing down on us, dressed in a drop-waisted floral-print dress with enormous shoulder pads.

"Constance! M-Ms. Baxter-Hicks! You're looking... fabulous," I managed to choke out when she paused beside me.

"Thank you, dear." She leaned in and added more quietly, "I thought quite a lot about what you said last night, about how style should reflect what makes you feel most confident, and this morning I decided to it was time for this little number to make a reappearance." She tweaked the skirt of her dress, making it flow around her shins.

Constance Baxter-Hicks felt most confident in late-eighties Laura Ashley. Good to know.

"Ma'am, this man is not Sterling... whoever," my accuser—Bernard—insisted. "He's the man who delivers my lunch."

Constance turned toward him and raised a single eyebrow. Apparently, Bash wasn't the only one who knew how to wield those like swords.

"*This* man?" Constance flung a hand toward me. "This gentleman wearing a vintage tweed St. Laurent blazer and last-season Ferragamo loafers delivers your lunch? *Really?*"

Beside me, Bash leaned back to scan me up and down, like he was appreciating my outfit for the first time. If he knew how many visits to Second Chance Savers it had taken for me to find these loafers for a *steal* or how many hours I'd spent polishing them, he might have appreciated them even more.

Before Bernard could utter another word, Constance spoke again. "Which is more likely, Bernard: that I don't know Sterling Chase, the billionaire founder of *Sterling Chase*, when I see him? Or," she said in a withering tone, "that this is a repeat of that unfortunate incident at Olivia's birthday party, where you tried to force Lord Piers Bishop to sing 'Rocket Man'?"

Bernard's mouth opened, then shut again. Several onlookers tittered. Bernard looked at me, frowned, and shrugged. His shoulders slumped.

Constance made a *tsk*ing noise. "Honestly, dear, you smell like a brewery. Your poor father will be *incensed*. Apologize to Mr. Chase for grabbing him without permission."

"Sorry," Bernard mumbled like a petulant child.

I stared at Constance in shock. I'd have bet money last night that she'd seen right through me. Instead, she'd come to my defense... *magnificently*. So fuck Joey and his "big brass balls" talk. From now on, when I needed confidence, I'd be channeling Constance Baxter-Hicks.

"Hon. Est. Ly," she said, watching Bernard walk away. She visibly shook herself, as though clearing away her negative emotions, then turned to me with a brilliant smile. "Now, Mr. Chase, you *must* come to the clubhouse with me." She pointed toward the low white building nearby. "I have some people who'd absolutely love to meet you. And Miranda, of course—"

I took an instinctive step toward Bash. I couldn't possibly go with Constance. I was already tired of playing this character, and I hadn't even encountered Dev or Justin Hardy yet. But how could I say no politely when she'd been so kind to me?

Fortunately, I had an assistant for this sort of thing. "I'm afraid Sterling and I are overdue at the stables," Bash said briskly, taking my hand to pull me away. "Perhaps another time."

"Bash." She inclined her head regally and eyed our joined hands, confirming my suspicion that this was not your average billionaire-and-assistant behavior. "I'm spearheading an equine therapy endowment..." She lifted an eyebrow. "I assume I can count on your support? Yours and Mr. Chase's?"

"Of course." Bash's words came out more like a sigh, like he was used to being hit up for donations in a casual conversation.

Honestly, rich people were worse than Bobby's daughter hitting up all the people at the Tech Barn every time her Scout troop wanted to go on a field trip. I could only imagine how often people hit up an actual billionaire like Sterling Chase.

"Come along, Mr. Chase." Bash marched resolutely down a dirt path toward the stables, his long strides eating up the dirt the only sign that he was annoyed by the encounter. With my hand in his, I had to trot to keep up, but it didn't occur to me to pull away, either.

He didn't say anything for a full minute, and neither did I.

Then, finally, "Are you alright?" he asked in a low voice.

"Y-yes." *No.* "I'm really sorry about that. I hope you don't feel obligated to donate any money to Ms. Baxter-Hicks's endowment thingy," I blurted.

I had no idea how much money Bash had, and it was none of my business. I figured it was more than me if his mom was vacationing someplace Constance Baxter-Hicks liked to go, but it couldn't be very much if the man was working as a billionaire's personal assistant. I really hoped he hadn't agreed to make a donation just to get me out of an awkward situation.

Bash blew out a long breath. "Nothing you need to apologize for. I'm sure it's an excellent cause, and I can afford it." He shot me a glance. "Sterling Chase pays me well."

I would hope so. "Doesn't matter. It's still wrong to, like, *expect* someone to contribute just because they have money."

He didn't reply. Instead, he gave me another of those side-eyed looks. His fingers clasped mine more firmly, and he slowed his pace so we were strolling, almost like... friends. Almost like *lovers*.

I could feel my pulse in my cheeks and knew my face had to be a concerning shade of puce now. Sadly, puce was *not* my color.

My conscience screamed at me to come clean. To tell Bash I wasn't Sterling and admit everything. To tell him exactly how naive and desperate and foolish I was. Bash seemed like a person who knew how to get things done, and he had a great sense of humor. If he could handle working for a man he'd never met until last night, whose mother scheduled his dates and who enjoyed coffee so full of carbohydrates it might evolve into a new life form, maybe he could handle the truth. He might even help me.

But on the other hand... what if he didn't? What if he was so loyal to the real Sterling Chase that he got angry at my impersonation? What if I'd cleared this many hurdles, gotten so close to achieving my goal, and lost it because I trusted the wrong person?

I thought of my sister and touched the tattoo on my hip. I couldn't take that chance.

More than that, the idea of confessing my lie to Bash made my whole body go cold with humiliation and fear. I liked him—liked the sound of Bash's laughter and the way he looked at me so intensely that my heart plinked around like pennies in a jar. Liked the way he'd protected me when he'd thought I was someone who deserved protecting and the soda pop fizz that had sparkled through my veins when he'd leaned close to me in the car.

I didn't want to lose any of that.

I didn't have a lot of experience with guys. Back home in Indiana, I'd shared a few longing looks and a couple of handjobs behind the bleachers with guys who'd gone on to very loudly proclaim their straightness by dating women. After I'd come up with the idea for Project Daisy Chain, I'd been too consumed with my research to spend time figuring out how to meet other gay men in rural Indiana. And since I'd arrived in New York, I'd been way too busy delivering burritos and trying to finagle a meeting to bother with Hornet or Grindr or any of the other apps Joey kept encouraging me to try.

But I knew that I was close to having a very real crush on my very fake employee. And, maybe selfishly, I wanted to keep talking and laughing and holding this sexy man's hand as long as I could...

Assuming, of course, that I didn't vomit on his shoes in the next ten minutes from nerves.

"I was a bit worried back there, honestly," Bash said after we'd walked in silence for another moment.

I looked up at him in surprise. "Worried... about me?"

"Obviously not," he scoffed. "Worried about Bernard. I was afraid you were going to let loose with the martial arts." He dropped my hand and mimed some sort of move that looked more like a person having convulsions than any of the karate moves I'd learned through after-school enrichment programs.

I snort-giggled inelegantly and pressed a hand to my mouth, startled by my own laughter... and by the fact that I *could* laugh so soon after the almost-debacle.

Bash glanced at me, and his lips twitched, exactly as they had last night. Then he repeated the action, jumping into an exaggerated crane pose before doing a high kick... right there on the track to the stables, where anyone could see him.

"Sterling Chase does not tolerate your disrespect!" he fake-yelled.

I burst into laughter then, so hard I doubled over and my stomach cramped with it. It was so *silly*—all of it, nearly every moment of the last two days—and my life had had a distinct lack of silliness for so long. The simple pleasure of laughing with him was like rain after a drought, soaking into all the dried-up parts of me, washing away the dust, and making me feel like something could grow there again.

Even if nothing else came of this weekend—of my whole damn trip to New York—I could almost, *almost* convince myself that this wonderful moment with Bash was enough to justify the cost.

I'm going to kiss this man, I promised myself. *Somehow, some way. He is going to be my first real kiss.*

When we neared the stables, Bash grabbed my hand again and gestured for me to follow him halfway down the row of stalls to the spot where a pretty brown horse with a white starburst on her fore-head stuck her head out curiously, like she'd been waiting for us.

"Ohhhh," I breathed. "How gorgeous."

"She is." Bash reached out to stroke the horse's nose. "These stables house more than the polo ponies. Several people keep their thoroughbreds here because of the trainers and facilities... Hey, sweet girl. I want you to meet a friend. Rowe, this is Starlight. Starlight, Rowe."

"How do you know her?" I asked before reaching out a tentative hand to rub the side of her neck. "You said you liked polo, but do you ride?"

"I do." He hesitated. "Silas and I have been friends with Dev since college, and Dev's a renowned horse trainer... among other things."

"Oh." Bash's answer explained why he'd been able to introduce me to these guys. It also probably explained how he'd gotten the job with Sterling Chase in the first place. He had connections to two of Sterling's—*my*—trusted board members.

"Where'd you go to college?" I asked just as Starlight swung her head around and pushed it into my face.

I hadn't realized how close I'd gotten to the horse while following Bash's lead, and I stumbled backward with a little yelp. Thankfully, Bash grabbed me before I got accidentally knocked down by another horse being led down the center aisle of the stables.

"Fuck," I croaked, trying my best not to let my fear of the giant animals overwhelm me. "That horse is really *exceptionally* large." I'd never been comfortable around livestock despite living near lots of farmland, a fact that Daisy used to tease me about constantly.

"Woah. Easy," Bash said, grabbing me out of the aisle and pulling me close. The warmth of his breath landed on my cheek, causing all the little hairs on my body to stand on end, and when I tried to suck in a breath to calm myself, I ended up inhaling Bash's expensive cologne... which had the opposite effect to what I'd intended. "Starlight," he chided the horse softly, "didn't anyone ever teach you to play hard to get? You can't just get right in a man's face and try to kiss him like that."

"Can't you?" I mumbled without thinking, taking another deep, drugging lungful of Bash's delicious scent.

A loud bang came from a stall door down the aisle, making me jump and Starlight blow out her cheeks with a disgruntled noise. My lips accidentally grazed the edge of Bash's jaw when I startled, and Bash's arms tightened around me in response. Our eyes met, and the air thickened around us.

What is this? I wanted to climb him, to kiss him, to full-out beg him to touch me anywhere and everywhere. My brain was clearly not looking out for my best interests since the last thing I needed to do was fuck things up with this guy and his rich friends, but I couldn't help myself. I brushed my lips across his jaw again, so softly it was almost like a phantom touch.

Suddenly, Bash's mouth crashed down on mine with firm possession, stealing the breath from my lungs and sending every drop of blood on the express train out of my brain and into my pants.

"Oh," I whimpered against his mouth. "Oh."

All I could think was *yes. This. Now I understand.*

This was what all the fuss was about.

This was what I'd been missing.

Kissing Bash was like having a portal open up to another world. A world where things were brighter, more colorful, and just all around... better.

My hands fisted in his shirt, and I realized I was pressing myself against him as desperately as I could. Was that bad? Was it okay? Was he having a kind of mental situation in which he was no longer in control of his own lips? Otherwise, why would a man like that be kissing a man like me? It made absolutely no sense.

"You're killing me," he murmured under his breath before his tongue snuck into my mouth and took ownership of the place.

My dick was leaking. It had to be. I was going to humiliate myself further with a giant wet spot on the front of the clearance rack

designer jeans I wore. I was going to get arrested for public inde-
cency, and the stupid story would get picked up by that tabloid that
people read on the subway, and I'd be ruined. *Burrito Bandito Gets
Extra Spicy on the Polo Field.*

I honestly didn't care. Kissing Bash was worth any creepy headline, especially when his hands moved down to cup my ass and pull
me even closer. I groaned into the kiss and ground my hardening dick
into his thigh. This was pure nirvana.

But when Bash's hand moved down to cup my hip, I froze. His
fingers had brushed over my tattoo, the exact same spot I always
touched to ground myself, and when my sister's image flashed
through my mind, I pulled sharply, guiltily away.

Where the fuck are your priorities, Rowe Prince?

"Sorry," I said, pulling back and heaving in some air. "Fuck. I—"

"That was a mistake," Bash said in a low, gruff voice. He backed
up half a pace. "Won't happen again."

I blinked. I mean, yes, he was right; it shouldn't happen again.
Not while I was lying. Not while I still needed his help. But I had to
wonder why *he* was pulling away.

"Did I... do it wrong?" I wondered. "It's okay. You can be honest."

If it was possible, Bash's eyes darkened even more. I felt like he
wanted to devour me... which was incredibly inconvenient because I
really wanted to be devoured against my better judgment.

"No. Not even close." He pushed a curl out of my eyes, but his
fingers lingered on my hair, chafing it between his fingers like he was
assessing the texture... and then he stepped even further back, out of
touching range. "You didn't do anything wrong. It's just... unwise.
You're Sterling Chase, after all."

My eyes widened in realization. "Oh, god. Oh, I am. I'm your
boss, aren't I?"

Bash's mouth opened, then shut. His lips were swollen and shiny
from our kisses, and I couldn't help tracing them with my gaze the
way I wished I could with my tongue.

He growled and took another giant step away—at this rate, he was going back himself all the way to Cleveland—but it did nothing to break the thread of pure *want* between us.

"I meant that you have business to attend to, sir. You're hoping to see Justin Hardy. You wanted me to introduce you to Dev. You were eager to talk to them about an opportunity. Remember?" Bash pressed his lips together and stared at the ground for a beat before looking up at me with fresh conviction. "So we should go do that and not allow ourselves to be distracted by... other things."

"No, of course," I said softly.

His hands were fisted by his sides, and I wondered what I could have possibly done to make him look almost angry, but maybe it didn't matter. I'd gotten the kiss I'd promised myself, and it had been better than I'd ever dreamed. It would be greedy to want more. And Bash was right—I did have a higher purpose.

"Nothing I love more than talking about an exciting new piece of technology," I assured him with a fake smile.

But for the first time in a very long time, when I said I was excited to talk about my project... I was lying.

SIX

BASH

He was lying.

I'd known it all along, and all along, I'd told myself it didn't matter—that I could fuck a handsome liar as easily and uncomplicated-ly as I could fuck anyone else. But then I'd kissed the man... and found myself forgetting.

Holding Rowe in my arms had sent shock waves through me. Like an idiot, I'd stood there indulging in the most passionate, incredibly overwhelming kiss of my life with a man who hadn't said more than a handful of truths in the few hours I'd known him, and every cell in my body had wanted to rub itself up against the tiny fraudster.

Even now, having put several feet of space between us and invoked the name of Justin *fucking* Hardy, which should have killed off any lingering lust in an instant, tension still saturated the air between us, and my hands ached to pull Rowe against me again.

It was a lowering moment... and an enlightening one.

There had been a small part of me, back when we'd first learned just how big an asshole Justin was and how comprehensively he'd screwed Silas over, that had been almost angry with my best friend. I'd never told Silas that, obviously, and I never would, but I'd wondered how the hell a man brilliant enough to win a full-tuition scholarship to Yale and people-savvy enough that Fortune 500 companies consulted him on their organizational structures could be fooled by a pissant idiot like Justin.

Now, I was starting to think I understood.

Maybe Kenji was right. Maybe sometimes you couldn't see the danger until it was too late.

Rowe stared back at me, swaying slightly on the balls of his feet. His cheeks were flushed a dark pink, and his hair was even more disheveled than before, like a pair of large hands had raked through them. *My hands.* A bolt of longing pierced my gut, and my dick, which still saw absolutely no problem with the situation, swelled uncomfortably in my pants.

When Starlight whickered softly, I seized on the excuse to turn my attention to the mare, stroking her head and ears soothingly.

"You're, uh... you're sure I didn't do anything wrong?" Rowe asked hesitantly after a moment.

Fuck, the man sounded nervous as a virgin. Like he'd never actually kissed anyone before today—and, Christ, if I spent any amount of time dwelling on *that* idea, I wasn't going to be able to turn around without embarrassing myself.

"Positive," I gritted out.

"Good. Okay. Only..." He swallowed so hard his throat clicked audibly. "Only you seem kind of upset? And I wonder if I might, ah, owe you an apology for taking advantage? I swear to you, Bash, I've never done that before with anyone. Anyone I *employed*, I mean," he tacked on belatedly. "And I am truly sorry."

I took a deep breath and let it out slowly. The man was apologizing for taking advantage of me, sounding genuinely, acutely miserable, when it was taking all my self-control not to grab him, shove him into the nearest empty stall, and kiss him until there was no doubt in his mind that he was doing it right because he couldn't possibly do it wrong.

"You didn't take advantage," I assured him. "It's like I said: we need to focus on the reason we're here." Unfortunately for me, it was getting harder and harder to remember what that was.

I'd originally intended to make Rowe squirm all day—to keep him out of his element, feed him ridiculous foods that were "Sterling Chase's favorite," flirt with him outrageously, and see whether I could make him confess everything before I got him into bed. Now, being within five feet of him felt like a threat to my equilibrium.

Thankfully, Devon McKay happened to be just on the other side of this barn. And for maybe the first time, I couldn't even be sad that life had hardened Dev into one of the most suspicious, grumpy men I knew. Thanks to Silas lighting up our group chat with a play-by-play from last night's gala like he worked for TMZ, Dev knew exactly who Rowe was, and he'd already given me a ration of shit about the situation via text this morning. Dev didn't suffer fools, he was impossible to con, and he'd have no trouble helping me rebuild my defenses against the sexy little liar... before I decided I didn't want to get rid of him at all.

After a final stroke of Starlight's blaze, I took Rowe's elbow and led him deeper into the stables toward Trigger's stall. Sure enough, Dev was crouched down on the floor, tending his precious stallion.

Dev turned when he heard us approaching, straightened to his full, impressive height, and for a single second before he pulled me in for a tight hug, his face lit with the broad, open grin he so rarely wore anymore.

"Bash," he said warmly, thumping my back. "Shit, it's good to see you."

"Same. How was your trip from Texas? "

"Eh." Dev shrugged and stepped away. "Little engine trouble outside Christiansburg, but we survived." He threw one heavily muscled arm around his horse's neck, causing the rolled cuff of his sleeve to ride up. "At least Trigger got to enjoy his new trailer."

Of course the horse got a swanky new trailer while Dev still drove the same beat-up truck he'd had for years. My smile slipped a fraction, but I knew better than to comment on how Dev spent—or didn't spend—his money.

"New ink?" I nodded at the lines of black on his forearm.

"Yep." He tugged his sleeve down before I could see the design and immediately shifted his attention to the man at my side. His smile disappeared as he folded his arms over his chest and gave Rowe a long, thorough up-down. "And who's this, then? New fuck buddy? Could you not afford a full-sized one?"

Rowe, who'd been steadily inching behind me, froze. His gaze ping-ponged from Devon to the horse and back, like he wasn't sure which was the greater threat.

I shot Dev a glare. I hadn't expected Dev to be friendly to Rowe—I'd even hoped he *wouldn't*—but fucking with Rowe was one thing. Being mean about it was another.

Dev gave me a blank look in return.

"I'm afraid you've misread the situation," I returned, warning in my tone. "This is *the* Sterling Chase, founder of Sterling Chase. My boss. Your boss, too, in a way. He goes by Rowe."

"Rowe." Dev made the word sound like a threat. "Middle name?"

Rowe blinked. "A-actually... yes." He sounded almost surprised that he was able to tell the truth for once, and my lips twitched. "It's a pleasure to meet you in person finally, Devon, after so many years of you serving on the... *my*... board." He leaned around me to offer Dev a handshake.

Dev's huge hand engulfed Rowe's for a second. "It's Dev. Nobody but my mother calls me Devon, Sterling. As I'm sure you recall from our many telephone conversations."

Rowe's face, which was still pleasantly pink from our kiss, went red, and he stepped back immediately. "Right. Yes. Sorry. Silly me. *Dev.* That's, um, a fine horse you've got there. Very..." He gestured vaguely with his hands. "Shiny."

Dev seemed unsure whether Rowe was making fun of him or not. He made a noncommittal noise and stroked the horse's flank. "Rowe, meet Trigger by Noble out of Zephyr Lake by Legendary Lake."

"Oh. Wow. I see now why he's so big. He'd have to be, to carry a name like that." Rowe gave the horse a tiny, formal bow. "Pleased to make your acquaintance. I'd love to introduce you to my own fine horses sometime. Perhaps we could have a small dinner party. Bash, please make a note."

Dev shot me a look—*Is this guy for real?*—and I shrugged minutely. None of Rowe was real. And, I was starting to think, *all* of him was.

"Silas mentioned that you had some business you wanted to discuss with me, Sterling." Dev set his jaw. "What's that about?"

"Oh, no, I... Well. Maybe? There's a project. Project Daisy Chain." He flushed hard and gnawed at his lip for a second. "That's just a working title, of course. I... I mean, *the inventor* will think up a much more professional title eventually. Right now, it's just a basic app and a whole lot of research and notes on ways to improve it so that it can be brought to market, but the inventor has, ah... reached the limits of their knowledge. They need help."

Dev glanced at me, but I could only shrug again. Rowe had just given Dev more information on this topic than he'd ever given me... though, to be fair, I'd been too mesmerized by the man to think about his business.

"And why not develop this project in-house at Sterling Chase?" Dev wondered.

"Good question. *Great* question. I actually, um, initially thought it would be a good fit for Sterling Chase. Did you know—*fun fact*—I founded the company because I created a prototype for a stoplight communication system that reduced the arrival time of first responders to emergencies? ETC is a killer innovation... Well, you know it, obviously."

"Of course we know," Dev said dryly. "Brilliant idea *you* came up with."

Rowe nodded, and just like last night when he'd started speaking passionately about fashion, once he'd warmed to his subject, all of his stuttering and hesitation disappeared. "It's an amazing tech. Recent studies have shown that response times are down by nearly thirty percent in municipalities that use the... *our...* system. Fatalities from auto collisions due to emergency response have gone down by nearly ten percent."

I frowned. Those specifics weren't a secret, but they weren't exactly available on our website. Rowe had done some research. I felt a frisson of mingled worry and excitement race down my spine.

"But as great as all that is," Rowe went on earnestly, "there's so much more to be done. So many other brilliant ideas out there to improve lives, if someone would just look for them instead of... spending their time sending out rude, terse form-letter rejections."

I wanted to tell him that people *were* looking for them. That Sterling Chase was, right then, working on technology that would help tremendously. But I held back. That was proprietary information, and it was none of his damn business.

"Of course, our company is already exceptionally busy right now." Rowe slipped back into his "quirky billionaire liar" voice, so different from his genuine excited tone that the effect was jarring. "So many great ideas, so little time, right? Like that app that interacts with your coffee maker to make sure your cup is brewed before you wake up. Really thrilling stuff."

I opened my mouth and shut it again. I wanted to inform him defensively that the CaffApp had been a highly profitable endeavor, and it *did* improve people's lives, and it was none of his business which projects Sterling Chase chose to contract for... but the words got stuck in my throat because a tiny part of me agreed with him.

"Now, I know I could simply ask you, as my loyal board of directors, to intervene and push my project through, but that hardly seems fair. That's why I'm suggesting that the inventor take his project elsewhere. To Justin Hardy, perhaps, or anyone else you believe might be interested." Rowe gave Dev a bright smile. "With Sterling Chase's personal recommendation."

The look of outrage Dev shot me should have sent the barn up in flames. "Bash, I need to speak to you a moment. Alone." He shoved me back toward the main area of the barn. "*Now.*"

Before I turned, I saw Rowe's smile turn to panic. "But... shouldn't you look after Trigger? He's not in his cage. What if he bites someone?"

Cage?

"He's a free-range horse," Dev said, rolling his eyes, though Rowe couldn't see. "Feed him an apple from the bag on the table, and the two of you can chat."

He dragged me away from Rowe and around the corner toward the trainer's office before hissing at me, exactly as Silas had the night before, "What the fuck?"

Since my insides were screaming the same question, I had no answer. "I know."

"*Sterling Chase's personal recommendation?* He's using you to gain access to people who can invest in his little project, and you're helping him. I don't care how hot a piece of ass he is, Bash—"

"Stop! It's not like that." I paused, then admitted, "Not *entirely* like that. And I'm not helping him do anything—"

"Silas said you spoke to the guy for twenty minutes last night. You showed up with him today. You don't think people noticed? You don't think that gives your little liar credibility?"

Christ. I remembered the way Constance Baxter-Hicks had looked at me holding Rowe's hand and groaned.

"I brought him here to figure out his game," I shot back, temporarily glossing over the other half of my plan for the day. "If he's targeting our business, shouldn't we figure out how and why?"

"Sure. What did he say when you confronted him?"

"I..." I opened and closed my mouth like a fish.

"Right." Dev folded his arms smugly.

"He's... I just... I like being around him." It felt like I was confessing a dark sin. "He's kind and ridiculously innocent. He lies through his teeth, but even that is amusing. He makes me laugh. He makes me want to make *him* laugh. He's... beautiful. And I keep putting things off because I... I want more time with him."

"Bash." Dev shook his head sadly. "You wanna fuck him, fuck him. But the more time you spend with him, the more chance you're giving him to dig his claws into you. There are lots of ways people lie about who they really are."

Shit. "Dev, your brother—"

He made a slashing motion through the air. "We're not talking about me. You gotta promise you'll confront this guy. Today. Ideally, right now."

I blew out a breath. As much as I hated it, this was the advice I needed to hear. There was a reason it had taken *all* of our brotherhood to make Sterling Chase successful. "Yeah. I promise. Today."

"Good. Now, let's go make sure your beautiful liar hasn't fucking *caged* my horse." Dev huffed in amusement and shook his head as we turned and walked back. "You sure know how to pick 'em, Bash."

But as we rounded the corner, we found Rowe stroking Trigger's neck and murmuring to him gently. Dev froze and yanked me to a halt, too, just out of Rowe's sight.

"You're actually a very good boy, aren't you?" Rowe asked, brushing his hand down Trigger's deep brown coat. "I apologize for misjudging you. It's just that my only experience with a horse before today was... not positive."

Trigger nickered.

"Yes, it *was* unfortunate. Thank you. His name was Apple Butter, and he was known far and wide—well, far and wide around Linden, Indiana, so not particularly far or wide—for being unfriendly." Rowe paused. "A *kicker*."

The horse whuffled, making Rowe chuckle, and beside me, Dev made a low, startled noise before covering his mouth with his hand.

"But maybe it's not all that surprising that he had a chip on his shoulder, now that I think about it," Rowe went on, stroking the horse's ears. "Since they named him for a breakfast condiment. Give a creature a name like *Noble* or *Legendary* or *Sterling Chase* and they're automatically taken seriously. But when you're named Apple Butter—or plain, old Rowe Prince—you've kinda gotta misbehave to get your point across."

Dev darted a look at me. I had no idea what expression my face wore, but it was probably something sappy and sympathetic. Whatever it was made Dev come to some kind of decision. Without a word to me, he stepped fully into the open with a deliberate clomp of his boots that Rowe couldn't miss. Frowning at his back, I followed.

Rowe turned, looking suddenly nervous again, and rubbed a thumb over a spot on his hip in that nervous gesture I'd seen him do before. "Oh. Hello. Trigger and I were just having a pleasant chat."

Dev took this in stride. "Trigger's an excellent conversationalist. Look, Sterling, I'm afraid I haven't really kept up with who's investing in what recently. I'm not the best person to help you make connections. It's possible that another member of the board would know better. I think most of us are going to be in town for the Innovation Awards in a couple weeks since Sterling Chase's projects have been nominated for several awards. You could maybe meet some of them then."

Rowe blinked. "I could?"

"He could?" I said at the exact same time. What had happened to *confront him immediately?*

Dev looped his arm over Trigger's neck and gave me a small shrug, and I thought I understood his sudden about-face. My friend loved his horse more than most people. Hell, maybe more than *any* people. Clearly, Rowe had made an impression on Dev without intending to.

A sound outside announced that the match was about to begin, and Rowe squared his shoulders resolutely. "Well. Thank you anyway, Dev. I'll take the Innovation Awards under advisement if I haven't managed to find another investor in the meantime. I suppose I should go... spectate now."

Now that Rowe's nervousness had returned, he sounded as enthusiastic about joining the crowd as a man facing a firing squad.

Dev regarded Rowe for a long moment. "No one will be interested in talking about business while the match is going on. If you'd rather watch from a quieter spot, you and Bash can head up on the roof." He pointed to the far end of the building. "There's a ladder that leads to an access door."

"Oh, I... yes." Rowe turned his huge brown eyes on me. "Could we? It feels like it's been a long day already."

More time alone with Rowe? It was the unwisest possible choice. "Sure," I found myself saying. "You're the boss."

"Oh, right." Rowe grinned. "I guess I am."

"I just need a quick word with Dev about... horses," I said. "I'll be up in a minute."

Rowe gave Trigger a final loving pat and took off in the direction Dev had pointed before calling over his shoulder politely. "Thank you so much, Dev!"

Meanwhile, I stayed where I was, arms folded, staring at my friend. "Confront him, *Bash*. He's a liar and a user, *Bash*. Don't spend time alone with him, *Bash*. But also, Bash, take him up on the roof."

"Wipe the stupid smile off your face," Dev grumbled. "Look, I'm still almost positive this guy's a duplicitous, scheming fraudster bent on destroying everything you've—*we've*—built..."

"But?"

Dev pushed past me to grab a currying comb. "But... he reminded me that maybe I should reserve judgment, that's all. Sometimes people do things because they don't think they have a choice." He shrugged, his back to me. "Besides, Trigger likes him."

"Oh, well, if *Trigger* likes him..." I rolled my eyes.

Dev shot me a look over his shoulder. "Go figure out what this guy's story is, Sebastian. What's his endgame? Why the fuck is he doing what he's doing? And," he warned, "for god's sake, do it without listening to his project pitch. You're already in way too deep with a guy you barely know. The only way you could make this clusterfuck worse is by getting into business with him, too."

"I wouldn't!"

"You would. If I know you—and I do—you're already dying to know what his project is all about and whether it would be a good fit for Sterling Chase. Am I wrong?"

Damn it. I set my teeth. "Curiosity is not the same as commitment—"

Dev shook his head, clearly amused, and turned away again. "You wanted more time with the pint-sized liar, so go have your day in the sunshine. But I'm warning you, it's not gonna last forever."

SEVEN

ROWE

I freaking *loved* polo.

There were parts of the match that I hadn't entirely followed
—*bumps* and *hooks* and how the penalties were determined since, in
my opinion, the blue team were a bunch of animals and the red team
had been *robbed*. But by the final chukker, I'd been so excited that I'd
pushed to my feet on the slanted roof, cheering my red players as they
galloped down the pitch toward the goalposts in the final moments.
Only Bash's quick reflexes had saved me from tumbling to my doom
Humpty-Dumpty style.

"Oh my god!" I exclaimed as he pulled me down by my waistband and my ass hit the metal roof. "Somebody needs to revise the
Top Ten Most Amazing Feats in Polo History video with new footage
because that was *epic*. Can you believe it?"

"Believe that you just attempted to jump up and down on a
pitched roof while wearing those shoes? Fuck no." Bash scowled,
breathing hard, his hair glinting in the sunshine. "What were you
thinking?"

"I... may have gotten a little caught up," I admitted. "I do that sometimes." I paused and considered for a moment and admitted, "Possibly *all* the time."

"I didn't know you were such a Kingmakers fan," Bash said.

"A... what?"

Bash shook his head, the corners of his mouth twitching up like he was trying to fight a smile but couldn't. I really loved that look.

"The red team." He lifted an eyebrow. "The ones you almost killed yourself over?"

"Ohhhh. The *Kingmakers*. Right, right." A warm breeze ruffled my hair, and I wondered if I'd just done something unforgivably un-Sterling.

In fact, I had all sorts of questions. Like, which team was Sterling Chase supposed to have played on in the match today? Who'd covered for me? Where was *my* polo horse? Why hadn't Bash mentioned any of that?

It was frustrating that I couldn't ask without giving everything away.

"Er, I wouldn't say I'm a *fan*, per se. I don't follow the rankings. I just like to see an underdog win."

"Me too." Bash's leg bumped mine, and my heart, which was already galloping from the thrill of the game, began to beat even faster with a very different kind of excitement. "The Kingmakers have a novice on their team this year, of course, which brought down their handicap."

"Mmm." I nodded sagely, like I hadn't learned about polo handicaps mere hours before.

"I'm curious, though," he went on, "how you knew they were the underdogs if you don't follow the standings."

"Oh. Their posture when they took the field." I shrugged. "Kinda nervous and determined but subdued. And the first time they scored, they were *really* excited. You could see how unexpected it was."

Bash's smile spread and softened slightly. "You're very unexpected, Rowe."

The furious beating of my heart must've been contagious because

my stomach began swooping and dipping like it was doing the tango.
I couldn't look at Bash without staring at his mouth, so I forced my
attention back to the field, where the spectators milled around in the
sunshine.

"Yes. Well." I cleared my throat. "Unexpected in a good way, I
hope."

"I hope so, too," Bash said cryptically.

I frowned and glanced at him, but he was already eyeing the
roof's access door. "You ready to go? I think it's time for us to discuss
a few things."

A few things?

As in, *things* on my Quirky Billionaire to-do list for the coming
week? Or as fraudulent identity *things*? Or as in... *things* that might
come after the kiss in the barn earlier?

My stomach fluttered nervously.

Sitting side by side with Bash in the sunshine had been wonderful, like a step out of time. When he'd leaned closer to point out
something on the field, his warm breath had brushed my cheek.
When he'd laughed at one of my fake-Sterling observations, he'd
thrown his head back, and our knees had knocked together. I'd found
myself relaxing further and further into his side as the match had
gone on, lost in my excitement about the match and the moment and
the man at my side. I'd let myself forget about Sterling Chase, and
Justin Hardy, and Project Daisy Chain, and the very real risk that all
of this was going to explode in my face.

Now, though, that worry was back with a vengeance.

Last night, when Joey and I had flopped on the futon and traded
stories—Joey's involving a *West Side Story*-esque rivalry he'd ignited
with a competing food delivery guy—I'd told him about my plan to
attend the polo match, and his eyes had gone wide. *This is bad news,
cuz. You were only supposed to be Cinderella for one night. You keep
pushing your luck, and you're gonna end up holding a pumpkin.*

I'd come anyway. Of course I had. I was on borrowed time, and
I'd told myself I couldn't pass up the chance to meet Justin or another

investor, which was true... But another, larger truth was that I couldn't pass up the chance to spend one more day with Bash.

For the last ten years, I'd thought of nothing but Daisy. I'd told myself I was living for the both of us since I was the only one who could. But until meeting Bash, I hadn't felt like I was living much at all.

As Bash climbed down the ladder, I touched my fingers to my mouth. When I closed my eyes, I could still feel the weight of his lips against mine imprinted there and taste his unexpected sweetness on my tongue. And I was very glad I'd pushed my luck.

"Rowe?" Bash called from below.

"Yes. Coming." I scrambled to the ladder and swung myself over.

Bash reached up to guide me, his hand sliding from my calf to my thigh to my hip. But instead of steadying me, his touch was electric. By the time I dropped to the ground inches away from him, sending up a cloud of dust motes and random bits of straw, I was breathless and half-hard.

"Thanks," I said softly, trying not to stare at his handsome face. "So, um... now we go up to the clubhouse and see if Justin is there?"

"That's up to you," Bash said. "We can, if you'd like. And there's a reception for donors later on that you could attend. Or..."

"Or?" I repeated with ill-concealed eagerness.

"This morning, I called and booked you a suite at your usual hotel, as well as a private dinner. If you're tired, we could head there. I wasn't sure if you'd be eager for more polo after..." He lowered his voice. "Sally Struthers."

"Ah. That." My cheeks warmed. "You know, I... may have been a bit hasty."

Bash nodded. "Caught up in things again?"

He was talking to his boss. To Sterling Chase. And I knew that. But when he gave me that knowing, half-amused grin, it felt as if he saw *me*. As if he knew the real Rowe Prince. And *liked* him.

God, I wanted that to be true.

"Definitely caught up," I murmured.

Bash nodded again and watched me expectantly, waiting for me to make a decision. Would we stay and mingle or leave? Take a chance at finding Justin or make our escape? Did I want the business deal or the fairy tale? This could be my last chance at either.

I took a deep breath... and Bash lifted his hand to gently touch my hair. My breath hitched, and my whole body leaned toward him, like Bash was an archer and I was a bow.

"Sorry. You had a little piece of..." He flicked a bit of straw off his fingers and let it drift toward the ground, but his eyes locked on mine. "Rowe," he began breathlessly.

"The hotel," I croaked. "We should go to the hotel."

Maybe it was reckless and shortsighted, but I chose the fairy tale.

————

Bash and I spent the short ride to the hotel talking about light topics that did little to diffuse the tension in the air between us. The best polo matches he'd seen. The weather forecast. The hit single from Zee Barlo on the radio, which I knew all the words to and Bash claimed was "not as good as his early stuff." I would have maybe argued with him about that, but by then, we were pulling up to a large inn that looked light-years out of my price range.

My stomach clenched. Of course a place like *this* would be Sterling Chase's usual hotel. I really hoped someone else was paying for it because I didn't even have a credit card to pretend to pay with. And I was going to have to save up for eternity to pay them back.

The realization was a reality check. Like Joey had said, I was Cinderella, and midnight was fast approaching. I couldn't afford— literally—to keep this charade up much longer.

"Welcome to the Malachite. May I take your luggage?" a uniformed porter inquired politely about items we didn't have.

"Yes, please," Bash said, gesturing to the driver. "Morris has them in the trunk. Thank you."

He did? Bash had somehow acquired Sterling's clothing? Was

there any use in hoping the real Sterling was thin and vertically challenged?

"Certainly, Mr. Dayne," the porter said, ushering us into the lobby. "Enjoy your stay, sir."

The porter's brief exchange with Bash faded to background noise as I stepped into the lobby's sitting area. Whoever had designed this place was a master of their craft. They'd married a plush Victorian velvet settee with a rolled-arm Chesterfield and a marble-topped coffee table with inlaid mahogany end tables. On the walls, sturdy gilt-framed English landscapes were interspersed with black-and-white photos of the hotel's famous guests, and dozens of informal tussie-mussie floral bouquets adorned every flat surface.

The style was perfect for the space—refined without being stuffy, exactly the look I tried to achieve in my own space back home on a much, *much* slimmer budget.

"Oh my god," I whispered, moving toward the reception desk before I'd made a conscious decision to go there. I ran my hand over the sleek surface. "Is this rosewood?"

If the woman at the desk was surprised by my enthusiasm, she didn't show it. "Yes, sir. I believe so."

"My favorite," I said reverently. "Did you know that rosewood actually has nothing to do with roses? It got its name because the wood smells so sweet. It's actually my favorite kind of wood to refinish because it—"

Bash strolled up behind me. "Is everything alright?"

I straightened and tried to feign boredom. "What? Oh. Yes. Just... admiring the beautiful table. I might, uh, acquire one like it." I sniffed. "Maybe more than one."

His eyebrows lifted. "Really? Where would you put them?"

Shit. How was I supposed to know where Sterling would put giant tables when I'd never been to his home?

Had *Bash* been there? Would he know I was lying? This whole secret-identity thing was becoming annoying on a whole other level.

"Oh, you know." I shrugged easily. "I might... buy a new house. Something small. Ten thousand square feet or so."

"To display your tables." Bash nodded solemnly. "Perfectly reasonable."

"If you'd like, sir," the friendly woman offered, "I can put you in touch with our designer."

"Oh, no, I—" I began.

"Yes, please. That would be very helpful," Bash cut in. "Whatever Mr. Chase wants, he gets."

If only.

I rubbed my temple slightly as we waited for the woman to provide contact information that my helpful personal assistant stored in his phone. It was definitely time to come clean before I ended up on the hook for more than just a swanky hotel room.

Bash was unusually quiet as we made our way upstairs, and the silence was impossible to read. It wasn't the same tension as on the ride to the hotel, but it for sure wasn't the easy camaraderie of the polo match, and it set me further on edge.

Was he quiet because he was thinking about kissing me? Because he was hoping I wouldn't kiss him? Because he knew I was impersonating a billionaire and he was planning to call the police?

"Rowe?" he called as we walked down a carpeted hallway. I turned around and saw that he'd stopped beside a heavy oak door, and I hadn't even noticed. "Are you alright?"

"Mmm. Yes. Perfectly perfect!" I sang cheerily.

Just thinking about kissing. And prison. As one does.

"You sure?" Bash raised one eyebrow, his hand on the doorknob. "Nothing you want to share with me?"

"Nope! Noooope. I'm *so* perfectly perfect, in fact, this moment eclipses my previous most perfect day, which was the day I spent chatting with, um..." I cast my eyes around, trying to think of *literally anyone*, and spotted a black-and-white signed picture from *Some Like It Hot*. "Marilyn Monroe."

What. The. Fuck?

Bash and I blinked at each other, and I immediately shook my head. "Not... not *the* Marilyn Monroe, obviously. I meant, um..." I scanned the hall again for inspiration and landed on an English landscape. "A... horse! A horse named Marilyn Monroe."

I could practically feel my ball gown turning into rags and a pumpkin materializing at my feet.

"Your most perfect day," Bash repeated with excessive patience. "Was a day you spent chatting with a horse named Marilyn Monroe."

I opened my mouth. Shut it again. Then said, slowly and miserably, "W-would you believe it's... one of my quirky billionaire eccentricities?"

"Right." He pushed open the door. "Would you like a drink?"

"Desperately," I croaked. I didn't even care which of "Sterling's favorite" concoctions he gave me.

He nodded and moved to the sleek kitchenette area of the suite while I glanced around at the spacious sitting room, looking for a place where I might quietly melt into a puddle of embarrassment on the thick carpet, but my attention was instantly snagged by the view. Clear glass windows lined one wall, showing off the neatly manicured lawn edged by a wilderness area dense with a mix of fir trees and hardwoods.

"So pretty," I breathed, wandering closer to the view. "I didn't realize you could be close to the city and feel like the rest of the world was so far away."

After a moment, Bash walked up and handed me a bottle of cold beer before casually leaning against the back of one sofa.

I blinked in surprise at the drink in my hand. Had he remembered what I'd said about beer at the gala? I tried for a joke. "Is this Sterling Chase's favorite beer?"

Bash tilted his head. "Shouldn't you be telling me?"

I glanced nervously down at the condensation-wet bottle before taking a deep gulp. It was cold and crisp and delicious and *normal.* Bash watched me drink with a kind of singular focus that made it impossible for me to think of anything to say.

"You should see this area in the fall when the leaves turn," he said finally. "I have some distant cousins who live nearby."

"Yeah? Most of my cousins are in Indiana," I said without thinking. *Fuck.* "N-not all of them, of course! My cousin Joey's family lives here in Quee—I mean." Sweat rolled down my back. "I mean the Upper North Side." Wait, was there an Upper North Side? "The Upper *West* Side. East. East of the Upper West Side. You know, the nice area? That one. That's where they live. Near the... park. Central Park, I believe they call it."

I took a large gulp of the beer, waiting for an invisible clock to strike midnight and wondering where I might find a fairy godmother. Out of the corner of my eye, I could see Bash shaking his head, wearing that half-smile I liked, as if he wasn't sure whether to be amused by me or not.

I understood completely. The lying was getting out of control, and nerves made my palms slick. I could hardly remember who I was supposed to be anymore.

"Nice that your cousins are close to you," Bash said.

"Oh yes. We've always been close."

Bash seemed like he was trying not to laugh... and failing. "I meant geographically close. If you live on the Park and they live east of the Upper West Side." He took a slow sip of his beer.

"Fine," I snapped. "They live in Queens. There, you happy? They're not rich. But they're hard fucking workers. And they love me. They'd do anything for me."

Bash's amusement fell away, and he looked at me intently. "Good," he said at length. "Everyone needs someone like that."

"Well, family is family, right?" The blank look on Bash's face made me ask hesitantly, "Is your family not that way?"

He shrugged and seemed to consider his answer before speaking. "I'm an only child, and my parents travel a lot. We get along fine, but they have different priorities. I don't really know how to explain it. We're not close."

I wished he wouldn't be so careful. I wanted to know more about the man behind Bash's beautiful face. But I was in no position to be asking the truth from anyone.

I picked at the label on my beer bottle. "You don't have to tell me. Sorry if I got too personal."

Bash reached out to pull the empty bottle away from my fingers. The warmth of that tiny touch made my whole body flush with heat. "My parents are good people but... shallow. They seem to care more about their reputation than truly making a difference in the world. That's all."

"Oh." I was surprised by his words. By the honesty of them. And I had no idea what to say next. Any more details about my own family would make it glaringly obvious I wasn't Sterling, but I couldn't stand to meet Bash's truths with more lies.

Everything up to this point had felt like playacting. Mostly harmless to anyone except myself. But the longer I kept things up, the worse I felt. Lying to rich people for a few hours last night for the sake of my project had been one thing. But lying to *Bash*, the man who'd been nothing but kind and helpful, when it was possible that he was feeling this connection between us, just like I was? Nope. I couldn't do it. The very idea made me nauseous.

"Bash, there's something I should probably tell you—"

A firm knock sounded on the door, breaking the tension and sending my newfound resolve skittering into a million pieces.

Fuck.

A room service attendant came in with a rolling table full of domed dinner trays at the same time some other people came to deliver the suitcases, and I took the opportunity to duck into the smaller of the two bathrooms, trying to catch my breath and calm down.

No more lies, I promised myself. *No more.*

When I emerged, Bash beckoned me toward my seat and poured me a glass of wine. "Sorry. What were you saying before we got interrupted?"

"I... I..." I gulped my wine greedily. "You see, the thing is..."

"Yes?"

"I want to tell you about..."

Bash tilted his head. His eyes were warm and patient, and his expression was kind.

"...that table downstairs," I said weakly. "Wasn't it lovely?"

"Yes, very much. I hadn't known you liked antiques so much. When did that start?"

Okay, *this* was a topic I could discuss with no lies whatsoever. Of course, it also had a tendency to bore everyone in my life to tears after mere seconds. "It's not antiques, really. It's interior decorating. I love finding beautiful pieces, especially ones that have a bit of a history to them. I think they add so much character to a space."

Hello. I'm Rowe Prince, the world's most boring human.

I felt my face heat. "Anyway. That's silly."

"Silly?" Bash frowned. "How could it be silly to want to make a space look and feel better? Expressing your personal style is important. Isn't that what you told Constance Baxter-Hicks?"

"It is," I said softly. Damn it, why did the one person who listened to my rambling and paid attention have to be a man I was never going to see again once he knew who I was? I took another big gulp of my wine. "So, um. Tell me about you. What are your hobbies? Do you have any close family besides your parents?"

Bash chewed a bite of food and shook his head. "I have friends I consider brothers. You've met Silas and Dev—"

"Oh, right."

"But there are five of us in total. We met our first year at Yale because we were all in the same residential college—"

A swallow of wine got stuck in my throat. "Yale?" I croaked.

"It was on my resume, Mr. Chase." Bash lifted that damn sexy eyebrow.

Fuck. "Oh, right. So! Five of you, you say? How wonderful! You all instantly bonded and—"

"No." Bash snorted. "Hell, no. We hated each other at first. *Loathed.* We were from such a variety of backgrounds we couldn't help it. Some of us were there on scholarships, others came from the families that *endowed* the scholarships. Some of us were used to quiet, some played fucking rock music so hard the windows rattled. Some of us were slobs who dared to leave dishes in the sink... some of us were picky assholes named Silas." He grinned. "Some were conscientious students who never missed class, and some tried to tempt the others away from studying."

I snorted. "I know which one you were."

He smiled delightedly—not the tilted half-smile I liked so much but a full-on grin that hit me like a shaft of pure sunlight. "What makes you say that?"

Because you tempt me to do all sorts of unwise things.

"Just the impression I get." I waved a hand through the air. "But go on. How'd you become brothers if you hated each other?"

"A massive blizzard that closed the school for two days... combined with a bottle of my father's best Scotch."

I laughed out loud. "You were the ringleader. I knew it!"

He smiled at me again, then shrugged like he was a bit embarrassed. "Anyway. After a full day of drinking games, we figured out we were all queer misfits in our own ways. And we became a unit."

"Misfits who fit together." I pushed aside my plate and set my elbow on the table so I could prop my chin in my hand and stare at him. I probably looked like a smitten idiot, but I'd had just enough wine not to care. "I envy you, having brothers like that."

Bash tilted his head. "Do you not? I think you mentioned a sister..."

"I... yes." I touched the tattoo on my hip reflexively. "But it's complicated."

I rarely talked about Daisy to anyone outside my family. The sweet memories that overwhelmed me and the heartache that hadn't ever gone away, not really, even in ten years, were just too much for polite conversation. But I would have liked to tell Bash about her... except I couldn't while I was being Sterling.

Bash simply nodded and refilled my wineglass. "Families often are. So, tell me something different, then. I know you love traveling all over the world, so... what's next on your bucket list? Someplace you've never gone."

I laughed, but it came out a little too high-pitched. Even talking about bucket list travel would require me to lie to keep up my charade. Was there a safe topic in the universe?

Fuck it.

"Probably Wheaton, Illinois," I said honestly.

Bash sighed at me, shaking his head. "Why am I even surprised anymore by the stuff you come up with? Okay, then, what's so special about Wheaton, Illinois?"

"Well." I leaned closer. "They have an all-night flea market. Can you imagine? Wandering the stalls under the moonlight, with artists, and cosplayers, and music, and all the good foods you get at carnivals? Things don't have to be complicated to be amazing, right?"

Bash stared at me for a beat, then pushed his plate away, too. "That's right." He stood and twisted his back in an exaggerated stretch, and my eyes caught on the thin band of tan skin on his stomach that peeked out when his shirt rode up. "Want to go sit on the sofa? It might be more comfortable."

My mouth went dry, and I grabbed my wine, gulping down the remainder of the glass.

Tell him. You tell him right now, Rowe Prince. Don't let another minute go by.

"Rowe? Everything okay?"

Oh, peachy. I'm pretending to be a billionaire when in reality, I don't have enough savings to pay for this bottle of wine. I'm supposed to be using this opportunity to get connections I can pitch the business idea I've spent years working on, but instead, I keep using every excuse I can think of to spend time with you. The fairy tale is ending, and I want so badly to just have a few more minutes with you. Another kiss from you. For you to know who I am and still look at me the way you're looking right now.

"Yes. Great." I cleared my throat. "I just feel like I'm talking too much. Am I talking too much? I don't want to bore you."

"You couldn't possibly." He held out a hand to me, but it was the look in his eyes that drew me toward him. "Come tell me more stories."

It turned out that Bash meant that literally. He settled me on one end of the sofa and took up a spot on the other end. Then he proceeded to ask me questions. My favorite movies. My favorite books. My favorite foods. My most embarrassing moment.

Just like earlier, at the polo match, I forgot to be nervous. I forgot I was supposed to lie. I forgot I was supposed to maintain distance. And that was when it all went wrong.

"So what you're telling me," Bash said mock-sternly, "is that you jumped on the horse because you wanted to impress a boy—"

"Hey! You asked for my most embarrassing moment, and that was it. And I'll have you know, I did it because I was *dared*. It was a debt of *honor*. It didn't impress anyone... especially after I fell sideways across the saddle with one foot still in the stirrup and bumping against Apple Butter's back while he went leaping through the neighbor's field. You'd be surprised how much it hurts to fall into a row of soybeans." I shook my head. "I was the king of misfortune."

Bash met my eyes. The edges of his lips were still turned up, and all I could think was how much I wanted to tease them with the tip of my tongue. We'd slid closer together, incrementally, until we were turned toward each other, our knees mere inches apart.

"On the contrary," he whispered. "You're the Prince of Lies." His voice was low, almost sultry, utterly compelling...

Which was why it took me several seconds to realize the slight emphasis he'd put on the word *Prince*.

My heart skipped a beat before thudding double time, and my glow of happiness burned off, leaving me with a cold flare of humiliation. "P-pardon?" I breathed.

"I thought you told me Sterling Chase has been a champion polo player since high school?"

Oh. Fuck. Pumpkins all the way down. My imaginary clock had struck midnight, and I hadn't even heard it.

"I... I..." I darted a glance toward the door.

Bash's hand reached out to clasp mine. "Easy," he said, gentling me like he'd done earlier with Starlight. "Answer me."

I licked my lips. "It could be that I like to tell tall tales," I whispered. "Maybe I told that story b-because it was more exciting than the boring life of an elite child in polo lessons."

He surprised me by letting out a laugh. "Now, *that's* the damn truth. Polo lessons are only fun if you aren't sharing them with your asshole neighbor Eric."

That was oddly specific. As if he spoke from experience. *Personal* experience.

I eyed the expensive clothes Bash wore. The shoes I really should have noticed were Italian leather. The elegant, subtle cologne that must have cost a fortune. And then the square, black watch on his wrist. With his hand so close to mine, I could make out the brand name on the watch face, which I'd never thought to look at before.

Hermès.

It was amazing how much a person could willfully not notice. How he could put facts together wrong in his mind. But now that I saw them, I couldn't unsee them. And the picture that was coming together now...

"You aren't really a PA, are you?" I accused.

Bash's big hand tightened around mine. "No, sweetheart." He looked up at me from under his eyelashes. "And you're not really Sterling Chase."

Ah, fuck.

EIGHT

BASH

I wanted Rowe Prince.

This wasn't a surprise—I'd wanted him from the moment he'd slid into my hiding place at the gala and told me he was a quirky billionaire. But talking with him, hearing the light, husky sound of his laughter and the stutter-gasp-sigh of his breath when we touched, seeing the way his brown eyes went soft and melty when he looked at me—all those things that couldn't be faked—had made me want him even more.

I'd found myself, for just a second, wishing that this could be real. That *he* could be real. And that had been a fucking shock.

Dev was right. I needed to know who this man was, to separate the lies from the truth, before this went any further.

"I, uh... I think I'd better go." Rowe's voice sounded thready with nerves, and his eyes kept darting from the window to the door like he thought he might be arrested at any moment.

"Please don't." I squeezed his hand in reassurance. "Stay. Tell me the truth."

"Yeah. I owe you that much." He let out a long, shuddering sigh, and his shoulders slumped in defeat. "I don't even know where to start. My name is Rowe Prince. I-I mean, I guess you figured that out already?"

I nodded. "I know who you are. What I don't know is why you did it. Why pretend to be Sterling Chase?"

"It's kind of a long story. I wanted to get into the gala so I could talk to Justin Hardy, like I told you. I really do have a project I want to pitch to him. That part was true." His eyes implored me to believe him.

I squeezed his hand tighter. "Christ, sweetheart, what did you think would happen when you actually met Justin and he realized who you were? Did you think he wouldn't care that you'd been impersonating someone?"

"I never intended to impersonate anyone, I swear! The project..." He blew out a breath. "I've spent years working on it, Bash, and weeks and weeks here in New York trying to get an incubator or development company to show an interest in it, starting with Sterling Chase. But one after another, every company's turned me down flat. I'm running out of money. Out of time. Justin is the last potential contact I have. So I figured, okay, maybe the project doesn't look great on paper. I don't have the right credentials or contacts. My cover letter's not exciting enough. But if I could talk to Justin face-to-face, if I could get him excited about the project, that could make a difference." Rowe chewed his lip. "So I got an invitation to the gala, I borrowed my cousin's tux, and I showed up. I didn't know whose invite I'd gotten until I was already wearing the name badge, and then it was too late. I fell behind a potted plant, and there *you* were, and..." He shrugged.

"And you got caught up."

Rowe gave a watery chuckle. "Yes. God. Worse than ever before, yeah. And suddenly, I was talking in a funny voice, and making up stories about Borneo, and giving Miranda Baxter-Hicks fashion advice, and riding in a fancy car, and staying at a swanky hotel, and talking to horses, and kissing in the barn... and I never expected it to go this far." His big brown eyes were wide and innocent. "You might find this hard to believe, but I'm not a very good liar most of the time."

I laughed out loud and ran a hand over my face. "God."

"And I kept saying to myself, 'You should tell him, Rowe. He seems like a nice guy. Maybe he'd get it.' But I couldn't, because..." His face, which had been pale with nerves, flushed pink.

"Because?"

"Well, two reasons, I guess. I kept telling myself it was because I just didn't *know* if you'd get it. Like, what if you were angry? What if I'd blown my opportunity to get this project made because I'd trusted you when I shouldn't? And I couldn't take that chance because getting this project made... I'm not just doing it for myself." He licked his lips. "Do you remember I mentioned my s-sister?"

He stumbled over the word, and I frowned. "Yeah. You said it was complicated."

"Not so complicated, really." Rowe's words came tumbling out of him like he'd been damming them up for an hour. "Daisy died. Ten years ago."

"What?" I blinked at him in shock. "She *died*?"

He nodded. "It was this random, fluke accident. She was playing softball at school, like she had a hundred times before, and a softball hit her in the chest." He rubbed his own breastbone and stared at the lamp over my shoulder like his mind was seeing something very different, then went on softly, "She was standing there smiling one minute, on the ground the next. And I kept waiting for her to get up and start screaming at the pitcher, you know? But..." He shook his head sadly. "She didn't. Later, they told us a million little electrical impulses misfired at once, and her heart stopped. The coach used an AED machine to shock her, but it didn't work. The ambulance came, and they tried, too, but..." He pulled his hand away so he could wrap his arms around his waist, curling into himself protectively. "It turned out she had a heart condition we didn't know about. It all happened so fast... Suddenly, it was just over. She was gone. We were fourteen."

We. Jesus Christ. Daisy was his twin.

"Rowe..." Not for one second did I doubt that he was telling the truth. Liar he might be, but the raw ache in his voice was unmistakable. I reached out to run a finger over his wrist, just a light touch because I couldn't resist connecting with him physically to make sure he knew I cared. To make sure he knew I heard him deep inside.

Rowe's voice shook as he continued. "We'd always been a team. The Prince twins, taking on the world. But Daisy was the brave one. The one with all the plans to save the environment, to achieve world peace somehow, to find true love. The one who'd pull me away from my sketchbooks and make me join the three-dimensional world again. After she died, I was... alone. And I didn't know how to navigate life when the best part of me was gone."

"That's not true. Fuck, Rowe, I'm so sorry you went through that, but you're wrong—"

He smiled a little. "I know. Or, more like, I figured it out eventually. One day after a counseling session, I was sitting outside, and this voice in my head that sounded exactly like my sister said, 'Listen up, dork face. If part of you died with me, part of me lives with you. So stop wasting our time and *do* something.' She always used to talk like that, you know? Wasting time, running out of it. Like she somehow knew she wouldn't have much."

I tugged on his arm until I had his hand safely gripped between both of mine once again. I wanted to take him in my arms, but I wasn't sure he'd welcome that. So many facts I'd accumulated about this man slotted into place. The things he'd said to Constance at the gala. Even the things he'd said to the horse back at the barn. Rowe had been crushed by the shitty hand life dealt him—just like Dev had, just like Silas had—but now he was using that loss to propel himself toward something better. To take his idea, whatever it was, and make it a reality.

He let out a shaky breath. "So I got off my ass. I got out the sketchbook I use for design ideas, and I started hatching ideas for this project instead. And when I tell you I had no idea what I was doing, I mean if I'd set out to learn rocket science in Russian, it might have been easier. I had to research the fuck out of things, and teach myself technical shit that still seems over my head sometimes, and be brave enough to ask for help. And once I got it to the point where I thought it could really be something good and useful, something that would help people like Daisy, I saved up my pennies and came to New York—"

"And then put on a tux and went to a gala." I nodded. "I get it now."

"I couldn't not *try*, Bash. And I can't fail. I don't want to let Daisy down."

The shell around my own heart cracked.

"I didn't set out to lie. Not really. I mean, not beyond getting into the gala," Rowe continued in a rush. "Just find Justin, beg him for a meeting, and leave. And if it had worked out like that, maybe the whole stolen-invite thing would just be a funny story I'd tell at parties." He scrubbed at his eyes with his free hand. "I mean, if you do something reckless and get caught, people call you a fool. If you do something reckless and succeed, they call you daring and brave. Right?"

I huffed out a laugh. "You might have a point."

"But anyway, Justin *wasn't* there, and you *were*, and you noticed me, and..." Rowe shook his head and stared at our joined hands. "Well, that's the second reason I didn't tell you the truth right away."

"Because I noticed you?" I wrinkled my forehead. "I don't get it."

"Ugh." He tugged on his hand, but I wouldn't let him go. "You gave me that smile. You were so kind, no matter how ridiculous I was. You did the eyebrow thing that made me go all hot. You made me laugh, even when laughing was the last thing I wanted to do. You brought me those damn prosciutto bites. And it felt like you were on my... my *team*, Bash, when I hadn't had a team in forever. I was caught up," he whispered. "Caught up *tight*. And if I told you the truth, all of that would have gone away. *Poof.* So I was Cinderella, telling myself just one more dance, just one more, just one, before I re-pumpkin-ated."

I sucked in a breath through my nose.

By the time he finished this diatribe, Rowe was breathless, his hair was a curly mess from where he'd run his hand through it, and he looked on the verge of tears.

Meanwhile, I felt his words like a hard jolt of caffeine to my system, making my heart beat faster and excitement buzz beneath my skin. *He felt this, too. He felt the connection between us as powerfully, as illogically, as I did.*

"And what happens now?" I made myself ask. Despite the man's heartfelt story, despite how much I wanted him, I forced myself to remember that he could still have ulterior motives—billions of them. Whether he was telling the truth now or not, how foolish would it be to trust him? "You've told me the truth. Aren't you afraid I might spoil your plan? I could go to Justin Hardy myself right now and make sure you don't get that meeting."

I wouldn't, and not only because I tried to pretend Justin didn't exist. But Rowe didn't know that.

He nodded slowly, his face pale. "I guess you could, yeah. You could tell the real Sterling Chase who I am, tell all the guys on the board since you're friends with a couple of them, and they could tell everyone they know." He drew himself up as tall as he could, like he wanted to meet his fate bravely. "But lying sucked, too. When you kissed me in the barn earlier, it was the most incredible—" He broke off with a headshake. "But it wasn't really *me* you were kissing, and deep down, I knew that. And even when I was telling myself, 'Just a little longer, just another hour or two,' I knew I was making things harder. Worse. Because the more time we spent together, the more I wanted... and the harder it was to remember that guys like you don't go around kissing guys like me. Not in real life. So, I'm glad you know everything now. I wish I'd made myself tell you sooner. And I'm sorry if I hurt you."

Ah, fuck. He sounded so freaking young. Because he *was* young.

What had I been doing at twenty-four? Well, not impersonating a billionaire, no... but only because I hadn't had to. Instead, I'd had the equally audacious idea of founding a company with my best friends, even though none of us had really known what we were doing. If we hadn't already had my family money and connections, it all might have ended very differently, especially for my friends who hadn't had trust funds to fall back on.

Rowe was right—the only difference between being labeled a reckless idiot and a daring entrepreneur was whether your plan succeeded or failed.

My heart gave up its last attempt to harden against him, and the need to hold him in my arms intensified.

"Rowe, do you know who I am?" I asked softly.

"Well, I know you're not a PA. But your name's gotta be Bash since that's what everyone..." He blinked, and I could see the gears in his mind turning. His forehead crinkled for a moment before his eyes widened in realization. "Oh, no. The woman downstairs earlier called you Mr. Dayne. As in *Sebastian Dayne*. I didn't put it together until now." He squeezed his eyes shut and thunked his head against the back of the couch, revealing the pale skin under his chin. "You're on the board at Sterling Chase."

The urge to run my lips across that skin and down over his Adam's apple, to nudge his collar down with my nose and inhale the intoxicating scent of his skin, was nearly overwhelming.

"I am," I agreed. "Which is how I knew you weren't Sterling Chase from the very beginning. From literally the moment you introduced yourself." I leaned toward him, no longer fighting the magnetic pull. "Because Sterling Chase is the name of the company, not a real person."

"I freaking *told* Joey—" He frowned. "Wait. So all this time, you knew I was..."

"Inventing a quirky billionaire persona who was a cross between British butler and someone on *Real Housewives*? Yes."

I expected him to be annoyed, but instead, he exhaled in shaky relief. "Oh, thank fuck. I was worried that when the real Sterling Chase came back, you'd be in trouble. Or that you'd have to call the

PRINCE OF LIES 105

police and testify against me for identity fraud." He covered his face with his free hand, then pulled it away a moment later. "Wait, *are* you going to call the police?"

"Rowe. You're not hearing me." I grabbed his hand, then the other, and brought both to my lips. "You remember I already knew your name before we started this conversation, right? I'm telling you, I knew *last night* that you weren't Sterling, and I invited you to the polo match anyway. As of this morning, I knew exactly who you were and where you were from, and I knew you'd been lying. When I kissed you... I was definitely kissing Rowe Prince."

"Oh." He looked up at me again while the air seemed to shimmer around us with heated possibility. "*Oh.* So, then..."

"Wait. One more thing." I took a deep breath and screwed up the courage to set a critical boundary even though my gut—and my heart —wanted nothing more than to make this man's dreams come true. "Look, I cannot hear your pitch, okay? I am not going to put in a good word for your project to the development group at Sterling Chase. I don't want that between us."

Big brown eyes blinked at me. "No, of course. Shit. I'd never ask you to do a special favor for me."

That was what everyone said. Maybe it was even what everyone wanted to believe about themselves. But I knew for a fact that people could and would and *did.*

Rowe, however different and special he might be, was not immune.

"Also... I can give you contact information for plenty of people at incubators here in town who are decent humans. Please don't pursue Justin Hardy anymore. He's unscrupulous, and I don't want him to take advantage of you."

Rowe bit down on his bottom lip... which made me want to free it so I could bite on it myself. "Thanks for offering, but you don't have to do that, Bash. I've already contacted more than a dozen companies, and there was no interest—"

"I know a lot more than that," I insisted.

"Now you're just bragging," he teased, but he sobered quickly. "I think you've got the right idea. Let's not talk about business or any of this tonight, except..." He twisted in his seat until he'd gotten to his knees and pressed a hand to my cheek, forcing me to look at him—as if I could possibly look away. "I know we've both told a lot of lies in the past day, but I'm truly sorry for my part in it, Bash."

I tugged on his hand until he got the message and moved over to my lap, straddling me and wrapping his arms around my neck. The edges of his lips turned up, and his eyes danced.

"I'm sorry for your part, too," I said with a grin. Rowe's mouth opened in indignation, but I pressed his lips with a finger. "Let me finish, tiger. I can't honestly say I'm sorry I pretended to be your PA. Truthfully, I wanted an excuse to spend more time with you. I find you incredibly, overwhelmingly attractive, Rowe Prince." I paused, watching the emotions play over his face. Shock, disbelief... hope. "I want you naked in my bed."

Rowe's eyes widened again, and his cheeks flushed. "You do?" His voice came out breathy and unsure.

I nodded and leaned forward to brush his nose with mine. He was intoxicating. My brain cells had clocked out and fucked off to god-knew-where. My body was now fully under new management, and it was taking all of my self-control not to start ripping Rowe's clothes off.

"That kiss in the stable," I murmured before brushing my lips along his jaw, "was entirely too short."

"Y-yes." His voice was even breathier now, and his chest heaved between us.

I kissed the edge of his lips. "Stay with me. Just for this weekend. No business. *No lies.* Just the two of us. Just... this."

"Yes," he breathed again, turning his face to brush our lips together more fully. "Please."

Kissing Rowe felt like a strange kind of high, one in which I was euphoric but still sharply lucid. I catalogued every detail, from the heady mix of soap and the faint trace of hay coming from him to the little sounds of submission he made in his throat. The tiny plastic buttons on his shirt were a Sisyphean task for my shaking fingers. When one finally cleared its buttonhole, another three seemed to take its place.

"Want you," I admitted, inhaling the warm skin behind his ear before pressing my lips there. "Wanted you from the moment you skidded into me at the gala."

His fingers tugged on the hair at the back of my neck. "I don't know what I'm doing," he admitted. "But I want you, too."

I cupped his face and met his eyes. "Have you been with a man before?"

His cheeks were already patchy pink from our kissing, but they darkened as he spoke. "N-not really," he admitted. "But that doesn't mean I don't want to, and it definitely wasn't for lack of trying." He let out a nervous laugh. "Back in Linden... well, there weren't a lot of opportunities."

Too bad for the assholes of Linden. Their loss was definitely my gain.

I ran my thumbs across his warm cheeks. Making him feel safe was a priority. "What do you want tonight? We'll only do what you feel comfortable with."

Rowe let out a soft laugh. "Uh... everything? My sex resume includes a couple of hand jobs with guys who turned out to be jerks. I promise anything we do tonight will be a thousand times better... Honestly, it already is."

I leaned forward to feel his cheek with my lips, murmuring against his skin. "Do you want my mouth on your dick? Or my cock pressing inside your tight ass? Tell me what you want, Rowe."

The strangled hitch of his breath almost made a laugh bubble up in my chest. He was so fucking sweet. My words had been a test, a small push to get his gut reaction. But his reaction hadn't been in his guts as much as in his pants. His cock tented the front of his jeans enough to draw my attention. I reached down to rub him through the fabric. "You like that, hmm? Like hearing me talk dirty? Like knowing what I want to do to you?"

He leaned forward and hid his face in my neck. "You're going to kill me. I'm going to come in my pants and humiliate myself before I even get to see you naked," he groaned.

I laughed into his hair, landing kisses in his soft curls and enjoying every second of teasing and touching him. This was a thousand times better than I'd ever anticipated.

"Come to my bedroom?" I whispered against his ear. "I'll take off my clothes before debauching you, I promise."

He arched against my hand and let out a whine. "Just... tell me it won't just be one time, okay? Because the second I see you naked, I'm going to come, I just know it, and the only thing that will help me overcome the horror is knowing I get another chance to try again."

I moved us forward to the edge of the sofa before hefting him up and walking toward the bedroom with him attached to my front. His erection pressed against my stomach, eliciting a breathy, sensual gasp from him with every movement.

He was the sexiest fucking thing I'd ever seen.

"Oh, there'll be more than one chance," I rumbled in his ear. "I damn well guarantee it. We have the whole night, and I'm thinking... one chance for every lie you've told."

"There were kind of a lot of lies," he reminded me doubtfully, wrapping his arms more tightly around my neck.

I bit down gently on his earlobe, and he shuddered in my arms. "Exactly."

NINE

ROWE

How was real life more unbelievable than any lie I'd dreamed up as Sterling Chase?

I'd confessed who I was to Bash, put all my cards on the table. This should have been the sad end of the movie—the scene where he kicked me out of his suite, leaving me to wander the streets alone in a bleak montage while Adele's "Someone Like You" played in the background.

Instead, he was carrying me to his bed like the hero in a rom-com —or a fairy-tale prince—growling erotic promises in my ear that made my dick leak as it pressed against the front of my jeans.

One of us had clearly gotten our lines wrong, but I wasn't going to question it. In fact, I wished this *was* a movie so I could rewatch it all later when my mind inevitably tricked me into believing it had never happened in the first place.

No, really, Rowe... you did once go to New York City and have wild, passionate sex with a rich beefcake. Here's the video to prove it.

Was it possible to wear out digital video from rewatching it too often?

"You look like you're scheming," Bash said, clearly holding back a laugh as he placed me on the bed. His heated gaze roamed my body, stealing all logical thought from my brain. "There's no need. I'm a sure thing, I promise."

I kicked off my shoes while his hands returned to finish unbuttoning my shirt. I shoved them away and tackled the buttons faster than he ever could. "You do you. Me do me."

He laughed, deep and easy, and it lit up his face—as if he needed to become more attractive. "You going to watch me, caveman?"

I scrambled up onto my knees and faced him, pulling my shirt off as if I was a brave Lothario who'd done this many, many times. "Yes. Me watch. Me like."

Bash's eyes roamed over my naked skin, and somehow, impossibly, something about my pale, scrawny chest made his eyes go dark with need. "Me like more."

My nipples tightened, and air became harder to drag into my lungs.

"Bash," I said almost under my breath. "Take off your clothes. *Please?*"

My whispered plea flipped a switch in him, but instead of hurrying, he began to move in a kind of sultry slow motion, removing his clothes one stitch at a time with a liquid rhythm that made me salivate.

"Wha... what're you doing?" I breathed.

"You wanted me to remove my clothes, correct? I'm removing them. Thoroughly."

Bash's fake-innocent act was like a stroke to my already hard dick. I let out a noise of need and idly wondered how long a man could go without blinking before it became a risk to his eyesight. Because I needed my eyesight very, very badly, if only for this one night.

His abs contracted and stretched as his hips moved to a slow, relentless beat only he could hear. Meanwhile, my own heart pounded frantically, shuttling all of my blood south, and I was so busy watching the play of his muscles as he caressed his own chest that I forgot to take off my damned clothes.

"Pants off, Prince," he reminded me with a smirk. "You do you, me do me, remember?"

Right. *Shit.* I had one job.

I attempted to yank down my pants but forgot I hadn't unbuttoned them. When I remembered, I found the mechanics of unbuttoning way too complex for my trembling fingers. I ended up with my pants around my hips, trapped in a pathetic heap of desperation on the pristine bedding, my eyes still glued to Bash's hypnotic movements.

"I... I think I changed my mind," I panted. "*You* should do me."

Bash laughed, and without missing a beat, he shucked the rest of his clothing. He yanked me to the edge of the bed and got my pants and underwear off in one smooth movement.

"You're so *good* at unbuttoning," I said reverently.

Bash laughed again and pushed me back on the crisp duvet, then climbed on the bed, holding himself directly over me like he was performing the world's sexiest push-up. "Jesus. I swear, I've laughed more in the past twenty-four hours than I have in... *months.* Who knew laughter was so damn sexy?" He leaned forward and kissed me, pressing the entire hot length of his body against mine.

My brain was overloaded, overwhelmed by sensation. I tried to focus on all that was happening—every single place our skin touched, every tiny, growly sound that emerged from his throat, the perfect taste and texture of his tongue as it tangled with mine. There was no room in my mind for the niggling thoughts and worries that kept trying to surface—like *Crap, has there been a horrible mistake? Surely a guy like Bash cannot be fucking Linden, Indiana's shortest and least remarkable gay man on purpose.*—so I let my doubts go and focused on the opportunity right... on top of me.

Bash's warmth covered me from head to toe, and my hands couldn't get enough of him. They roamed over his back and shoulders hungrily while my lips mapped his throat and chest. He sucked on my earlobe and tugged it between his teeth while his hard cock dug into my upper thigh.

It was so much sensory input I realized I was making whimpering noises while trying to take it all in. But one thought emerged insistently: I wanted to see his cock. I wanted to feel its weight on my tongue and see his face when I sucked on the tip.

"Suck you," I gasped, falling back into the brain-dead one-syllable words from earlier.

Bash seemed to be totally on board with this. He flipped us over so that he was lying on his back while I was draped on top of him like a blanket. As delightful as it was to have him as my personal mattress, his erection pushing insistently against my leg reminded me of my quest, and I quickly moved down to kneel between his thighs and surveyed the terrain.

God, that was some good terrain. The best.

My new favorite kind of terrain, if I had to select one.

I glanced up at him and wondered how I could obsess over his package without seeming creepy. The look on Bash's face was intense enough to zap me right in the chest.

"Good enough?" he asked in a rough voice.

"It'll do," I said, sounding not at all cool.

I leaned closer and breathed him in, closing my eyes in pleasure and relief. He smelled so good, *felt* so good, and was about to taste amazing.

"You're driving me batshit," Bash gritted out. "Christ, Rowe."

"Am I?"

My breath against his skin made his dick jump in a very satisfying way. Well, satisfying for me, at least. Bash let out a frustrated groan and shifted his head on the pillow.

His big hand reached down to thread into my curls, tugging gently, but the words he spoke were not gentle at all. "If you don't put your hand or your mouth on me in the next five seconds, I'm going to have to find someone who will."

Bash's deep rumble made me light-headed, even as his words made me want to laugh out loud.

I leaned in and ran the tip of my tongue over the soft warmth of his cockhead. My eyes were still locked on his, and it took me a second to notice he'd started running his fingers through my hair, carding them over my scalp. Goose bumps prickled on my skin.

"You're fucking beautiful like this," he murmured.

I felt the truth and conviction of his words deep in my gut. This wasn't some kind of joke or payback or even simple convenience. He was really here for me, *with* me. He wanted *me*.

I wrapped my tongue around him, savoring the taste and the weight of it, the *aliveness* of it. The sounds of his irregular breathing and grunts of pleasure spurred me on until I was slurping and gagging like some of the men I'd seen in videos online. Holy shit, I'd been missing out all these years.

Or maybe not. Maybe it was only this good because it was *Bash*.

"That's it," he ground out. "Fuck, Rowe. *Fuck*. Don't tell me you haven't done this before."

I blinked up at him, my wet lashes sticking together. Before I could move off him enough to speak, he brushed his giant palm along my cheek. "Fuck, you're gorgeous. Get up here."

He pulled me back on top of him until our mouths crashed together in a hungry series of deep kisses. "Haven't," I heaved between kisses. "Haven't done it. Promise."

"Shh. 'S'okay. C'mere. More." Now who was the caveman? Hearing how affected he was by this, by *me*, was heady. It made me want to do whatever I could to drive him even crazier.

Bash's hands gripped my ass and squeezed roughly, making my dick painfully hard. I arched into his belly with a whine, seeking friction. I wasn't exactly sure what was supposed to come next, but I knew it needed to include an orgasm. Preferably quickly.

He hooked a muscular leg behind mine and pulled it, rolling us both over until he was on top of me again. He ground his cock into my hip and reached down to stroke me with his large fist.

"Bash," I croaked. "Want to come. Make me come."

His hand moved down to my balls before one of his fingers brushed behind them and across the tender skin of my hole. The needy sound I made would have been humiliating if I'd still given any fucks at that point.

"So empty there, isn't it? Poor Rowe. Don't worry, sweetheart. I'll fix that."

He knelt up and spat into his hand before gripping my cock again and sucking on the middle finger of his other hand. When he slid the finger inside of me and jacked me at the same time, I untethered from Earth completely and flew straight into the stars. Hot fluid landed across my chest and belly as I arched up and cried out.

The orgasm was as different from anything I'd experienced before as... well, as Linden was from New York. Rather than a simple release, it felt like my entire mind had separated from my body, leaving me loose-limbed and euphoric.

In a dim part of my brain, I wondered if I'd inadvertently unlocked a happy whore from inside of myself who would wander the world from here on out in search of greater and more mind-melting orgasms now that I knew what was possible.

Bash released his hold on me to shuttle his fist over his own cock while hungrily eating me up with his eyes. His gaze flicked from the jizz splattered across my skin to the little tattoo on my hip to the patchy flush that surely mottled the skin of my chest and neck to the glassy eyes I probably blinked at him dreamily. I couldn't imagine any of that was particularly sexy, but the total picture seemed to be working for him. His breath went choppy, his fist flew faster, and my breath caught at the pure want written on his face.

I reached out to run my fingers over the tight skin of his balls, and that was it.

When his release hit, the view was enough to perk my dick up again in a pathetic attempt to get back in the game. Bash barked out a curse, the tendons in his neck stark and the look in his eyes wild. The rhythm of his pumps faltered as his cock erupted all over me, mixing with what was already there—physical proof that the dirtiest, sexiest interaction I'd ever imagined *had actually happened.*

"Fuck," I breathed, trailing my fingers through the combined fluid. "Oh my god."

Bash hovered above me, and his eyes met mine for a long beat while the air around us seemed to pulse with... something. Attraction. Pleasure. *Connection.*

It was enough to make me wish I could erase the past couple of days and be honest with him from the start. Enough to make me wish I could actually be Sterling Chase, just so I could have the possibility of a future with a man like Bash.

"Already scheming again?" Bash accused fondly. He flopped down on the bed beside me, still breathless, eyes closed.

Could you scheme about telling the truth? I didn't think so.

"No scheming. I... I like you," I blurted.

He chuckled. "Believe it or not, I figured that out, sweetheart. Somewhere between 'want to come' and 'oh my god.'" He smirked. "I like you, too."

I shook my head. I didn't mean that I liked sex with him—although, Jesus Christ, *that, too.*

I wanted him to know that I liked who he was as a person—intelligent and protective and irreverent and kind. I wanted him to know that talking with him had felt so comfortable I'd ended up telling him truths I couldn't tell anyone else, even when I should have lied. I wanted him to look at me and see someone who wasn't out to use him —not for donations, or to green-light my project, or even to give me contacts, no matter how badly I needed them.

"Bash. Sebastian. I... I meant..."

"Mmm?" He turned his head toward me, eyes still closed, breathing still a bit ragged. "I came so hard I can't feel my toes, and my brain short-circuited. Go ahead and confess whatever you like, sweetheart. I promise, right now, nothing can shock me."

My courage deserted me entirely.

"I'm the Burrito Bandito!" I blurted.

Bash's eyes popped open, and we stared at each other as my confession landed with an awkward clunk between us.

"Well," he said slowly. "Apparently, I was wrong."

TEN

BASH

I stared at Rowe, chest heaving and heart squeezing painfully.

Had the man just confessed to being a fast-food thief? Was I experiencing oxygen deprivation? Was this how death by epic orgasm happened?

If so, that would explain a lot of things. For example, why my heart was trying to convince my brain that what I'd just experienced with Rowe was something way bigger and more life-altering than an orgasm.

"Repeat that?" I said, trying to make sense of his words.

Rowe covered his face with both hands like he was trying to conceal his blush, but it wasn't working. "That wasn't what I meant to say," he groaned.

I leaned up on one elbow and brushed his damp hair away from his forehead before I could remind myself that being sweet and schmoopy was not a good idea, and then I pulled one hand away from his face.

He peered up at me, flushed and wild-eyed, sexy as hell and so damn sweet.

I wanted to devour him. To keep him in my bed for days with

nothing available to him but the touch of my hands and lips, food fed to him from my fingers and tongue, and water only taken in furtive sips in the shower while I plastered him against the wall and fucked him long and hard into the cold tiles.

The fact that I could envision *all* of this with perfect clarity suggested my response to him was about ten notches past insanity levels, so I forced myself to shove those feels deep into a box in the back of my brain.

I cleared my throat. "Are you... are you trying to tell me you're hungry?" I asked, still not sure why he was talking about burritos. "Do you want me to order something?"

"No! I meant..." He sighed and shook his head slightly. "You know what? Yes. Yes I'm hungry. I didn't eat much dinner because I was too busy talking. Thank you, and please."

I heaved myself out of bed and reached for the phone on the nightstand to call room service, ordering a variety of desserts and snacks. While I did, Rowe sat up in bed with his hands in his lap and very pointedly didn't look at me.

"Thirty minutes," I told him after I hung up the phone. "Want to shower before they get here?"

He nodded, summoning a brief smile as he hopped out of bed.

I could tell his nerves were returning as the afterglow wore off, and part of me wanted to scoop him up in my arms and reassure him. Fortunately, the rest of me was far more wary.

Now that Rowe knew I was wealthy and had the connections he needed to get his project seen, how long before he forgot our agreement and started dropping hints about his mysterious project? How long before he started manipulating the connection between us in order to get what he wanted?

I'd seen it happen over and over again—to Dev with his family, to Silas with Justin... hell, even to me, every time my parents reminded me what I owed to the Dayne name. With connection came the poisonous creep of expectations. The deeper the connection, the deeper that poison would spread... and the more pain it would cause when things inevitably went bad.

I liked Rowe a lot—a remarkable amount, really, for a man I'd known twenty-four hours, who'd lied to me nearly the entire time—and I admired his strength and resilience, too. It was no wonder I wanted to be close to him. But I couldn't afford to have any illusions that the outcome with him would be different. In fact, knowing his story with his sister, knowing how desperate he was to get his project made, it seemed even more inevitable.

The smart thing to do would be to hold him at arm's length.

But when Rowe leaped out of bed and headed to the second bedroom to take his shower—after tangling his foot in the bedsheets and doing a hop-slide-shimmy that had no right to be as sexy as it was —I couldn't help watching him walk away... and wanting to snatch him back.

If he thinks he's spending the remainder of the night in the other room, he's mistaken, I thought to myself. I wanted him at arm's length, figuratively but not literally.

I cleaned up as quickly as I could before putting on a pair of joggers and a comfortable T-shirt. When I made my way to the main room to wait for the food, Rowe was already walking out of the other bedroom wearing similar comfortable clothes, running his fingers through his wet hair until the strands fell back into their tumble of curls.

"You'll never believe it," he announced, "but I found Sterling Chase's suitcase on the bed in the other room, and his clothes fit me perfectly."

I laughed. The shy smile on Rowe's face was worth the huffy, disapproving texts I'd gotten from Kenji when I'd asked him to coordinate the clothing. "*Seriously? We're buying him a wardrobe now? You don't even know his size, Bash!*" But it turned out, as with so many things regarding Rowe Prince, I *had* known, though I couldn't say exactly how.

"I'm glad," I said gruffly, trying to ignore the strange, proprietary feeling that swamped me when I saw him wearing those clothes. "You want a drink?"

"Sure." He shifted his weight nervously from foot to foot. "Uh. I don't know what happens now? I mean, not just because I've never, you know, *done that* with a guy, but also, like, what is the protocol for when you've lied to a guy about who you are, and he lied about being your personal assistant, and then he takes you to the most beautiful hotel, and then you tell him all your secrets and way too much about your family?"

Damn it. How was I to keep him at arm's length when every nervous word he babbled was a lasso pulling me to him more tightly?

"Definitely starting with a drink is the right thing." I feigned an easy grin and squatted in front of the minibar to grab a beer for each of us, trying to think of a topic that was light and casual. Something bland that wouldn't lead to any more interesting revelations. "So, Rowe, do your, uh... do your parents have curly hair?"

If Rowe thought that was a fucking ridiculous question, he was far too nice to say so.

He touched a hand to his curls and gave me a grateful smile as I handed him one of the beers. "Yeah. At least, my mom does. Daisy did, too, but she hated it. And I... well." He cleared his throat and blushed rosily. "I have a love-hate relationship with my hair, thanks to the picture incident."

Picture incident? "What's that mean?" I demanded, intrigued against my will.

Rowe shook his head again insistently. "Nope. Can't tell you. See, I was kinda hoping to have sex with you again before the night is over, and if I tell you, that dream will die."

"Rowe?" I whispered. "There is not a single question about whether we will have sex again tonight. I promise."

He swallowed hard. "Do you *pinky* promise?"

I laughed out loud. Jesus, this guy. This stupid attraction was welcome to fade any minute now. *Any minute.* "Yes. Pinky promise."

He sighed, certain I'd doomed us both. "When I was a toddler, I was kinda blond, and my hair was *so* curly. Like, little corkscrew ringlets? And I was a bit... chubby. You know, before I grew into my full height?" He straightened his five-and-a-half-foot frame and tried to look imposing.

"Right," I agreed gravely. I could envision this perfectly.

"And my mom... I cannot believe I'm telling you this... she took me to get my picture done at the mall, and the photographer dressed me up in, like, wings and a diaper thing? And my mom insisted on hanging the photo in the living room, and she... *callsmeherlilbaby-cupid.*" He downed half the beer in one gulp. "So! Let's talk about other things. *Sexy* things. O-or polo, my new favorite sport. Aren't horses wonderful?"

"Wait," I said, unable to help the delighted smile breaking over my face. "Wait, wait, wait. Your mother dressed you in wings? She calls you her little baby cupid? Present tense?"

"Shush." He clapped a hand over my mouth. "Not important. I blame the picture lady at the mall. And Daisy, who encouraged my mom to keep the picture up—"

I dragged his hand away. "Is the picture still there?"

"No. Maybe." He swallowed. "Yes. Why?"

"Just curious." I took a casual sip of beer. "And also filled with the sudden need to go to Indiana and begin a collection of Cupid-inspired artwork."

To my surprise, he laughed out loud. "Yeah, right. Like you'd ever go to Linden. You wouldn't last a day."

"Excuse you?" I moved closer until I was standing right in front of him. "I have traveled around the world. I think I could survive rural Indiana."

The research Kenji had done on Rowe suggested that his father worked at a chemical plant and his mother was a receptionist for an excavation contractor. The difference in our upbringings was night and day, but I was confident I could charm his parents.

"Linden doesn't have a single restaurant with tablecloths." He tilted his head back so he could look up at me defiantly. "There's one stoplight. One bar. One tiny grocery store. Closest decent hairstylist is thirty minutes away." He lifted a hand to brush a strand of hair off my forehead before snatching his hand away like he'd touched a flame. "There are no endowments or galas. No polo fields. Folks who are well-off there only have to work one job, but lots work two. My parents need my help so they can pay off their house and retire some-day." He shrugged. "Not your kind of place, that's all I'm saying."

I wanted to argue with this. To tell him that I'd been to lots of different places, and not just on exotic vacations—Landry had grown up with less than nothing; Silas, Zane, and Dev with only slightly more—but being familiar with it didn't mean I'd experienced it. Didn't mean that I knew at all what it had been like for him to grow up in a town like that.

"Isn't Purdue University nearby?"

Rowe took a sip of his beer and nodded. "Sure. I've gone there a couple of times to, uh... you know, try to hook up or whatever." His cheeks turned a delicious shade of pink.

"*Try?* Why didn't you succeed? I would think a college town would be a fairly good place for hookups," I said carefully, trying to ignore the feral banshee inside of me who suddenly wanted to kill every Boilermaker on the planet.

"Maybe it would have, but I kept chickening out," he said softly. "The only thing I knew about those guys was what their abs looked like in a Grindr picture, and all I could picture was my broken body thrown into an empty oil barrel and tossed into the Wabash River."

"Wow." I bit my lip. "Does that... happen a lot in Indiana?"

His eyes lit with amusement. "Well, no. But only because people like me remain ever vigilant and don't allow ourselves to get distracted by lusty hookups, you see?"

"I do see." I nodded slowly. "You're right. I wouldn't last a single day." I gave in to the temptation and raised my free hand to bracket one of Rowe's lean hips, then lowered my head to nibble at his lower lip. "If you were anywhere nearby, I'd be far, *far* too distracted."

Rowe's breath caught. I set our beer bottles on a side table, then did what I'd been longing to do since the moment he stepped into the room—I grasped the back of his damp curls and pulled him in for a hard kiss. "You're fucking irresistible," I murmured against his mouth, the words coming out like an accusation.

When I pulled back, Rowe's eyes were a little glassy, the same way they'd been earlier during sex. The front of his joggers tented out, and his neck was mottled again.

I was in trouble with this guy. I wanted him again, and it had only been fifteen minutes since I'd had him the first time. Men did *not* tie me into knots like this. Not ever. I'd always been way more interested in what I could do with my life than *who* I could do. But with Rowe... it was like my brain was covered by a thousand stickers of him and then covered with a permanent top coat that would make removal completely impossible.

"More," Rowe begged, grabbing the front of my T-shirt. "Please." But before I could agree and rush him back to the bedroom, there was a knock at the door.

"Hold that thought." I opened the door so the staff could deliver our snacks and perform their turndown service. It felt like they were all moving with exaggerated underwater slowness, but I told myself that was a good thing.

Arm's length, Sebastian. Light and easy.

But when the last of the room attendants left a few minutes later, my arousal hadn't let up in the slightest.

"Come eat," I suggested, gesturing toward the array of desserts, wines, and snacks that had been laid out for us. "I can't have you fainting on me."

"Fainting," he scoffed. He puffed his chest out. "I'll have you know I reached level six on Gym Joe's YouTube Bulk-Up challenge."

"I... don't know what that means," I said, but when he passed in front of me to get to the table, I couldn't help reaching my hands under his shirt to feel the muscles of his abs and chest... and if my thumbs happened to brush across his nipples, then so be it.

"It's... uh..." His breathing increased as his nipples hardened. "It's..."

I leaned in to kiss his ear before stepping away. "Eat," I repeated. "Then you can tell me more about it."

After I pulled back, he wobbled for a moment before seeming to snap out of it and reaching for the snacks. I poured myself a glass of wine, handed him his beer, and led him to the sofa, where we resumed our seats from earlier.

Between bites of a fruit tart, Rowe told me more about how he motivated himself through his workout videos, and I found myself promising I'd try one. And he told me about his adventures as the Burrito Bandito... which made me laugh so hard I snorted wine through my nose for the first time in my life.

"It's actually really fun," he admitted, crunching a handful of rosemary sea salt mixed nuts. "The tips aren't great, but it's nice to know you've brightened someone's lunch break with a little song and dance. I might even miss it a little when I'm back in Linden in a couple months."

"So why go back?" I asked lightly. "I mean, couldn't you stay—?"

"No way. I'm barely making ends meet here, even sleeping on Joey's futon. I couldn't afford to rent a tux last night, which was why I was wearing Joey's."

"The bunny tux was your cousin's?"

"Better than his stripper tux, or so I'm told." Rowe grinned. "Anyway, I told you, I have to go back to Linden so I can help my folks. They don't have much money, and my job at Bobby's Tech Barn pays pretty well. And it's fun, too, in a way."

"So you're interested in technology, then?" I asked, unable to stop myself from edging closer to the topics I'd promised to avoid.

Rowe snorted. "Nah. I'm the opposite of a tech geek. But I don't need to be. Most of our customers are sweet grandmas who don't remember how to get into their email and clueless middle-aged guys who *thought* they knew what they were doing but ended up downloading a bunch of viruses while trying to stream movies. Bobby and some of the other techs get impatient with them, but I know what it's like to be technologically challenged and learn things as you go."

He set his empty beer bottle on the side table, licked the last bits of salt off his fingers, and scooted closer so our knees touched. "Okay, enough. I feel like you know way too much about me now," he teased. "All the mystery is gone."

I'd hoped that would be true. Instead, I felt like we'd barely skimmed the surface, and I had a thousand more burning questions about him and the way he saw the world. This attraction was definitely not going away.

"What about you?" Rowe asked. "What was it like where you grew up? Who's got the unfortunate photos of *you* in their living room?"

I propped my feet on the coffee table. "Daynes don't take silly photos, Rowe," I said mock-severely. But as to the rest... it was hard to talk about the privations of growing up incredibly wealthy after hearing about Rowe's childhood.

"I'm not sure what to tell you," I said finally. "I had a very privileged upbringing. My parents both come from old money. My dad's great-grandfather founded a lumber company that put sawmills all across the Midwest—"

"Dayne Lumber," Rowe said, putting it together. "Holy fuck. Dayne Lumber has been around since Jesus's time."

"Slightly longer." I reached for a handful of nuts, more for the distraction than because I was hungry. "My family doesn't deal with any of the day-to-day operations anymore, though. My parents socialize and travel and donate money to many, many different causes they know little about. I take my work seriously and spend a lot of time in the office. I prefer to be more hands-on with the things I'm involved in."

Rowe's nod made the light from the lamp glint off his curls. "So what *do* you do for work, exactly, other than having a seat on the board at Sterling Chase?"

I hesitated over how much of a connection I wanted to reveal, and Rowe immediately tried to backtrack. "Are we getting too close to things we shouldn't talk about?"

We were. We definitely were. But I plunged right ahead anyway, like I was hang-gliding off a cliff.

"It's not really a secret. I work closely with some of Sterling Chase's clients to support and nurture early business ideas," I admitted. "Fledgling entrepreneurs need a lot of help to get their businesses off the ground, as you know. I help them find money and connections, to hone their ideas. I meet with their developers, match them to the right resources, mentor their leaders, note places where their progress is lagging, and find ways to help them improve their processes to help bring their projects to market."

"Ah."

I could tell Rowe knew exactly what I was describing since he was one of the people who needed money and connections. I braced myself for him to cut in excitedly and give me his own pitch, despite our agreement, or to give me puppy dog eyes and reiterate how badly he needed me to fulfill my promise and give him contacts, preferably *now*. I was mellow enough, charmed enough, I'd probably even go along with it. But he didn't do either of those things. Instead, he shifted his weight, settling more deeply into the sofa, and nodded again, encouraging me to continue.

My stomach swooped again, harder this time.

"It's a lot of work. I feel a huge responsibility to the people I'm helping, obviously. I want the best for them, to respect their goals and vision. And then, of course, there's my responsibility to uphold the Sterling Chase brand. To make sure that all the financial dealings are fair while keeping an eye on costs and profit margins. It means a lot of long hours, but I enjoy it." I hesitated, then said honestly, "At least... most of the time."

"Shit," Rowe murmured, almost to himself. "Profit margins."

"Well, yeah. Obviously, that's not the company's highest priority —" I broke off, thinking of Austin. "Or not the only high priority, anyway."

"But Sterling Chase probably signs the projects that have the strongest potential for profitability because it's a for-profit company." Rowe shook his head ruefully. "Don't mind me. I'm just realizing how little I know about the business aspect of business, that's all. It's a little embarrassing how naive I've been. I'm so excited about my project and its potential impact on *people* that I didn't understand why the folks at these development companies weren't getting excited, too. I didn't really think about how much work is involved on the back end. Of *course* a company only wants to invest their money in something if it'll make them money."

"That's not entirely correct," I argued, stung by Rowe's easy acceptance of this as a normal business practice and more by the fact that I couldn't really argue with him. "The projects Sterling Chase has green-lit recently have been more commercial, I suppose. But money isn't my goal. The projects I get involved with personally are the ones that are the most challenging and which have the highest impact on people's lives. That's what I find rewarding."

"But..." Rowe wrinkled his nose in thought. "If you're saying you pick *your* projects from the ones Sterling Chase already green-lit, but Sterling Chase focuses on things that are commercial and profitable, doesn't that mean the ones you're working on are gonna be the most profitable and not necessarily the most rewarding, just by default?" He grimaced. "Sorry, maybe I'm misunderstanding the whole thing."

Or maybe *I* was.

His words hit me in a way I hadn't considered before. I thought about how much less passionate I'd been lately towards my work.

"Well, shit." I sat forward, my hands on my knees.

"What's wrong? Are you okay? Should we not be talking about this—?"

"No. Not that. I'm just having a revelation." I laughed weakly. "For months now, or maybe even years, I've noticed myself getting restless. Bored. I'm dedicated to the projects I'm working on, and they *are* challenging, and I do enjoy them, but they don't hold my attention the way they once did. So I started throwing myself into other stuff, too—adventure sports, travel to far-off places—and even *that* hasn't been working anymore. So I started taking on more projects, poking my nose into ones I'm not even supposed to be involved in, which annoys the fuck out of Sterling Chase's head of development, looking for a challenge..."

Rowe continued to munch on the snack mix and take sips of his beer like he hadn't quietly set off a chain of small earthquakes in my brain. "Okay. And?"

And this one simple conversation over snacks, with a guy who didn't understand business at all, had shone a bright light on *why*. Because Austin picked the projects, and Austin didn't take risks.

"And you just helped me realize that's not enough for me. I need to make a change. I need to be working on bigger stuff. Ideas that are more important to me, personally." I grabbed his face with two hands and pulled him in for an impulsive kiss. "And now *I* feel like I've been naive."

For people like Austin—and my father—profitability was about numbers. But my own definition skewed slightly from theirs in a way that I couldn't fully explain... or hadn't been able to, until right now, when Rowe had helped me put it all together. It was about knowing the investment of my time and energy would yield something I could be proud of.

I wasn't sure exactly what that would look like, practically speaking, but it felt like I was finally looking in the right direction.

He gave me a hesitant smile and settled in against my side. "Well, good. I bet work's way more satisfying when you know in your heart that the project is worthwhile, right? I mean, it is for me."

"Yes. Definitely. And to be fair, it's not like most of the stuff Sterling Chase is working on currently isn't also great. Not everything is the CaffApp—" I gave him a side-eyed look that made him laugh out loud.

"Is there a TeaApp in the works, too?" he teased. "A CocoaApp?"

"No, Sassypants," I growled, poking his side. "One of the projects

Sterling Chase is working on right now is amazing. Very tied in to the ETC program."

"Really?" He lifted his head, and his excited eyes met mine. "Okay, that's legitimately great because I know for a fact that there's so much more that can be done with emergency services. You know I... Ah..." He blinked and shook his head, his smile dimming a fraction. "I'm really pleased Sterling Chase is working on that."

I wondered at his change in attitude, but I decided not to call him on it. He was probably thinking of his sister. "The project was developed by one of our own employees, which makes it even more exciting, on a personal level."

"And does that mean only Sterling Chase will profit?"

I snorted. "Sterling Chase will make bank, yes." I didn't explain that this meant only me and the others on the board and that none of us were particularly money-motivated anymore.

Rowe's mischievous grin was like sunshine breaking through clouds. "Well, *this* Sterling Chase is *very* proud of you for making me a profit, my boy," he said, pulling out his drawling Sterling voice.

I spluttered out a laugh. "Oh, thank you so much, sir." I reached over to pull his bare feet into my lap. "Does this mean I get a prize?"

Rowe yelped and laughed as he nearly spilled the snack bowl. He quickly hugged it to his chest and leaned his head back on the arm of the sofa.

"Sterling Chase might buy you a new polo pony... after I splash out with some undercarriage lights for my old Corolla and some new Anchor-Hocking casserole-ware for my mother, of course."

I let out a low whistle. "Lifestyles of the Rich and Famous right there. And you could always pick your dad up a six-pack of the fancy stuff while you're at it."

"Budweiser instead of Pabst?" His eyes danced. "That's a bridge too far, Bash. Way too expensive."

I tickled the bottom of his foot until we were both sprawled against each other, breathless with laughter, smiling sappily.

"You're a really great guy, Bash," he said softly. "Not everyone wants to do the right thing the way you do."

Hearing those words from him meant a lot. Way too much for someone I'd known for less than a day.

"What would you do, if you had money?" I asked without thinking. "If you won the lottery, let's say. Enough to fund your own project idea, with a ton left over after."

I'd expected Rowe to smile or laugh, but instead, he frowned seriously, like the very idea was insane. "I don't know. Not worth thinking about, really."

"Isn't it? You'd take care of your parents, right? And then what?"

He hesitated, not as though he didn't know the answer, but as though he wasn't sure he should share it. "This is going to sound ridiculous."

"Nobody's dream is ridiculous," I said softly. Hell, it was the tenet of my life's purpose.

"I like decorating houses." Rowe studied the half-empty beer bottle on the table like it might contain the secrets of the universe. "I haven't actually done it, other than my own family's house, which doesn't really count since we didn't have a budget worth shit. But..." He darted a glance at me like he was making sure I wasn't going to make fun of him, then went on. "I've studied it so much, and I have hundreds of notebooks full of sketches. Bobby gave me a good deal on a used iPad, and I downloaded design software onto it. It's my favorite thing to make up a room in the software and then decorate it. I have hundreds of Pinterest boards for my made-up clients. So, yeah, I'd design beautiful spaces for people if I could do anything I wanted. And not just rich people, either, because everyone deserves to enjoy their home."

Ugh. How was it that every word this man spoke made him *more* attractive? Somehow, every unexpected answer just made me want to know more.

"Would you ever want to share some of your designs?"

He glanced up at me, and I saw his cheeks were flushed again, hopefully from excitement rather than insecurity. "With you? They're probably horrible compared to the things you've seen. I'm sure your house was decorated by a big New York stylist."

It was true, but that didn't mean I loved it. "Well, I have... more than one place, actually. But my Hamptons house *was* done by a big New York stylist, and I hate it. The entire thing is done in modern minimalism."

Rowe's fingers twitched. "Oh. Yeah. The Hamptons is the beach, right? You don't seem like the kind of person to want something so reserved. Especially for a place you're meant to relax in."

I imagined taking Rowe to my beach house and showing him around. Getting him naked and holding him in the swimming pool at night. Taking him to my big bed and making love to him in front of the giant windows overlooking the ocean at night.

The idea should have been ludicrous—I rarely had guests in my space, let alone hookups—but instead, it stuck in my brain.

"True," I agreed, taking another sip of beer to distract myself from mentally calculating how quickly Kenji could arrange a helicopter to fly us to Southampton. "Do you suppose the designer realized I'm not great at relaxing?"

"Oh, I don't know about that. You're doing a pretty good job of it right now." He laid a hand on my stomach, and the warmth of him stole through my shirt and into my skin. "All those things you invented about Sterling Chase... the mountain climbing, the polo playing, the adventuring. That's you. The stuff you did."

I nodded.

"So... were you supposed to be climbing that mountain this weekend?"

"I was. My parents asked me to attend the gala to represent the Daynes, so I changed my plans." I darted him a look. "Poor Bubbles must be there all alone, pining for me."

Rowe's eyes crinkled, but he bit down on his lip, stopping his smile. "Are you disappointed you missed it?"

I opened my mouth to say *yes, obviously*. Instead, I found myself admitting, "Not a single bit. If I'd been in Borneo, I would have missed meeting *the* Sterling Chase. And I wouldn't have wanted to miss that for the world."

His smile lit up his face, enough to make me yank him by the legs even closer and dive on top of him to kiss his adorable mouth again. Snack mix and empty glasses went flying all over the place... and the sound of his delighted laughter had the same effect on my heart.

We have until tomorrow, I told myself. *Maybe this thing will burn itself out, and then I'll cut the sexy liar loose.*

As I shoved his shirt over his head and nipped at his full lips, I ignored the little voice in the back of my head suggesting Rowe wasn't the only Prince of Lies in the room.

ELEVEN

ROWE

Being naked with Sebastian Dayne was... unbelievable. Unreal. Mind-blowing. Insanely hot. I could hardly breathe with his hands on me. And they were everywhere, touching me as if he wanted to map my skin with his fingertips. By the time we stumbled back into his bedroom, I was rock hard again and willing to sign my freedom away for another orgasm at his hand.

This time, I felt like I knew him a little better, which was devastating. It made me like him more, want him more... and at the same time, it made me know, without a shadow of a doubt, this was going to end soon and hard.

Men like Sebastian Dayne, the crazy-wealthy heir to the Dayne Lumber company with his *multiple* homes and his adventure trips to Borneo, would never end up with the Burrito Bandito from tiny Linden, Indiana. Real life didn't work out like that. Cinderella had gotten a deferment—one more night—but that was all.

Earlier, in the shower, that realization had made me pitiful. It wasn't fair that the first guy in forever who'd made me feel smart and funny and sexy was meant to be the handsome prince in somebody else's fairy tale. It wasn't fair that I couldn't keep him.

But on the other hand, this one night was more—better—than I'd ever expected to have with anyone. And if life had taught me anything, it was to enjoy what you had while you had it.

Tomorrow, I was going to walk away. I wasn't going to wait for Bash to have to kick me out or do some awkward thing where he promised to call and didn't. And I sure as heck wasn't going to ask him for business contacts for my project, either. Two days ago, I wouldn't have hesitated, just like I wouldn't have hesitated to blurt out all the details of my project while we were cuddling on the couch and he mentioned ETC. But two days ago, I hadn't realized that the least remarkable things about Sebastian Dayne were his money and influence. Now I did, so I was going to keep to the boundaries he'd drawn—no business talk, no pitch—and find a different way to get my project funded.

But all of that was a worry for tomorrow. For after the spell wore off and the world stopped being so shiny.

In the meantime...

"Can we have sex?" I asked, pulling back from a brain-melting kiss.

Bash looked at me, then down at our naked bodies, our clothes long abandoned in the living room. He lifted his eyebrow, which was even more compelling up close. "Aren't we already doing that? I thought—"

I lurched forward and kissed him again for a long moment before pulling back with a gasp. "*Sex*, sex. The... sex kind. Of sex."

I couldn't bring myself to say *anal*. In the back of my head, my middle school PE teacher said, *If you can't say it, you shouldn't be doing it.*

I shook my head to rid myself of Mrs. Colling's voice. "Sex," I repeated for clarity.

Bash's smirk was stupidly adorable, and his eyes shined with affectionate amusement. "Say it again? I didn't quite catch *mppfh*—"

I tackled him again and kissed his fucking face off through his laughter. When we both had to pull away or suffocate to death, Bash cupped my cheek. "Are you sure? And do you want to be the one who gives this sex or the one who gets this sex?" The smirk was still there.

"Both," I said honestly. "Both."

My head was spinning, but I was just so freaking happy I didn't even care.

Bash's eyes went from being lit with laughter to dark with desire. "I'd really like to fuck you."

I sucked in a breath so fast it nearly made me pass out. "Yes." I also nodded just to make it crystal clear how strong my agreement was.

This time, when he kissed me, it was tender and gentle. "I'll go slow," he promised.

I shook my head, breaking the kiss. "Not too slow."

"You've never done this before. I need to prep you—"

I blinked away from his intense eye contact. "I've never done this before... with a *human*," I corrected.

His nostrils flared either in amusement or lust. Possibly both since he seemed to keep confusing the two. "Are we talking extraterrestrials or toys?"

"Second one," I admitted, feeling my face get even hotter. The pulse at Bash's neck fluttered wildly. I reached out to run my fingertip over it. "A lot. I really like them."

What happened after that was a cross between being ravaged by a wild beast and being treated like a precious treasure. Bash muttered to himself while prepping me, and I took the opportunity to squeeze the ever-loving fuck out of the base of my dick to keep from spilling into his hair. Just the sight of him between my legs like that, laser focused on me, was such an incredible turn-on I could barely stand it.

"Look away," I cautioned myself under my breath. "Do not stare at the sexy man and his sinful lips. Do not—*ohhhhh, fuck!*"

The feel of his fingers moving inside me made me whimper and toss my head on the bed. None of my toys could compare to this warmth and intensity. I needed more.

"Sebastian. *Bash*. Hurry. Please..."

"Need to make sure you're prepped." His voice was rough with need but gentle, too. I could tell he'd rather do anything other than hurt me.

"I'm prepped. I've *been* prepped. In fact, I have spent twenty-four years preparing for—*hngmpfh!*"

Bash cut off my protest by taking my cock into his mouth and sucking it halfway down his throat, his eyes on mine the entire time. I screamed and arched into him, torn between letting myself come and trying so hard not to.

The scream turned into a whimper as he pulled off quickly and reached for a condom. "Still sure, sweetheart?"

"Super sure," I breathed.

When Bash began to enter my body, I had to admit I was grateful for the time he'd taken to prep me. He was big—bigger than any of the toys I used regularly—but the burn was oddly satisfying. It was proof I was finally here. Finally experiencing something I'd wanted for so long. I was with someone I trusted not to hurt me, someone I was strongly attracted to.

"You okay?" Bash asked. I could see sweat beading on his forehead as he fought to go slowly.

My knees were bent up by my shoulders, and when Bash turned his face to brush a kiss on the inside of one, I reached out to run my fingers through his hair. "Yeah."

He continued going slowly until I finally felt comfortable enough to tell him to move. He propped himself up with one arm while his other hand held my face. His thrusts started off gently, but as soon as he brushed against my gland, it lit a spark in both of us.

My dick came roaring back to life, and I let out a sound that expressed just how okay I was with all of this. Bash thrust in and out of me while alternating kisses with curses against my lips. It was hot and fast. My ass stung and my cock throbbed until my senses completely overloaded and shorted out.

"*Fuck*," I cried, arching into him to take him even deeper. Bash's fist shuttled over my cock with the perfect amount of pressure and shoved me over the edge into free fall. My entire body sang as the warp stars shot past the edges of my vision. Bash cried out, too, and hearing my name in his broken voice made the whole world contract to the precise size of this bed, then smaller—to every tiny place where his skin touched mine.

After, I didn't want to move. Even breathing felt overrated. I wanted to stay suspended in that moment with Bash forever.

His lips brushed against my temple. "Careful," he whispered before pulling out of me.

I sucked in a breath. The loss of him hurt far worse than having him inside me had, and I immediately wanted him back. I wanted another chance to feel him the way I'd felt before, feel the sharpest, edgiest orgasm I'd ever imagined.

"Stay right here," Bash murmured, moving off me carefully. My eyes roved over his naked body, sweat-damp and flushed. The thick muscles of his pale ass bounced as he walked to the bathroom, and the clench and flex of his thighs as he climbed back onto the bed a moment later was possibly even better.

I closed my eyes with a happy sigh, committing it all to memory. Years from now, when Bash had forgotten all about the time he fucked the Burrito Bandito, I'd still be savoring this moment.

"You have a dopey grin on your face," he said with a smile in his voice. I opened my eyes to see him return with a wet washcloth. "You look like I feel."

That was probably the sweetest thing anyone had ever said to me. I winked at him, still too come-drunk to feel shy. "Then you must feel *amazing*."

He leaned over and cleaned me off. "Even better than that," he assured me. He dragged the cloth over my hip, then traced his finger over the damp skin. "Tell me about this?"

I knew without looking down that he was tracing the simple black lines of the tattoo on my hip.

"It's a caduceus," I explained. "And at the top of the rod is a..."

"Daisy," he concluded. "You got this for your sister?"

I nodded. "Funny thing. The caduceus is commonly thought to represent medicine now, but that's kind of a mistake. For the ancient Greeks, it was a symbol of Hermes, the messenger god, who was also the god of negotiations and commerce and eloquence and..."

"Lies?" Bash said, amused. His fingers playing over my skin made my very satisfied dick want to try for round three.

"Yeah. I mean, that's not why I got it. The guy at the tattoo shop was the one who told me that," I confessed sheepishly. "I got it because it symbolizes, uh..."

Shit. Just like before, I wanted to tell Bash about my project—about how I hoped it would change processes in emergency medical response so that people like my sister get more accurate trauma care, and maybe some other brother wouldn't have to lose his twin. I wanted to share my excitement over everything I'd learned about emergency processes and hospital administration and budget cuts, and to hear Bash's feedback since I knew he would probably have a thousand intelligent thoughts that would help me refine it.

It felt strange that we'd shared so much, talked about my mortifying toddler pictures, for heaven's sake, but not discussed this crucial thing that had consumed my life for the past few years. Not talking about it felt almost like another, bigger lie.

But it also seemed wrong to bring that up now, in this bed. Like it was the sort of thing that would steal the light from Bash's eyes and make him pull away from me.

You only have a little longer, I reminded myself. *What's one more lie?*

"It symbolizes hope," I said because it was partly true.

"And that's why you touch it when you're nervous." He brushed his thumb over the lines once more, then lowered his head and kissed it so tenderly my breath hitched. When he lifted his head again, his eyes met mine and caught. *Held.* A tiny frisson of something passed between us but was gone before I could name it.

I froze, my mouth suddenly dry. I had no idea what to say or do. No idea what was happening between us or if Bash felt it, too.

After that one fraught second, Bash cleared his throat, stood up, and returned the washcloth to the bathroom without a word. When he strolled back in, he began rooting around in his open suitcase for his phone charger and plugged it in while giving an exaggerated yawn. "I don't know about you, but I'm going to sleep like the dead."

Idiot. You're starting to believe your own fairy tales, Rowe Prince.

I swallowed down a bubble of disappointment and turned my face into the pillow. "Same. And you promised me we'd have all night. I'm not leaving this bed," I warned. "If you were planning on sleeping without a leech stuck to your side, you might want to switch bedrooms with me."

Bash yanked the covers from underneath me, then crawled into bed before settling them over us both. "Fortunately, I have no problem with leeches. They're fascinating creatures. Remind me sometime to tell you about the time I went kayaking in Patagonia and how you should always listen to the locals, especially when they tell you to put tobacco in your socks."

Sometime? There wouldn't be other times when Bash and I would be together trading stories, unless he actually made that trip to Linden someday. But I wasn't gonna say that and ruin the mood.

"Ew," I said with a shudder that made him laugh out loud.

Bash's laughter was the best sound in the world, and I reveled in it. Another memory from my fairy-tale weekend.

"Now I'm going to have nightmares," I informed him. "I think you need to clean my brain with a better story."

Bash gathered me in his arms and pulled me close until my head rested on his chest. His skin smelled familiar to me now, which made me feel relaxed and safe.

"How about I tell you about the time I went to Antarctica?"

"No leeches?"

"Not unless you count a certain minor Danish noble who tried sneaking into my tent to cuddle me for warmth."

I chuckled and burrowed further into his chest, and with his voice a warm rumble in my ear, I slipped into a delicious, deep sleep.

Which was why, when a phone's ringtone split the midnight silence in the room a few hours later, I had no idea where the hell I was or whose hairy chest I was lying on.

TWELVE

BASH

Rowe had fallen asleep quickly, snoring lightly on my chest while I held him and ran my fingertips over his back and shoulders. Instead of feeling the deep, sated relaxation I would have expected to feel after a night of incredible casual sex, I felt restless and edgy...

Because this sex hadn't been casual.

Rowe Prince was casual like a lightning strike.

Like a supernova.

Like free fall, in that heart-stopping moment before the parachute opens.

I couldn't imagine how I was supposed to wish him well after this weekend, leave him with a few contacts for his project, and let him slip back off to Noplace, Indiana, without me.

The way he talked, the way he laughed, the way he saw the world, the way he let himself be trusting and vulnerable with me... all of it was electrifying and addictive. More thrilling than a hundred adventures to far-flung places because Rowe was endlessly unpredictable. Every part of him, right down to the freckles on his cheeks, was fascinating.

Which was a real problem because casual was all we could ever be.

I had no interest in an actual relationship. This wasn't because I'd sworn them off after some terrible breakup, like Silas had, or because I was busy fucking my way through all fifty states like Landry. It was because I was already *in* a relationship with Sterling Chase—the company, not the adorable liar—and I liked it that way.

And even if I didn't? Even if I was prepared to somehow make room in my life for a—my brain caught on the word—a *boyfriend?* How could I do that in good conscience when I would have to hide so much from him about my role at Sterling Chase, about my brotherhood and our money and our secrecy pact? I'd end up telling more lies than Rowe in his bunny tux... only worse, because I'd be lying to someone I cared about.

There was also the tiny matter of Rowe having family obligations calling him back to Linden, where the only thing that interested me was a certain Cupid picture hanging on his mother's living room wall.

The last thing I wanted to do was lead Rowe on or hurt him in any way, which meant I had to end this immediately. But—my arm tightened around Rowe's shoulders, and he nestled closer with a sleepy sigh—I didn't know how.

The mind-numbing circular thoughts finally lulled me into an uneasy sleep, and when the phone rang sometime later, I was groggy and disoriented.

"Bash?" Rowe mumbled into my chest. "Wha—?"

I grabbed my phone from the nightstand. "Shh. It's Kenji, my assistant. Go back to sleep, sweetheart."

It was just after two in the morning, not a time for social calls, and panic slithered through my mind as I remembered a different phone call several years ago, when Dev's brother had died in a terrible car crash. Nudging Rowe's warm body off mine as I slid out of bed left me feeling even more uneasy and wrong-footed.

"Kenji?" I croaked into the phone. "Who's hurt? What's wrong?"

"Everyone's safe," Kenji said immediately. Under his breath, he added a menacing, "Until I get a hold of them, at least. Fucking Landry, Bash. I swear to Christ."

I ran a hand over my face, trying to shake off the remnants of sleep. "What'd he do? Does he need bribe money or bail money?"

"The second. This time for property damage and public intoxication." Kenji's voice was nearly vibrating with anger.

I sighed. I had no idea why Landry pulled the stunts he pulled or why he almost seemed to enjoy being a thorn in Kenji's side. "Okay —" I began.

"No. No, it is definitely *not* okay, Bash. Because this time, he took our favorite rock star along for the ride. And of course he waited until I was already in Florida for my grandmother's birthday so I can't even make this go away before the media gets a hold of it."

"Zane, too?" I closed my eyes and groaned. "Fuck."

"Precisely." Kenji took a deep breath and let loose, his words practically tumbling over themselves he was so worked up. "They're in Philly. Zane played at the Tower Theater last night, so I booked him into a nice hotel near the venue. But then fucking Landry showed up to watch him play—which, like, did Landry bother to *tell* anyone where he'd be? *Noooooo*, of course not, because then someone might get to enjoy their weekend in Florida without needing to send him a hundred 'Where are you and who are you fucking?' texts on a daily basis so I can make sure I have the NDAs ready and/or a description for the police when one of these randos murders him in his bed—"

"Kenji..." I said, trying to calm him down.

But Kenji was too upset to be calmed. "Zane's publicist already has him convinced that a rock star needs to be freaking *nocturnal* and either fighting or fucking someone every waking moment, which is bad enough— like, are you a musician, Zane? Or a horny, rabid raccoon?—but you just know that once Landry was on the scene, he made sure things got dialed up to eleven. The two of them ended up in some groupie's hotel room on the other side of town, where they proceeded to engage in Landry's *other* favorite activity—when he's not fucking anonymous strangers, that is—getting drunk and trashing a hotel room." Kenji blew out an aggrieved breath. "They're cooling their heels at the police station now. And here *I* am, stuck in Boca Raton..."

While Kenji continued to bitch, I glanced over at Rowe. He'd sat up in bed, gorgeous curls going every which way, and furrowed his eyebrows in worry. "Everything okay?" he whispered.

I covered the phone. "Define okay." I rolled my eyes. "No one's hurt, but there's been a huge clusterfuck, and I need to drive down to Philly to bail my friends out. You can go back to sleep."

Instead of snuggling back under the covers, though, Rowe squeezed my hand, then moved off the bed and out to the other bedroom, like maybe he didn't want to be disturbed.

"Bash?" Kenji demanded. "Are you still there?"

"Yeah, sorry. I was talking to... never mind." I shook my head, still staring at where Rowe had disappeared into the darkened living area. "I'm gonna go get them. If the guys call back, tell them I'm on my way."

"Oh. Oh, shit. You're with Rowe," Kenji said in a hushed voice.

"You knew I would be. You arranged—"

"No, I mean... you're *with* him. Like, in *bed* with him. Post-sex *sleeping* with him. *Together*."

Kenji had traded his anger for pearl-clutching. I couldn't help chuckling as I headed into the bathroom, blinking under the bright overhead lights as I retrieved my toothbrush. "Did you think we were going to tell ghost stories and braid our hair all night?"

"Well, no, but I thought... Actually, I don't know what I thought," he finally admitted. "Spending the whole night with someone isn't a thing you do... is it?"

The last thing I wanted at that moment was to be reminded of how unusual—and impossible—this situation with Rowe was... especially now that it was coming to a disappointingly quick end.

I cleared my throat. "If I leave now, I should get to Philly in an hour and a bit. Text me the location. I assume you've already contacted Bruce?" I asked, mentioning the expensive attorney Kenji had finally put on retainer to deal with Landry's messes. "*Shit*. And I forgot I didn't drive out here. I need a car—"

"Morris will be waiting outside. I've been texting him as we talked. And yes, Bruce is already involved—he should have the guys processed out before you get there." Kenji paused. "Sorry, Bash. Genuinely. I wish you didn't have to be the one to handle this. But somebody needs to have a come-to-Jesus with Zane, and he'll listen to you. He can't jump on Landry's fuckery train and expect it not to catch up with him."

"I get it. It's fine." It really wasn't. I wasn't ready to say goodbye to Rowe, to leave the little bubble we'd created in this hotel room. But that wasn't Kenji's fault. "I'll text you when they're out. Put this out of your mind and enjoy the rest of your weekend, okay?"

He snickered. "Oh, yeah. You know me—living it up here at the Vista Bonita Active Seniors community. I've finally found my people. See you Monday... And FYI, I'll be making another large deposit to the Fake Sterling Chase Escape Fund before then. Just in case of disaster."

"Great." I wanted to tell him that I wasn't going to need any special coping mechanisms to deal with the fallout of spending a single weekend with a sexy man... but that would be a lie.

After Kenji and I disconnected, I splashed some water on my face, ran a hand through my hair, and pulled on some clothes. I made a point of *not* looking at the bed as I walked through the bedroom on my way out of the suite.

Rowe appeared in the doorway of the second bedroom with a towel slung around his waist and a shy smile on his face. "Hey! Just let me throw on my clothes, and I'll be ready for our next adventure, okay?"

He walked back into the bedroom, and I stared after him, too busy admiring the way the towel dipped over his luscious ass to process his words for a long moment. Then...

"Wait. You're coming with me? To Philly?" I trailed after him.

"Sure. You said we had all night, right? Still looks like night to me. Besides, you looked like you could use a friend or at least a distraction." Rowe grabbed a shirt from the open suitcase triumphantly and turned toward me. His sunshine grin fell the moment he saw my face. "Or maybe not. Oh, god, I'm such a dork." He rolled his eyes. "You'll already *have* friends there. What would you need me for? Never mind. I'll just catch the train back to New York in a little while. And I, uh... I'll settle up for the room in a couple weeks, if that's—"

I stepped across the room and took his face in my hands so he would have to meet my eyes. "Please come. I'd love your company. I figured a middle-of-the-night trip to a Philadelphia police station wasn't on anyone's adventure bucket list, and I didn't want you to feel obligated—"

Rowe lurched forward and kissed me. It was awkward, with bumped noses and lips pinched between teeth, but it was real and heartfelt and... and definitely not casual.

"I'm not ready to say goodbye yet," he admitted, and hearing him speak my thoughts aloud made my heart squeeze painfully. "Besides, I'm not sure if you've noticed, but ordinary stuff just *becomes* an adventure when you're around. You're kinda magic that way."

I was pretty sure it was the other way around.

I kissed him again because I couldn't help it, savoring the flavor of toothpaste and Rowe. I was very, very close to tumbling Rowe into the bed and letting my idiot friends figure out their own shit, but finally, I set a hand on his chest and pulled my lips away reluctantly. "My dick wants to stay here very badly and continue this conversation with you in bed, but we need to go."

Yet we both watched my fingers trace down his chest, over the smooth skin of his lean stomach toward the knot in his towel. Rowe's breathing hitched, and he turned those big brown eyes up at me. "Bash?"

"*Fuck.*" I stepped further away, out of touching distance.

Rowe gave me a wry smile.

"Later," I promised, though I still had no fucking idea how that was going to work.

Once we were dressed, we gathered up our things and met the driver out front of the inn. "Sorry to wake you, Morris."

The older man held out a tray with two cups of coffee while taking a third for himself. "As soon as Kenji texted, I figured we'd be bailing those two knuckleheads out."

"Again," I muttered, taking the tray and offering one of the cups to Rowe.

We huddled together in the back seat of the car as it made its way down the driveway and into the deserted country roads of early morning.

"Does this kind of thing happen often?" Rowe asked hesitantly.

I huffed out an almost-laugh. "Me making midnight rescues? No. Kenji usually takes care of it. Landry getting into trouble, though? That's pretty common. And Zane..." I hesitated, but if Rowe was coming with me, there'd be no way to keep certain things a secret. More than that, I didn't want to. I wanted Rowe to know about as much of my life as I could share, even if it wasn't wise. I took a sip of coffee and casually asked, "You know Zee Barlo?"

"Uh, yeah. I made you listen to 'The Solo Hour' on the way to the hotel earlier, remem— wait." Rowe's eyes got wide, and he shifted in his seat to face me, his whole body practically humming. "Are you telling me Zee Barlo is your college friend Zane? You actually *know* him? Bash!" He thumped my arm lightly. "You *scoffed* when I played you that song."

I snorted and ran a hand through my hair. It was funny which things actually got Rowe excited. Powerful socialites, ritzy galas, untold wealth? Meh. But give the man a good snack mix, show him an old desk, or tell him you knew an up-and-coming musician and watch him come alive.

"Zane was a business major in a previous life." I stared out the darkened window of the car and couldn't help smiling as I remembered how buttoned-up he'd been freshman year. "That was his grandmother's influence. She wanted him to be a banker or a lawyer. Something stable. But music has always been Zane's passion, so that's what he devoted himself to after we—*uh*..." I bit my tongue. *Jesus*. I'd been about to say *after we sold ETC* and just casually break a secrecy promise I'd sworn to the brotherhood. I was tired, and Rowe was dangerously easy to talk to, but I knew my friends wouldn't consider those good excuses. "After we graduated."

"That's awesome." Rowe's smile was genuine... and a little wistful. "I love hearing about someone who decides to just go for the thing they want. And Zane succeeded."

"Yeah. He's worked hard, and I'm happy for his success. But..." I took another sip of my coffee and tried to determine how much I could share. "Once he started getting some airplay, Zane's agent and record label hooked him up with this PR company, and they decided he needed a total image overhaul. 'Rock stars are edgy. You're too sweet and clean-cut.'"

"Ooof. And now you need to bail Zane out. No wonder you weren't super enthusiastic when I played you the song."

"I love Zane's music," I said quickly.

"No, I get it. You just love your friend more, and you're worried they're trying to change him." Rowe chewed his lip thoughtfully for a moment. "Seems silly to me. Zane's already got that raspy voice, and those poetic lyrics, and those broody, soulful eyes." Rowe's own eyes got a little shiny and dreamlike. "A bad-boy image seems like overkill."

A curl of emotion slithered through my gut, and it took me a second to recognize it as jealousy. I wasn't normally a jealous person, but the idea of introducing Rowe to model-gorgeous Landry and talented Zane made me want to shove the curly-haired angel behind me and hiss at anyone who came near. To mark him up with a giant hickey or a T-shirt that said *Property of Sebastian Dayne*. Something subtle like that.

Jesus, my friends would give me shit forever if they realized I felt this way. And Rowe would...

Well, Rowe would be very confused since it wasn't like that between us, and I didn't want it to be.

Did I?

I cleared my throat. "Zane was playing a show in Philly, and he and Landry ended up trashing a hotel room somehow. I'm gonna try to talk some sense into him."

"Right." Rowe tried and failed to hide his grin behind his coffee cup. "So you decided to bring *Sterling Chase* along to prove how sensible you are?"

I rolled my eyes and stretched my legs out, tilting my head back against the leather seat. Rowe wasn't wrong. I was sure there'd be hell to pay when my friends saw that I wasn't alone, and I knew I was only delaying a difficult conversation with Rowe himself. But being with him felt so good I let myself tuck those things away to worry about later.

As we drove south toward Pennsylvania, the sky lightened outside the windows. The space between us on the seat seemed impossibly large, so I shifted a little to get closer to him. When that didn't ease the aching in my chest, I pulled him closer until he was up against my side with his head on my shoulder and his curls tickling my stubbled chin.

"Thank you for coming with me," I said, feeling suddenly awkward, like I needed to explain my desire to touch him.

"It's no problem. Really. Sun's still not up," he reminded me with a yawn. "I'm still not a pumpkin. And I've never been to Philly."

Strangely enough, I was able to follow his disjointed thoughts, which should have been a sobering reminder that I'd gotten too close to Rowe too fast—*How's that arm's-length thing going, Bash?*—but when Rowe gave a breathy little snore, I decided that for now, I didn't give a shit. I wrapped both arms around him and for a moment let my worries fall away.

Morris woke us when we hit the outskirts of Philly a little while later, and I tried to tell myself it was a good thing when Rowe instantly moved away to his own side of the seat. We pulled up to the police station and went inside while Morris waited with the car, and we began the process of collecting my misbehaving friends.

Sure enough, Bruce had sorted the paperwork, and Rowe and I only spent a minute in the dank precinct lobby before Zane came shuffling out of a side door, looking exhausted and cracking his knuckles guiltily.

Landry, who came strolling behind him, didn't look guilty at all.

"Where's Kenji?" Landry demanded. His eyes roamed the room like maybe I'd stashed our assistant in a closet somewhere.

"In Florida with his grandmother, which is a little more urgent than saving your ass for the twelfth time this month," I said sourly.

Landry glared at me—at least as much as a person *could* glare when their eyes were bloodshot and couldn't seem to open more than halfway. "So he sent Big Daddy to lecture the riffraff on appropriate comportment for highbrow gentlemen? Delightful."

"I'm happy to take Zane and let you languish if you can't be civil," I warned.

I yanked Zane into my arms for a hug, and he trembled a little. No matter how hard he tried to be a bad boy, to me he would always be the shy, buttoned-up kid from a small town in Georgia who only felt like his true self when he was singing.

"Hey. You okay?" I murmured against his pot-scented hair.

He pulled away, nodding slightly.

Landry ignored me as soon as he caught sight of Rowe, and he managed to summon a sultry smile from somewhere. "Well, well, well. Hello, gorgeous. Looks like Bash brought me a reward for keeping Zane alive while we were locked up."

I snapped at him without thinking. "Take one step closer to him and it will be your last."

Landry and Zane both looked at me like I had twelve heads and they were all wearing crocheted bonnets. Then Landry smirked.

"Ohhhh," he singsonged. "You must be the guy who's kept our group chat popping for the last couple days. Sterling Chase, isn't it?"

Rowe glanced at me nervously, and I shot Landry a killing look that finally—temporarily—seemed to shut him up.

"Rowe Prince, this is Landry Davis," I cut in smoothly. "And he's cranky when he's hungover, so ignore him. This is—"

"Hey, Rowe," Zane said, stepping forward with a sweet smile. "I'm Zane." Genuine kindness and authenticity radiated from him, drawing Rowe in like a tractor beam.

"Wow. It's... really nice to meet you. Your music is phenomenal. I-I'm Rowe... wait, you said that already." The familiar blush emerged on his cheeks, which made my jealousy roar back to life.

Those were *my* blushes, damn it.

Landry's smirk deepened, suggesting some part of my jealousy had shown on my face, which was the last thing I wanted.

"What the hell were you thinking, Landry?" I demanded, going on the offensive. "You wanna be a magnet for trouble, fine. But don't rope Zane into your shit."

Landry's eyes narrowed, but Zane cut in before Landry could speak.

"That's not what happened," he said tiredly. "This isn't Landry's fault."

"Like hell it's not—" I began.

Zane looked furtively around the lobby. "Can we... not do this here?"

It seemed the media hadn't caught wind of his release—at least, I couldn't see anyone nearby who showed a particular interest in him—and I spared a moment of gratitude that his popularity was only just moving out of certain key demographics and more into the mainstream. There were still plenty of people in the world who had no idea what he looked like, even if they knew all the words to his song.

I lowered my voice. "Fine. Yes. Get in the car. We can talk about it on the drive back to the city."

Zane shook his head. "Can't. My people are waiting for me at the hotel here. I need a shower and a change of clothes."

I wanted to strongly argue with him labeling the PR company "his people" since they didn't seem to be looking out for him in the slightest, but this wasn't the time. "Fine. We can talk there. Let's go."

The three of them followed me out like tired little ducklings, filing one by one into the town car until Landry and Zane were in the rear-facing row staring at Rowe and me.

"Champagne, anyone?" Landry said with a teasing grin as soon as I closed the door. "We can celebrate Zane's first arrest in Pennsylvania. Huzzah."

Zane elbowed him in the ribs and slumped down in the seat. "Shut it, Landry. I have a headache."

I reached for a couple of bottles of water from the built-in cooler and handed them across. "Tell me what happened exactly."

Landry ignored me, sucking down the cold water, while Zane proceeded to explain things mostly the way Kenji had laid them out. "It was stupid," he said. "I see that now. But we didn't damage anything on purpose. It was the others. They kept knocking things off the walls and screaming out the window. And it wasn't Landry's idea. He just went along with it."

Landry looked affronted. "I did *not* go along. I don't go along with things, Zane, and most definitely not a plan to spend an evening yukking it up at some no-tell motel in Philadelphia with a bunch of strangers. In fact, if you'll recall, I strongly argued that if you needed to blow off steam—and who doesn't, from time to time?—there were better ways and better people to do it with." He examined his nails. "I also told you to hurry up and run when they announced that the cops had arrived, but you didn't do that, either." He rolled his eyes and hooked a thumb in Zane's direction. "Our boy here's hella slow."

I leaned forward with my elbows on my knees. "Zane. You are on the cusp of having everything you ever dreamed of. You're being booked into huge fucking venues all over the world. What happens if you're stuck in a holding cell and can't do one of those shows? Or if you have a court appearance on the same day a big media group wants you to do a photoshoot?"

Zane shook his head firmly. "That's not gonna happen. Noelle said—"

"Fuck Noelle," I hissed, trying not to shout in the small, enclosed space. "Was Noelle there when you did dangerous tree work in the Georgia summer heat to earn money for guitar lessons? Is Noelle the one who's going to explain to your granny that you can't be there for Hoppin' John and cornbread on New Year's because you were partying with drug users and making hotel messes she herself would have had to clean up back in the day? Huh? Tell me that, because I fucking knew you before this." I gestured to Landry. "So did this asshole. We remember that kid who swore to fucking Christ he wouldn't be that guy if he ever became famous!"

I felt Rowe's soft fingers grip my biceps and turned my head. His face looked sympathetic, but his eyes urged caution. Landry, too, though he didn't disagree with me, was raising an eyebrow at my delivery.

I rubbed my hands over my face and blew out a breath. "I'm sorry. I just..."

Zane nudged my foot with his. "Nah, don't apologize. You're right. I can't imagine what Granny would say if she knew I'd made a mess like that. Noelle said it would be good to work on my local fanbase, so when those guys asked me to hang out..." He shook his head. "I should have cleared out once I saw how things were going down, though. That was my bad." He twisted to face Landry. "And I should have listened to you. I'm sorry, Landry. I didn't mean to get you into trouble, too."

Landry squirmed in his seat and blinked at Zane like he'd been speaking in a foreign language; clearly, the idea of someone apologizing to *him* for causing trouble was beyond his comprehension since the shoe was so often on the other foot. "Yeah, well. Not my first rodeo. Won't be my last. But listen to Big Daddy." He tilted his head toward me. "He's talking sense for once."

"It's under control," Zane assured us. He tapped out a quick text and a moment later reported, "Noelle will be waiting for us in the lobby to get us upstairs as quickly as possible."

"Good." I sank back in my seat and stretched out, letting myself get comfortable. "Crisis averted, then, it sounds like."

Landry pursed his lips, and then he and Zane exchanged a speaking glance.

"What?" I demanded. "Is there something you're not telling me?"

"I think *you* should tell *us*," Landry drawled. He looked pointedly at the seat between me and Rowe, and I realized that part of my "getting comfortable" had been grabbing Rowe's hand and threading our fingers together like we'd done it a thousand times before. "Care to explain why you're holding hands with the guy who's been impersonating a guinea pig?"

A thousand responses flashed through my head, but in the end, I merely gripped Rowe's hand more firmly when he tried to pull away. "No. Would you like to hear more of my thoughts on spoiled dilettantes who waste their lives and talents by getting into trouble so often that we have a lawyer on retainer?"

Landry folded his arms over his chest sullenly, closed his eyes, and pretended to sleep.

The silence as we rode through the streets of downtown Philadelphia was definitely not comfortable. When we arrived at Zane's hotel, the four of us climbed out and dragged our way inside. I was too busy wondering how many rooms Kenji had reserved for Zane—and whether Rowe and I could snag one so that I could curl up with him for another few hours and maybe figure out what the fuck I needed to do about him—to notice at first that the lobby was excessively crowded for this hour of the morning.

And then the chaos began.

"Zee! Zee, look over here! Philadelphia Daily Inquisitor—"

"Zee? Celebrity News Online. Could you give us a sound bite—?"

"Mr. Barlo. Rumors are circulating that you've been on a drug-fueled rampage all over Philly. Are you pleading guilty?"

Zane's eyes went wide. "Drugs? No way. I—"

I grabbed Rowe's hand and pulled him behind me while also thrusting out a hand to block Zane from view. Landry stepped in front of Zane also, shielding him from the other direction as we moved in a group toward the bank of elevators.

Finally, several minutes too late, Zane's PR manager arrived to whisk us upstairs.

"Zee, where the fuck have you been? I was so worried," she hissed in a stage whisper. Then, to the clamoring reporters, she announced, "Mr. Barlo has no comment at this time. The Night Agency will be releasing a statement on his behalf later today. That's Night with no K."

But as soon as the elevator doors closed on our group, she turned to Zane with a grin. "Oh, my god, they bought it! Great job. And nice touch, bringing an entourage of hotties!" She squeezed Landry's biceps appreciatively. "I'm Noelle, by the way."

Landry, Rowe, and I exchanged a glance. *Entourage?*

"So, *you* I recognize," she told Landry. "Cover of *Vogue Hommes* last fall, right?"

Landry ignored her, but Noelle didn't seem to mind. She turned to me. "And you are?"

"That's Bash." Zane stretched his neck like he was trying to ease stiff muscles.

"Bash, as in... Sebastian Dayne?" she asked breathlessly. "The investor?"

"Noelle," Zane sighed, rubbing his eyes. "Later, okay? We're all really tired."

"Sure, sweetie." Noelle keyed us into a huge modern suite, where a team of five people sat around a large glass dining table and sprawled along twin sofas in an eye-watering neon green.

I wondered what Rowe thought of the decor, but his face was closed off and gave nothing away.

"Zane, this room is for you." She gestured to a door off the living area.

"Thank fuck," Zane muttered. He gave me a one-armed hug. "Love you. Promise I'll be more careful, 'kay? Thanks for coming to get me."

I was still angry, still worried, but what could I do? I blew out a breath and nodded as Zane shuffled away.

Landry watched him go, shaking his head, a little smile on his lips. "Somebody needs to bring the rock star some oatmeal and chocolate milk," he said softly.

I narrowed my eyes at him, feeling my anger rise now that it had a convenient target. "At least Zane knows he has responsibilities—" I broke off when I noticed Noelle watching us avidly and gestured to another room off the living area. "Is this room for Landry?"

Noelle blinked rapidly. "Well, I..." She noted the expression on my face and swallowed hard. "I suppose so."

"Great." I pushed Landry in that direction. "We'll be back."

"Bash, Bash," Landry fake-chided. "Pushing me into bed? Won't your boyfriend get the wrong impression?" He snickered under his breath at his own joke as he wandered off in that direction.

"He's not my boyfriend," I snapped after him. "Asshole." But before I followed, I glanced back at Rowe, who hadn't moved from the entryway. "Rowe, I have to..." I gestured helplessly toward Landry.

"No, no. I completely understand. Go. Do what you have to do." Rowe's big brown eyes were wide. He looked tired and a little lost, and I wanted to hug him. I wanted to kick Landry out and take Rowe to bed for a week. I wanted...

Christ. I had no fucking idea what I wanted anymore.

"Will you be okay on your own?" I asked him with a pointed look at Noelle, who still watched us like the concept of privacy was more complex than brain surgery. I didn't plan to leave him for long, but I didn't trust her not to try to torture him for information during that time, either.

Rowe did that little thing where he straightened his posture, extracting every quarter-inch from his small frame, and shook the curls out of his face. "Of course I will. Don't worry about me, Bash."

Despite my anger at Landry, Rowe made me smile. I took a step toward the bedroom—

"Bash?" Rowe called.

"Yeah?" I stopped and turned my head.

"N-nothing, just..." He shrugged a little and shot me a bright, sunshine smile. "Good luck."

"Thanks." I was definitely going to need it.

By the time I got into the room, Landry had already undressed into a hotel bathrobe and slippers and was reclined against the head-board of the king-sized bed, fiddling with his phone. He glanced up when I came in.

"Look, whatever you want me to say here, Bash, can we pretend I've said it? *Mea culpa, mea culpa.* Landry's fucked up again."

"Landry," I said between clenched teeth.

He sighed and made a production of turning off the phone and setting it on his lap. "Fine, then. Scold me if it'll make you feel better. I warn you, you're not as pretty as Kenji, so I probably won't tolerate it for long."

I shook my head. "What the hell is wrong with you? This..." I gestured up and down his frame. "This whole spoiled-dilettante thing? Dragging Zane along with you? That's not you, Landry. That is not the man I knew back in the day, who was on fire to make a name for himself, to change his situation, to help people. That guy didn't dream about going around breaking hearts and causing scandals, including being banned from a major commercial airline—"

"That incident was blown wildly out of proportion, and you know it," Landry scoffed. "Besides, you're not one to talk. The Sebastian Dayne who founded Sterling Chase with us was a leader. A guy who wanted us to be in control of every corner of our business, right down to where we kept the pencil sharpener. *That* guy wouldn't fuck off on a safari and let other people run his company. People change. Not always for the better. Are we done now?"

I set my front teeth together and exhaled through my nose. "*No.* I had reasons for the things I've done, Landry. I didn't want to be the public face of Sterling Chase anymore. I didn't want to be the one people were always fucking *asking* for things. And I realized recently that maybe... maybe I've backed off a little too far. Maybe it's time for me to change things up and take a more active role in things again—"

"Big Daddy admits he made a tiny error?" Landry rolled his eyes. "Alert the media."

"But that is not the same thing as what you're doing," I insisted. "I'm not hurting anyone, for one thing."

"Except yourself." Landry yawned. "And possibly the Sterling Chase impersonator out in the living area you so loudly proclaimed was *not* your boyfriend, after leading him on a merry chase all weekend, sleeping all night with him—according to Kenji's texts, dragging him to Philly with you in the dead of night and holding his hand while he stared at you with big puppy eyes like he thought you were personally responsible for the sunrise. Gotta say, for all my faults, I've never treated *anyone* I slept with quite that shittily, so well done, you, for setting that bar so low."

"Shittily? He wanted to come with me," I corrected.

"No, I mean barking at me about him not being anything special. About not being your boyfriend. You didn't need to be so callous about it. Way to claim your real feelings."

"That's not..." I began, then hesitated, feeling my face go hot. "It isn't..." I tried once more, running a hand through my hair. "We aren't..."

My thoughts were tangled inside my brain. I wanted to deny all of what he was saying—that I hadn't done any of those things and that Rowe definitely hadn't looked at me that way, but the words stuck in my throat. I *had* denied Rowe the chance to talk about his project, the one thing that meant almost the most to him in the world.

And that was shitty.

Landry narrowed his eyes, and for the first time all morning, I felt like he really looked at me. "Are you alright?"

"Yes. No." I blew out a breath that sounded like a frustrated groan and sank down onto the side of the bed, near Landry's knee. "I don't know."

He sat forward, bending his legs. "Talk to me."

I opened my mouth. Shut it again. "I don't even know where to start. God, this is so absurd. Seriously, the most overly emotional, ridiculous—"

"All my favorite things. You came to the right place." Landry prodded my shoulder. "Go on."

"I like the guy," I admitted. "I... care about him. I'm attracted to him, yes, but it's... more than that. I think. And I know what you're gonna say, okay? I've known the guy for a day and a half. And none of it was real—he lied about being Sterling Chase nearly the whole time; I lied about being his assistant, too. And even though we talked about all that and why he lied, he still has a project he wants funded—"

"I know."

"What? How?"

"From Dev." Landry rolled his eyes. "Honestly, do you never check the group chat?"

Rarely, and especially not this weekend. "Then you know what all the others—Dev, Silas, even Kenji— are saying. Rowe can't be trusted. I'm getting in too deep too fast. I run a billion-dollar company, and he delivers burritos. There's no future between us—I can't fathom what one would look like, even if I were sure I wanted one. I assure you, I know all of that. I *knew* this weekend with him was a one-time thing."

I waited for Landry to say something cutting, but all he said was "And?"

"*And?* Nothing." I worried my top lip and stared at the artwork over the bed without really seeing it. "*And* I don't know. I mean, Jesus, what do you do when you feel drawn to someone, but the situation is all wrong? When you feel like you know someone, and they know you, but it was probably all just the heat of the moment or the novelty of the thing? What do you do when you don't want to let someone go, but there's no room for them to stay because you already know what your priorities are? The potential for this to go staggeringly wrong is just... enormous."

Landry watched me pensively for a long moment before speaking. "You remember the night before we sold ETC?"

"Huh?" I blinked and focused on him. "What's that got to do with anything?"

"You were a nervous wreck." He grinned suddenly. "We were still crammed into that little office over by the Flatiron that barely fit three desks for the five of us because it was all we could afford when we left New Haven, and we'd stuck there because it was easier than moving, remember? The other guys were exhausted that night because you'd made us go over *everything* for the hundredth time—the system, the notes, the contracts that our lawyer had already gone over with us. Finally, Silas went to grab food, and Zane and Dev went back to that shitty apartment we were renting, but you were still working, working, working. Compulsively."

"Yes, I know." I scrubbed both hands over my face. "I'm a workaholic. Sterling Chase is my life. That's the *problem*."

"Shhh. Don't interrupt. So, that night, I was waiting around for you, but you kept biting my head off. '*Five more minutes, Landry. Five more minutes. Can't you see I'm busy?*' without even looking up from your desk. And finally, I snapped. I was like, '*I am hungry. I am tired. It's the middle of the night. What the fuck, Sebastian? There is no more to do here.*' And you looked up at me, right? And you said, '*But what if I'm wrong, Landry? What if we weren't supposed to sell? What if there was more for us to do?*' I was so used to seeing you as this guy who was born with money and privilege, who had confidence baked into his pores, and you were practically paralyzed by second-guessing yourself. I'd never seen you like that before or since. Freaked me out."

I grunted. "I remember you decided the best course of action was to fuck up the router so I couldn't get online anymore and force me out the door because your pizza was getting cold. Thank you for reminding me of this happy time in our history. Why are we still friends?"

Landry laughed—not mocking or self-deprecating, but a real, genuine laugh—and shoved my shoulder. "My strategy worked, didn't it? You do supportive friendship your way, and I'll do it mine, m'kay? My point is, you were nervous because you cared, Bash. You didn't want to make a mistake or let anyone down. And so, if this thing with that guy out there—" He nodded toward the living area. "—has got you this unsure? I say that's a good thing. It's easy to take risks when you're not so invested in the outcome, but the biggest payoffs happen when you are. And I trust your instincts. I always have. So if you think there's something there, or there *could* be something there? Then go after it with that single-minded Sebastian Dayne intensity that made us billionaires, man."

He made it sound so easy. "But... how? It's way more complicated than you're making it. Rowe doesn't know about ETC or who founded the company, and I can't tell him. I've only spent a handful of hours with him. I don't know if I can actually trust him not to be using me for contacts or social capital, like—"

"Like Justin." Landry's voice hardened. "Yeah, that's valid. Has Rowe been asking you for shit, trying to get you to give him money for his project? Because that's a whole other situation."

"He hasn't asked me for anything." I swallowed, remembering last night. How close I'd been to telling Rowe truths. How much we'd talked about my work, even when I'd made him promise he wouldn't talk about his. "The opposite, actually. I asked him not to talk about his project with me, and he didn't. At least not yet."

Landry nodded slowly. "So why not get to know him? Bash, that promise we made to our brotherhood... It was never supposed to be a forever thing, was it? If we can't ever share our lives with anyone else, that would really suck since I'm not remotely attracted to any of you fuckers, and none of you have ever had the good taste to be attracted to me."

A startled laugh erupted from my chest. "No. I... I don't know."

"And how are you supposed to tell if Rowe's trustworthy unless you take the chance of trusting him, at least a little?"

"I don't know that, either," I admitted.

"All this not-knowing," Landry teased. "No wonder you're going out of your mind, Big Daddy."

"You've gotta stop with that nickname," I said severely. "That's not going to be a thing."

Landry's mischievous smile told me he was going to ensure that it *was*.

"You're such an ass."

He plumped the pillow behind him, closed his eyes, and settled in, like he was about to go to sleep. "I know. I love you, too. Do you feel better?"

"Shockingly? Yes." I hadn't come to Philly expecting a pep talk, and sure as hell not from Landry, but he'd delivered in spades. "I'm still worried about you. The stuff you've been doing—"

Landry sighed and opened one eye. "I promise, Sebastian, I have things under control. Mostly. And I would never let anything happen to Zane or to any of you. Okay?"

My chest squeezed at the sincerity in his voice. "Okay."

"Now, go forth and fuck the sweet young thang who's waiting for you." Landry shut his eyes again. "He probably likes hearing you talk a lot more than I do."

I snorted. I was pretty sure Landry was right about that. And there was for sure no shortage of stuff for Rowe and me to talk about. I took a deep breath and pushed to my feet, feeling a surge of hopeful energy despite my fatigue.

I wanted to know about Rowe's project. I wanted to hear about this big idea that had gotten him so excited he'd saved up all his pennies and come to New York to make it happen. I wanted to help him with it if I could. I wanted to hear more about his sister and their antics as kids. I wanted to tell him about my friends and how amazing they were. I wanted to show him the most beautiful places I'd ever been so that I could enjoy them again through his eyes. I wanted to pull him into my arms and kiss his gorgeous face until he was breathless.

I was ready to stop holding back. And I was ready to tell Rowe so.

But when I got out to the living area, he was gone.

THIRTEEN

ROWE

I was afraid I was getting a little too good at the lying thing. When Bash had locked himself away in the room with his friend, I'd assured him I was fine, but as I retreated to the sitting area and perched awkwardly on the arm of one of the horrible sofas, I realized that was the opposite of the truth.

During the hour-long ride to Philadelphia, I'd nestled up against Bash's chest, pretending to sleep, listening to his heart thump steadily beneath my ear, and tried to remember how I'd gotten to this place. Everything had seemed so simple two nights ago—sneak into the gala, sweet-talk Justin Hardy into a meeting, make him fall in love with Project Daisy Chain, then resume my perfectly good life in Linden, with my job and my aging parents and my secondhand furniture and an iPad full of interior designs that might never become reality.

It had seemed like enough.

But then there'd been Bash—gorgeous, brilliant, funny, deeply kind Bash—who'd gone along with my schemes, and listened to my truths, and made me feel like my dreams weren't distant twinkling stars but ripe fruit just waiting to be picked. I could feel myself falling for him, and it scared me. A lot.

"Here you go, cutie. You look like you need this." Noelle, the PR person, wandered over with a friendly smile and a can of energy drink she thrust into my hand. "Are you a friend of Zee's? What did you say your name was again?"

"Rowe." I took the can and fiddled with the tab uncertainly. "And no, I've never met Za—Zee before this morning. Love his music, though."

"Interesting." She cocked her head thoughtfully. "You must be friends with the male model, then? Or with Bash Dayne? Are you two dating?"

"Ha. No." Only in my dreams. "I'm just here as Bash's moral support, kinda." I shrugged.

"Aww. That's sweet of you." She smirked a little. "What do you do, Rowe?"

"I..." I opened my mouth to answer, then shut it again with a clack. Belatedly—and I blamed this on how damn tired I was—I noticed the gleam in Noelle's eye and realized she wasn't asking a friendly question. More likely, she was working on a press release.

Zee Barlo Rescued from Jail by Male Model, Wealthy Investor... and Part-Time Burrito Bandito.

I felt my cheeks go hot.

In real life, I rarely felt bad about myself. I was a good person. I worked hard. I tried my best to help people. I never worried about how much money I had, except when I didn't have enough of it to make ends meet, or how I didn't have a fancy degree, except when it prevented me from getting the meetings I wanted. I was proud that I'd grown up in tiny Linden. I liked that most of my clothes were high-quality designer labels I'd gotten from a thrift store.

But suddenly, I felt mercilessly exposed and vulnerable, worse even than at the polo match or the gala. A headline like that would make a laughingstock out of everyone involved. A giant game of *one of these things does not belong.* And worst of all, it would be true.

A clock somewhere in the suite chimed the hour, and I felt a bubble of frantic laughter erupt from my chest. *Midnight's come, Cinderella. Isn't it time you were going home?*

I shoved the unopened can toward Noelle, and she took it in surprise. "Sorry, I... I just remembered I needed to do... a thing."

"But... don't you want to wait...?" Noelle called to my back.

I ignored her.

I hightailed it out of the suite, and instead of taking the elevator to the lobby, where the press had been camped out, I pushed open the heavy door to the stairs and clattered down them, breath heaving like something might catch me and drag me back.

I should be used to disappointment. I *was* used to it.

Let the boy do his thing in New York, Muriel, if he's bound and determined. It's never gonna go anywhere. He'll be back home with us soon enough.

Whoa! No kissing. This was just a handjob. I'm not gay, Prince. There's no future here.

Dear Mr. Prince, Thank you for your interest in Sterling Chase. While we commend you on the thoroughness of your research, we do not feel that your "Project Daisy Chain" merits further development by our company at this time. Sincerely, Austin Purcell.

But this disappointment was worse than anything that had come before because despite my best efforts, sometime in the night, I'd allowed a tiny germ of hope to set down roots in my heart that, just this one time, things would work out. That finding a way to keep Bash in my life would be as easy as falling for him had been.

"Rowe Prince," I whispered to myself angrily, blinking away hot tears. "Of all the ridiculous things you've done this weekend, this might be the worst."

I got caught up.

A-fucking-gain.

When I ran out of stairs to descend, I leaned against the wall in the stairwell and took stock of the situation.

I was a mess. Two days of lies and impersonations, heartfelt confessions, brain-melting longing, heart-pounding sex, zero actual sleep, and way too many feelings had left me completely empty. *Stick a fork in me, I'm done*, as Daisy used to say.

I had no reserves left for goodbyes that were bound to be awkward (for Sebastian) and painful (for me). I wasn't up to the task of riding in his car back to New York, trying not to look at his handsome face while forcing cheerful conversation to hide my feelings. And I absolutely couldn't handle him offering me business contacts out of pity or obligation.

It was better this way. Safer for everyone. Bash would feel guilty when he found that I'd left—he took his responsibilities to people seriously, after all, which was why he'd come to Philly in the first place—but ultimately, I hoped he'd be glad.

Of course, that meant I was now stuck here with nothing but the clothes on my back, seventeen dollars in my pocket, no leads for my project, and no way to get home, which meant that my feelings were the least of my worries.

I ran a hand over my face and straightened, then took out my phone and dialed Joey's number.

"Rowe!" he exclaimed excitedly. "Thank fuck you called."

"Hey—" I began.

"Shit, I was getting worried. You went radio silent. And I was like, is he okay? Is he just too busy fucking the rich guy to call me? But also... I have *so* much to tell you, bro. The fast-food delivery game moves pretty fast, and if you don't keep up, the Sandwich Shark will take you down. Damn sexy motherfucker," he muttered.

"What? Joey—"

"No, no. It's cool. It's fine." He hesitated. "Mostly. I think. But FYI, I had to add a couple moves to the Burrito Bandito delivery dance. You know, so I could win the dance-off? There's, like, a hip-shimmy now after the toe-kick and then kind of a bump-and-grind thing? I'll demonstrate later."

Dance-off? What the fuck? "Joey."

"Oh, and I'm playing around with lyrics for a second verse of the song. I just need to figure out something sexy that rhymes with salsa. Falls-*ah* is as close as I've gotten. Like, *when you taste our salsa, in love you're gonna falls-ah.*"

"Joey, stop."

"I know, I know, it's shit. We can workshop it when you get back. I just wanted you to know—"

"Joey!" I yelled. "Chill for a second. I need your help."

Joey paused for a beat, and when he spoke again, his voice was serious. "Whatever you need, Rowe. You know that."

"I need you to come get me," I blurted. "I'm in Philly. I came here with Bash, and we... I... he..."

Joey blew out a breath. "Bro."

"No, I know. It seemed like a good idea at the time. But it's done now." I sniffed, swearing at myself under my breath.

"Are you okay?" Joey demanded. "'Cause if that fucker laid a hand on you—"

"God, no! I just... I confessed everything. He knows who I am now. And it was kinda time for me to go. But I don't know if I have enough money to catch the train back, and I haven't slept, really, and I'm afraid I'll fall asleep and end up at the wrong stop or something, and..."

"Say no more. Lea let me have the Burrito Mobile for the day so I could go on a supply run. Pretty sure I officially work here now. You're lucky it's Sunday. Text me an address, okay?"

I couldn't even care that Joey was driving down to get me in a red-and-yellow food truck. "Yeah. Thanks, Joey. I owe you big."

I took a deep breath and emerged from the stairwell into the lobby. Fortunately, all the newspeople from earlier had dispersed already, and I didn't see Bash or his friends, so I strolled directly out the front door. A block down the street, I spotted a used bookstore and texted Joey the address before ducking inside and attempting to lose myself in the stacks.

In the back of the store, I found an empty reading nook with an overstuffed armchair in the self-help section and sank down grate-fully to wait, but the books mocked me from their places on the shelves. *When Sorry Isn't Good Enough. I'm Telling the Truth, But I'm Lying. The Key to Success: Stop Trying So Hard!*

My phone buzzed with a string of incoming texts from a number I didn't have stored.

> UNKNOWN
>
> Rowe? What the fuck? Where did you go?
>
> UNKNOWN
>
> Did Noelle say something to you? She claims you freaked out for no reason, but I don't believe her.
>
> UNKNOWN
>
> Come back. Please. We have things to talk about.

I felt the tears coming again and blinked them back as I shoved my phone away without responding.

No more tears. Not for this. I'd been through shit things before. I *knew* what terrible loss felt like. And this was not it. It wasn't. This was the consequences of my own actions, inevitable as gravity.

Of course Bash was being wonderful. Protective and sweet. I'd expect nothing less. But it wasn't real. There was no universe where his life and mine would ever have intersected if I hadn't told the biggest lie of my life.

I blew out a breath, feeling my whole body flash hot and then cold. What was I doing?

The whole time I'd been developing Project Daisy Chain, I'd focused solely on the project itself. If the EMTs had access to her medical records or communicated with an ER doc during the trauma response, she might have lived, so ambulances needed better ways of communicating with area hospitals to optimize treatment in the field, not to mention delivery to the best hospital for the problem rather than the closest one. The amount I'd known about emergency communications, hospital resources, and even the technology involved in designing a solution to the problem could have fit in one of my mom's collectible thimbles. So I'd focused single-mindedly on learning what I needed, on *creating* the solution by improving what was there.

I'd been so focused on the overwhelming *goodness* of what I'd been trying to achieve I hadn't let myself think about who I was becoming. I'd decided that the end justified the means, even when it meant lying.

And this was where I'd ended up.

I'd never considered what it felt like when Cinderella crashed back to Earth after her one brilliant night of dancing. Of how much more terrible it felt to put your rags back on when you knew for a fact how amazing the life just out of your reach could be.

For the first time since... well, since I'd dreamed up Project Daisy Chain, I wondered if maybe it was time to pack it all in and head home.

Bobby would happily give me my job back at the Tech Barn, and the guys would only give me shit about my "pie-in-the-sky" idea for a little while. I knew my parents would be happy to forget I'd ever had a business idea, just like they'd be thrilled if I finally started dressing like a normal person and stopped cluttering the garage with cast-off furniture that needed love. After I'd worked for a few weeks, I'd mail Sebastian a check for at least part of the money he'd spent on me, and I'd try, somehow, to apologize for pretending to be someone I wasn't, even knowing he would have easily moved on by then.

I could have a good life. A stable life. An honest life.

A booooring life, Daisy's voice in my head insisted, but I ignored it. I was going to tune that voice out entirely from now on. Daisy had been built for adventure, not me.

When my phone buzzed to tell me Joey was out front, I stood up and made my way to the front of the store on shaky knees. I grabbed a dog-eared paperback off the table before I left and plunked it down on the counter in hopes of justifying my protracted stay in the woman's store.

"That'll be three-twelve," she said with an understanding smile. It wasn't until after I walked out into the bright sunshine that I looked down at my purchase.

You're Not Enough (and that's okay).

Great.

I looked up at the sound of the familiar Mariachi jingle that took the place of the horn on the Burrito Mobile. Joey danced in the driver's seat like the song was a sick beat, and I couldn't help but breathe out a little laugh. No matter how shitty of a hand he'd been dealt—like having to drive to Philly in a half-broken-down food truck —Joey always found joy in the moment.

I envied him that.

"Hop in," he called out the window, the hip-hop music on the radio warring with the Mariachi jingle playing outside. "We're going cruising in this bitch."

I hauled my dejected ass up onto the torn vinyl passenger seat and yanked my seat belt on. "It's ten in the morning, Joseph," I reminded him. "Not the best time for cruising. Besides, don't you have a supply run to do?"

"*Eh.*" Joey shrugged as he pulled back out into traffic. "I had to take a little detour. Lea will understand."

The hotel loomed large halfway down the next block, and to my horror, a sleek, black car was parked out front.

"Shit." I ducked down in my seat. "Turn left! Turn left! Don't go past the hotel!"

He side-eyed me. "You want me to turn left in downtown Philly traffic in a 1985 Chevy P30?" Before I could answer, he swore under his breath. "You could kill someone with those puppy eyes. Swear to fuck."

The sound of tires screeching and horns blaring barely reached my ears as Migos's "Taco Tuesday" blared from the speakers with its rich deep bass.

We hurtled onto the side street, cutting off prim hybrids and causing a few pedestrians to step a little livelier. The song was replaced by Kap G's "José Got Dem Tacos," which made it very clear there was a horrific playlist theme going on here.

"No," I said, trying to turn off whatever tricked-out contraption he had connecting his phone to the truck's old speakers.

"Hold, hold, hold," he said, flapping my hand away. "It gets better. Wait for it."

Rhianna's voice began to croon, with Eminem's following soon after. I glared at my asshole cousin. "'Love the Way You Lie'? Really? Are you trying to make me open the truck door and dive into fucking traffic?"

His familiar chuckle was comforting despite my annoyance. "I made a playlist for you. I didn't know I'd get to play it for you on a road trip, but life is always full of unexpected good shit, isn't it?"

Was it? I remembered I used to think that, but the memory felt faint and old.

Selena Gomez began singing "Bad Liar," so I grabbed his phone, yanked out the cord, and threw it behind us, deep into the bowels of the food truck. The silence lasted a beat before I could have sworn the tinny sound of Beyoncé and Shakira's "Beautiful Liar" made its way out of the shadows.

"I hate you," I said.

"Don't diss the Queen." He glanced over at me, twin lines of concern marred the space between his messy brows. "I hope you know the way home because that phone was our navigator."

After I pulled up the nav on my own phone and connected it to his cable, I closed my eyes in hopes of catching some sleep.

That lasted less than three seconds before my cousin nudged me. *Hard.*

"Nah, nah, nah. No sleeping until you spill."

"Don't wanna," I murmured without opening my eyes. "Tired."

"Oh, you don't *wanna.* I see." His oddly soft voice trailed off before he barked, "Too bad, cuz! I stayed up late last night watching a hot twink get dicked down by a pair of gym bros, and I'm about to fall asleep at the wheel if you don't give me something to stay awake for."

My eyes flew open, and I stared at him in shock. "G-gym bros? Dicked *down?*" I shook my head, fighting off my fatigue. "What happened to the Sandwich Shark? What happened to Chloe? What happened to *you being straight?*"

His mouth widened in a *gotcha* grin. "Woke your ass up, now, didn't I?"

"Wait. Was that all a lie? Are you straight?"

"Bro. It's a new millennium here. I like to think of myself as free from the encumbrance of labels."

"Uh. Okay. But, like, you and Chloe..."

He shrugged a little dejectedly. "Chloe likes to think of herself as free from the encumbrance of me."

"Ouch." I reached over and gently punched his shoulder with my knuckles. "But wait, the gym bros..."

He waved this off. "It was some high-quality porn. And my story time will come later. It's your turn now. And I made a mad dash to your rescue, princess, so you can at least tell me why."

I sighed and told him what happened, leaving out graphic details with a mumbled "And then we hooked up" before continuing on to the reasons I'd left and the fact that Bash had tried to reach out.

"I'm thinking it's time for me to grow up," I concluded. "To stop wasting time with this project, once and for all. This is not gonna end happily."

Joey held up a finger. "Okay, pause. First, if the musician you're talking about is Zee Barlo, we're going to put a *giant* pin in that for later discussion. And put a pin in the hookup thing, too."

"Right next to the pin for the gym bros?"

Joey ignored me. "Now, let's focus on the part of the story where my favorite cousin, Rowe, Aunt Muriel's li'l baby cupid—"

"Oh, Jesus, do not bring that up."

"—decided he wanted to be a sad sack of self-pity and bullshit excuses."

I shot him a glare. "That's *not* what I said."

"You sure? 'Cause that's what I heard you say. Walking away from your business idea because of a setback—?"

"It was a little more than a setback," I said angrily. "Did you hear the part where I failed to talk to Justin Hardy, my last hope? And I can't ask Bash for contacts, Joey. I refuse. I don't want him to think this was all about using him."

"So we find another way! Dude. *Dude.* We're Princes, and Princes don't quit. This is the part where the story is getting good."

I shook my head. "I'm out of ideas, Joey. I'm out of money. I'm out of... energy. And I feel like shit for lying. This isn't quitting. It's moving on."

"Nope. Unacceptable. You've got at least one more try in you."

I leaned back into the lumpy headrest, stared out the windshield, and groaned. "You don't know that. I've contacted so many people already. It's not that easy."

He huffed out a laugh. "No, you know what's not easy? Doing a backflip while holding a tiny guitar and a bag of burritos. But some of us manage it."

I blinked at the road for a moment, then turned fully in my seat and gawked at him. "A backflip? What the *hell*?"

"Shhh. It's all under control. The point is, Princes know how to do hard shit. You got a crush on someone you think is out of your league, and that sucks. Now, maybe he is and maybe he isn't, but that's a problem for another day. Don't tie all that up with whether you can or can't succeed with your project, Rowe. Focus on one problem at a time. Don't just turn tail and run back to Indiana." He shook his head. "Jeez. And people call *me* a Drama Llama."

"No they don't." I tilted my head. "Who called you that?"

"I dunno." Joey's cheeks went red. "People." He cleared his throat. "Anyway, let's get back to the original plan. You need to talk to Justin Hardy, so let's figure out a way to get that done."

I shook my head. "Bash said he's not a good guy. He's a user."

Joey made a rude sound with his tongue and shot a bird over his shoulder in the general direction of Philadelphia. "Well, fuck Bash. He could hear your pitch anytime, and fund it, too, but he wouldn't even listen."

"Stop it." I pointed a finger at him angrily. "Bash is generous to a fault. He gives to charities. He devotes his time and energy to helping small businesses succeed. When his friends need him in the middle of the night, he *runs* to help. But he's not an ATM machine, and he doesn't owe anyone his money or his contacts or his influence."

Joey rolled his eyes. "God, you've got it bad. Okay, fine, he's a lovely human. But he's still on the board at Sterling Chase, and Justin Hardy is one of their biggest competitors. Asking him if you should pitch to his archnemesis is like asking me if you should eat at Sandwich Shark. Which you should *not*. No matter how tasty their chicken parm is or how generous their portions. Understand?"

"No... but I'm kinda craving Italian now. Kidding, kidding," I said when Joey glared at me. "You're saying Bash is biased against Justin Hardy because they're competitors."

"Doesn't that make sense? I mean... did he tell you why he didn't like Justin? Specifically?"

"Well... no. There's history there, but I don't know what it is."

"So, there you go. When you make your pitch to Justin, you can form your own opinion. We just need to think of a way to get you inside his office."

"Right." I huffed. "Back to the drawing board, in other words?"

Before Joey could retort, his cell began playing "The Imperial March" from *Star Wars* somewhere in the back of the truck. "Shit. It's Lea. Call her on your phone, will you? Tell her I'm just about to start the supply run."

I dialed Lea, and the phone barely rang before she answered. "Rowe! Thank goodness. Are you with Joey?"

"Yeah, we—"

"Listen, stop him before he goes shopping. We just got a *huge* lunch catering order for later this week, so I'm texting him an updated supply list. And I need all hands on deck Thursday for delivery. You, Joey, everyone."

"Not a problem," I told her. I relayed the information to Joey, who grunted. Apparently he really did work there now. "We'll be there—"

Joey pulled over, braking so hard my phone flew out of my hand, and I'd have hit the windshield if I wasn't buckled in. "Holy shit!" he cried. "Holy shit, I've got it! The way into Hardy Development. It's so fucking obvious. Rowe, why didn't we think of this?"

"Think of what? Joey, you nearly killed us!"

"You deliver him a burrito," Joey said, eyes wide like this genius plan had just been delivered to him in an ayahuasca vision. "You find yourself the best outfit Second Chance Savers has to offer, then make a burrito delivery to Justin Hardy. Hit him where it counts. *In his belly.* Then, once you've got him where you want him, *boom*, pitch the deal and leave him gagging for more."

I blinked. Why the fuck *hadn't* I thought of that? Joey's metaphors left a little to be desired, but I could see the spark of brilliance in the plan. And, hell, desperate times truly did call for desperate measures. If this was going to be my last chance before giving up and moving back home to Indiana, I needed to make it count.

"That... that might actually work." Optimism flooded through me like oxygen after a long time underwater. "I need to try, right?"

"Fuck yes."

"And also... one thing I learned from Bash is that I've been thinking about this pitch all wrong. I've been hoping people would be bowled over by the idea of improving emergency response outcomes, but I need to be more convincing about how it could potentially be *profitable.*" I chewed my lip. "I can try to figure that out. I just need some time, and I don't know if I have it."

"You do. Bro, you have no idea how many tips I've scored delivering burritos this weekend. I can float you for a week or two."

"I can't let you—"

"Yeah, you really can. For this? For Daisy? I insist."

Another week or two. Time to hone my pitch and make it count. To give it one final shot, for Daisy's sake. Time to focus on what I could have and not what—and who—I couldn't. I could absolutely do that.

Or so I thought.

Until Thursday came.

FOURTEEN

BASH

I stared out the window at the city skyline stretching out in front of me. Normally, the view from my office window was invigorating. New York was a place where anything could happen, where any dream could become reality if you worked hard enough, and the eight million souls that called this place home filled the air with a frantic energy that made it impossible not to try.

Today, though, there was only *one* person among the eight million that concerned me. One angelic liar who'd returned my many, many texts over the past four days with only one simple *"I'm safe, Bash. Thank you for everything."* Sunday night.

The words rang with finality. It was clear Rowe meant them to be a period at the end of our story. Instead, they only made my longing for him that much deeper.

There was so much fucking potential there, and I hadn't seen it for what it was until Landry opened my eyes. There was so much more I wanted with Rowe, *for* Rowe, but I'd held myself back until it was too late.

"Bash. *Sebastian.*"

"Hmm?" I startled, turning away from the window, and shot an apologetic glance at the man standing in front of my desk. "Sorry, Kenji. I was just... thinking over that last point you made. Very thought-provoking."

He pursed his lips. "That shit doesn't work on me, remember? You're daydreaming again," he accused. "This is becoming a problem."

"It's not a problem. I'm thinking. Thinking is an important part of my job."

"Not when you're *thinking* of ways to get me to run a deeper background on Rowe Prince. I told you yesterday, the answer is no. I will not be a party to stalking. Consent fucking matters, Sebastian. The information in that background report was meant to determine whether Rowe was a security risk to the company, not so you could stand outside his cousin's place holding a boom box in the rain."

I rolled my eyes. "As if I would. The initial report was sparse, that's all I said. I wanted to learn more about the man."

But Kenji was right. The things I wanted to know—more stories about his sister, his family, the way he'd grown up, his hopes for the future and whether they might include me—couldn't be found in any background check. They were the sort of things I'd have to hear from Rowe himself...

If the man ever gave me the opportunity.

Kenji sighed and sank into a chair, giving me a look of concern. "You knew the man for two days. It's been four days since you saw him, and you're acting like you've just been through the worst breakup of your life. You're being ghosted, Bash. It sucks, but it happens to the best of us. Some more than others," he added under his breath. "Is it time to use the Fake Sterling Chase Escape Fund, do you think? Why not reschedule that Borneo trip? Change things up a little. Get your mind clear again."

I shook my head. "Believe it or not, Kenji, I'm thinking more clearly than I have in a while." At least about things that didn't involve the sexy man who'd pulled a disappearing act on me. "I might be done with adventure trips for a while. In fact..." I squared my shoulders. "I think it's time to take on a more active role at Sterling Chase."

"Bash. You cannot possibly work more hours than you already do —" Kenji began.

"Not that. I mean, I think it's time for me to start vetting projects again from the very beginning. At least the projects I'm going to be working on."

The conversation with Rowe the other night had been enlightening in a lot of ways. So had the unexpected come-to-Jesus with Landry. When I'd shifted responsibility for vetting projects to Austin and Clarissa several years back, I'd told myself it made good business sense. Now, I was starting to see it was at least partially motivated by fear. Fear of being taken advantage of. Fear that all anyone saw when they looked at me was an opportunity or an open wallet. I was still worried about those things.

But giving up authority meant that I'd allowed other people to determine the guiding principles of the company I loved. Without any input from me, they'd naturally focused on profitability... and I'd let it happen. Instead of freeing me, stepping away had weighed me down. It was time for a reset.

I expected Kenji to frown in disapproval, to tell me all the reasons that would never work, but instead, his eyes widened, and a slow, delighted smile broke out on his face. "Thank fuck," he breathed. "Look, I know you like Austin, and I'll admit the man's devoted to his job, but... he's not you. When I started working for you, Sterling Chase was all about supporting advancements that weren't necessarily commercial. Projects that were complex and had a global impact, like the one Clarissa's been working on in Sierra Leone for the past year. Over time, they've become more... instant gratification, I guess? Like that HungerGamer device that integrates your gaming console with an air fryer. It's cute, and it sells, but it's not a thing you point to and say, 'We made people's lives better.' Or the CaffApp..."

I snorted. "Yeah, I've heard people's thoughts on the freaking

CaffApp. But if you were feeling this way, why didn't you say anything? God knows it's not like you to hold back."

"What was I supposed to say? 'Hey, Bash, so you know how you consciously stepped down from having a public role in the company? Well, I really feel like you need to put your own emotional well-being aside because Sterling Chase shouldn't be making kitchen appliances.' How could I possibly do that? You deserve to have more in your life than this company, Sebastian. I hoped stepping back would help you get it."

I felt a surge of overwhelming fondness for Kenji. "I'm starting to see that I overcorrected," I admitted. "I stepped back too far and forgot my purpose. I was trying to fill the void with travel..."

"But that didn't work. And you came to this realization thanks to Rowe Prince?"

"Rowe was definitely a catalyst."

Kenji looked thoughtful. "*Hmph*. He might not be so bad after all."

"You'd like him." I found myself smiling. "He's... hard not to like."

"Sure." Kenji's voice had warmed a fraction, but he was clearly reserving judgment. "Remember that's what you said about fucking *Landry*."

It took an effort not to smile when Kenji sounded so put out. "Landry's behaved this week, hasn't he?"

Kenji grimaced. "If by *behaved* you mean propping his feet on the corner of my desk, chewing gummy bears so loudly my noise-canceling headphones are useless, and trying to inject himself into my personal phone calls until I'm ready to scream."

I ran a hand over my mouth to hide my smile. "Better than having to negotiate bail, right?"

"Debatable. At least *that* Landry is a known quantity." He shook himself slightly, like he was trying to clear all thought of my friend from his mind. "Anyway, Austin Purcell is coming by in an hour for that meeting you put off Monday. You wanna give him the news?"

I considered for a moment, then shook my head. "I might mention it, but I'm not presenting it like a done deal. First, I need to talk to Clarissa when she gets back. And since I'm technically just a member of the board, I think an official announcement needs to come from all of us. But there *is* one project I'd like to look at in the meantime."

Kenji frowned, then rolled his eyes as understanding dawned. "Lemme guess... Rowe's project?"

"Yes. I'm not saying I'm going to sign him to Sterling sight unseen," I argued quickly. "I'm not going to give his project special treatment simply because I'm attracted to the man. But the other night..." I shook my head, frustrated with myself. "The other night, I turned down his project sight unseen simply because I was attracted to the man, and that's just as bad. I essentially said, 'I want to know everything about you, Rowe, *except* the thing you're most passionate about,' because I got stuck in my head about things. And that's unfair. Worse, I didn't even realize how unfair I was being until the man left. So, no." I looked at Kenji seriously. "I'm not signing him to Sterling right now. But if I can help Rowe somehow, then I'm going to consider it. Not because I think he expects it but because I like him, and it feels good to help good people. Okay?"

"Yeah." Kenji smiled slowly. "I think I'm going to enjoy this new and improved Bash."

I rolled my eyes. "Step one, let's pull whatever information Rowe submitted. He requested a meeting within the last couple of months, so we shouldn't have to go back too far. Let's also pull any notes that Austin or anyone on his team might have made about why we rejected it."

"Easy enough," Kenji agreed. "We document everything."

But after searching the submissions log for an hour, both of us were frustrated to find that there was no record of any submission by Rowe at all, even as far as six months back.

"Bash," Kenji began hesitantly. "Is it possible that Rowe wasn't being truthful? Don't give me that look, okay? He lied before."

"Only because he thought he had to. I know when he was telling the truth," I said with a confidence I rarely felt.

I remembered how his face looked when he talked about decorating a home, when he spoke of his sister, when he admitted he'd never had sex before. The precise texture of Rowe's curls against my fingertips. The light in his eyes after I'd kissed him. The sound he made when he came. No, there were some things that couldn't be faked.

"He definitely submitted his idea and requested a meeting," I concluded. "He mentioned a 'terse' rejection letter from Austin, too."

"Okay, so did he submit it under a different name? Maybe he's put things under an LLC?"

"I don't think he's business savvy enough to open an LLC." I pushed a hand through my hair. "Look, do me a favor? Get someone in IT to search the whole corporate file system for any mention of Project Daisy Chain. That's Rowe's name for the project."

"Might as well," Kenji agreed, getting to his feet. "That's going to take at least half an hour to complete, though."

"Fine. I'm not leaving town anytime soon." And if I had anything to say about it, neither was Rowe.

"Or you could just ask Austin—" Kenji began.

"Hey, hey!" Austin's familiar voice called, followed a second later by a knock on my open door. "Ask Austin what?"

Austin, who always dressed impeccably, had outdone himself today. He wore a charcoal three-piece suit and a smile brimming with excitement. Belatedly, I remembered that he was counting down to the big beta launch of his own project. It was nice that things were swimming along for someone around here.

"For an update on MRO," I lied smoothly, deciding the man should be able to celebrate his victory for the day without distraction. "Come sit down and tell me how everything's gone. Kenji, you can go get started on that... other thing."

Kenji nodded and ducked out while Austin took the seat he'd vacated.

"Today's the big day, right?" I prompted. "You got the approval from Legal? Beta's about to launch?"

"Yup. Everything's on track." Austin relaxed back, propping his ankle on his knee and his elbows on the chair arms. "Lonnie had some interesting things to say, actually, about the prelaunch response from the testing sites..."

Austin updated me on the details of our next steps, and I quickly settled into the conversation, feeling my excitement build as I thought about the far-reaching implications of what we were doing. I knew in my bones that we were on the cusp of something amazing with this project, just like the brotherhood had been when we were developing our stoplight communication system, and when the clock on my wall chimed the hour, I was shocked to find that I'd spent thirty minutes talking without feeling the time pass.

This was precisely the kind of project I wanted to be working on. The kind that stretched me and challenged me in a way that felt *right*.

It was the same way I felt about Rowe.

"I'm continually impressed, Austin," I told him. "Your team has managed this well, but the real brilliance was in the idea you had in the first place and the research you did on your own."

Austin shrugged modestly. "It feels like this launch has been a long time coming, and I couldn't have done it without Sterling Chase. I'm treating my team to a little celebration at lunchtime to thank them. You should come. It would mean a lot to everyone."

"Sure. I'll try to make it down if I'm free."

"Great! Oh." Austin snapped his fingers. "I forgot to mention there was one tiny, silly hiccup with Legal filing the provisional utility patents. Because the patents will be solely in my name, the company has an internal review. Normally, I just sign off on this stuff and that's good enough for them, but they're pushing back since the patent is in my name. Can't sign off on my own patent." He sighed and rolled his eyes. "Lawyers."

I snorted. "Figures. What do they need?"

"Documentation from earlier in my development process. The initial brainstorming notes I made. Though why they want to see my chicken-scratch scribbles on notebook paper is anyone's guess. If you want to do me a solid..." He gave me a shameless grin. "I'm thinking a quick email from someone on the board verifying the documentation exists would probably be good enough to settle their feathers. That would save me a bunch of time combing through my files so I can focus on all the other projects I'm supposed to be managing."

I laughed. "I would if I could, friend, but Clarissa was the one you first brought the project to, so I never saw that documentation." I hesitated for only a second before adding, "Speaking of your workload, though... I think I'm ready to step back into the fray. In the next few weeks, I'd like to start reviewing some proposals and being part of the selection team again. I'm not sure exactly what that process will look like, but you and I work well together, so I'm sure we'll figure something out. And hopefully, that'll free you up a bit."

Austin's smile dimmed a fraction. "Sure... assuming the rest of the board agrees and the owners don't have an issue with it. But there's a reason they wanted you to step back in the first place, isn't there?" He raised an eyebrow. "Or is there something you're not telling me?"

I bit my tongue against a snappy retort that Austin didn't deserve. He had no idea that the decision to step back had been mine. And giving up the reins had been difficult for *me*, even when it had been my choice. I couldn't expect him to be immediately enthusiastic about it.

"No, you're right. We'll see what they say," I agreed. "Sorry that doesn't save you from having to find the documentation for Legal, though. Is that going to present a problem for Sterling Chase moving the project forward?"

"Of course not." He picked at an invisible piece of lint on his pant leg. "The testing might be delayed a day or two, but no more. I swear, I copied every piece of documentation to my work system after we signed our contract, but in one of my attempts to get my files organized, I must've deleted them, assuming no one would ever need them. Now I need to find the original scans on my personal system. The price of organization, right?" He grinned.

I chuckled lightly, though I wondered what Kenji would say about Austin admitting he'd deleted a file that way. Our attorneys required us to keep a meticulous paper trail in case our patents were ever challenged. Everything that had ever been created, from handwritten notes to product sketches to meeting minutes, was kept in the project folder on our server. As someone who dealt with these things all the time, Austin should have known better.

"Well, don't forget the entire Sterling Chase system is backed up regularly. If you can't find it on your home computer, we can talk to IT and see if they can restore the files for you," I offered.

Austin's eyes widened, and he smacked his forehead. "Right. Of course. God, I'd forgotten about the backups. Good idea. I should be able to get all of that sorted within the next day or two, then."

"Perfect. Frustrating to face a setback when you're so close to the finish line, though." My thoughts immediately turned to Rowe—because *of course they did* since the man seemed determined to sit at the center of my brain this week. The way he'd spoken so passionately about his sister. The way his eyes had burned when he said, *I couldn't not try, Bash.* "What's kept *you* motivated with this?" I asked Austin suddenly.

He stared at me like I'd sprouted horns. "Motivated me? Aside from wanting to do a good job for Sterling Chase? That's always my primary motivation."

"Not that." My cheeks felt warm, and I wondered if Rowe's blushes were contagious. "You could have an amazing career at Sterling Chase without ever needing to invent your own project, to jump through these hoops. So I was curious what made you dream up the concept for MRO. What's kept you pushing, even when you faced setbacks?"

"Oh. That." His face cleared, and he shifted in his chair. "It's...

it's actually a very personal story. I, uh... lost a friend when I was young."

What a fucked-up coincidence. I blinked at him in surprise for a moment before I managed to get out, "God, I'm so sorry."

He nodded stiffly. "Thank you. My friend died due to something called commotio cordis after being struck in the chest with a ball during a baseball game. She had this heart defect the EMTs didn't know about. If they'd had access to her medical records, they might have responded differently. Instead, she died. It was really... tough."

The blood in my veins went cold, and my scalp prickled. There was no way that was a coincidence. It couldn't be. Could it?

"Yes, I bet it was," I agreed softly. "And this was in New Hampshire? Where you grew up?"

He shrugged, almost but not quite agreeing. "It happened a while ago, but it's still pretty painful. If you don't mind, Bash, I'd really rather not talk about it."

"No, of course. I don't mean to pry."

"I just thought," Austin went on bleakly, "that if emergency response had been better coordinated with doctor communication and a real-time data collection and assessment tool... maybe things would have been different. And then when I started thinking about it, it seemed like a natural companion piece to the stoplight communication technology that launched Sterling Chase years ago." Austin met my eyes with stark sincerity. "I realized just how many people we could help with something like this."

"And I'm so glad you did," I managed to choke out. I pushed to my feet. "Well. I won't keep you any longer. I know you've got a celebration to get to."

Austin stood and gave me a brave smile. "I do. And I'll see you there later?"

"I have a few things to tie up here first," I said vaguely.

The minute Austin cleared the doorway, I stood and paced the area in front of my desk. "Holy shit," I muttered under my breath. "Holy shit."

"What's going on?" Kenji stood in the doorway, frowning at me. "Is everything okay?"

"Close the door," I told him. Then, "Kenji, if two people told you the same exact story, and one of them was almost definitely lying, would you believe the man you'd worked with for years—someone you liked and admired and *trusted*—or would you believe a guy you'd known for two days, who'd lied to you repeatedly, and who... who had every reason to lie to you again?"

Kenji sucked in a breath and then pulled out a chair and sat down. "I'm going to need more details."

I filled him in on everything Austin had said, along with the story Rowe had told me.

"That would be an incredible coincidence." Kenji pulled at his lip. "It could simply *be* a coincidence, Bash. I mean, how many cases of that heart thing occur every year in the United States?"

"But both Rowe's sister and Austin's friend had a heart defect that medical records would have notified EMTs about? This was the motivation *both* of them had for coming up with their projects?"

"Okay, yes. That's slightly more suspicious." He nodded slowly. "You think Rowe's lied to you again?"

It made the most sense. Maybe that was the logical conclusion here. After all, why in the world would a well-educated, experienced, successful businessman like Austin Purcell—with so much to lose—have stolen an idea from someone like Rowe Prince. But...

"No," I whispered. "I really don't. If you'd seen his face, Kenji..." I dropped heavily into my chair. "What do I do? How do I prove that Austin stole Rowe's project?"

Kenji shook his head. "Bash, you're three steps ahead of yourself. I'm not defending Austin, *believe me*, but you don't even know for sure what Rowe's project is—"

Except I did. I remembered, way too late, how excited he'd been last weekend when I talked about Sterling Chase working on a project that dovetailed with ETC. It had been on the tip of his tongue to tell me about his project then, and looking back, I knew it. But I'd let the moment go.

"Fine," Kenji said, tapping on his tablet. "Step one, we go back to the initial documentation Austin submitted with this project. There are records of everything, and Clarissa must've reviewed it all. So, we'll look through it and see if there are... *clues*." He rolled his eyes. "And just like that, I'm Jessica Fletcher. Working for you people is never dull."

I laughed and ran a hand over my eyes. "Christ. I think you'll find there *aren't* records. Not all of them, anyway. Austin was just telling me he's misplaced several key pieces of documentation from his early research. *Oops*."

Kenji froze, his jaw hanging open. "He fucking knows better."

"Yes, he does. Put that together with the fact that Rowe's submission seems to have been misplaced—"

"Don't jump to conclusions. I'm serious, Bash. There are legal issues at play here, okay? Patent issues, Human Resources issues, not to mention your reputation, Austin's reputation, and the reputation of the company. Contact Legal before you do anything."

I swallowed. "No, you're right. I know you are. Okay, why don't you do that. Quietly. Ask them to slow-roll the patents and beta testing until we get this squared away. And we need a background check on Austin. Find out where he grew up and see if we can confirm that his story about his friend is true." Kenji nodded. "While you're at it, get a deeper background on Rowe—not for stalking purposes."

"On it," Kenji agreed, standing up.

"I'm going to start checking through the remaining files on MRO." I turned to my laptop. "I really, really hope you're right and there's a reasonable explanation for all of this."

"Same. I, uh... take it you're skipping Austin's celebration lunch, then? If you want, I can go snag you a burrito before the festivities begin. I think they're setting up soon."

My head shot up and whipped to Kenji. "Say that again?"

"I said, I can go grab you a burrito...?"

I pushed to my feet. "Austin ordered his team burritos."

"Yes? That Burrito Bandito truck that sometimes parks over on West Forty-Seventh. Why? Bash? Where the hell are you going? Since when are you so passionate about burritos?"

"Since very recently," I called over my shoulder. But as I made my way down two floors to the large conference room where Austin was scheduled to have lunch with his team, searching everywhere for a colorful, gaudy sombrero, I smiled to myself because the burritos were definitely not what I was feeling passionate about.

FIFTEEN

ROWE

My hands were shaking, rattling the cardboard box of burritos I carried through the gleaming front door of the office building. Avoiding Bash Dayne was supposed to have been easy—no matter how badly I missed him, our paths were never destined to cross, right? Except apparently, the universe had other plans because suddenly here I was, wearing my freaking sombrero and making a special lunchtime catering delivery to Sterling freaking Chase. And my presence, according to Lea, was not optional.

Certain people did not seem to care that there was no part of the fairy tale where Cinderella was forced to bring lunch to the palace.

This whole past week had sucked. I hadn't been able to eat, and I'd barely slept since leaving Philly the other day. Instead, I'd been working double shifts in an effort to make up for lost time and tips. I'd even stayed up all night figuring out how to repack the trick pocket square in Joey's tux. And when I should have spent every damn minute preparing to ambush Justin Hardy with my project proposal, I'd found myself daydreaming about Bash. It was like all my focus had evaporated the minute the man had touched me, and I wasn't sure how to get it back.

The only thing that had kept me from sending Bash a text begging him for one more night was the knowledge that I'd done the right thing by walking away so Bash wouldn't have to. But being so close to him now—just a few floors away, probably—made the ache in my chest swell until I was nothing but a giant blob of *want*.

"Rowe! Don't drop those burritos!" Lea warned, marching along behind us, carrying her own box of food.

Correction: I was a giant blob of want *and burritos*.

"You got this, cuz," Joey muttered. "We get in, we sing, we set up the burritos for the nice folks, we collect our tips, and we're out, okay? I told you, you don't have to do the toe-kicking. And even if someone here spotted you at the gala, nobody's gonna recognize you in that mustache and sombrero."

I gave Joey a look that said listening to him was *exactly* how the trouble at the gala had started. "Yeah," I said softly. "Let's just get it done, okay?" Hopefully, with no Bash-related run-ins this time.

The receptionist on the ground floor gestured us toward the conference room, which was filled with an assortment of corporate types and computer geeks, laptops and whiteboards. No Bash.

I mentally crossed myself and hoped for the best. *Jesus, if you exist, please help a bandito out...*

Joey, bless him, didn't hesitate, jumping immediately into the song, and all I had to do was sing along. "My name is Burrito Bandito..."

Several people turned their heads to stare at us, which should have been fine—that was part of the job, and I was used to it—but suddenly, I felt anxious. I held my box of burritos so high it blocked half my face. I'd never known true anxiety until I imagined someone recognizing me as the guy Bash Dayne had been hanging around with all weekend.

Joey finished his dance with a truly epic twirl that had the businesspeople clapping, and it was time to pass out the food. *Nearly home free. And then you can go back to preparing to impress Justin Hardy. Focus, Rowe—*

"Oh my god, I love burritos." A woman stood on her tiptoes in front of me, trying to peer into the box. "Could you maybe lower that a bit?"

I swallowed. "Oh, uh... of course." I set it down on the table and adjusted my mustache. "Help yourself."

"Austin, this lunch was the best idea," she called to a man down the table who wore a high-end three-piece suit.

The man turned, and I recognized him as Austin Purcell, the head of development, from his corporate photo on the company website. A guy who worked directly with Bash. *Shit.*

"As much as I'd love to take credit for it, I can't," Austin returned. "Remember my college roommate Bernard? He kept raving about this place. Orders from here once a week. Claims he and one of the delivery people watched polo together this weekend." He looked Joey up and down. "Don't suppose it was you?"

"Nah, man, I don't do polo," Joey said easily, but he darted a shifty look at me that might as well have been a giant neon sign saying, *"but my cousin Rowe does."*

Before I could duck under the table, or lower my sombrero, or melt into a puddle of embarrassment, Austin followed Joey's gaze toward me. "Oh." He frowned. "Wait, I know you, don't I?"

"Me?" The word came out incredibly high-pitched. "N-no. Nope. Not unless you've gotten a burrito delivery recently."

He shook his head. "That's not it. I saw your picture somewhere, I'm almost sure. I never forget a face." He tilted his head. "What's your name?"

"Ha. *Ha.* No. I don't give that information out to customers," I lied. The truth was, no one had ever asked. "Would you like a burrito, sir?"

"I bet you'll give out your name if it'll mean a bigger tip," Austin said with a smile that managed to be friendly and weirdly menacing at the same time. What a fuckwad. *This* was the guy who'd turned down Project Daisy Chain?

"Nope. He definitely won't. Company policy," Joey interjected.

"We are alllll the Burrito Bandito, *señor*. Isn't that right, everybody? Sing it with me! And free burrito coupons for whoever sings loudest! *Our name is Burrito Bandito...*"

Austin scowled at Joey but refused to be distracted by his singing. I could sense him searching his memory banks, and I second-guessed my decision not to triple-swipe my deodorant this morning. Would it be worse for him to remember me being with Bash? Or for him to somehow figure out my name and remember I was the guy he'd sent that rude rejection email, even after I'd taken the time to send him all my project notes?

Oh, who was I kidding? Both would be equally awful. I needed to get out of there, immediately.

I ducked behind the table so I could lean closer to my boss. "Lea, I'm really sorry, but I need to find a restroom. I'm not feeling so great."

"But, Rowe—" she began.

Joey sent a quick glance in my direction and must have seen that I was planning a retreat. He danced around the table without missing a beat, jammed his sombrero on Austin's head, then grabbed Austin's hands and pulled the man into an impromptu burrito jig.

I didn't wait for Lea to finish speaking. I ran out of the conference room and headed left down the hall past conference rooms and offices, all of which seemed to be occupied. It wasn't until I got to a bank of elevators that I realized I had no idea where I was going. When the elevator dinged and the doors began to slide open, I skidded around the corner and found myself in a little reception area with a single sofa, an office phone, and a giant potted tree in the corner by a curtained window. Without pausing to think, I squeezed into the space between the tree and the curtain and took a deep, shuddering breath.

Who knew burrito delivery could be so hazardous to your health?

I pressed a hand to my stomach, turned my face to the wall, and told myself to calm down. I was fine. I wasn't injured. Even my mustache was intact. All I had to do was stash my sombrero, and then I could escape—

"Another impressive move," a deep, sexy, way-too-familiar voice said from behind me. "But Rowe, sweetheart, we've really got to stop meeting like this."

I squeezed my eyes shut and locked down my muscles as every single cell in my body tried to jump backward into Bash's arms. "I'm imagining this," I told myself sternly. "When I turn around, I will be all alone. Or, possibly, the tree is speaking to me."

"You'd rather talk to a tree than to me?" Bash asked softly.

I inhaled sharply and nearly whimpered when the fresh, expensive scent of his cologne assaulted me. I didn't know shit about science, but I knew it had to be impossible for that smell to have imprinted on me in just a couple of days or for it to be so instantly arousing. I was glad the pantalones de charros I wore were constructed of thick enough fabric to hide my rapidly growing interest.

"Rowe, can we please talk? Look, if you don't wanna talk about us, that's fine. But I have questions for you about Project Daisy Chain."

That got me to turn around. "Daisy Chain?" I repeated in surprise, scanning his face, searching for a hint that this was a trick.

His eyes roamed over me at the same time, from the bits of curl escaping my sombrero, down the exposed skin of my neck. Every place his eyes landed felt like a physical touch. And when his gaze finally landed on my mustache, his lips twitched up in that amused-against-his-will smile that would never *not* make me want to fall to my knees.

"Hi," I breathed. I sounded besotted.

"Hey," he replied, the lip twitch becoming a full-on smile. He darted a glance out to the corridor, where the burrito song was growing louder and louder, as if his employees had started roaming the halls in a lunchtime conga line. "Come with me so we can speak privately." He held out a hand. "Trust me?"

This was an absolutely terrible idea, but there really was no decision to be made. If Sebastian Dayne held out a hand for me, I was going to take it.

He threaded our fingers together and pulled me toward the elevator, taking a second to check that the hallway was clear first. The elevator was already occupied, but the passengers' conversation quickly cut off when they realized they'd been joined by someone from the board of directors... and a man in a fake mustache.

Bash swiped his key card and hit the button for the top floor, then leaned against the wall, facing me. His eyes met mine, sending a hot flush racing across my skin that made my clothes itch.

The woman beside me darted a look up at my sombrero—which was taking up a significant amount of space—before quickly glancing away.

"I brought burritos," I explained.

I carried a watermelon.

Belatedly, I realized this didn't really explain my presence since there were no burritos on my person. The woman snorted softly. The man next to her hid his laugh behind a cough.

Bash's lips quirked like I'd been talking to him. "Thank fuck you did. You're a hard man to get hold of."

Was I? Since I was forcibly restraining myself from jumping into his arms, I didn't think that was accurate.

I glanced at the woman and swallowed hard. "Yes, they *are* good burritos," I said with a strangled laugh. "It was very kind of you to offer a tour of your office, Mr. Dayne."

Bash shook his head, still wearing that little smile, still lounging against the wall with casual elegance. His eyes caught the light in the elevator, and I thought for a minute I might turn into a sombrero-topped puddle right there at his feet. It would serve me right for being harebrained enough to go with him when I should have buzzed right out the front door and burned off my need with a long-ass walk back to Queens.

The silence in the elevator was electrically charged and excruciating. I couldn't imagine what the people stuck with us were thinking.

"If you ever wanna see the inside of the Burrito Mobile," I went on, "just let me know, and I'd be happy to repay the favor." My nervous babbling was reaching entirely new heights.

Thankfully, the elevator doors opened before I could say anything more, and the other passengers hurried off. Unfortunately, it turned out to be our stop, too.

"Where are we going?" I asked, following Bash down the hall to the right when the others had turned left. "I should probably get back downstairs before I miss my ride. Lea doesn't take kindly to rogue banditos."

When he passed the open door to an office, a dark-haired man jumped up from his desk and called out. "Bash, did you get a burrit —*oh*," he finished when he clocked me trailing along in Bash's wake. "Well, damn."

"Kenji, hold my calls," Bash said without slowing down. "I'm about to get some answers."

"Okay, but—" Kenji began.

Whatever he'd been about to say was cut off when Bash dragged me into his office and slammed the door shut. His hand shoved my chest until my back hit the closed door, and then his mouth crashed down on mine like a lightning strike. My sombrero went flying... and so did all the reasons why being in Sebastian's space was a tragically terrible idea. Bash was hard and hot and strong, pressing me into the door with his hips and chest, grappling with me until he had my arms crossed above my head, wrists clasped in one of his large hands. His other hand gripped my throat just firmly enough to tilt my face the way he wanted it.

I kissed him with a hungry intensity I seemed to only feel in Sebastian Dayne's presence. The room spun wildly around us as his scent and touch and the sounds of our desperate kisses filled what little space remained between us.

When he finally pulled his head back, it was only so he could run his thumb over my fake mustache, his eyes sparkling with silent laughter.

I'd forgotten I still had the damn thing on, and my face went hot. "Shoot. Sorry." I peeled it off and stuffed it in my pocket. "Was it weird kissing a man in disguise?"

Bash's voice rumbled with sensual promise. "Kissing you always feels incredible, no matter what identity you're using."

The man needed to stop saying such sweet things. How was I supposed to convince myself that none of this was real when he looked at me like that?

"I thought you said you didn't want to talk about u-us," I accused.

"I lied." He leaned closer again, running his nose along the edge of my jaw and inhaling deeply. I prayed he was smelling soap and not extra-spicy red sauce.

"Bash," I protested, feeling my knees go weak. I needed to leave or for him to throw me down on the nearest surface and have his way with me and *then* leave. At this point, I wasn't sure which would hurt more.

He heaved a heavy sigh. "I very much want to talk about *us*, Rowe. But first..." He let me go, then stepped back. When he gestured me toward one of the chairs in front of his desk, I was finally able to get a glimpse of his office. One whole wall was windows, looking out over the city. Reflected light from the nearby buildings made the whole office sparkle. On the wall by the door was a large seating area with a couch. And in front of the window sat an enormous black desk. It was stylish and modern without being cold. Very perfect for Bash.

Instead of going around the desk to his office chair, Bash dropped into one of the visitor chairs and pulled me into the other. But he gripped my hand in his, like he thought maybe I'd run away if he let go.

"I'd like you to tell me about your project. About Daisy Chain. I should have let you tell me last weekend, and I regret—"

I started shaking my head before he could finish. "No. You said you didn't want that between us, and I agreed. I *still* agree. I'm desperate, I admit that. But I didn't spend time with you because I wanted an investor, Bash. I didn't h-have sex with you," I stammered, "because I wanted you to put in a good word with the Sterling Chase people—"

"I know."

"I don't want money from you. Not even for Daisy's project. I spent the weekend with you because you're fun and smart and seriously fucking kind. Because when I'm with you, I feel like you *see* me, even when I'm not *being* me. Because you make me laugh, and you don't get impatient when I babble like an idiot. Because I like you...*mmmph.*"

Bash grabbed me by the back of my neck and hauled me in for another kiss, even more drugging than the last. Oh, god. The taste of him, the feel of his tongue brushing against mine, turned my spine to liquid. By the time he pulled back, I was slumped in the chair.

"You really need to stop kissing me, Bash Dayne," I whispered.

"Then you need to stop being so fucking kissable, Rowe Prince."

I squeezed my eyes shut. My brain spun like a Tilt-A-Whirl at the fair. "What do you want from me?"

When I peeked up at him, Bash's lips were wet and red, and his eyes were intent, like he was giving the question a lot of thought. "For now? Exactly what I said. Tell me about the project, Rowe. Please."

"You want a... a pitch?" I asked anxiously. "Because I'm still working on some revisions to that. After our conversation, I realized I needed to focus on how it could be profitable, so I started making a PowerPoint—"

"I don't want a presentation." He slid his chair closer to mine and took my hand again. "Just talk. I really, really want to know."

In general, I never needed coaxing to talk about Daisy Chain. In fact, my mom sometimes said I was like a person who'd just come back from a vacation and needed to show everyone his photos, "even though I don't understand above one word in ten that you're speaking, Rowe, dear." I usually tried to *stop* talking about it.

Bash was different. He was maybe the best listener I'd ever met, which made it hard to hold back, even when I'd had every reason to keep my mouth shut. Now, with him holding my hand in both of his and his eyes locked on mine intensely, I didn't need much convincing to spill my guts.

When he looked at me like that, like the whole world could fall to ashes around us and he'd still be hanging on to my hand and my every word, it was beyond my capability to deny him anything he wanted.

I took a deep breath and held it for a moment before letting it out in a *whoosh*. "Right. Okay. Project Daisy Chain is my idea for an emergency response communication system that connects EMTs to medical records, local hospitals, and physicians to improve trauma response outcomes—"

Bash inhaled sharply—the exact inverse of the breath I'd just exhaled—and I could feel his tension ratchet up in the way his fingers clenched on mine. "Well, *fuck*."

SIXTEEN

BASH

"P-pardon?" Rowe stammered.

From the moment Austin had told his sad story—a story suspiciously like Rowe's, with all the supporting documentation conveniently missing—I'd known this was coming. But until Rowe spoke, I hadn't realized I'd been holding on to a sliver of hope that, despite all the circumstantial evidence, this might just be a coincidence. That Rowe's project might turn out to be a jewel-matching game, or a dating app, or... Christ, anything but what it was.

Earlier, I'd focused on my need to hurry downstairs and find Rowe—to set eyes and *hands* on him again—and I'd let that distract me from the enormous potential fallout of this situation. If Rowe's project really was *exactly* like the one Austin was taking credit for, I didn't know what it meant for Sterling Chase, or for me, or for Rowe himself.

Legal and HR would need to conduct a huge internal investigation, for sure. We'd have to comb through every contract Austin had ever signed—every emailed meeting request he'd ever received—to see if this was an isolated incident. There could be press releases and media scrutiny on the company that would set us right in the public eye—which was the last thing any member of my brotherhood wanted...

You should probably get more information before jumping to conclusions, Dayne.

Right.

I blew out a breath and summoned a smile. "Sorry," I told Rowe. "I was just startled. Keep going. How'd you come up with the idea?"

Rowe looked confused for a moment before he recovered. "Okay, um. I told you how Daisy died—"

"You did. A softball to the chest," I said gently, playing with his fingers. My heart hurt for him. I couldn't imagine what it must have been like for him to experience such a traumatic loss.

He nodded and ran a hand through his hair, sending his adorable curls tumbling around his face. "The technical name for what happened is commotio cordis. It's when a blow to the chest disrupts the heart rhythm. It's pretty rare for someone to die of it because usually when someone performs CPR or the paramedics bring a defibrillator, they can get the heart back into normal rhythm. But that didn't work with Daisy. We found out later she had a heart defect called dextrocardia—her heart was on the right side of her chest instead of the left. If the EMTs had known about it, they could have adapted the typical CPR position to accommodate that—"

"And they could have saved her?"

"I don't know," Rowe admitted. "Maybe? But better trauma response could save *someone*. There are a ton of emergency response situations that would benefit from a real-time assessment communication tool. If EMTs and physicians could communicate during the initial response and that critical time be used to make decisions about where to route a patient, imagine how much better the outcomes would be."

"I can imagine," I said grimly. It was one of the reasons I'd been so excited about the MRO project when Austin had first brought it to Sterling Chase. "Go on."

"So, I was watching a rerun of an old medical drama about a

similar situation when the idea came to me that there could be a data-secure mobile device— but maybe with a satellite connection, which would make it more useful in rural places like Linden that don't have a lot of cell towers—that EMTs could use to access medical records but also communicate with the hospital in real time during the initial trauma response. And at first, I figured there had to be some reason that wouldn't work because otherwise, someone else would've come up with the idea before I did, right? But then... well, I told you, I heard Daisy's voice in my head, and I... I decided to look into it more. To develop it into an actual business plan."

"Whoa. I know you said you had to teach yourself all kinds of stuff to get your project off the ground, but..." I shook my head in disbelief. "With no science background, no business background... The kind of process you're talking about requires extensive research and knowledge of emergency response protocol, patient medical record data security, not to mention the GPS and mobile software integrations needed—"

"No shit." Rowe's ears were already red, and now the blush spread to his cheeks. "I didn't do great in school—partly because of what happened with Daisy and partly because it just wasn't my thing. But that doesn't mean I'm stupid. When I'm passionate about something, I go all in, whether it's interior design or reading dry medical journals with a dictionary app open on my phone."

"You got caught up," I whispered.

"Yeah, and I guess it's not always a bad thing," he said with a little smile. He pushed his free hand through his curls. "But, yes, I was way out of my comfort zone on this, and everyone I talked to knew it. Took me ages to get people to take me seriously because no one wanted to waste their time on what they figured was the equivalent of a little kid working on a science project." He picked at the silver-studded side seam of his black uniform pants. "Eventually, though, I got through. I interviewed EMTs, firefighters, and dispatchers. I researched the existing dispatch software and the other technologies used in emergency response. I had sit-down meetings with emergency room administrators at two area hospitals and brought lunch to a group of trauma specialists to beg their thoughts and ideas on a system like this."

I was impressed. The report Kenji had pulled together on Rowe Prince had indicated he'd been a mediocre high school student who hadn't been on a college track, but I'd known already that was bullshit. Academic success wasn't an indicator of career success... and I knew plenty of underemployed Yale grads to prove it.

"What did you come up with? A process or a software system?" The idea Austin brought to Sterling Chase had been both.

He stopped picking at the seam on his pants and leaned forward. The light from the window danced through his hair and lit up one side of his face as much as his passion for the subject lit up his eyes.

"It's actually got three key components." He pulled his hand away from mine so he could count them off on his fingers. "First, communication from dispatch, which begins with emergency response. Then, using an app to access medical records and track critical data like vitals, medical history, and preliminary treatment, which will then be sent to the nearest trauma centers. And finally, coordinating through the app between the EMTs and the trauma centers to create a care plan for the patient based on which center has the right staffing and resources and how long it will take to get there, because it doesn't matter that the hospital in Timbuktu has the best resources if you're gonna die before they can get you there. Once they have the plan, the EMTs can begin treatment in the field. The parts connect and build on each other, you see? Like a..."

"A daisy chain," he and I finished together.

"Yeah." Rowe's brilliant smile broke out, warmer than the sunlight. "It fits, right?"

"It definitely does." And wiped away any lingering doubts I might have had about whether Rowe had authored this plan.

"I know this all probably seems pie-in-the-sky," he went on. "I've already heard that from my parents and the Tech Barn guys from day one. My mom says it's not healthy for me to be so obsessed. She'd like me to forget all about this and just find someone nice to settle down with. My dad says it's irresponsible of me to devote so much time and money to this when I need a new car and when I'm leaving Bobby short an employee by 'traipsing off to New York.' And I know it's gonna take a lot of work to make it marketable and profitable, but it *can* be, Bash. I really think it can, if I can get someone else to be passionate about it."

"I know," I agreed. "But, Rowe—"

"A-and I'm not asking for a lot of money. I just want to get this out there in the world." His excitement drained away, and he straightened in his seat, like he was trying to appear more professional. "When I sign a contract, I'm going to insist on the kind that guarantees the company will produce a working product within a certain timeframe, or the rights will revert to me. That way, I can make sure there's forward progress. And if I can eventually get back the money I spent so I can get a car, I'd really like that also." He chewed his lip uncertainly. "I... I guess I did get a little pitch-y there at the end. Sorry about that."

Oh, god, he was planning to *give* the idea away? The man had no idea just how profitable this idea was going to be. None whatsoever.

I stared at him for a long moment, not sure how the hell I was supposed to tell him what had been going on behind the scenes. And as I stared, his face fell further.

"Crap. Is it... terrible? Like, no hope at all?" he asked in a small voice. "Maybe I'm just not explaining it well. If you let me get my PowerPoint— I have *charts*. Data I've collected. Screenshots from the app I built, which are pretty trash right now, but... Just... shit, Bash, say something. Tell me what you're thinking. Don't sugarcoat it."

"What I think," I said slowly, "is that you are amazing. Inspiring. And a little bit brilliant."

Rowe's cheeks flushed, and his eyes went shiny. "Really? Oh, shit. Wow. Okay."

"I think Project Daisy Chain is amazing, too." I set my jaw. "And that's exactly what I thought the first time I heard it... When someone else presented it to me."

"The same idea?" Rowe stared at me in shock, and his brown eyes filled with tears. "What?"

I was a man who'd never had a Kryptonite, an Achilles heel. There'd never been a button anyone could push to bring me crashing to my knees in despair... until now, apparently, because seeing Rowe so upset made me want to burn the fucking world down.

Hearing his project pitch, knowing just how much effort—how much of his heart and soul—he'd poured into the concept for Project Daisy Chain, had made me ready to sign my fortune over to him if that was what it would take to take the look of desperation off his sweet face. Now, seeing his entire face crumple in confusion made me want to go downstairs, find Austin Purcell, and assault him... possibly with a burrito.

"I don't understand how this is possible. I swear, Bash, this was my idea. I know I lied before—about being Sterling, and playing polo, and... and... *Bubbles*—but I'm telling the truth now."

"I believe you."

Rowe didn't seem to hear me. He jumped to his feet and began pacing, swiping an impatient hand under his eyes. "I have every bit of my research, starting with the first scribbles in my design notebook. I even wrote down the episode of the show I was watching when the idea first came to me." He patted his pockets and seemed distraught to find that he didn't have his notebook on hand.

"Rowe, I believe you."

"And you can ask anyone. I have witnesses. My parents will confirm it." He paced as far as the window and turned back. "I mean, granted, they have no freaking clue what I was actually doing since they never really paid attention, and I guess they're not great witnesses since they're my *parents* and not exactly impartial, which is the same reason Joey wouldn't be a good witness either, but— Oh! Bobby and the guys at the Tech Barn! They could vouch for me, at least partly. And one of the hospital administrators—her name's

Tracey, and we got to be friendly when we talked about her office redesign—she could tell you—"

I stood up, blocking his path, and grabbed both of his biceps as he prepared to turn toward the window again. "Rowe. I *believe* you. I don't need to talk to any of them."

Though our corporate lawyers certainly would. They'd want every scrap of evidence they could get their hands on.

Rowe looked horrified by my response. "But you *shouldn't* just believe me, Bash. You should demand proof." He shook his head like *he* was the old and wise one of the two of us and I was hopelessly naive. "You're so kind, and I lo—like that about you, but you really need to stop letting people take advantage of your generosity. You know?"

I opened my mouth, then shut it again. It was a novel thing to have someone be protective of me that way, but I kind of liked it... even though it was wholly unnecessary. It was true that I was generous when it came to money, but only because I had more than I could use in several lifetimes. With other things, though—with my time, with my effort, with my true feelings—no. There were very few people I would give those to unreservedly, and even my own parents didn't make the cut. The short list included Silas, Dev, Landry, Zane, Kenji...

And now, it seemed, Rowe Prince.

The realization made me a little light-headed.

I was a risk-taker by nature, but usually, those risks were carefully calculated based on my own knowledge and experience. This thing with Rowe was like nothing I'd ever experienced before, and there was a cacophony of voices in my head—voices that sounded like Kenji and Silas, mostly—reminding me that I should pull back *now*, but... I didn't want to.

Scary as it was to feel this way, it had been scarier still when I'd thought Rowe had walked away from me for good. I wanted a chance with him. A chance to get to know him for more than two quick days.

To see if this instant chemistry and attraction—this *potential*—between us could actually develop into something real.

Landry had reminded me that I had good instincts. It was time I trusted them.

"Come here." I led Rowe to the sofa and sat down beside him. I wanted to pull him in my arms, but I also knew that once I did, I wouldn't be letting him go, and we still had a lot more to talk about.

Of course, because he was Rowe, in spite of the seriousness of the situation, he couldn't help running a hand over the cushion like he was admiring the lines of the furniture. "This is really nice. And I love the color. Someone who really knows your style picked it out. Was it you?"

I shook my head, amused despite myself. "No, Kenji."

He nodded, then frowned as a thought occurred to him. "Do all the board members have offices here in the building? Is that common?"

Not unless you were more than simply a board member. "No. Only Silas and me, though Silas doesn't spend much time here these days. Look, Rowe—"

"I'm gonna get my notes and send them to you," he interrupted. "It's important to me that you know for a fact I'm not lying, in case later you start to wonder. I... it's stupid, maybe, but I don't want you to remember me that way... after."

"After," I repeated, not understanding. "After what?"

"After I'm back in Indiana." He folded his hands primly in his lap and kept his gaze fixed on them. "I mean, if you're saying someone's already working on an idea like this... then that's great. That's all I really wanted, you know? To have someone care about this and take the time to improve the system. And since there's no sense in me bringing it to Jus—uh, to anyone else—if Sterling Chase is already taking care of it, then I don't need to stick around New York anymore." He shrugged. "It's not the way I expected things to go, but my parents and Bobby will be thrilled I'll be home sooner than I planned, and I... I'll be content."

"Well, I fucking won't." Not with any of it. Not with someone else taking credit for Rowe's brilliance, and sure as hell not with Rowe being a thousand miles away from me.

His gaze flew to mine. "But—"

"That is not how this ends, Rowe." I gripped his chin firmly so he couldn't look away. "Before, you told me that you wanted more time with me—more time to get your project seen—before you turned back into a pumpkin. But you've gotten it all wrong from the very beginning. You're not the fucking pumpkin of this story. You're the *Prince*. And you're not going to fade back into obscurity in Linden and take all your beauty and intelligence and light with you. I won't let that happen. Do you hear me?"

He shook his head. "Bash, there's no sense in—"

"There is *every* sense. Because you deserve better, Rowe. Not for Daisy. Not for your parents. For *yourself*. It's time that both of us stop worrying about what the world wants and expects from us and start thinking about what we want for ourselves. *You only get one life, and if fear holds you back from living it the way you want, you're wasting it.* Isn't that what Daisy said?"

"Y-yes. And I want to believe that. But Bash... how am I supposed to fight this?" He threw up his hands in frustration. "Proving to you that I'm telling the truth is one thing. Proving it to everyone else in the world? Proving it to people who'll take one look at my resume and know how unlikely it is that a guy like me could come up with an idea like this? That's gonna require lawyers, and money, and time... all things I don't have. I'm just... one person."

"You aren't." I shifted closer, cupping his jaw with both hands. "Not if you don't want to be. You don't have to do any of this alone."

I could see the hesitation in his eyes, and it nearly killed me, but I understood it. It was too much to expect him to have faith in me this quickly. Not when it seemed like he hadn't had anyone who believed in him for a long while. But I would show him.

"Start with this," I said, sitting back just a little but setting a hand on his knee because I couldn't stand to break our connection entirely. "Tell me who else knows about your project."

Rowe ran a hand over his forehead, disordering his curls again. "I guess... a lot of people know *about* it. Know the general gist of it. Like I said, I've talked to my parents about the research, but they don't really get it. Same with Joey and his parents. Uh. Bobby's helped me out a little bit with the app-coding aspect, but we never really discussed the process part. And the medical people I talked to know about the research and maybe some of my ideas about the process, but not about the app, so... I don't think anyone back home really knows about the whole thing. Definitely not enough to steal the idea."

I nodded. "That's what I figured from what you explained so far." And it was too bad because it would have been convenient if there'd been a plausible explanation for how Austin had gotten the idea that wouldn't mean someone on my team—a person I'd *trusted*—had masterminded the theft of intellectual property. "Who have you shared your research with? I know you said you sent out a lot of meeting requests. Maybe you don't remember all of them—"

"Oh, no, believe me, I remember each and every one. It's almost embarrassing to admit this, but I was so new to the process that, at first, I was sending out letters one at a time, like otherwise there might be this mad stampede of people clamoring to get at this project—"

"That's not impossible. It does occasionally happen. But with Sterling and our competitors, there's a certain level of professional courtesy, mostly because it's good business strategy. If one company has already studied the feasibility of a concept with an eye toward getting a patent, it's rare that another company will pursue the same idea since that would result in a lot of legal wrangling."

"So I accidentally did the right thing? That's comforting, I guess." He rolled his eyes. "So, the first request I sent was to Sterling Chase a while ago, specifically to Austin Purcell since he's the head of development. I waited about a week, and when I hadn't heard anything back, I sent a second letter. A whole big packet of information this

time, with some background on the project and a heartfelt letter."
Rowe groaned. "If only I'd known at the time that Austin was the
kind of entitled asshole who'd threaten to withhold a burrito delivery
person's tip if the delivery guy didn't give him personally identifying
information. Anyway, then—"

"Wait, hold up. Austin did that. Just now?" My voice vibrated
with outrage.

"Yeah, downstairs. I think your guy needs some sensitivity
training."

Oh, Austin certainly needed something. I added a large black
mark to my mental tally of his offenses.

"Go on," I all but growled.

"Uh... okay. Well, three days later, I got a form-letter rejection.
Dear Mr. Prince, blah blah blah, *we do not feel that your 'Project
Daisy Chain' merits further development by our company at this time.*
It was disappointing, but I figured—ow!" Rowe winced and pushed at
my hand. "Bash, I'm gonna need this knee later."

I realized too late that I'd been squeezing Rowe's leg with
possibly bruising force. I instantly snatched my hand away. "Christ,
I'm so sorry."

"What's up with you? You were okay, and then I quoted the
rejection letter, and your face just got all..." He blinked. "Oh. Fuck.
It's Austin Purcell, isn't it? He's the one who had a similar idea to
Daisy Chain? Do you think that's why he rejected me?"

Rowe was so fucking sweet. Instead of immediately jumping to
the conclusion that someone had stolen his idea and passed it off as
their own, he was giving Austin the benefit of the doubt.

I was way past that.

Still, though, I tried to speak diplomatically. "I'm concerned that
it's a bit... worse than that."

"You think he stole it."

Okay, so maybe I hadn't spoken as diplomatically as I'd thought.

"Yeah," I admitted. "That's exactly what I think. I think he's
passing your idea off as his own."

"But... why?"

"Rowe, sweetheart." I huffed out a laugh and cupped his cheek. "You really *don't* know much about profitability, do you?" I smiled to take the sting out of my words. "MRO or Medical Response Optimization—what we've been calling the project in-house—was going to make a ton of money, and Austin was going to own the patents."

"Was?"

"Yes. *Was.* I already told Kenji we were putting the project on hold the minute I first suspected what was happening. There's no way I'm profiting off *anyone's* stolen idea. It's going to take some work to get to the bottom of everything, but we will. And Austin doesn't know it, but he made a huge fucking error when he targeted you —*ooof.*"

This time, it was Rowe who kissed me—kissed me with utter abandon, locking his arms around my neck and throwing himself bodily against me. His kiss, like so much about him, was artless and enthusiastic... and utterly devastating. I gave up the rest of my self-control and pulled him onto my lap, holding him against me and breathing him in.

The person I'd been just a week ago would have been shocked to see me now, grabbing onto the liar from the gala with both arms, embracing the chaos my life had become. But as long as I had Rowe in my arms... I didn't give a shit.

SEVENTEEN

ROWE

Being held in Bash's strong grip made me feel treasured, protected, *safe*. Like anything was possible and I was strong enough to take on the world. I wanted to stay exactly like this for hours. Days. I didn't want to question any of it... but I couldn't help it.

"How can you believe me so easily?" I asked into the side of his neck. His cologne smelled amazing, and I didn't want to pull away from him, even though I knew I should. "I lied to you most of the time we were together."

To my surprise, Bash laughed. "Rowe, I truly hate to break this to you, but you're a terrible liar. Not only did I know you couldn't possibly be Sterling—"

"Since there is no Sterling..."

"Right," he laughed. "But also, your whole body tenses up when you lie. Your voice changes. Which is how I know you told the truth a lot more than you lied."

He was right, and I really loved that he knew that. "There go my dreams of being an international spy," I mock-sighed. "I've been a horrible liar since childhood. Remind me sometime to tell you about the time I nearly drowned while pretending to drown."

He laughed again, and it rumbled through me, lodging deep in my chest. "I definitely will. For now, just know that I trust you. And we're going to work together to get as much evidence as we can for the legal team. I don't suppose you happened to secretly watermark any of the documents with 'Property of Rowe Prince'?"

"Uh, no."

"I didn't think so. Know why? Because you're the most honest liar ever." He gave me a pointed look, and I flushed. "At least Austin doesn't know we're onto him, which might make things easier."

I chewed at the side of my lip for a minute. "He recognized me, sorta. Downstairs. Even with the mustache on. He said he'd seen my picture and wanted to know my name, but I didn't tell him."

Bash's face was stormy for a moment. "Good. We'll figure out a way to get you out of here without him seeing you." He touched my face in a way that suggested he wanted to be touching other parts of me but was holding back.

I hadn't even thought of how I'd get out of here, and it melted me more that Bash had. It had been a long, long while since I'd felt like someone was looking out for me. Like I was part of a team. But nothing had really changed from that hotel back in Philly—this was all still temporary, all going to be snatched away any moment.

The only difference now was that running away wasn't an option as long as Bash needed me to prove his case.

"I can get all of my research and notes," I volunteered. "I have a ton of information Austin wouldn't have, along with all my contacts. That will help." I started to climb off Bash's lap, ready to go and collect all the notes and files from Joey's place that would now be evidence.

"Not yet." Bash grasped my hips, trying to hold me in place.

During the brief, halfhearted (on my side, at least) struggle that ensued, someone knocked on the door, and the dark-haired man from the hallway pushed his way in and leaned back against the door to close it.

"My eyes are closed," the man said in lieu of a greeting. "Super tightly closed. I'm seeing nothing."

"Kenji," Bash growled. "I told you—"

"Not to disturb you. Yes. But Silas is here, and he's on the way up."

"Silas? Why would he— Oh, for god's sake, open your eyes! Nobody's naked, *unfortunately*. Why the hell is Silas here?"

"Because Dev called earlier, and I may have mentioned the situation with Austin..." Kenji opened his eyes and saw me half-perched on Bash. "And your new friend Sterling Chase. And then he lit up your group chat, and Silas got involved."

Bash sighed, letting his head fall back onto the sofa cushion. "Kenji, this is Rowe Prince. Rowe, this is my assistant, Kenji. Do not give him that look, Kenji," he warned. "Rowe's had a fuck of a day already, okay?"

Kenji's skeptical expression didn't waver one iota. "So, then, I shouldn't observe that Mr. Prince has royally disordered everything around here?"

"Kenji, shut it."

"Or that you've been walking around here like a sad Bella Swan since Rowe did his disappearing act?"

"I have not." Now, Bash used his grip to push me off him, like he was going to jump to his feet and kick Kenji out bodily.

Before he could, I jumped up and extended a hand to Kenji. "Hi. It's nice to meet you. Sorry if I've messed things up."

Kenji glanced from my hand to my face for a moment before shaking it. "You don't need to apologize to *me*. But you'll find that I'm very—"

"Protective of Bash." I nodded. "I get it. He's way too nice."

Bash made a disbelieving noise, but Kenji's lips twitched. "I'm glad you realize it."

"Kenji," Bash said, exasperated. "Did you hear back from Legal?"

"I did—"

"Bash! What the fuck is this nonsense I'm hearing about Rowe—" Bash's friend Silas walked into the office, dressed in perfectly tailored jeans and a button-down, and stopped short. "Prince," he finished in a smaller voice.

"Hello." I felt my face go red. "Nice to see you again."

"Lock the door behind you, Silas," Bash instructed. "Since you're here, you can help us plan."

"Plan *what?*" Silas demanded after making sure the door was secured. "What's going on? Kenji said something about intellectual property theft."

"Exactly. MRO was not Austin Purcell's idea." With a hand on my shoulder, Bash led me across the room to lean against the front of his desk while Kenji sat in one of the visitor chairs, and Silas stood in the center of the room with his arms folded over his chest. My discarded sombrero lay on the floor by his feet, and I had to swallow down a nervous bubble of laughter.

Bash quickly filled both of them in on everything I'd told him, as well as some things he'd learned from Austin earlier that day, keeping me pressed against his side the entire time. I hadn't heard about his conversation with Austin, and the idea that he'd not only stolen my project but my story—Daisy's story—made my blood pressure spike.

I'd been willing to let my claim to the project go—I didn't need to get the glory, and the money still seemed impossible to me—but the idea that he was taking on my pain, my sister's death, as part of his act? That wasn't something I could let slide.

As Bash spoke, Silas's gaze flickered between us, and though he nodded along to show he was listening, the look he gave me was distinctly unfriendly. I could tell he didn't believe what he was hearing. Though I hadn't expected any different, it made my stomach queasy. Bash had sounded so firm before when he spoke about believing me, but I knew how much he loved the friends he considered his brothers. How likely was he to stay on my side if it meant risking their disapproval?

When Bash was done, Silas set his jaw. "You know, I heard from

Landry about your plan to take a more public role at Sterling Chase again. That you're dissatisfied about the direction the company's going in—"

"That has nothing to do with this," Bash insisted.

"Doesn't it? It's very convenient that all of this is happening at once, Bash. Almost like someone's been putting ideas in your head."

Bash ran a hand over his face. "Rowe isn't Justin, Silas."

"How would you know?" Silas threw out an arm toward me. "You've known this man a week—"

"And you knew Justin a whole hell of a lot longer than that," Bash shot back angrily. "And he *still* fucked you over."

I had no idea what they were talking about—Justin? As in, Justin Hardy? Whatever it was, Bash seemed to score a direct hit. Silas's face registered shock and hurt before he smoothed it out into the polite, urbane expression I remembered from the gala.

"Silas," Bash said apologetically. "I didn't mean—"

"No, of course," Silas said stiffly. "Perhaps we should all just become irrationally attached to perfect strangers. Perhaps that's where I went wrong last time."

Bash closed his eyes and tilted his head back, like he was silently begging the ceiling for patience.

"I understand why you don't believe me," I offered in a small voice. "I'm not asking you to take me at my word. I have proof. Extensive notes. Research. Contacts. Recorded interviews from as far back as five years ago. An app I coded. I can provide you with all of that."

Silas nodded once. "Good. But proving you came up with Daisy Chain is a very different thing than proving Austin did anything wrong." My confusion must've shown on my face because Silas huffed impatiently before explaining, "You can't trademark or patent an idea. And people come up with similar ideas all the time. Austin can, and probably will, claim that he was working on MRO long before he ever heard of you."

"But he stole the story about my sister!" I insisted.

"Or he had a similar experience with a friend, exactly as he told Bash. It would be very hard to prove he didn't."

I knew Silas was right, that what he said made sense, but I could feel my anger ratcheting up anyway in the face of his cold, emotionless presentation.

Bash put a hand on the small of my back and rubbed his thumb in soothing circles. "It's convenient that Austin's earliest documentation is missing from our servers when he should absolutely know better than to delete anything."

Silas inclined his head, granting Bash that point. "Still doesn't prove anything." He looked at me, narrowing his eyes. "What specifics can you provide showing that Austin personally received the paperwork you submitted?"

I blinked. "I have his rejection emails."

"Which only shows that he rejected a project called Daisy Chain. You can't prove he received your second packet containing all the background documentation. You can't prove that he stole anything. It would be his word against yours, and frankly..." He shrugged.

I knew exactly what Silas wasn't saying out loud. That anyone looking at my lackluster resume, especially someone who knew that I'd lied about being Sterling Chase, would give my claim serious side-eye.

Bash's arm closed around my waist protectively, and he bristled with anger, but I laid a hand on his thigh before he could say something he might regret. "Silas is right. We need to connect Austin to Daisy Chain somehow."

"Still no results on the search for the term Daisy Chain in our current project files," Kenji inserted quietly. "If there ever was any, it might have been in Austin's missing documents—"

Kenji broke off as someone knocked on my locked door.

"Hey, hey!" a voice called from the hall. "Bash? I was sorry you couldn't make it downstairs, but I brought you a burrito. Do you have time for a quick chat?"

"Austin," Bash muttered under his breath. "Fuck."

Kenji's teeth ground together audibly. "It's like the man doesn't understand what a closed door means. *Insufferable.*" In a louder voice, he called, "Bash and I are in a meeting, Austin. Drop the burrito on my desk and walk away."

I pressed my lips together to keep from laughing. Kenji reminded me of Daisy. I thought he was someone I might like to be friends with, under other circumstances.

"Rowe and I need to get out of here if we want to keep Austin from getting wind of this," Bash said, nodding toward the door. "We'll work remotely."

"You mean from your apartment?" Kenji rolled his eyes. "Where I can only assume Landry is, at this moment, throwing a sex orgy for every male model in the area since that's his favorite pastime when he's not gorging himself on my desk candy? I don't know why you didn't insist on him getting a hotel when he followed you home from Philadelphia."

"Shit. I'll take Rowe to my Hamptons house instead. It's private there."

Bash looked at me as if waiting for an argument, but he wasn't going to get one. For one thing, I was *in* this now, and I didn't want Austin to get away with his crimes. For another, I'd googled the Hamptons this week after Bash mentioned having a house there and found some interesting information thanks to *Real Housewives* that made me really want to see the place for myself.

And, okay, yes, I also wanted to spend every possible second with Bash while I could, but I was going to pretend that wasn't actually a factor in my decision.

Silas's exhale had attitude this time. "Sebastian, can I speak to you privately?"

"Fine." Bash gestured Silas toward the door. "Make sure Austin's not out in the hall, and I'll meet you in Kenji's office." He kissed me softly on the cheek. "I'll be back in a minute, then we'll swing by your cousin's place to get your stuff, okay?"

I nodded and tried to give him a smile, though my stomach roiled with nerves.

Once the two of them left, Kenji remained seated, his eyes on me. "Bash likes you," he said at length. It sounded a little like an accusation.

"I like him," I admitted. My gaze darted toward the closed door like I was searching for one more glimpse of Bash. "Possibly too much."

"Then you should know Bash doesn't do relationships. He doesn't fall for people. Not in the whole time I've known him."

I nodded. "And he certainly wouldn't fall for someone like me. I get it. You don't need to warn me off, Kenji. I'm very aware that he exists in a different world than I do. I don't have any long-term expectations. No hopes of a fairy-tale romance."

Oh, look who's decided to be a lying liar again. I only hoped Kenji couldn't read me as well as Bash could.

He leaned closer. "I'm not warning you off. Not at all. You seem... nice. Dedicated. Despite the lies—metric fuck tons of them, mind you—there's something strangely authentic about you. And I have to admire the way you knocked Bash's perfectly tailored life off kilter. He needed some excitement."

I snorted. "We're talking about a man who climbs mountains and jumps off cliffs. I don't think he was lacking excitement."

"Mmm. Maybe. But I think that stuff was just a mask for what he was missing: something, *someone,* in his life who was worth taking a *real* risk."

My heart beat faster with a combination of fear and excitement, but I shook my head firmly. "This... Bash and me... it's not like that. We barely know each other. It's not real at all."

"Isn't it?" He tilted his head. "Well, if that's the case, I *am* warning you off. Sebastian's falling for you. And if you don't feel the same, you need to tell him so immediately... Because if you hurt him, Rowe Prince, be aware that I have a line item in my budget dedicated to you and a bunch of contacts Upstate who can make a body disappear."

I knew exactly which part of that statement sent a shiver through my body... and it wasn't the part about me likely ending up in a shallow grave.

Still, I threw back my shoulders. "Bash is an adult. And his personal life is his own business. He's strong, and smart, and more than capable of taking care of himself. I appreciate that he has people who care about him and want to protect him, Kenji—*really*, I do—but he's too nice to draw boundaries with you, so I will: you need to mind your own beeswax and back off."

"The kitten has claws." Kenji's face creased in a smile, and he pressed his hands to his knees before standing up. "Oh yes, you'll do," he murmured nonsensically. "You'll do just fine."

I was still blinking at him in surprise when the door opened and Bash and Silas walked into the office, still arguing.

"No, Sebastian, I do *not* understand. Running off to the Hamptons right now is the worst thing you could do. If you want to get rid of Austin, fire the asshole and be done with it," Silas said angrily.

Kenji scooted behind them to close the office door before glaring at Silas. "Would you like to give the entire office a heads-up that this is happening? Keep your voice down."

Bash rounded on his friend. "And I told you, this isn't just about getting rid of Austin. Jesus, Silas. I liked Austin. I trusted him. I would much rather that none of this had happened, but it did. He stole this idea—I'm convinced of that, even if you're not—so the person you should be angry at is *Austin*, not Rowe."

"I'm not angry at Rowe!" Silas yelled back. He caught himself and gave me a look that was half-apologetic. "I'm not. Your story is very plausible, Rowe. I believe you invented Daisy Chain. But... I'm worried about all of this. I'm worried about the attention it's going to bring to the company and any legal exposure we end up battling because of all this."

"So am I." Bash propped his ass against his desk again and crossed his arms. I took a moment to appreciate how sexy this man's forearms were in a business shirt with rolled-up sleeves. Linden, Indiana, didn't have much of that, so I may have stared a little too intently at his exposed forearms. "Which means we need to do things by the book. We need to remove critical documents from Austin's reach and prove that he stole Rowe's IP *first*. If we fire him now, he'll think he has a perfect right to take his MRO idea with him to his next company. And he might even pursue a wrongful termination case. A very *public* one."

Silas's shoulders fell. "You have a point. But... shit, Bash, I want to be involved. I want you to stay in town so I can help," he admitted quietly. "I can't believe another jackass is threatening our company—*your* company—even if this one wasn't due to my fuckup."

Silas's words took a minute to sink in. *Our company. Your company.* As in... Silas and Bash felt proprietary since they were on the board of directors? Or were they shareholders in the companies that owned Sterling Chase? Or... my breath caught as the idea hit me, so clear and so *right* that I knew it was a fact immediately.

Bash and his friends had invented ETC. They had *founded* the company. And they'd hidden it from everyone.

Holy fucking shit. That explained so much, particularly why such a random group of people—a thrill seeker, a horse trainer, an uptight businessman, a rock star, and a dilettante—had been selected for Sterling Chase's board of directors.

I must've made a startled noise because Bash tugged me closer to his side.

"The situation with Justin wasn't your fault, either, Silas," Bash said. "You trusted him because that's the kind of man *you* are. Justin was an asshole who was willing to lie, cheat, and steal to build his company. That's the kind of man *he* is. I really wish you could find a way to let it go."

"Yeah." Silas blew out a breath, but the tension in his shoulders didn't change. "I'd rather *go* kick his ass."

Bash snorted. "I'm down. Though I don't think you'd need help unless the asshole fights dirty."

I barely paid attention to the conversation. I was pretty sure they were talking about Justin Hardy, and I was distantly glad I hadn't followed through on my plans to pitch my idea to Justin. He sounded like a douche—a dangerous one. I couldn't muster much curiosity for the full story, though, since I'd already reached maximum capacity for shock.

Sebastian Dayne and his friends own the company. That meant he wasn't just a millionaire from family money; he was a... a... a *billionaire*... in his own right. The divide between us had already seemed wide as an ocean. Now... now it was something that would require rocket fuel to cross.

"One last thing," Kenji said, "before Silas and I leave you to all your Mission Impossible covert operations... I do believe Austin needs a new project."

That got my attention. "Unless Dev needs some horse shit mucked, I wouldn't trust that guy to do a damn thing," I said.

Silas snorted. "Dev wouldn't let Austin near Trigger. Especially not since he's already decided he's very Team Rowe."

"He is?" I looked at Bash, but he seemed as surprised as I was.

"Jesus," Silas muttered. "Sebastian, you really need to pay attention to the group chat. But yes, he, Zane, and Landry all suggested I calm down and give you the benefit of the doubt."

"How's that working for you?" I asked sweetly.

"Don't fuck with my friend, Bandito, and you and I won't have any problems," Silas shot back.

I had the momentary urge to tell Silas off the way I had with Kenji but quickly dismissed the idea. I wouldn't be around long enough for Silas's opinion of me to matter. Bash might be "falling" for me, but who knew what that even meant for a billionaire? He'd told me in his own words that he owned entire *houses* he rarely visited and traveled around the world whenever he grew restless. What if it was only a matter of time until he lost interest in me, too?

"As I was saying, boys," Kenji cut in, "Austin can't just be left to his own devices. Legal has been informed that you're delaying MRO, but it won't be long before Austin questions it." He tapped his lip thoughtfully. "You know, I bet Clarissa is getting pretty lonely in Sierra Leone."

Bash laughed. "Devious. But it's true that she could use the help. Send Austin out to Sierra Leone tomorrow, and make sure he stays gone for a couple weeks."

Silas shook his head. "He's going to want to be here for the Innovation Awards presentation at Lincoln Center a week from Saturday. Austin was nominated for his work on CaffApp, remember? He won't miss it."

"Fuck that." Bash grimaced. "He doesn't get to receive awards. Let Clarissa have his ticket. Austin can fly home Sunday. We'll call a board meeting for Monday, where we can present our case against him. Kenji, notify the others as well as HR, okay? And follow up on those background checks. We need them ASAP."

Silas and Bash shook hands, which quickly turned into a back-slapping hug that showed all was forgiven. Silas held out a hand for me, which was probably a huge concession since I knew he still didn't trust me fully, but I couldn't make myself feel much of anything about it.

A billionaire. The guy I lo—liked more than I'd ever liked anyone —was a freaking *billionaire.* That was a number I couldn't even comprehend. That was more hairs than I had on my head. More stars than I could see in the sky. More minutes than I'd been alive. Enough money to buy the entire town of Linden, Indiana.

I vaguely heard Kenji promise to order Bash a car and Bash telling Kenji that he'd be bringing a plus-one to the awards thing before Kenji led Silas from the room.

When we were alone, Bash turned and studied me for a long moment.

"Okay, what's going on in your brain right now?" he demanded.

"Did I do or say something to upset you? Because if you're punishing me for Silas's paranoia, you might want to reconsider."

The low, commanding tone of his voice made me shiver against my will. It also made me imagine him taking that tone with me in bed while I was naked and eager to please him in any way he wanted.

"Guh." I made another embarrassing sound before blinking rapidly while trying to get my mind out of the gutter and retain my dignity.

"Silas was hurt very badly by Justin Hardy, and he doesn't trust easily anymore. This issue with Austin and the IP is bringing up a lot of things for him," Bash went on.

I nodded. "Understandable." Frankly, I understood Silas's mistrust a lot better than I understood how everyone else—including Bash himself—seemed to be taking it in stride that Bash Dayne had allied himself with Rowe Prince, the criminally poor guy from Bobby's Tech Barn and occasional Burrito Bandito.

That wasn't me feeling sorry for myself, either. I knew exactly who Rowe Prince was, and I liked him fine—nervous rambling, terrible lying skills, impetuous hyperfocus, and all. But I also knew I wasn't meant for a life centered around galas and polo matches and air-kisses.

"Are you worried about the awards banquet? Because it won't be worse than the Coalition for Children gala, and you survived that."

"No, I hadn't even thought about... wait." I frowned. "I'm the plus-one you told Kenji you were taking?"

"Of course." His lips tipped up in that irresistible smile. "You really *have* to be there. Constance will expect a certain quirky billionaire to approve her outfit."

"Oh, god," I groaned. The idea of impersonating a billionaire while on the arm of an actual billionaire fried my brain. I was going to have to beg Joey to borrow the bunny tux again.

"You'd better not be thinking of running away again," Bash warned softly.

I glanced up at that. "I didn't *run*. I made a logical, rational choice to leave you in Philly." And if I were smart, I'd have stuck to that decision. But I couldn't make myself regret it, either. Not when Bash was close enough that I could smell his cologne and feel the intensity of his gaze on me. Not when I could have one whole *week* with this man that would sustain me through a hell of a lot of lonely nights to come. I swallowed. "I'm not going anywhere. I'm going to see this through."

"Good." Bash gripped my jaw in both of his hands and pressed a slow, gentle kiss to my lips. "Because if you run from me again, Rowe, I'll come after you."

EIGHTEEN

BASH

Bringing Rowe to my house in the Hamptons was fantasy fulfillment at its finest. My only regret was the look of disappointment on his face when he saw how sterile the decor was in my house.

"Everything is... white," he said, staring at the simple squared-off sofas and matching chairs.

"I warned you. Maybe when all this is over, I can hire you to redecorate for me," I said, wondering what kind of colorful jumble he'd create in the open-plan space. I could use a few more refinished antiques. And if he wanted to do the work himself, there was a large storage shed in the backyard that the previous owners had referred to as a "chicken coop," which would be plenty large enough for him to set up a workshop.

"Maybe I won't wait that long," he teased. "Maybe I'll accidentally-on-purpose smear raspberry jam on these cushions just to give the place a little life."

I remembered the night of the gala when he'd come alive while talking to Constance Baxter-Hicks about fashion and decor. While Rowe was shy and insecure about many things, he was 100 percent himself when talking about style.

And god knew the man was good at bringing things to life.

"Stain away," I said with a laugh. "If it makes you happy, Jackson Pollock the hell out of this stuff with whatever you find in the fridge. Or order something online. Make yourself at home." He had no idea how badly I meant that. "Trying to relax in this space has always felt like putting on a tie that's a little too tight. It's hard to breathe."

Rowe's eyes softened. "We can definitely fix that." He pulled out his phone and began tapping it. "Oh, thank god. There are plenty of vintage and thrift stores around here. I hope you have a little money to spend on throw pillows at the very least."

I opened my mouth to offer him everything I had—the billion I'd made myself and the fortune I was due to inherit one day—when I closed it with a snap. This man didn't want money. He wanted many things, but wealth didn't seem to be one of them. "I believe I can afford a few pillows," I said with a straight face. "As long as they're used. Nothing I love more than putting my face somewhere a stranger has put theirs."

Rowe waved his hand at me in a dismissive gesture. "Snob. Haven't you heard of a washing machine? Or do you have a laundress of some kind?"

Before I could admit I did, indeed, have a laundress, Rowe finally caught sight of the view through the wall of windows that led to the back deck. "Holy fuck," he breathed reverently, moving closer to the expanse of dunes and wild waves.

I moved up behind him and snaked my arms around him. "Better than the white sofas?"

"So much better than the white sofas."

We watched the ocean together for a while. The rhythmic ebb and flow of the tide was soothing, reminding me that there were bigger things in the world than Sterling Chase—bigger even than the knowledge that yet another person I'd trusted had betrayed me *and Rowe* right under my nose. A reminder, too, that not everything in life was predictable or understandable, but that didn't mean it couldn't be beautiful and *right*... like the way I'd met the man beside me under the most ridiculous circumstances and the way I felt about him now.

I turned my face to press a soft kiss behind Rowe's ear. "Thank you for coming out here with me," I murmured into his sweet-smelling skin. Holding him in my arms made me feel both anchored and restless. I wanted him with a solid desperation that was crawling under my skin, but I was in no hurry since we had an entire week together away from the rest of the world.

Rowe tilted his head to give me more access. "It was hardly a sacrifice," he said with a smile in his voice. "It was this or ramen noodles and a futon. You won by a hair."

I continued nibbling on his neck. "Who says I'm not serving ramen noodles?"

Rowe's laughter was warm and easy. There had been a moment, after Silas and Kenji had left my office, when I'd felt Rowe pulling away from me, even though he was right beside me. I still wasn't sure what had been going through his mind, but knowing he was relaxing now helped calm me further. "Have you ever even *had* ramen noodles?" he asked.

I'd eaten them plenty in college, but because I was addicted to seeing Rowe's smile, I said haughtily, "I'll have you know I've eaten ramen at Mr. Taka in the Lower East Side."

Rowe spun in my arms. "Isn't that the place that has a freaking Michelin star? That hardly counts."

His grin was contagious. I leaned over to press my lips against it and taste him. "You're so easy to rile."

We kissed for a long, unhurried moment, letting ourselves settle into it. I'd kissed Rowe enough that the taste of his mouth and the feel of his body under my fingertips were familiar, but that familiarity only made it more exciting.

My hands snuck under his shirt to spread across the warm skin of his back. His hard cock pressed into my inner thigh. I was torn between taking my time with him and ripping his clothes off like a savage beast. In the end, I found a sweet middle ground, undressing him quickly with my hands while teasing him slowly with my lips and nose.

Every time I ran my nose lightly under his ear or against his cheek, he shuddered and let out a delicious noise of submission and abandon.

I moved him over to one of my sterile white sofas with the sole purpose of acting on every single sex fantasy I'd had about the man since the moment I'd met him.

"We're going to mess up your perfect furniture," he said in a gasp as I bit into the tender skin of his bare neck.

"Good."

"We... we're going to horrify the neighbors with all these glass windows and doors." Rowe ended with a long, drawn-out groan as I moved my hand down into his briefs to fondle his dick. "Oh. God. *Fuckkk.*"

"Neighbors can go fuck themselves," I said before sucking on one of his nipples.

"Just like that." He reached his fingers into my hair and scratched my scalp lightly, which made my skin prickle with need. "Touch me."

I fondled his balls and tried to remind myself we had an entire week together. "You smell fucking amazing," I said, moving my mouth down across his stomach to his happy trail. The top of his tattoo peeked out over the waistband of his briefs. I ran a thumb across it and down below the elastic. "I want to lick every inch of your skin."

"Start with my penis. Just a suggestion." Rowe's voice was rougher and deeper. He sounded more confident than he had before. I hoped the experience we'd already had together had contributed to his comfort with me. "Not a suggestion, actually," he hissed as I teased the area around his cock without touching it directly. "Command. Superstrong command. Suck me. Please. Pretty please."

I adored this man. He was sexy and sweet, an intoxicating blend of vulnerability and masculinity that fired all my engines.

My mouth hovered over his cock, and the warm, humid air from my exhales made the fabric of his briefs damp. Rowe's entire body thrummed with anticipation.

"I hate you," he said. "This is torture. This is horrible."

I yanked down his underwear and sucked the head of his cock into my mouth. Rowe yelped.

"I fucking love you," he cried. "This is heaven. This is the best."

I wanted to laugh. He made me feel so many things all the damned time. Suddenly, it felt like my life was about someone else. Pleasing him. Reassuring him. Impressing him. Listening to him. Learning about him. Adoring him.

All of it seemed possible. A fantastical future laid out before us on the golden trail of sunlight that danced across the ocean water outside the windows. In that moment, I felt like I could have it all.

And I could have it with Rowe Prince.

My mouth held him while my tongue danced around his shaft. I proceeded to defile him, sucking his cock and fucking him with spit-slick fingers. The sexy flush mottling his neck and chest made my dick hard as granite, so I yanked at the button and zippers on my pants until I was fisting my dick while sucking him off.

Rowe grabbed my hair and pulled as he shouted his release into the room. The sound of his broken voice crying out my name was enough to make me come all over myself and the stupid white sofa. I lurched up to take his mouth in mine and roll us until we were side by side, a dirty mash-up of panting breaths, sweat, saliva, and semen.

"More," Rowe said with a cheeky grin.

I barked out a laugh and leaned back with a groan. "You're with an old man, cutie. There's no more in the tank for a little while."

He reached out and ran the tip of his finger across my forehead and down my temple to my cheek and jaw. The tender affection in his expression didn't help my breathing slow down in the least bit. "Thirty's not so old," he said dreamily. "Seems like you're just right."

We lay there staring at each other and sharing small touches and kisses until I realized someone's phone was buzzing insistently from wherever we'd dropped our clothes.

"Real life is intruding," I murmured, unable to take my fingers out of his adorable curls. "Make it stop."

He groaned for a long moment before smacking a quick kiss to my lips. "We did come here with a plan," he reminded me. "Maybe we should execute that plan."

"Or what if we make a new plan? A plan called Sebastian and Rowe Christen Every Room of This House."

"Hmm. I like it. How many rooms here?"

"So many," I said fervently.

Rowe's light laugh was enough to keep me there in his arms for a few more minutes before I finally pushed off the sofa and reached out a hand to pull him up. "Duty calls. And let's order some food, too. I haven't fed you in a while."

"Good idea." He looped his arms around my neck. "I could go for a beer and some of that snack mix we had last weekend."

"Hmm. I dunno. I'm craving *burritos—*"

Rowe snickered, pressing his face to my chest.

"Do you suppose Burrito Bandito delivers out here? I heard they have this hot-as-fuck delivery person who does a little toe-kick move, but I haven't seen it yet..."

Rowe pinched my waist, and I jumped back. "I'll show you a toe-kick," he threatened, eyes dancing as his fingers made grabby motions toward me. He chased me into my bathroom, where we spent long, gorgeous minutes teasing each other under the hot spray.

It was a long time later when we finally dressed, ordered our food —burgers, not burritos—and settled at the kitchen table with our laptops to return Kenji's calls.

"Bash, made much headway on your research?" Kenji said over the speaker, his voice just a shade too innocent. "Since you didn't return my call immediately, I can only assume you've found a crucial piece of information and you've been working tirelessly."

Rowe blushed and bit his lip, looking a bit guilty, but I didn't feel guilty in the slightest. Despite my very real concerns about Sterling Chase, with Rowe at my side, none of it felt as overwhelming or heavy as it might have even a few weeks ago. Only the knowledge that this mattered to Rowe, too, had kept me from dragging Rowe out onto the balcony so I could make love to him until the sun set.

"Stop teasing, or I'll tell Landry you're bored and need him to come keep you company," I said blandly.

Kenji sobered quickly. "Our investigator already found some interesting information about Austin." I could hear the familiar tap of his fingers on his tablet. "First of all, he's exactly who he claims to be. All of his education and work experience from his resume are accurate. However... did you realize that Austin got his MBA from NYU's business school five years ago?"

I frowned, though he couldn't see me. "So?"

"So, that was the same year Justin Hardy got his MBA from the same school. Not something I would have put together," he admitted, "but the investigator we're using is the same one we used when we investigated Justin after he and Silas broke up, so it pinged for her right away. Turns out, Austin and Justin worked with the same professor as partners on a special research project for Troy Innovation Lab about boosting profitability of startups."

"Huh." It wasn't a surprise that Austin knew Justin somehow, but discovering they'd worked closely together on a graduate studies project *was*. "Is there a way to find out if they're still in regular contact?"

"There is, and they *are*. Both of them are registered mentor alumni at NYU Stern, and they're still working with that same professor. And what's even more interesting? Austin's latest HR recommendation—Felicia Ullney—was recruited from that program. It also looks like several of the grad students have been recruited to work at Hardy Development."

I couldn't decide if that was suspicious or not. "They might just be loyal to their grad school. Why wouldn't they recruit from its program?"

Kenji made a sound of agreement. "Exactly what I'd think, but get this... apparently, Austin and Justin have helped not one but *three* other sets of partners who worked on the Troy project. In every case, *one* person from the partnership got recruited by Sterling Chase, and the *other* went to Hardy Development. That makes three people at Sterling who are close to Hardy employees. Almost like Justin and Austin planned this out. Interesting, no?"

"Very," Rowe agreed. "How did the investigator discover this so quickly? Finding out who was paired up for a school project doesn't seem easy."

"Ordinarily not, but this professor has published his students' group projects on a departmental website, so it's very easy to see who was paired up, as well as the title of their project." He paused. "Wanna know the title of the project Austin and Justin co-authored?"

Rowe and I exchanged a glance. "I'm gonna hate this, aren't I?" I sighed.

"*Using Strategic Teaming, and Power and Professional Influencing to Facilitate Out-of-the-Box Acquisitions.*"

Out-of-the-box acquisitions. My stomach dropped. "You..." I didn't even know where to begin. "You're shitting me. They wrote a paper on how to steal clients?"

"I'm trying to get my hands on that project or at least find more information on it. In the meantime, I'm pulling records from any of our employees who have any relation to NYU Stern, and the investigator is trying to find what she can on the ones at Hardy. That's obviously more difficult."

"What can I do from here?" I asked, reaching over to squeeze Rowe's hand. "What can *we* do?"

"Other than getting all of Rowe's material together, I'm not sure." Kenji sighed. "Legal is opening up an investigation. They'll be getting access to Austin's files as early as tomorrow, and with any luck, there'll be backup of one of the documents he 'deleted' that will be a smoking gun. But god, what wouldn't I give to be able to get into his emails and see what the hell he and Justin Hardy have been talking about. If only it wasn't, you know, illegal."

"It's not illegal. All employees know Sterling Chase email

accounts are subject to oversight by management and HR," I reminded him.

"Yeah, but would he be stupid enough to use company email?" Rowe asked at the same time Kenji said, "I mean his *personal* email, Bash."

"Oh." I thought about it for a moment. "Do we have any hackers on speed dial?"

Rowe opened his mouth like he was about to say something, then shut it again.

"What?" I prompted.

"Well... if Austin's stupid enough to use his work computer to check his personal email or messages—like, from Slack, or Facebook, or even his texts—you could remotely install a keystroke tracker and see his activity." He held up a hand before I could pepper him with questions. "Yes, it's legal to install a keystroke tracker on company-owned computers. I don't know specifically about New York laws, but most employee privacy laws don't protect personal email if it's accessed on a company-owned computer or on a company-owned network. In other words, the company has a legal right to all data created, viewed, or managed on the computers they own."

"Holy shit. Thank you, Bobby's Tech Barn," Kenji said excitedly.

Rowe laughed. "Bobby acts as the IT department for a couple of local companies. Miss Melly was very concerned that one of the ladies from her yarn shop was watching porn during work hours. It turned out that she hadn't accessed anything more exciting than cat videos. But we did the same thing at one of the local credit unions, and they were able to prosecute a teller for fraud," he said proudly.

"Kenji, who do we trust in IT who could do this?" I asked.

"Rachel Reynosa," he said without hesitation. "She can help us, and she's no fan of Austin's."

"Perfect. See if she can call us today. I'm happy to authorize overtime."

While we waited for Rachel to contact us, Rowe pulled up his cloud storage account to walk me through his research for Project

Daisy Chain and even showed me his early notebooks of ideas. If I'd been impressed with the man before—and I fucking *had*—it was nothing compared to how I felt after seeing the enormous amount of research he'd compiled. Document after document, page after page, told the story of his dedication to making this project a reality. There were articles from medical journals, screenshots of newspaper headlines, reams of notes from his conversations with the Montgomery County and Tippecanoe County Health Departments, email after email from hospital administrators. And that didn't even begin to touch the literal hours of interviews he'd recorded.

Still, when he showed me the earliest incarnations of the app he'd coded, Rowe seemed almost apologetic. "It's so basic and clunky. I really had no clue what I was doing—"

I grabbed him by the back of the neck and kissed him on the mouth, stopping the apologies with my lips. "Rowe, some people go to school for *years* and don't manage anything this incredible. The idea that you managed this on your own... is there nothing you can't do if you put your mind to it?"

He gave me one of his gorgeous blushes. "Some things are still pretty hard for me to understand," he whispered. "Like how I slid into an alcove behind a potted plant a week ago and ended up here with you right now."

"I'm just glad that you did," I said firmly.

Our burgers arrived, and we worked as we ate, taking turns stealing each other's french fries as we carefully assembled the key pieces of information to send to Sterling Chase's head attorney. At my urging, Rowe also copied all of his data to an additional cloud storage account to make sure it was well backed up for his own protection.

By the time Rachel contacted us, Rowe and I had finished cleaning up our meal—a process that took a lot longer than it should have since my wet, soapy hands insisted on going lots of places besides the kitchen sink—and he was standing in my personality-less living room, gesturing wildly as he talked about feng shui and golden ratios with every bit of the same excitement that he'd talked about polo hooks and penalty points.

Every word out of his mouth, every second in his presence, made me feel alive. Like the world was filled with more possibility than I'd ever let myself recognize. And for the first time, I started to see how my own attitude toward money had held me back. I was like Aladdin's genie—phenomenal power and money at my fingertips but shackled by my own ideas... until Rowe had set me free.

"I love it," I told him when he finally finished speaking, before his nerves rushed back. "I agree with everything you're suggesting. Let's make it happen."

"You sure?" Rowe asked, waving around the room as if his ideas had already manifested inside the space. "I mean, you're gonna have to do some of the work."

"Positive," I assured him. Because the picture Rowe had painted with his words was of something much bigger and wilder than a new living space—it looked like my future. And I couldn't wait.

Rachel's call was another sobering reminder that we had stuff to deal with first, though. While she and Rowe videoconferenced at the kitchen table for an hour, speaking in a technical language that would have made way more sense to Silas than it did to me, I made notes and took a few more calls from the attorneys. The patent applications in Austin's name hadn't been submitted yet, which meant we could pause them indefinitely. Applying for the patents on Rowe's behalf would have been my ideal next step, but it wasn't something I could or would do without his consent.

By the time he wrapped up his call with Rachel, Rowe was red-faced with excitement. "Sterling Chase already uses keystroke tracking, so Rachel had access to the data without having to install it. She was able to pull his recent history, and guess what? Rachel discovered several texts between Austin and Justin."

He looked down at his hastily scribbled notes on the back of the brown paper takeout bag. "There were three in particular that caught our attention. One arranged an introduction between Justin and someone named Inessa. Not much info to go on for that one, but Rachel said she thought the name was familiar. One was a text exchange where Austin seemed to be congratulating Justin on something called 'the Odegard matter.' The third was—"

"Wait," I said. "Odegard? You're sure that's what he said?"

"Yeah." Rowe typed a few keys on his laptop. "She sent me the logs. It's... here." He turned the computer in my direction. "See? 'Congrats on the Odegard matter. You owe me dinner at Mastros. Name the night.' Does that mean something to you?"

"Yes," I said grimly. "It means that all this time, Silas thought Justin used *him* to steal a client Silas was trying to sign to Sterling Chase. But it looked like Silas wasn't Justin's only source of information." I picked up my phone to text Kenji. "Send those keystroke logs to me?"

ME

> Ask the investigator to see if she can find a connection between Austin, Justin, and Odegard.

KENJI

> Silas's Odegard?? WTF??

ME

> This is getting dirty. Sending you transcripts from Austin's computer.

KENJI

> On it.

I tossed my phone on the table and rubbed my hands over my face. "Do I even want to know what the third text said?"

Rowe's forehead crinkled in concern, but he glanced back at his notes.

"The third thing was Austin messaging someone else about Justin. Rachel doesn't have an ID on the number yet, but the message read, 'Hardy's so into the game, he's legit marrying some chick for her IP.' Is Justin engaged? Was he... didn't he... date Silas?"

"Yes. He did." Adrenaline spiked in my gut. Even though Silas hated Justin now, hearing that Justin had moved on would probably crush him. He'd also want to kill the man for using someone else like this. "Just when I thought I couldn't loathe that fucker any more than I already do."

"You should tell Silas. He should hear it from you and not through the gossip mill."

I nodded. "I'm ninety-nine percent sure Kenji will already be relaying this information to the brotherhood. And we'll be there for Silas if he needs us."

"I know you will." Rowe stood and came around the table to rub my shoulders. "I'm sorry. This whole thing sucks. Money doesn't buy happiness, huh?"

I snorted tiredly. "Definitely not."

"But it does buy nice beach houses." He slid his small frame between the chair and the table, straddling my lap. His grin was pure playful temptation. "Beach houses with a truly excessive number of *rooms*, many of which haven't been christened."

I pulled him closer and slanted my mouth over his before filling my hands with his delectable ass. "We're gonna have to rectify that right away," I told him, breaking away only long enough to suck on the long column of his neck. "Starting with this one."

NINETEEN

ROWE

In all the sexual fantasies I'd had about being with a man I cared about, I'd never imagined falling off a chair mid-grind and laughing my way through a dirty sixty-nine with a billionaire on the dining room floor of a multimillion-dollar beach mansion.

But then, I'd never, ever, even in my wildest dreams, imagined Bash.

"Oh fuck, *yes*, just like that," he grunted as I practiced my newfound oral skills on him. "I think I'm lying on your shoe."

I sucked the head of his cock and jacked the shaft with my hand just as he swallowed me to the back of his throat. "Shit, fuck," I gasped. My knee scraped along the area rug and knocked the leg of the chair behind me, which then bumped the table and sent a pen and notebook tumbling over the edge to land on my shoulder. "Your interior designer should be drawn and quartered. The sisal rug isn't functional."

Bash snorted. His face was flushed and his lips slick with spit. "I don't think she was imagining the dining room would *function* quite this way. You have ink on your shoulder."

"Don't care," I said, breath heaving between sucks and licks. "Shut up and keep going."

As soon as I saw him take my dick back into his mouth, I let go. A cross between a grunt and a whimper left me as my orgasm struck. I did my best to keep jacking Bash, but I wasn't the best multitasker. Within seconds, Bash shoved me onto my back on the rough rug and bit out a quick "Can I?" before putting his cock against my lips.

I opened happily and sucked him down again, grabbing his bare ass with my fingers and encouraging him to fuck my face. It was a filthy scramble on the floor, the two of us sweaty and grunting as he thrust deep into my throat, causing me to gag, but as soon as I swallowed his release and tried catching my breath, Bash lay propped beside me, slowing his touches down to a gentle caress, a sweet tenderness that made my eyes sting.

"You okay?" he murmured between soft kisses to my cheek and neck.

"Mmhm."

"You did so good. You sure I didn't hurt you? Is your back scratched up?"

It was. It definitely was. And I was going to feel it in the morning. But...

"I liked it." My voice was wrecked. "A lot," I said, just to hear the result of the experience again. It made me feel grown-up somehow, which would have made me sound hopelessly childish if I'd tried explaining it to anyone. But I was finally here experiencing sexual pleasure with another man. And not just any man.

Sebastian Dayne was gorgeous and sexy. Smart and strong. He was an intoxicating combination of confidence and charisma. It wasn't that he was too good for me—Daisy would have hated my insecurity, so I fought it—but it was impossible not to think that his life full of mansions, and cars with drivers, and high-powered corporate negotiations, and billions of dollars was not where I belonged.

"What are you thinking?" Bash asked. His fingers moved gently through the damp hair on my chest, and his spent cock lay sticky against the outside of my thigh.

"I want to do everything with you," I said, admitting a different truth because I couldn't bring myself to spoil the moment. "I like seeing you come. I like sharing that with you. There's nowhere I'd rather be right now."

Bash's face lit up enough to strike my insecurity down. Seeing the joy on his face was worth exposing my vulnerability to him.

"Nowhere else?" he teased, glancing up at the table beside us and the chairs that had been knocked askew. "I was thinking maybe next time we could aim for someplace less dangerous, like a nice comfy bed. But I should have remembered how fond you were of furniture."

"What can I say, Bash?" I said in my quirky billionaire voice. "Sterling Chase lives on the edge. You should see him under an antique desk."

"Oh, believe me, that's on the list, sir." Bash sighed happily. "Bubbles's loss is definitely my gain."

I laughed out loud, then winced as the motion did not-great things for my abraded skin.

Bash rolled, pulling me on top of him, and stroked my cheek. "I feel exactly the same, you know. As much as I hate the reason we have to be here, there's nowhere else I'd rather be."

We stayed like that for a while, touching and teasing and flirting until the discomfort of dried sweat and semen mixed with the hard floor finally urged us to get cleaned up.

Thankfully, the ease between us continued over the next several days. In fact, he was so sweet, and things were *so* easy, it was hard to remember all the reasons I shouldn't get too comfortable.

In this bubble, just Rowe and Bash, it was easy to forget about pesky real-world things, like the people in Linden, Indiana, who were expecting me back any day now. Or how many favors I was going to owe Joey for taking over all my shifts for the week. Or the responsibilities that came with Bash's wealth, like running Sterling Chase. Or the knowledge that all of this peace would end in a disastrous blaze once Bash confronted Austin back in the city next week.

Over the next few days, we returned to our work pulling data together, taking breaks now and then to walk hand in hand on the beach and enjoy every hot inch of each other's bodies in bed at night. Sleeping with Bash was a dream... one I didn't want to wake from *ever*. His warm, solid presence, usually with strong arms wrapped around me or thick thighs thrown over my legs, was better than any fantasy.

Unlike that first night we'd spent together, nothing was off-limits anymore. With no lies between us, we were free to be entirely ourselves. And every minute I spent with the real Bash Dayne, I liked him more.

One silver lining of Austin being a thieving asshole was that he'd proven Daisy Chain was a viable product, and I peppered Bash with a million business questions while we showered or relaxed on the sofa with our laptops: What was needed to bring the idea to the market-place? What would be involved in the municipality beta test? What would the future stages of development look like?

Bash didn't merely humor me with his answers, either. It was clear he knew a lot about the project already and had brainstormed dozens of ideas for improving it. On some points, like the need for a satellite uplink, we agreed completely. On others, like the amount of training the system would require, we argued passionately, but even *that* was kind of great because it showed how invested he was in this concept that, for so long, had felt like my burden to bear alone.

Also, I couldn't lie—it was hot as fuck to see how his brain worked. I hadn't known I had a competency kink until I heard Bash effortlessly calculate potential return on investment and expose pitfalls of my idea I'd never have anticipated myself. Watching his eyes spark and his face flush as he argued made me rock hard.

"If you think the interface will be complex enough to require training, I'd contend that we need to change the interface rather than

—what are you doing?" he demanded as I moved his laptop to the coffee table and slid to the floor in one smooth movement.

I knelt between his knees, pushing them wide, and yanked his legs, forcing him to slide down the sofa.

"Say ROI again," I whispered, running my palms up his thighs through his thin sweatpants. "Tell me more about cost-benefit analyses."

Bash's eyes sparked with a fire that had nothing to do with training protocols.

"If this is your attempt to win the argument—" Bash began, but he broke off in a moan when I mouthed his cock through the fabric. His hands flew to the back of my head, holding me in place as his hips instinctively bucked.

I pulled back so I could grasp his waistband with both hands... then paused. "Sorry, what were you saying, Bash?" I prompted, all wide-eyed innocence. "I didn't mean to interrupt you."

"I believe I was admiring Sterling Chase's oral negotiation style," Bash said roughly. "Very effective, sir. Please continue."

"Do you think?" I let the backs of my fingers graze over his happy trail, and his cock twitched. "I'm happy to take the lead in any client meetings if my skills would be helpful—"

Before I knew it, I was on my back on the pristine white sofa with a very possessive, very aroused Bash looming over me. "Absolutely fucking not," he growled. Then he proceeded to thoroughly prove his point.

In the end, I liked to think we both won.

In the back of my mind, I knew this was all too good to be true—that Bash had never mentioned anything long-term, and we were once again on borrowed time—but I forced myself to stay in the moment, to enjoy every single second of him while I could.

On Tuesday morning, when Rachel was out of the office, Kenji was busy working on something for Silas, and the stress of waiting to hear back from the investigator had started getting to both of us, I convinced Bash to leave the house and visit a thrift store with me.

"The white and beige is hurting my brain," I insisted, looking over at the boring living room from my spot at the kitchen table. "I'll think better after shopping. And we won't spend much, I promise."

"What if I told you I like neutral tones?" he said grumpily.

I nudged his leg with my toes. "I'd say you're lying. You hate it more than I do."

He snorted and shoved a bite of toast in his mouth.

I sipped my second cup of coffee and scrolled through my phone, reading a string of texts Joey had sent.

> **JOEY**
>
> Dude. This Sandwich Shark guy is like a fucking Visa card—he's everywhere I wanna be.

> **JOEY**
>
> I park the truck for the Monday lunch rush? Guess who shows up a minute later and parks right beside me.

> **JOEY**
>
> I go to the Glass Elephant Tuesday night to meet Chloe for a beer? Sandwich Shark's already drinking with his friends.

> **JOEY**
>
> I park the truck in the lot last night after the longest day in Burrito Bandito history? Fucking Sandwich Shark's there, too, and he hands me a Chicken Parm with extra mozzarella, WHICH HAPPENS TO BE MY FAVORITE, and it's still warm.

> **JOEY**
>
> And he says... get this... he says, 'Sleep well, Joe.'

> **JOEY**
>
> Like, WTF is that even? Fucking diabolical, that's what. How can I sleep with his song in my head?

JOEY

BTW, what kind of lube do gay guys use?
Just curious.

JOEY

Also... how do you know if a guy likes you?
I mean, the kind of like where he wants to
rail you into a mattress? Everyone says girls
are hard to read, but dudes are waaaay
more complex.

I tried hard not to connect these dots to form a picture... and failed.

The texts from my parents were a whole lot less amusing. And in fact, I found myself stifling a groan.

"Problem?" Bash asked. "Something from the investigator?"

"No, no, nothing about that at all. Just messages from my parents."

"Ah. They must miss you."

"Maybe. My mother's worried that I've joined a cult or 'fallen in with a bad crowd.' Dad says Bobby needs another guy at the Tech Barn, and he's talking about hiring one of our neighbors." I clicked my phone off and slid it into my pocket. "I need to call them, but not right now." That would pop this bubble instantly. "Wanna go?"

"Yeah." Bash carried our dishes to the sink.

"No second thoughts?" I teased.

"About letting you have your way?" He shook his head as he walked back to me. "I know what I'm in for. Remember, I've seen you in a bunny bow tie, pulling rainbow-colored hankies out of your pocket at the MoMA."

I stared at him. No doubt my face was turning scarlet right before his eyes. "You... you saw that? Oh my god. I was so embarrassed. Stupid Joey and his stupid magician tux." I took a breath. "At least it was colorful."

Bash's bark of laughter made my heart skip several quick beats like a smooth stone skipping brightly over still water.

This. Him.

Him.

I wanted more time with him like I wanted to breathe clean air... like I wanted to splash bright colors across this stark house, like I wanted to run pell-mell down the beach with Bash hot on my heels, like I wanted to put Project Daisy Chain out into the world and watch others thrive.

"You ready?" he asked, pushing back from the table and raising his eyebrows.

"So ready," I said, and in that moment, I meant it. If Bash wanted to fly me to the moon, I would go.

I pushed the inevitable goodbye out of my mind.

————

"Absolutely no. Not in my house," Bash insisted. "Not now, not ever."

I looked at the turquoise rotary telephone in my hands. "It's a 1973 floral Empress. How could you not want this? It's a steal," I teased. "Do you have any idea what an incredible conversation piece this would be?"

I would say this for the Hamptons—even the items in the thrift store here were higher quality than most of the stuff I found in Linden. My fingers itched to buy some of these pieces, restore them to glory, and decorate some of the nearly empty bedrooms in Bash's house. Unfortunately, the price tags on these items were higher, too, and it was hard to stop counting pennies, no matter how many of them Bash had.

"It's ugly and hasn't seen a dustcloth in the new millennium. I can't even imagine how many smears of lipstick have touched the mouthpiece. Pick something else. Hell, anything else."

I set the phone back on a shelf and patted its handset. "Someone will love you again one day," I murmured. "I promise."

"Weirdo," Bash said with an affectionate grin. He pointed to a stack of colorful but inexpensive throw pillows. "What about these?"

"Pfft. Cheap reproductions," I said in a low enough voice to not be overheard by the employee at the counter. "Move along."

We came to a vintage velvet-and-silk throw in deep green, Kelly blue, and rich berry colors, which was being sold for a song—possibly because it didn't coordinate with anyone's minimalist decor. I couldn't help my happy sigh. "We're getting it. If you don't like it, don't tell me. Get it anyway and consider it my payment for sexual services rendered this week."

Bash grabbed it and bundled it under his arm without even looking at the tag. "Done. What else?"

"You're not going to argue about how many people's skin cells have sloughed off onto it over the years?"

He made a face. "Are you trying to gross me out?"

I nudged his arm with my shoulder. "No. I'm just surprised at how quickly you agreed."

"I'd do anything to put the look on your face you got when you saw this," he said.

I wanted to tell him he already did. That I couldn't remember the last time I'd let myself enjoy anything as much as I was enjoying this time with him, even though the unanswered messages from my parents made my phone feel like a lead brick in my pocket.

Instead, I leaned up to press a kiss against the edge of his mouth. "You're an easy mark," I whispered.

The sound of his laugh was enough to convince me what he'd said was true. If making me happy felt anything to him like the way making him laugh felt to me, I could understand his willingness.

And if it soothed some little place inside me to think that Bash might think of me every time he saw this throw on his couch, long after this week was over and I was back in Linden... well, that was my own business.

After selecting a pair of abstract paintings of colorful flowers from a local artist, we checked out and put our selections in the Land Rover Bash kept at his Hamptons house. We walked through a few more shops and made our first major purchase—an Art Deco walnut armoire with a hidden compartment that had made me catch my breath at how stunning it was... and then again once I saw the price tag. I tried to hurry Bash along, but it was too late. He'd already noticed my one-sided love affair with the piece and arranged with the clerk to have it sent to his house later in the week.

"You can tell me where it needs to go and what needs to be done with it then," Bash insisted, strolling me out of the store and down the street. He paused in front of a quaint-looking cafe and inhaled the yeasty scent from inside. "Let's get lunch."

Bash is a grown man who can decide how he spends his money, I told myself repeatedly as we walked inside. The decor was charming —funky and colorful, with gleaming wood tables and sunshine streaming in the windows—exactly the sort of place I loved. *Relax and enjoy this, Rowe.*

But all my bold self-talk evaporated when the host handed us menus.

"Twenty-five dollars for a turkey sandwich?" I squeaked when I saw the prices. "Let's go home."

"It's a panini." Bash's calm response was betrayed by his grin. "On rustic, artisan bread."

"Does grilling the bread truly cost the extra twenty bucks? Seriously? Who the hell wants to live in a town that—" I stopped abruptly when I realized the server had arrived. An older woman with laugh lines next to her eyes asked if I preferred still or sparkling water. "Which one is free?" I asked.

Bash's feet trapped mine under the table, and his soft laughter surrounded me, so infectious our server joined in.

"Neither," she said with a wink. "If you want free water, the restroom taps are your best bet."

My jaw dropped, and Bash grinned. "She's kidding. Still is fine. I'll also take a limeade. Rowe, would you like wine or a cocktail?"

I glanced at the drinks menu and tried not to choke at the prices listed. "No, thank you."

"He'll try the rum punch," Bash said, raising that devastating eyebrow and daring me to contradict him. "Thanks."

Once she'd left, he met my eyes. "Lunch is on me. I should have said that before."

I felt a hot flush of embarrassment and stared out the window at the shoppers strolling by. "I hope so," I grumbled, "or else I'll be washing dishes in the back room after this."

He reached across the small table to grab my hand. "I'm sorry you feel uncomfortable. I should have thought about it before I suggested this place. I thought you'd like it."

"I did. I *do*. I like it so much, Bash, and I love that you picked it. I just..." I swallowed my pride and tried to set my nerves aside. "Last Monday night, I went on the website for the Malachite and nearly had a heart attack when I realized how much I have to pay you back for my half of the night we spent there. And the stuff for the house is one thing, since that's yours, but this lunch... I don't want you spending money on me, Bash." I chanced a saucy grin. "Sterling Chase is a sure thing. You don't need to wine and dine me. Okay?"

"But I like it," he said slowly. "I like seeing you smile. Giving you new experiences. And there's no way you're paying me back for the hotel when that was my idea."

"It's easy to say that when you have money. Not being able to pay my way makes me feel..." Inadequate. Useless. Like a freeloader. "Like a turtle in the wrong shell. You live in a very different world than I do."

Bash pulled my hand up to kiss my knuckles. "I like your shell. I want you to wear whatever shell you want and know that you are a one-of-a-kind turtle."

While his words warmed me, I had to doubt them. "You've known me for a week. I don't want you to look back and think I'm using you—" I broke off at his intense gaze.

"It's been twelve days," he corrected. "But you bring up a really good point. For twelve days, you've made me laugh more than anyone I've ever met, you've given me better advice than any corporate coach ever could, and you spent hours working to correct a problem that *my* company—a company I'm on the board of directors of—caused when their employee attempted to defraud you of your life's dream. We need to figure out how I'm going to repay you for all of that."

"What?" I demanded, affronted. "I would never want repayment —" I caught myself and sighed. "Which is your point," I grumbled.

"Yup. Rowe, I told you—there's nothing I like better than seeing you smile, whether we're watching polo, or sitting on the couch, or eating overpriced paninis. Being with you isn't something I could possibly put a value on. You use your talents to help people all the time, and you give that gift freely. Money happens to be one of the things I have to give, and choosing to share it doesn't have to create entitlement or negative feelings. *You* were the person who helped me realize that. So, I don't want to dismiss your feelings about this, but I'd really like you to try to understand mine. Okay?"

What the hell was I supposed to say to something that heartfelt except... "I'll try." And then, because I didn't know how long this moment of bravery and maturity would last, I found myself blurting out the hard questions. "Then what? What happens after Monday, after the board meeting where you confront Austin with the evidence of his fraud? What happens to... to me? What happens to Project Daisy Chain?"

Bash leaned closer and cupped the side of my face. His touch was so affectionate and gentle I closed my eyes to savor it. "Anything you want."

We were interrupted by the server delivering our drinks. I hid my goofy adoration for Bash behind the Mason jar of sweet punch topped by a stack of fresh fruit and a floppy flower of some kind.

"Motherfucker," I groaned after taking the first sip. "I would sell that antique throw blanket for another one of these if I had to."

"But you don't have to. Because you know that I'll buy you as many as you want, just for the pleasure of watching you enjoy them." Bash leaned in to kiss the sweetness from my lips. I tasted the lime and vodka on his and thought for a split second that I'd never been in a more perfect moment than this.

And then it got even better.

Bash said, "Of course, Sterling Chase would be honored to continue bringing your concept to market, if you'd trust us to. I would make sure you got the best possible terms."

I gaped at him, unable to say a word.

"Before you tell me to fuck off," Bash said quickly, "hear me out—"

What? "Why would I tell you to fuck off?"

"Because Sterling Chase was the company that defrauded—"

I clamped a hand over his mouth. "We've already established that wasn't on you or the rest of the board. As long as anyone involved in the fraud isn't part of the project moving forward—"

"Fuck no," he muttered against my palm before pulling my hand away. "I will get to the bottom of this and root out everyone who was involved. I promise."

I took a deep breath and felt the stress of all the years of pursuing my dream begin to chip off of my shoulders and fall away. "And you wouldn't be doing it because you felt like you had to?"

Bash set down both of our drinks and took my hands in his. "Austin brought the idea to Sterling Chase because it's a winner, Rowe. I knew it the first moment I heard about it. This idea is going to save lives and help optimize emergency services. You know that's a mission near and dear to my heart. I'd be thrilled to be a part of bringing it to fruition."

His words felt like an oath, like a promise. There wasn't a part of me that didn't trust him to keep it.

And if getting Project Daisy Chain made—the one and only goal I'd focused on for years—no longer felt like quite the happily ever after I'd dreamed of, well, that was my own stupid fault. Cinderella only got *one* wish.

"Thank you, Bash," I whispered. "Truly."

Bash leaned over to kiss my cheek. "You thrill me," he said softly before nuzzling the side of my face and brushing his lips under my ear. "Landry was right. I've been looking for excitement in all the wrong places. You inspire me to remember who I am and who I want to be."

As always, proximity to Bash made my mouth start running independently of my brain. "I'm actually pretty boring when you get to know me."

Way to sell it, Prince.

Bash pulled back and met my eyes. His shone with life and happiness. "A quirky billionaire like yourself, Sterling Chase? Never in a million years."

We talked through turkey paninis and dessert cocktails. We talked until the sun dropped low in the sky.

We talked until even the tap water was at risk of running out.

And then we went back to the house and let our bodies do the rest of the talking for us.

TWENTY

BASH

I was falling in love with Rowe Prince. I knew it, Kenji knew it, and all of my friends knew it, too.

If I ever got up the nerve to tell him, poor Rowe would be the last to know. Hopefully, he could feel my affection through every touch and kiss between us because thinking about actually saying the words out loud to him terrified me.

It was too much, too fast. He had obligations to his family back in Indiana that he couldn't and wouldn't put off forever. He had major insecurities about money, like he hadn't put together what I'd told him about Daisy Chain's potential profitability with the concept that soon *he* would hold the patent. And I didn't want to make him any promises, to get his hopes up about anything, until we could clear Austin Purcell out of our lives forever.

So I kept my feelings to myself, held it close and tried to appreciate these "between" days where we were no longer simply fucking but not quite officially together. It was quietly exciting, the closeness that built between us as we lived and worked together. A glimpse of something real that I wanted profoundly. But there was a stubbornly transient quality to it, too, that made me hold my breath when we encountered a setback with IT or when Rowe had a long, stilted call with his parents where he told them he needed more time in New York, wondering if that would be the thing that tipped the balance. I held him tight every night, hoping he didn't run away before we could get this sorted.

And then, like a plague of locusts in ridiculously expensive cars, my friends descended.

Early Thursday morning, Rowe perched on a stool in the kitchen, checking his email. I'd positioned myself behind him, nominally waiting for the "jazzed-up TikTok cinnamon rolls" Rowe had baked to cool so he could ice them, but mostly enjoying the excuse to wrap my arms around Rowe's waist, kiss the skin behind his ear, and make him shiver.

"What's that noise?" Rowe asked, his voice breathy from the kissing. "That thumpy sound?"

I was on the verge of saying one of the unforgivably cheesy things that started popping into my head this week, like "that's my heart, beating for you, baby," when I heard it, too. An unmistakable *thunk scrape thunk scrape*, coming from outside.

I barely had time to straighten up before the side door opened, and Kenji and Landry invaded our space without even saying hello.

"...*not* buying me a Louis Vuitton suitcase," Kenji insisted. "You can replace the exact one you just destroyed."

"I didn't destroy it! I lifted it out of the trunk of the clown car you insisted on driving down here—"

"And the back wheels just decided to swan dive to the pavement? No. Don't blame the car for your lack of spatial awareness, Landry Davis. And you can march your ass right into Target and buy me a new one."

"I hate Target. I always leave with toilet paper," Landry whined. "I don't even go to the toilet paper department!"

"Oh hey, guys." Kenji set a bunch of grocery bags on the other end of the kitchen island and belatedly noticed Rowe and me staring at him. "There's a bunch more groceries in the car, Bash, if you wanna help unload."

I blinked. "I... don't recall asking for groceries?"

"No, well, with five extra mouths to feed, I figured..." Kenji shrugged. "Easier to just get it on the way. Hey, Rowe."

"Uh... hey?" Rowe said, at the same time I said, "Five extra mouths?" both of which were practically drowned out by what sounded like a jet airplane landing on the lawn.

"Sick," Landry said, running to the door like a little kid. "Zane brought the Spider."

"Zane?" I demanded.

But Zane wasn't the next person in the door. That was Silas, carrying a giant leather duffel bag he threw onto the living room sofa... right where I'd planned to get Rowe naked before continuing our room-by-room christening tour of the house.

"Why buy an Aston Martin if you're going to end up with a car that sounds like a leaf blower?" he demanded of no one in particular before walking directly to the coffeepot. "Hey, is this still fresh?"

Dev appeared right behind him, looking shaky. "At least the Spider isn't made of tissue paper and daydreams, like the Smartcar you just made me ride in. I swear they designed it with no legroom so passengers are forced to sit in the crash position the whole time." He plopped on a stool, gave my arm a friendly shove, and said gruffly, "Hey there, Rowe."

Rowe lifted his hand in a tiny half wave.

"You can ride home with Zane, then," Silas said, grabbing a mug from my cabinet. "Good luck getting *him* to listen to your sad-as-fuck country ballads the whole way."

"Holy shit, you guys!" Zane appeared in the doorway, face flushed and dark hair mussed. "I only rolled out of bed twenty minutes ago! That car broke the fucking sound barrier. It's a great day to be alive! Oooh! Cinnamon rolls!"

I grabbed the spatula I'd set next to the frosting container and brandished it at my friend warningly. "Not another inch closer, Zee

Barlo. I haven't even iced them yet! Would someone like to tell me what the fuck you're all doing here? And how you got inside?"

Five pairs of eyes blinked at me in surprise. Then Silas snorted. "Someone didn't check the group chat again."

"Are you fucking kidding me?" I demanded, but it was hard to be as angry as I might have been when Rowe's shoulders began shaking with laughter. "You don't just invade a man's house on a whim—"

"We've been talking for days about preparing for the board meeting Monday," Kenji explained. "Silas said..."

"I said we need a power strategy session on how to handle Austin." Silas began opening and closing cabinet doors. "And we do. Where's the sugar?"

Kenji dug through one of the shopping bags and handed Silas a small container.

"Don't blame me. I was practically kidnapped and forced to come." Landry lifted himself up to perch on the counter and gave Kenji a glare.

"We wanted to make sure you were okay, too," Zane said, his eyes still on the cinnamon rolls. "So, like, were you gonna frost those now, or... Hey! Easy with that spatula, Bash. I was just asking."

"Looks like things are going pretty well from where I'm sitting." Dev had turned on his stool to look at the living room, and everyone else did, too, staring in stunned silence for a moment at the bursts of color and kitsch Rowe had added to the Hampton house decor.

"A hot-pink French bulldog." Landry hopped off the counter and ran a long finger over the back of the porcelain figurine standing on top of a new stack of colorful art books on a nearby shelf.

"I like the turquoise lamps," Silas said with a nod of approval. "Definite upgrade from the glass ones that were here before."

"I love it all," I said, setting my hands on Rowe's shoulders and letting my thumbs drift against the soft skin at his nape. "Rowe really does have an eye for this stuff. If I'd tried decorating this room, it would have been a disaster."

"You *did* try," Landry pointed out. "And it was."

"Only because the designer Bash hired didn't take the time to get to know him." Rowe stood, grabbed the spatula from my hand, and began icing the cinnamon rolls. His cheeks were rosy under his freckles, the way they always were when he was praised, but he seemed to be taking the invasion of our private time in stride...

Which was more than I could say about myself.

"Speaking of disasters..." Silas took his mug of coffee across the room to the bar cart near the dining room table and added a generous pour of whisky. "The text you found about Justin was true. Rumor has it he *is* engaged. To a woman." He lifted his mug in an ironic toast. "May the poor lady come to her senses faster than I did."

"Thought he was gay," Landry said, leaning his head against the cabinet.

"Same," Silas agreed wryly. "Because that's what he told me."

Dev made a disapproving noise. "People's sexuality can change. You know this."

"Or they can lie," Zane added, reaching for a handful of grapes from a bowl on the counter. "Sorry, Rowe."

I shot him a glare, but Rowe only smiled. "No, it's fine. I did lie. But so did Sebastian. Motive matters."

"Oooh. Score one for the Indiana boy," Landry said under a laugh.

"Look, I don't know the exact details of what happened with you and Justin," Rowe said. He grabbed a stack of plates, dished a gooey roll onto one, and walked it over to Silas. "But I do know beating yourself up over something only makes *you* feel bad. It's what you do next that counts." He squeezed Silas's forearm sympathetically before returning to the kitchen to dish up more plates.

Silas stood still, plate in one hand and mug in the other, and watched Rowe for a long moment. He flicked his gaze to me and let out a deep breath.

"That segues nicely into what we most need to discuss." Kenji took one of the rolls Rowe dished out and brought it to the dining table, then grabbed his laptop from his suitcase. "What happens next?"

"Rowe comes first," I said before anyone else could speak. "I'm as eager to kick Justin's ass as any of you, especially after hearing he and Austin might've been neck-deep in some kind of conspiracy, but we need to protect Rowe's IP and Sterling Chase's own interests before we ride in to save this woman from making a mistake or doing anything else about Justin." I looked around at my friends. "Agreed?"

Zane licked icing off his thumb. "Yes. I think we all agree." He pulled a bottle of water from the fridge and sat down beside Kenji. "Right, Silas?"

Silas gritted his teeth but nodded, taking a seat across from them. "Fine. What's the plan?"

We all took seats around the table. I sat down next to Dev and motioned Rowe to the chair beside mine at the head of the table.

I let Rowe take the lead in outlining the plan we'd come up with to confront Austin as a group quietly, in a way that would minimize the chance of media exposure that none of us—including Rowe—wanted. I felt an unexpected pride and *rightness* at the way they all nodded along with what he was saying.

"A couple of people from Legal will be there, of course, to keep an eye on everything," he finished. "Margot said she knows tensions will be high, but if you want to keep Austin from contacting the *Post* to air his grievances, everyone needs to stay calm and professional—"

"Easier said than done for some of us," Landry interjected, raising a sculpted eyebrow at me.

"Oh, I'm cool as a cucumber," I lied. Just thinking of the way Austin had defrauded Rowe made my fists clench. "Worry about that one." I tilted my chin toward Silas, whose jaw ticked with anger.

"Oh, Bash." Dev draped an arm over my shoulder and pulled me against him. "You've never been cool, baby, but I love you anyway."

Rowe's eyes narrowed on Dev's hand with laser focus. It took me a moment to realize he was jealous or possessive. Whichever emotion it was, I liked it.

I liked it *a lot.*

I grabbed Rowe's hand and kissed it before holding it in my lap. The pink flush on his neck and cheeks thrilled me, as usual. Would that ever get old? Would he give me enough time for it to even be a concern?

Silas's eyes rolled. "Can we focus, please? You had a conference call with Clarissa yesterday, Bash. Walk us through it."

It was on the tip of my tongue to tell him off, but I knew what he would say. His opinion about my sudden "relationship" was clear on his face. And up to now, it had made me doubt my feelings for Rowe. But I didn't *want* to doubt them. After the days we'd spent alone together, I wanted him now more than ever.

I launched into a long explanation of my video call with Clarissa the day before. It had been a difficult and emotional one—Clarissa blamed herself for not seeing the signs and not supervising Austin more closely, just like I did, even though I'd assured her no one held her responsible.

"And we're sure she wasn't involved? Zane asked. "I mean, I like her fine, but she and Austin started at the same time..."

I spread my hands. "As sure as I can be. There's no evidence tying her in, and she seemed genuinely upset. But really... I don't know. I don't know how many people at the company are involved."

Rowe must've heard the catch in my voice because he took my hand this time, holding it firmly. "I don't know her at all, but I can tell you, she looked genuinely shocked. She offered to resign, and Bash told her not to. I believed her."

The others nodded thoughtfully.

"Tomorrow, she's flying back for the Innovation Awards, so you can try to get a word with her Saturday night. I warned her to keep things normal with Austin between now and then." I took a deep breath. "But that brings up another subject. I asked Clarissa to make a list of all Austin's current projects. I'm going to reach out to the contacts there personally next week and transition them to someone on Austin's team or take them on myself if necessary. But his team's primary focus of late has been Daisy Chain—formerly known as MRO. We hit pause on beta testing, but we're going to need to make some decisions about the project."

Rowe squeezed my hand before standing up. "That's my cue to leave. I'm going to go for a walk on the beach and give you guys a chance to speak privately." He looked around at my closest friends. "Just know that I believe strongly in this project, and I'm not about to abandon it. But I will understand completely if it's not the right fit for Sterling Chase moving forward. Either way, thank you for helping me protect the intellectual property. I appreciate it."

Once he'd left through the glass doors and began making his way down the boardwalk toward the beach, Dev exhaled. "He's different than he was when I met him at the stables."

"How do you mean?"

"Gutsier," Dev said with a shrug. "Just as sweet but more confident. I think you're rubbing off on him."

"Twice a day, if the scene we walked in on was anything to go by," Landry said dryly.

Kenji elbowed him remorselessly.

"I didn't talk to him much the other day, but he's really cute," Zane added. "Very hot in a Disney princess kind of way. And his cinnamon rolls are orgasmic." He gave me a mischievous look. "Maybe I'll write a song about him. Guys *love* when you write them a song."

I glared, and everyone burst into laughter. Landry leaned over to give Zane a knuckle-bump.

"Ah, Bash is so fucking satisfying to tease," Landry sighed. "And we so rarely got an opportunity before now."

"Rowe's a good person," I said, sounding petulant. "He's kindhearted and intelligent and dependable."

"Then maybe we should add *Rowe* to the group chat," Silas said mildly.

Everyone stopped their laughter and stared.

Silas shrugged. "At least he'd check it periodically. And it's not like he's going anywhere anytime soon, is it?"

I ran a hand over my hair, feeling unusually nervous. "I don't know. I mean, I know I don't want him to. That's for damn sure. But... he's got shit in Indiana that's tying him there. Parent stuff."

"Rough," Dev said because he knew about parental expectations better than anyone.

"And I think... the shit that comes along with me is... a lot. All of this..." I waved a hand in the air to encompass the expensive beach house and all that it signified. "The galas, the money, the backstabbing employees. I don't blame him for not being all 'sign me up.'"

"Poor little billionaire Bash," Landry said, half-mocking. Then he shrugged. "I don't blame him. It *is* a lot to take in when you're not used to it."

"And that's another thing," I said, picking up on Landry's comment. "I haven't even told him I'm a billionaire. I haven't told him about us owning Sterling Chase or creating ETC. He knows I come from the Dayne family, and even that level of wealth is problematic."

"Meh, millions, billions," Zane said. He'd gotten up to get another cinnamon roll but seemed to be spooning cinnamon goop straight out of the baking dish. "I doubt the extra zeroes will matter much when you tell him."

"It matters that I *can't* tell him." I looked around the table. "Rowe and I have been discussing Daisy Chain all week, and I keep wanting to mention ETC or tell him he has the full backing of Sterling Chase, but I can't. I have to act like I'm just a member of the board."

Zane and Landry looked at each other, then at Dev. Dev pursed his lips for a long moment, then shrugged. As one, all eyes swung toward Silas. Silas was the one of us who'd been burned by a lover most recently—was *still* feeling burned, if his current level of anger was anything to go by. Silas, who'd made his distrust of Rowe very obvious just a week ago.

Shocking us all, Silas sat back in his seat and folded his hands over his lean stomach. "So tell him, then. Jesus, why's everyone looking at me? I *said* to add him to the group chat, didn't I? And Zane's right. He makes a good cinnamon roll."

I couldn't have kept the smile off my face if I tried.

"You all are forgetting Rowe's about to be pretty dang rich in his own right," Kenji piped up, "once he gets his IP back and Daisy Chain is on the market. When he sees his own bank balance, I think the shock of finding out Sebastian isn't just wealthy but wealthy *as fuck* will pale in comparison."

"True story," Dev grunted.

"I don't think he's put that together yet," I agreed. "That would solve a lot of problems. He could buy his parents' house or move them wherever they wanted to be. He wouldn't have to worry about his job back in Indiana. He can go to design school, or... hell, he can choose to do whatever he wants." And I prayed that choice would involve being with me. "But I can't talk to him about any of that yet. I don't want to get his hopes up until we know what's happening with Austin."

"Fucking Austin. I can't get over that guy's balls," Dev said. "Stealing blatantly, thinking he'd get away with it."

"Austin Purcell has no balls," Silas corrected. "And he might very well have gotten away with it if Rowe hadn't been willing to go to extreme measures." He snorted to himself, shaking his head. "I'm still annoyed that he lied, but I've gotta give the man an A for effort."

"Agreed." I stood and walked to the windows in the living room. In the distance, I spied a lone figure standing atop a sand dune, watching the waves with a hand up to shade his eyes from the glare of the sun. The ocean breeze whipped his curls into a wild mess around his head.

I yearned to be out there with him. To have him in here with me. To follow him to Indiana or that nighttime flea market he'd mentioned. The where didn't matter; all that mattered was the way I felt when I was with him. Settled and seen. Protective and protected. Challenged and accepted.

Home.

"Sit your ass down, Sebastian," Landry said. "Let's talk about the terms we're offering Rowe."

I turned from the window and gave him a speaking look. "Pardon me? You haven't attended a board meeting in a year. Since when do you take an interest in the running of Sterling Chase?"

"Since our head of development became a criminal, our CEO is out of the country, and the guy on the board who usually handles this shit is currently suffering from a debilitating case of Heart-Eyes Syndrome." He held up a hand before I could protest. "To be clear, I'm not worried you'll be biased, Bash. I'm worried that *you'll* know you're biased, and once all this panic is over and you actually sit and think about it, you'll wonder if you handled everything in a way that was fair to the brotherhood."

I stared at Landry long enough for him to huff and roll his eyes. "What?" he demanded. "I have *depths*, fucker. You should know this."

Kenji patted his hand soothingly. "Don't worry. Half the gay population of Manhattan knows about your depths, Landry."

Dev threw back his head and laughed, Zane snickered, and even Silas cracked a smile. But Silas quickly sobered. "Landry's thinking smart. I say we make Rowe a solid offer that allows him to retain the patent, like the one we made on the Hegel Project back in the day. Remember? It was lucrative for everyone. This project might be a harder sell since it involves local government budgets, but..."

And like that, we were off, discussing business the way we used to when Sterling Chase was brand-new, weighing pros and cons and the legal organization of IP ownership. I was impressed and relieved that they handled Rowe's project the same way they would have discussed any other project proposal at one of our board meetings. I hadn't realized how badly I needed that connection, that support, until my friends had provided it without my having to ask.

When we adjourned, Landry, Zane, and Kenji moved to the kitchen to make lunch, Dev wandered off to check in with someone at the stables, Silas made some business calls, and I watched Rowe trek back from the beach with a dopey smile on my face. We had a plan to handle Austin and Sterling Chase, the brotherhood had opened their ranks to Rowe, and it felt like puzzle pieces I hadn't realized were misaligned had begun clicking into place. But there was one more thing I had to do.

As soon as Rowe stepped in the door, all sun-warmed and disheveled, I immediately pulled him into our bedroom, shut the door, and lavished his face and neck with the hours' worth of kisses I'd been storing up.

"Bash! *Mmmpfh.* Your friends are right th—*shit...* right there! And I... *oh! Oh god.*" He tilted his head to the side, panting slightly. "I... you... what was I saying?"

"You were worrying about my friends' delicate sensibilities." I bit his earlobe lightly. "Don't."

"But I get so *loud.*"

Yes, he really did... and I really fucking loved it.

But tempting as it was to take him right there against the bedroom door—Rowe would require almost no convincing, and I'd make sure he loved every noisy second—I knew he wasn't secure enough around my friends to appreciate the teasing that would ensue. Besides, he and I had other things to discuss first.

Reluctantly, I stepped away. "Sorry. I really did have a reason for hauling you in here." I ran my hands down my shorts nervously.

Rowe remained standing against the door. He ghosted his fingers over his lips dreamily. "I thought kissing was a solid reason, just so you know. I would not be averse to more kissing."

I laughed, but it came out short and tense, and Rowe straightened up right away. "What's going on?"

"Nothing bad," I said quickly. "I promise."

But of course, Rowe wouldn't be pawned off so easily. "Is it about Daisy Chain? About your meeting with your friends? Because as much as I'd love to work with Sterling Chase, I knew it wasn't a given, Bash. You don't need to let me down easy. You guys have processes, and the legal ramifications are probably a nightmare. I get it. I don't expect—"

"We founded Sterling Chase," I blurted.

"What?" Rowe whispered.

Jesus. I could have handled this so much better. I wondered for a second where polished, urbane Sebastian Dayne who had no fucks to give had wandered off to.

And then I remembered. This was scary *because* I gave a fuck.

"Those guys—not Kenji; he came on board after—but my other friends and I, we developed ETC our final year at Yale." It felt weird to say it out loud. Like a dark confession and a vow to Rowe all at once. "We own Sterling Chase together, through various pass-through companies. We've kept that knowledge away from the public for a lot of reasons, some of which you can probably guess and others that aren't my story to share. No one outside this house knows the whole truth, though."

Rowe's eyes were huge. "But you're telling me."

I nodded. "Because I know I can trust you. Because I want *you* to know that I trust you. And because..." I took a deep breath. "Because Sterling Chase is going to offer you a deal for Daisy Chain, and I want you to know that's not because I brought undue influence on anyone as a board member. It's because I, and the other four guys who founded the company, believe in you and in your project."

"Bash," Rowe said softly. He took a step toward me and then another, like he was a lifeline towing me to safety. He lifted a hand to cup my cheek. "Baby. I already figured it out."

I froze. "What? How? There's no way..."

"Silas mentioned something in the office the other day about Sterling Chase being 'our' company. I put two and two together." Rowe shrugged. "As soon as the idea occurred to me, I realized *of course* you'd invented ETC. You're passionate about emergency medicine. You've invested your soul in the company. You care about people. And, honestly... you're one of a very strange mix of people on the board of directors. I bet it's not as much of a secret as you think."

I huffed out a laugh. "Oh, I assure you, it is. No one else knows. Not Clarissa or Austin or any of our employees. Even our lawyers don't talk about it openly." Another thought occurred to me, even more overwhelming than the last. "Wait, so if you knew—"

"Well, *strongly suspected* might be more accurate—"

"Then you know that when we sold ETC, I—"

"Became a billionaire?" Rowe took a deep breath and smoothed my hair behind my ear. "Yes. Yep. That was... trippy."

"And you're fine with it?"

"I mean, no? Because I still cannot comprehend what a billion of *anything* would be like, let alone a billion *dollars*. But also, yes. Because I like you. *You*, Sebastian. And I'd like you even if you didn't have a cent—"

"You'd probably like me better."

"Not better," he insisted. "I like you the way you are. Confident. In charge. Very, devastatingly..."

I lifted an eyebrow and asked hopefully, "Sexy?"

"Kind," Rowe said with a grin. He pushed up on his toes and kissed me, and my arms instinctively went around his waist. "And sexy, obviously. Goes without saying." He sank back down but linked his hands behind my neck. "Thank you for trusting me with this. I promise, I will keep your secret safe."

"I know you will."

"But let the record show," he teased, "I trusted you first."

I snorted. "Is that right, *Sterling Chase*?"

"Mmhmm. I told you about the li'l baby Cupid picture," he said loftily. "There is no greater trust than that."

I covered his smile with my lips and took his laughter deep inside.

"Your friends are pretty great," he said a long moment later when we came up for air. His hands roamed over my chest, lighting tiny fires everywhere he touched. "I'm glad. You deserve them."

"They are," I agreed. "I'm glad they came—"

Down the hall, a smoke detector began to wail, followed instantly by Kenji yelling, "Everything's fine! Silas doesn't understand how toasters work, but otherwise, we're all okay!"

"—and I'll be very glad when they go away," I grumbled.

Rowe stifled his laugh in my chest. "Come on. Let's go rescue them. It's the least we can do."

A little while later, I found myself perched on a stool, watching in amusement as Kenji tried to ride herd on all the sous chefs in the kitchen while Zane strummed his guitar at the kitchen table. It was chaos... and I thought I could get used to it.

Eventually, Silas, who'd been exiled to the living room for crimes against food preparation, came and stood by my shoulder, watching the spectacle with me.

"I told him," I said simply.

"Good. And you two are together now?"

I shook my head. "He can't make that decision yet, so I didn't ask. He's got too many other things to focus on. But after Monday..."

Silas nodded. "And if things don't work out? If he makes a different choice?"

"He still won't tell anyone." I'd bet my fortune on that. In a way, I had.

Silas fell silent for a moment, but it was the kind of silence that I knew meant he was churning things over in his mind methodically, logically.

"Spit it out," I prompted easily.

"Are you gonna be able to handle this and stay professional? Because I can take point on the Austin fiasco. Fuck knows you did it for me when things with Justin went to shit."

I raised an eyebrow at him, and he shrugged.

"Yes, I know I was the one who just wanted to fire Austin in the first place, but now, after talking to Legal..." He shook his head. "You were right. That would have been the worst possible course. We need to pull Austin's fangs by reminding him of the nondisclosure agreement he signed *before* he does anything rash that would earn Sterling Chase media scrutiny—like complaining about his wrongful termination at the same moment your new boyfriend is applying for a patent on the project Austin's trying to take credit for." He shoved his hands in his pockets. "Zane's career is taking off, Kenji's barely keeping Landry's behavior off the radar, Dev's in no shape to have people poking around his personal life. I don't want this to blow up in our faces. And more than all that, I don't want you to have to worry about all this when you've already got enough on your plate."

Silas had always been the mother hen of our group, and I appreciated that he was concerned about my emotional well-being, but...

"I'm fine," I assured him. "I care about Rowe a lot. I want to build something real with him. But Silas, Sterling Chase is still my baby. It means more to me than anything."

I said the words with confidence, believing them to be absolutely true...

But less than twenty-four hours later, I realized I'd become a bigger liar than Rowe Prince ever was. Because when I had to choose between Sterling Chase and... *Sterling Chase*, there was hands down no question which I'd choose.

My Prince of Lies would win every time.

TWENTY-ONE

ROWE

I'd worried that having Bash's friends come to the Hamptons would pop the iridescent bubble we'd been floating in, but it hadn't. Not at all. The brotherhood were nothing but kind, and Silas had even pulled me aside to apologize for being slow to trust me.

"It wasn't personal. I'd side-eye anybody these guys got serious about," he'd admitted, gesturing to the men laughing in the living area. "Wouldn't matter if you came with a PhD and a recommendation from Lin-Manuel Miranda. Besides," he added with a grin, "Bash always said he'd end up married to Sterling Chase. Now maybe he will."

I laughed at the time—a kind of frantic laugh, though Silas didn't know me well enough to recognize it. *"Serious about"*? *"Married to"*? I couldn't pretend that I didn't realize Bash had feelings for me, not after he'd done something as heart-shatteringly, mind-bendingly wonderful as telling me the true story of the founding of Sterling Chase, but I still couldn't comprehend what anything beyond this week with him would look like. Me, showing up at his penthouse apartment with my delivery sombrero after a shift? Him, coming over to chill on Joey's futon after a long day of buying and selling small countries? What about my parents? What about the Tech Barn?

So I simply didn't think about it. I focused on preparing for Monday, on the future of Daisy Chain, on making sure the bubble didn't pop.

But when we arrived back in the city on Saturday afternoon and the elevator doors opened into the palatial entrance hall of Bash's Park Avenue apartment, I felt the bubble pop anyway, trampled beneath the feet of commitment and lost in the shuffle of reality.

A reality that included ten-foot ceilings and a private elevator.

"Hey!" Kenji said, materializing out of nowhere. "You guys made good time."

"This... what... is...?" I didn't even know where to begin in my quest for answers about Bash's living space. If his Hamptons house had screamed wealth to me, this pretty much deafened me. The furnishings alone were probably worth millions, and that was before I even began asking about the art on the walls.

"Rowe, you're set up in the guest room. Third door down the far corridor on the left," Kenji said, waving in the general direction of an honest-to-god gilt-framed mirror hung over an antique mahogany console table in a hallway carpeted by a luxurious Persian runner.

"Set up?" I repeated, still gawking like a tourist at Versailles. "I have my suitcase here."

"Keep moving," Kenji said, barely holding back a knowing smirk. "You can gawk after we see how well the tuxedo fits."

"Joey sent over his tux?" I asked a split second before I entered the guest room and saw an Alexander McQueen garment bag hanging from a small rolling clothes rack.

"Not exactly," Kenji called down the hallway after me. The laugh in his voice wasn't funny.

"Fuck," I whispered, reaching into the garment bag like it held a venomous snake but instead pulling out the most gorgeous tuxedo I'd ever seen. "We aren't in Kansas anymore."

"Please don't tell me this is the thing that finally makes it all too weird for you." Bash walked into the room behind me and gave me an uncertain smile. "It's off-the-rack."

"An off-the-rack *Alexander McQueen*," I squeaked, running my hand over the ultra-smooth wool. "This had to cost... five thousand dollars?" That was enough to buy a used car. To pay my parents' mortgage for months. "I... I..."

Bash's smile fell. "You don't have to wear it," he said quickly. "I'll be proud to have you on my arm wearing the bunny tux. Or those pajamas with the goldfish that you wore at the beach. I just know you like beautiful things, and I thought... But it doesn't matter. My date's going to be the most gorgeous, quirky man at the banquet. And I care about the man inside the tux, not whose name is on the jacket."

I squeezed my eyes shut for a second. *Rowe Prince, what the fuck are you doing?* Daisy's voice was clear in my head. Hadn't I been the person, two weeks ago, telling Miranda Baxter-Hicks that she needed to wear dresses *she* liked and not to worry about whether they were good enough for anyone else?

And here I had the man of my dreams, a guy whose only goal was to make me happy, handing me a tuxedo beyond anything I could have imagined for myself. And instead of thanking him for being so thoughtful, instead of *rejoicing* that I got to wear something I loved on the arm of the man I'd fallen head over heels for... I was worrying that *I* wasn't good enough for the fucking tuxedo.

I touched the tattoo on my hip. For years, I'd worked hard, focused exclusively on Daisy Chain, and told myself I was doing it for my sister. But that tiny, lightless existence was never what Daisy would have wanted for herself. It wasn't what she'd want for me.

It was about time I did the *brave, exciting thing*.

I turned to Bash and kissed him fiercely, with all the love in my bruised and hopeful heart. "Thank you. For the tuxedo. For putting up with my nerves. For being so much more than I ever expected." I kissed him again. "I can't wait to wear it, Sebastian. I can't wait to be on your arm."

That might have been overstating the case somewhat—I was still a jangly mass of nerves about the party—but Bash was too kind to call me on it. Or maybe I'd simply exploded his brain with the force of my kisses. "But I'm putting Joey's magic scarves in the breast pocket," I added breathlessly.

"Uh, yeah," he said, eyes glassy. "Yeah."

Kenji barked from somewhere out in the hall. "Sebastian Dayne. Focus."

Bash almost ran into the doorframe on his way out of the room, and it was enough to help me let go of some of my nerves. If the world's hottest billionaire was a regular guy who could be knocked senseless by a hot kiss, then maybe we weren't so different after all.

Maybe, just maybe, we could find a way to work things out.

I ran my hand over the buttery wool and satin of the jacket once again, then closed my eyes and prayed to my imaginary fairy godmother.

Let tonight go smoothly. No pumpkins.

But a few hours later, it became clear that my fairy godmother was a deceitful troll—or she was adhering hard to that one-wish-per-customer rule—because there were no happy endings in sight.

———

"Darling, who are you wearing?" a familiar voice asked from somewhere behind me.

I hadn't expected an industry awards banquet to be quite so crowded or quite so filled with random socialites. I'd spotted at least two A-list actors and a politician just in the short time that Bash had stepped away to greet a colleague he recognized, and my nerves were back in full effect.

The throng of people had closed around me so thickly I didn't realize the words were meant for me until a hand touched my arm.

I spun around and saw Constance Baxter-Hicks wearing a strapless black satin bombshell gown that made her look like she'd stepped out of an old Hollywood film. She was pure understated elegance, and it suited her to perfection.

"You're outshining us all tonight, darling," she said, air-kissing my cheek.

"Who, me?" I shook my head. "Look at *you*."

She poked me with a jewel-encrusted clutch purse that matched the beading along the bust line of her gown. "This old thing?" She preened. "Don't be silly. That tuxedo is to die for."

Constance wasn't wrong. As soon as I'd seen myself in the mirror, I'd vowed never to be caught dead in Joey's bunny tux again. The look on Bash's face when he'd first seen me in it had made me consider turning tricks if that's what it took to keep dressing so fine. Second Chance Savers castoffs were great, but they couldn't hold a candle to this.

"It's McQueen," I said with a sniff, feeling the familiar armor of my Sterling Chase persona fall over me. *If you can't beat 'em, join 'em.*

"*Really?* I would have imagined you in something a little more... *quirky*," she said with a sparkle of understanding in her eye. "A Siriano tux gown perhaps... or at least a vintage Alberta Ferretti. Something with flair."

I held out my arm to her. "Butter is better than flair. Feel this."

Her grin widened when she ran her manicured fingers down my sleeve. "*Grain de poudre*... and surely it's made from virgin wool. How... appropriate."

My face heated. I'd been so intimidated by the woman at our first meeting I'd taken her at face value. Considering my own circumstances at the time, I should have known better than to assume that anyone at these parties was truly who they appeared to be. After the incident at the polo field, I'd started to wonder whether Constance was more aware than I'd given her credit for—which was both interesting and off-putting. Now I was pretty sure she'd confirmed it.

"I'll have you know this is no longer virgin wool," I said, my gaze searching the crowd for a particularly tall and handsome head... or, in a pinch, any of the other members of the brotherhood who were supposed to be attending. "It's thoroughly debauched wool. The debauchiest."

"What is going on over here?" Bash's murmur made my skin prickle. He handed me a glass of wine and slid an arm around my waist. "Constance. How are you this evening? Exciting developments with your topiaries?"

Constance laughed delightedly. "So thoughtful of you to ask, Sebastian. I'm doing much better now that I've run into Sterling here. The man brings life to a party."

Bash's hand tightened on my waist. "I couldn't agree more."

She pursed her lips, and her eyes danced. "He was just bragging about his... wool. It seems the man... excuse me, his *tuxedo*... has been through some things since we last met."

I tried not to choke on my wine. "Yes, well. You know McQueen." I waved a hand in the air, trying at the last minute not to slosh out my wine. "He likes to make a statement."

"Indeed." Constance looked around the room. "Bash, please tell me there's going to be entertainment tonight. I can hardly stand these awards banquets. The least they can do is roll out a dance floor and strike up an orchestra. Or maybe have Zee Barlo sing. I swear I saw him around here somewhere."

"There'll be dancing after dinner," Bash said with a knowing smirk. "Why do you think I brought a date?"

I elbowed him while secretly bouncing with excitement over the idea of dancing with Bash after the awards ceremony. I'd never been to a party like this—not as an invited guest, anyway—and I'd certainly never danced with another man in public before.

Constance waved to someone across the crowd. "Pearson, darling!" Then she leaned in to whisper, "Insufferable ass but serves the most delightful Coquille Saint-Jacques at his Memorial Day fête every year, so I can't help but maintain the connection, you understand. Until later, mon cher! Save a dance for me, will you?" She floated away into the crowd with a heavy waft of Chanel No. 5.

"Force of nature," I murmured.

"We should have told her your real name," Bash said. "She's a good connection to maintain."

"Pretty sure she somehow knows it," I admitted softly. "The woman seemed to see right through me." I gave him a look. "Not easy to keep a secret in this crowd."

Bash threaded his fingers through mine and tugged me in the direction of the banquet tables. Rows and rows of tables sparkled with silver and glassware, rich floral centerpieces, and lit votive candles. My eyes took in every inch of the exquisite surroundings from the elegant clothes to the pristine table displays. Near the side of the room, he found the tables with Sterling Chase's logo on a card in the center and led me to them.

Landry was already seated at the first Sterling Chase table, slumped in his seat with a glass of wine in his hand. His date, a model-gorgeous man, sat beside him, talking to his phone like he was making an Instagram reel and ignoring everyone else around him. When we approached, Landry winked and raised his glass to us.

Silas waved from another table and elbowed Dev, who was hunched awkwardly over a tumbler of whisky like he was attempting to appear invisible. Dev up-nodded us.

"Thank you for bringing me," I said impulsively, pulling Bash to face me before we took our seats at Landry's table. "I'm glad I'm getting the chance to experience something like this." Not just being at the glittering party but the chance to be part of his brotherhood, even temporarily.

"First of many, I hope," he said, giving me a half-smile that made my knees go weak.

"Huh?"

"I mean... I hope this is the first of many boring awards banquets you experience with me." He leaned in close to my ear and whispered, "Ducking behind a potted plant *alone* seems like such a waste now."

My heart beat fast, and my stomach dropped. "Are you... are you saying..." I licked my lips. "Do you mean while I'm living in New York? Or, like, you'd want me to maybe come back to the city sometime? O-or..." I trailed off, unable to think of a third option.

"No." Bash set his hand on my waist. "I'm saying I'd like you to consider—"

"Bash." Austin Purcell stood behind one of the empty chairs. "Hey, hey. Sorry to interrupt, but there was a mix-up with my ticket tonight. The people at the entrance said—*oh*." He noticed Bash's arm around me and broke off with a frown.

Bash stiffened and turned, blocking Austin's view. "Austin. I thought you were in Sierra Leone until tomorrow."

"Well, I was, but I changed my flight. I assumed it was an oversight on Kenji's part since I was meant to be *here*." He peered around Bash, his attention fully on me. "Are you...?" His eyes widened in recognition. "Your picture was up on Bash's wall screen." He looked to Bash for confirmation.

Bash ignored him, instead smiling broadly at someone near the entrance. "Oh, look, Clarissa's arrived. We should take our seats." With a hand on my shoulder, he finally took his own seat.

Austin plopped down into the chair on the other side of me. "What's your name again?"

My stomach gave a sickening swoop. I didn't want to give him my name and possibly start something. Would Austin remember the name of the man whose project he'd stolen? Possibly not, but I couldn't take the chance of tipping off Austin before the board meeting on Monday, when Bash and the others would confront Austin with the legal team present.

My best option was to lie low.

"I'm Bash's date." I managed a tight smile. "Nice to meet you." I turned to Bash. "What were you saying again? Something about polo, I think?"

Under the table, Bash grasped my hand tight enough to cut off my circulation. Thankfully, someone stopped by the table to greet Austin, and he stopped talking to me. But as the uniformed servers began delivering dinner and an older man in a sweet navy tux stood up at the podium to make his opening remarks, I felt Austin's attention on me again, like he was trying to figure out a way to ask my name without being overtly rude.

I straightened my posture, ignored the keynote speech I couldn't care less about, and tried to look like I belonged.

"Bash, darling." Constance Baxter-Hicks appeared next to Bash. "They've seated us at the Loringtons' table, and that just won't do. I've asked them to switch us here. You don't mind, do you?" Without waiting for Bash's confirmation, Constance took the seat beside him. Her daughter, Miranda, took the chair next to hers, and a nice-looking guy around my age took the next seat down—after holding out Miranda's chair for her.

I shot Miranda a covert thumbs-up, gesturing to her elegant, understated green dress, and she blushed and smiled hugely.

"Always happy to have you with us," Bash said with a genuine smile. "Miranda, Hank. Nice to see you both."

The man nodded, then leaned toward Miranda like he was continuing a conversation while Miranda cheerfully munched her dinner roll.

Another pair of women arrived and took the remaining seats at the table. They both appeared to be in their forties. One had a pale complexion with a short platinum pixie cut, and the other was dark-skinned with long mahogany hair that tumbled in shiny waves against the red satin tux she wore.

Bash stood and went around the table to help the ladies with their seats, then returned and put a hand on my shoulder. He gestured toward the blonde woman first. "This is our CEO, Clarissa, and her wife, Kamaria. Ladies, I'd love to introduce you to my date. He's—"

"The Burrito Bandito!" Austin blurted triumphantly, like he'd finally come up with the answer that had been eluding him. "You're the one who does the dance!"

Bash's fingers tightened on my shoulder, and I knew my face had to be fire-hot.

What was I supposed to do now? Would it cause more of a scene to confirm or deny?

"See, I know him as the brilliant inventor of—" Bash began in a low growl, but I set my hand on top of his to stop him.

"Don't," I said softly. "Don't."

"And you are?" Constance leaned forward to look down her nose at Austin like he was a lower life form she'd only just deigned to notice.

But Austin wouldn't be distracted. I could see the scales falling from his eyes like dominos, *plink plink plink.*

"Rowe!" he accused, pointing at me. "That was the name on the wall screen. I knew I'd remember it eventually. I *told you* I never forget a face. Bash investigated you! You're the funny little man who delivered the food the other day, but you refused to tell me your name then. You're Rowe Pr—*uh.*"

Austin hesitated and swallowed hard, like he hadn't made the connection between the picture he'd seen in Bash's office and the letters where he'd first seen the name Rowe Prince until the words had been in his mouth. Then he darted a glance at Bash's hand on my shoulder, recognizing what it might mean that the real inventor of Daisy Chain was attending this function on Bash's arm.

I saw the moment he decided to go on the offensive in an effort to save himself.

"Bash, your date is a security risk!" Austin flushed as red as my own face had to be. "He was at our office the other day in a disguise, a-a-acting extremely suspicious. He refused to identify himself, then he ran off into the building, and our security team couldn't find him. I wouldn't be surprised if he... if he *stole intellectual property!* We need to have him removed right now and investigated thoroughly. I'll take on the task myself. This man is a danger. A thief. A *liar.*" He looked around the dining room frantically. "Somebody find security!"

Bash's voice was low and full of command, the kind of voice that might have melted the clothes right off me if we hadn't been surrounded by a couple of hundred businesspeople in formalwear.

"Keep your voice down, Austin. I know exactly who this man is. And I'm crystal clear on who at this table is a thief."

Austin's chest expanded and contracted rapidly. In the face of Bash's uncompromising refusal to act, he turned toward his CEO. "Clarissa, Bash's judgment is clearly compromised. You have to believe me."

Clarissa was already aware of the situation. And while she might not have known who the true owners of the company were, she knew that Bash, as the person who acted as a liaison from the board of directors, was very much in charge.

Fortunately, she had also been well coached on the need to act clueless about Austin's treachery until the official board meeting on Monday morning.

"My goodness, Austin," she said, managing to sound shocked. "Have you had too much wine? We have no proof anything's been stolen, and this man is Sebastian's friend."

"But—"

"Let's table this until Monday," she said firmly. "They're getting ready to begin the awards."

Austin straightened in his chair. "I will not sit here and be accused of stealing my own idea!"

Clarissa blinked at him. "Accused?" She gave Bash an incredulous look, like she wondered if he could shed light on Austin's strange theories. "No one's accused you of anything. And what idea could you have stolen?" She frowned, as though the idea had only just occurred to her. "Wait... you don't mean the idea for MRO?"

The woman deserved an Academy Award. Or a promotion. Or... all the burritos she could eat for the rest of *ever*.

"I... I..." Austin seemed to realize that in his haste to shift blame onto me, he might have unwittingly revealed his crime. "Maybe, yes! I remember this man's name. He sent letters to me. Months ago. H-he's a rival inventor. He warned me he'd try to steal my plans. To claim that he came up with them himself."

"This man?" Bash took his seat and grabbed my hand, holding it on top of the table in a gesture of support and connection that would have made me fall in love with him... if I hadn't already been there. "The one you just claimed was a burrito delivery person? Now you're saying he sent you letters warning you that he was going to commit a crime?"

"He is! He did!" Austin insisted. "He... I..."

Silas wandered over from the next table, a politely chastising look on his face that hardened when he looked at Bash. It was almost like he knew Bash was going to have a hard time holding his temper. "Is there a problem over here?"

"Not at all, Silas. Austin appears to be confused about some things. Maybe it's jet lag." Clarissa lifted a hand to Austin in a soothing gesture. "Your claims are easily proven, Austin. On Monday, you'll provide us with copies of the letters you claim this man sent you, and the truth will come out. Now, please don't make a scene."

Around us, there was a scattering of applause as the first awards were presented.

"Well, I don't *have* the letters. I-I-I threw them away! But still—"

"You threw away letters that threatened corporate espionage?" Landry wrinkled his perfect nose and took a deliberate sip of his drink. "Is that normal operating procedure?"

Austin glared at Landry angrily before turning his glare on me. "The situation was mine to handle as I saw fit. The patent applications have gone through in *my* name."

"Have they?" Bash's voice was deceptively mild. "Last we spoke, you needed to provide some documentation to Legal in order to pass our internal reviews."

"A formality," Austin whispered, like he could feel the net closing on him. "I have the documentation."

"Of course you do," Bash agreed. "That's what you said. Which is why I asked IT to search all the files you've deleted in the last six months. Thank goodness for backups, right? Now, we will resolve *all* of this on Monday. But in the meantime, I will not tolerate another accusation against my date without proof. Understand?"

Bash's tone suggested there would be consequences if Austin did not.

"The MRO is my project. I've worked countless hours on it," Austin gritted out, his eyes still on me. "I've developed it into the market-ready program it is today—"

He sounded like a petulant child whose toys had been taken from him. Part of me wanted to be sympathetic—there had to be something broken inside him to have done such a terrible thing with no apparent remorse, right?—but I couldn't. Instead, I thought of how he'd stolen the story of Daisy's death and given that to Bash as his own. How he'd lied to Bash and was potentially conspiring with Justin Hardy behind Bash's back.

I didn't want him to have the opportunity to hurt Bash again.

"That doesn't sound like proof to me," I said softly.

Bash huffed out a startled laugh but didn't let go of my hand.

Constance Baxter-Hicks, who'd been watching the conversation like she was at a tennis match, pressed her lips together to hide a smirk. And Clarissa's wife tilted her head, presumably to hear better since she was furthest away from me.

Silas leaned in between Bash and me and spoke in a warning whisper. "Sebastian, stop this immediately. We're in public, for Christ's sake. And you've known Austin for years. Every report the board of directors has received shows that Austin's excelled in his role. Surely you'd take his word over... this person's." He tilted his head in my direction.

I glanced up at Silas in dismay. Had he been lying when he said he believed me?

"Thank you," Austin breathed, sitting back in his seat in relief. "Finally, a voice of reason."

Silas nodded. "But since I happen to know Landry's date is an Instagram influencer and this whole thing will be on his stories in an hour—"

All eyes swung toward Landry's date, who shrugged unapologetically over the top of his phone. "What? My followers want content."

"—you might as well tell us how you came up with the idea for Daisy Chain in the first place." Silas sounded bored and annoyed. "The last thing we need is rumors circulating that you were dishonest."

He directed this comment toward Bash, who gripped my hand but kept his gaze on the tabletop.

"As I already explained to Bash, Daisy Chain came about because someone dear to me died of commotio cordis, and I recognized a need," Austin said primly.

I sucked in a breath. Now I was the one squeezing Bash's hand. I'd been afraid I'd be thrown out of the gala for lying. Now, just a couple of weeks later, I was getting ready to be thrown out of an awards banquet for assault.

"Did you hear that, Bash? He came up with Daisy Chain because he lost someone. Very noble."

Austin nodded in satisfaction.

"Just one more question, Austin. When did you start calling Daisy Chain MRO?" Silas asked softly.

Silence descended on the table. I imagined only half of us understood the importance of what Silas had engineered—what Austin had admitted when he didn't challenge my name for the project, the connection he'd drawn—but even if they hadn't understood the words, there was no missing the expression of shocked guilt on Austin's face.

The tide had turned.

Silas had turned it.

"I... it... I didn't." Austin flushed pink, and his eyes looked panicked again. "I was confused. I was repeating what you said. I..."

"Save it. That might not be enough admission for a court of law, but it's plenty for me," Bash hissed. "Your employment at Sterling Chase is over, and you will *never* get your name on the patent for this project."

Austin's breath came in shallow pants. Like a gazelle surrounded by lions, his gaze pinged around, from unfriendly face to unfriendly face, and then to the phone Landry's date held. He inhaled sharply. "You know, Bash," he said, lowering his voice at last, "I don't believe you have the authority to fire me. You're just a member of the board, right?" He conjured up a smile that was half sneer. "Unless you're telling me you're *more* than just a board member? Silas, Landry, care to weigh in? Just how much power do you have?"

Bash froze, and I heard Silas suck in a small breath as he straightened.

As last-ditch efforts went, Austin's was devastating. For so long, Bash and his brotherhood had kept the truth of their relationship to the company hidden, not wanting to be publicly associated with ETC and the insane wealth it had brought them. But how well had they really guarded it if I'd figured it out in a matter of weeks? How many people, like Austin, had suspicions? Had Justin guessed when he was spending time with Silas? Had Constance, who seemed to know everything about everyone, ever wondered? How long could their lie stand if anyone had a reason to look?

Already, Clarissa's eyebrows furrowed as she glanced back and forth from Austin to Silas, to Landry, to Bash, and I could tell by Silas's angry stillness and Bash's slackened grip on my hand that both of them realized it.

Suddenly, the award announcer's voice caught everyone's attention. "And the winner of the Innovation Award for Food and Beverage Project Development goes to... Austin Purcell on behalf of Sterling Chase, for their work on the CaffApp!"

The audience applauded, and Austin laughed lightly, holding Bash's gaze as he stood, daring Bash to object, challenging him to make a scene that would end with Austin publicly questioning—in a room full of their peers—who owned Sterling Chase and had created ETC.

Bash and Silas exchanged a look with Landry. Being revealed as the owner of Sterling Chase and the inventor of ETC would change the course of his—and his friends'—future in ways I couldn't even comprehend. What privacy they had would be gone; Zane's music career would be overshadowed; shy Dev would be forced into a lime-light I instinctively knew he'd hate; and Bash would be hounded by every fledgling entrepreneur, every charity, every greedy soul he'd ever encountered, who'd treat the man like he was nothing more than a walking checkbook.

It was a bell that could not be un-rung, and I could tell by the helpless fury on their faces none of them were prepared. Tension thrummed through Bash's body, and he gave Austin a look that promised retribution, but he didn't protest when Austin waved and grinned, then began the long walk to the stage.

Anger surged in my gut, pulsed all the way through to my fingertips.

That smarmy, self-serving asshole thought he could go up there and claim a prize after he'd threatened the man I loved—a man who'd accepted me, cared for me, protected me, and helped me from the first moment we'd met? No.

No.

I'd stood helplessly by while too many things went wrong in my life. While too many risks went untaken. Not this time.

I pushed to my feet also. And for once, I didn't cower before the crowd of well-dressed socialites and industry executives. I did not babble, and I did not stammer.

Instead, I did what any self-respecting quirky billionaire would do when he had the honor of protecting the man he loved. I bent down, pressed a quick kiss to Bash's unsuspecting lips...

And lied my ass off.

TWENTY-TWO

BASH

"Thank you, Austin," Rowe called in his quirky billionaire voice, grinning forcefully. He buttoned his tuxedo and stepped around the table. "But you can step down now. There's no need for you to accept this award for Sterling Chase." He took a deep breath. "Sterling Chase can accept his own award."

In the stunned silence that followed, Rowe stalked to the center of the banquet hall with the same spark in his eye as when I'd met him at the gala—the one that had first drawn me to him and had kindled a fire inside me wilder than anything I'd ever believed I could experience.

It had left me speechless then. It left me speechless now.

Silas dropped into the seat Rowe had vacated without taking his eyes off the spectacle. "What the fuck is he doing?" he whispered.

"I think he's saving our asses," I whispered back. And he looked magnificent doing it. His spine was straight as an arrow, his shoulders thrown back. His curls gleamed under the lights, and his tux caressed every inch of his frame exactly the way I wanted to. Exactly the way I *would* once this shit-show was over.

"Jesus, Bash. Should we stop him?" Silas demanded.

I shook my head. I trusted Rowe. Trusted him with my secrets. With my company. With my heart. And just like the first night we'd met, every cell of my body hummed with energy, waiting to see what lie he came up with next.

Austin's eyes narrowed, but he tried to cover his anger with an uncomfortable chuckle. "Very funny, Rowe," he said into the microphone. He glanced around, inviting others to share the joke. "He's a burrito delivery guy, everyone, and he has a terrible sense of humor. Pay him no attention."

My fists clenched on the tabletop.

"I'm not joking, Austin." Rowe's voice rang with authority—enough to startle the MC, who snatched back the award he'd been about to hand to Austin and stepped away. "And you're the one who hasn't been paying attention. Sterling Chase invented ETC and founded this company with a mission to foster entrepreneurship around the world. To support education. To save lives. To make the world better. You don't *deserve* to accept this award on behalf of Sterling Chase."

Shocked whispers flew around the room.

Oh my god, I had no idea.

Karen, didn't I tell you there was something hinky like this?

I mean... he's young, but like, look at the youngest Kardashian, right?

Does he always talk about himself in the third person like that? Rich people are so extra.

Austin shook his head. "You're a fraud named Rowe Prince from Indiana, and I've never met you before tonight—"

Rowe shook his head sadly. "We met just last week, if you recall."

"Ohmigod! You carried the chicken burritos!" Irma, one of our account managers, cried before her coworkers could shush her. "I recognize you!"

Rowe nodded. "Yes, madam, that was I. Sterling Chase goes by many names and wears many hats. I've chosen to live a more simple life because I find it fosters my creativity without distraction. But it's also particularly handy when I want to observe my employees without calling attention to myself—"

"Ohhhh, fuck! He's like that guy from that show who does the thing," Landry's date gushed, snapping his fingers. "Yassss!"

"Bet that's one of his quirky billionaire eccentricities," Miranda Baxter-Hicks suggested to no one in particular. "Sterling Chase is a Renaissance man."

Rowe—*Sterling*—glanced over his shoulder and nodded gravely at her, accepting this praise. "Indeed, Miranda." He turned back to the podium. "And I'm sorry to say that you, Austin, have disappointed me greatly with your attitude." He clucked his tongue. "And your lack of scruples."

"There *is* no Sterling Chase!" Austin shouted into the microphone. "Everyone knows that."

Except everyone didn't. Rowe was the sort of person everyone wanted to believe could be the billionaire founder of a company—young and angelic, a little outrageous, and drop-dead gorgeous. It didn't matter what his real name was or where he came from. In fact, that would all add to the mystique. This audience *wanted* to believe.

When Austin looked around the room for allies, he found none. Even Clarissa was watching Rowe with surprise... but not a shred of suspicion. "My god," she breathed. "This explains so much."

"He's Sterling Chase, alright!" a woman near the door volunteered. "I worked the reception desk at the Coalition for Children gala just like I'm doing tonight and gave him his name tag. *And* he said he liked playing pranks on his friends!"

"Good god, of *course* he's Sterling Chase," Constance Baxter-Hicks said, managing to sound both imperious and incredibly weary of the conversation. "Why are we even discussing this? I've known the man for simply eons. I was friends with his mother back in Illinois—"

"Indiana," Miranda murmured.

"You know how bad I am with flyover states," Constance sighed. "In any case, Sterling and I are quite, *quite* close. In fact, I credit him for my new fashion evolution. We're having lunch at *Jean-Georges* next week. Bettina, dear, you'll join us, won't you?" She waved to a woman at a nearby table who looked delighted at the invite.

For the first time since he'd stood up, Rowe blinked uncertainly before he schooled his features back into his Sterling Chase expression and nodded politely.

I felt a brilliant smile break out on my face that I couldn't restrain. The man was impossibly talented. Incredibly dedicated. Genuinely himself, no matter who he was impersonating. And yet he still couldn't seem to wrap his head around how many people had fallen for him in such a short time.

Particularly *me*.

Constance winked at me, and I had only a second to marvel that Rowe had been right—the woman knew a lot more than she let on—before she said in a ringing voice, "Why not ask his boyfriend. Bash, darling, you're on the board of directors at Sterling's company, aren't you? Do clear up this confusion so we can move on to the dancing."

"I can't believe anyone would accuse Sterling Chase of lying," I said, rising to my feet and defying anyone to contradict me. "Sterling is the purest soul I've ever known and the greatest adventure I've ever encountered. That's what first drew me to him. That's what made me fall in love with him. It doesn't matter what name he goes by. Sterling Chase is the love of my life, and I'm proud to serve at his side for as long as he'll have me."

Over-the-top? Yes.

Cheesy romantic? Fuck, yes, and Landry's gleeful smile told me he was memorizing every word of "Big Daddy's" big love declaration so he could quote it back to me.

But I meant every damn word.

And when Rowe's big brown eyes went wide and shiny, when his lower lip trembled, then curved into the widest smile I'd ever seen, I didn't give a fuck who else was listening or what they thought.

Rowe pressed a hand to his heart, right over the pocket where only he and I knew he'd tucked a bunch of brightly colored scarves—a hint of magic, hidden just out of sight. "Sterling Chase loves you, too," he said softly, and I took a deep breath as something deep in my soul clicked into place like the dial on a telescope, shifting my whole future into focus.

Rowe turned to Austin. "The board of directors has been concerned about you for quite some time. We've set up a meeting for Monday. Ask any of them."

"Oh, yes," Silas said, his voice rumbling ominously. "I plan to be there, Sterling."

"Same," Landry agreed. "Even if I have to cancel my training session with French Alex."

I had no idea who Alex was, but Landry's date gasped, clearly impressed.

"But that's not— The entire board is made up of liars!" Austin insisted. "Bash and the other members aren't who they say they are. *They* are the ones who—"

"Please, Austin." Rowe held up a hand. "You're only making this worse for yourself. No one here wants to listen to your ramblings. I'm sure at this point there's nothing you wouldn't say or do to discredit me or the company, including lying about the board of directors."

I ran a hand over my mouth, trying to smooth away my smile. The irony was so, so sweet. Austin, the asshole who'd been lying for his own gain for months, was finally telling the truth... but no one would listen.

"It's not just me!" Austin insisted. "Justin knows! He's the one who told me. Justin!" He used his hand to shade his eyes from the bright lights in the room. "Justin, I know you're here! Come tell them what you told me about Sterling Chase."

I glanced over at the Hardy Development table, which I'd avoided looking at all night, and saw Justin Hardy looking red-faced and unhappy. Seated next to him was an attractive woman with intelligent eyes who looked eager to see what would happen next. I wondered idly if this was the woman he was supposedly marrying for her intellectual property and whether she knew what she was in for.

Justin shook his head like the Judas he was. "Austin, buddy, you must be mistaken. I have the highest respect for Sterling Chase. The company's been nothing but helpful to me in growing my business."

Though Silas hadn't so much as glanced at the Hardy table, I felt that seemingly innocuous comment hit him directly in the solar plexus, and he let out a shaky breath. After a beat, he turned to Landry's date and yanked the phone out of his hands. "Sorry, bro," he whispered, pocketing the video evidence of the drama.

"Jesus Christ, you're all so fucking *stupid*," Austin wailed, running his hands through his hair. "This guy is *nothing*, and he's manipulating you all—"

"Enough." I stood up from the table and moved to where Rowe stood in the middle of the banquet hall. As soon as I reached him, Rowe turned and pressed his face into my lapel. I wrapped my arm around his shoulder and kissed his unruly hair, inhaling just enough of his clean soap smell to make my fists unclench. "You've made a mockery of this event long enough, Austin. Everyone here tonight has seen exactly what kind of person you are, and they've seen who this man is, too. *This* is a man whose selflessness and loyalty are unparalleled. He's sacrificed years of his life to create Project Daisy Chain, a project that will revolutionize emergency response and make ETC look like just the beginning. And tonight, he sacrificed his privacy in an effort to protect this company. That is who Sterling Chase is. That's who Sterling Chase was always supposed to be. And you should never have been a part of it."

Exit music swelled, and the presenter yanked Austin off the stage with the help of two burly security guards. It took a while for the poor presenter to get the crowd under control enough to continue the awards ceremony, but by then, it didn't matter. I'd gotten my quirky billionaire out of the banquet hall and managed to find us a convenient potted palm just off the main lobby. I dragged him behind it and wrapped him up in my arms, right where he should have been all along.

"Oh, fuck. Holy shit." Rowe trembled slightly as the adrenaline coursed through his system. "We did it. Didn't we? I mean, that's it, right? You're safe?"

"We're safe," I confirmed. "Thanks to you. Austin's suspicions will be meaningless after this. And come Monday, he'll be reminded of the NDA he signed when he joined our company. He's done." I clasped him tighter until there wasn't a millimeter of air between our bodies. "But you and I aren't. Not by a long shot."

"Did you mean it?" Rowe demanded breathlessly. He wrapped his arms around my neck and stood on his tiptoes, peppering kisses over my face and neck, everywhere he could reach. "What you said back there?"

"The part where I said you were the love of my life? Where I said you were my greatest adventure? Where I said I planned to be by your side forever? Fuck, yes, all of it. And don't you dare make a liar out of me, Sterling Chase."

He laughed out loud and looked up at me, eyes shining with a kind of unconditional love I couldn't have purchased with all my billions, couldn't possibly have earned in the short time we'd known each other, but which Rowe had bestowed on me anyway... and I would do my best to deserve.

"I'm still scared, you know. I still have no clue what our future might look like... but I want it. This. *You.* I want to join your group chat and let you buy me ridiculous tuxedos. I want you to meet my mom and talk to me for hours about Daisy Chain or whatever project we dream up next. I want to make sure Silas never gets near your toaster again, and I want to spend some more time talking to Dev's horse. I want us to be *together.* Rowe and Bash. No matter which mega mansion we end up in."

"Wherever we live, you'll make it a home." I pressed a soft kiss to his head before moving my lips down to his ear. "Whatever Sterling Chase wants, he gets."

"And if Sterling Chase wants a fairy-tale ending?" he whispered, running his thumb over my cheekbone. "With a handsome prince, and true love forever, and the whole shebang?"

"Then I'd say we're halfway there." I grinned, feeling his body relax against mine as it began to move to the beginning of music coming from the other room. "Because I've found my Prince. And I could not love him more."

EPILOGUE
ROWE

"Babe, the estimated income to you from the sale of Daisy Chain is in the *billions*," Bash told me for the thousandth time. "Can you please tell Lea to find someone else to deliver burritos on your birthday? I'd like to take you out. Hell, I'd like to take you to the Caribbean, honestly. But I'd settle for a nice dinner here in the city."

He looked up from his phone with an accusatory glare.

Seeing him sitting at the rough wooden picnic table in my parents' backyard was still a mindfuck. I couldn't believe we were here in Linden. My parents seemed to like him, even though they took everything he said with a grain of salt. Apparently, rich folk from the big city were known as big talkers. *All husk and no kernel, if ya know what I mean,* my father had said with a knowing nod after Bash had bragged about how big Daisy Chain was going to be in the market.

I knuckle-punched Bash's arm. "Stop saying the word 'billions,' or I'm going to puke all over you. You know how that much money makes me feel."

It had been three months since the fiasco at the Innovation Awards. Three months since the Sterling Chase legal team had discovered clear evidence of Austin's conspiracy to commit fraud in three other projects at the company. It had been enough to negotiate a settlement along with his silence to ensure the company and its owners would be protected.

Thanks to the legal team's efforts, spearheaded energetically by Bash, we'd been able to move forward with Project Daisy Chain at lightning speed. I was thrilled with the result but completely overwhelmed by the realization of what it all meant for me personally.

My life as I'd known it had changed in the course of one summer. I'd gone from a dead-broke Burrito Bandito to a rich-as-god tech startup entrepreneur almost overnight. My parents didn't believe any of it. Bash had offered to fly them to New York to show them around the office and talk to them about the project's future, but they'd refused.

My father had claimed he couldn't take the time off work, and my mother admitted to not wanting to miss the summer craft fair season where she sold the handmade crocheted items she'd spent all winter making.

Instead, Bash had flown us to Linden. The plan was to spend a few days decompressing after our whirlwind visit to Wheaton, Illinois to enjoy the annual all-night flea-market Saturday night. I wasn't sure which part of the weekend had been the bigger culture shock for him—shopping for antique home furnishings while eating fried dough and listening to a Backstreet Boys tribute band, or meeting my parents and driving through Linden's single stoplight on the ride from the airport.

Either way, the shock didn't seem to faze him much. Bash was still determined to have me officially move in with him in the city, which was something of a joke since we hadn't spent a night apart since the original Hamptons trip.

During the summer, we'd spent almost every weekend at the Hamptons house, soaking up the sun, sand, and each other with more passion than I ever could have imagined. But since Bash had finally convinced me to take the interior design class I'd been eyeing for weeks and Constance Baxter-Hicks had a year's worth of design clients lined up for me, I had a feeling our lives were about to become much busier this fall. Knowing I'd come home to Bash each and every night to ground myself made all these big changes feel exciting rather than scary.

"Who told you about that shift?" I asked. "Are you texting with Joey?"

Bash nodded and tapped on his screen. "He said you'd promised him the use of the beach house during Labor Day weekend and that if he goes, you'll have to work his shifts." He looked up at me. "I thought he worked for that events place. Whatever happened to that job?"

I grabbed the phone out of his hand and typed out a message.

BASH

stop blabbing to my boyfriend.

JOEY

your boyfriend, my cousin? Blab about what?

I rolled my eyes.

BASH

this is Rowe. If you want me to work your Burrito shifts, you might not want to piss me off by getting all up in my shit.

JOEY

Sorry, bro. He wanted to plan a surprise thing for you. I had to tell him you were working.

I looked up at Bash. "You were planning a surprise for my birthday?"

Bash pursed his lips in annoyance and grabbed the phone back. "Give me that. Stop reading my messages."

"That's so sweet!" I began to climb into his lap to give him proper appreciation when my mom walked out of the house through the sliding doors. I scrambled back onto the bench. Bash snickered.

Mom set a plastic tray of brownies down on the table before handing Bash a tall glass of icy lemonade. "What's so sweet?"

"Thanks, Mrs. Prince." Bash smiled before taking a deep sip. "This hits the spot."

"Bash was going to plan a birthday surprise for me," I said. "But Joey ruined it."

Mom shook her head. "Typical Joseph. Takes after his father. Impulsive. Doesn't think before he acts."

Dad came out of the sliding glass doors and set a cold beer in front of Bash. "Because Laura isn't impulsive in the least, taking off on the back of a motorcycle when he came through town all those years ago. Pfft."

I looked at the noticeably empty area of the picnic table in front of me. "Where's my beer and lemonade?" I asked.

Mom lifted an eyebrow. "I would imagine it's in the kitchen where it lives."

Before I could stand up to go serve myself, Bash slid the beer over to me. "You take this one. I'm keeping a clear head for later."

"What's happening later?" Dad asked, pulling brownies out for each of us and setting them on paper napkins.

"I'm taking him on a tour of Linden," I said with a snort.

Mom let out a huff of laughter. "Don't blink, Sebastian, or you'll miss it."

Bash squeezed my leg. "He's taking me to meet Daisy. Would you two like to come with us?"

Mom's eyes filled, and she clapped a hand to her chest. "That's so sweet. Oh! He's a keeper, Rowe. What a sweet boy. And you should have seen how he reacted to seeing your portrait."

I whipped my head around mid-brownie-bite. "What portrait, Mother? What. Portrait." It hadn't been easy to convince my father to hide the embarrassing photos of me before we arrived home, but I'd done it.

At least, I'd thought so.

Bash's eyes danced while his mouth turned up in a cocky grin. "Li'l... diaper—"

I clapped a hand over his mouth and glared at my father. "You are a failure as a wingman. You are fired from any future winging. You have failed your son and heir, and this will not be forgotten."

Bash's arm came around me, and he managed to pull my hand away enough to whisper in my ear. "He sold it to me for a dollar. It's going over the fireplace in the penthouse."

If his voice in my ear didn't override all of my brain cells with *want* cells, I might have argued with him. Instead, I let out an embarrassing sound and inhaled the familiar scent of him. "Gotta go. We... gotta go..."

When I pulled away from Bash, my parents were howling with laughter. "Gotcha," Mom said, pointing at me. "You're so predictable."

When Dad finally caught his breath, he walked over and squeezed Bash's shoulder. "Thank you for including us, but we're going to let you boys go on your visit without us." He turned to me. "Be sure to drive him out past Luna Farms. There's something out there I want you to see."

"What is it?" I asked, standing up and gathering the napkin and crumbs from my brownie.

Dad shot Bash an enigmatic look. "You'll know it when you see it."

I grabbed Bash's hand and led him through the house and out to the driveway. "I think he wants me to introduce you to Apple Butter. Apparently, my father doesn't mind sending me to revisit childhood trauma."

Bash leaned over to press a kiss to my temple. "Poor baby. I was thinking we could buy Apple Butter so Starlight would have a friend."

My heart went all goopy when he used "we" like that. He was

doing it more and more lately, and it made me both nervous and excited for what our future held.

"You're a sentimental sap," I accused. "Sticky sweet and super sappy."

Before we reached my mom's minivan, Bash pulled me into his arms and smiled down at me. "You make me that way. Silas says it's disgusting. Zane thinks it's sweet. Dev still can't believe there's actually a soft side to me, and Landry hasn't said a word. He just struts around in a T-shirt that reads *the purest soul*. As if I needed reminders of my giant cheesy love declaration, considering I did it in front of two hundred industry peers."

"Wasn't cheesy," I said. "It was everything."

"You really are the purest soul," he murmured with a soft kiss.

"And Kenji?" I teased. I already knew Kenji was the leader of the Rowe Prince fan club. He'd started prioritizing all Daisy Chain tasks above Bash's other stuff and came to me for decisions now before involving Bash.

"Kenji's not allowed to speak your name aloud," he said, losing his smirk. "He's on P-Rowe-bation after having the audacity to tell me that he spent my Fake Sterling Chase Escape Fund money on Taylor Swift tickets for the two of you."

I stood on my tiptoes to kiss him. "You don't like Taylor Swift. Besides, there wasn't enough money in the fund for three tickets, and you know how much of a penny-pincher I am."

Bash's eyes widened. "Were the tickets that expensive? Jesus. Are they made out of diamonds?"

I nodded excitedly. "Front-row ones are. With backstage VIP passes and custom merch packs."

"Give him several billion," he mumbled, pinching my side and shoving me away from him, "and he thinks he's the freaking queen."

We hopped in the van and started the three-minute trek through town. I showed him my elementary school, the post office, the Depot Museum, the pizza place, and the church. When I pulled around to the cemetery, we got out and walked together through the wide-open space. The air was August-hot and heavy with humidity. When we finally arrived near the shade of a large tree, I let the peaceful surroundings ground me.

"There," I said softly, pointing to her large granite headstone. The town had come together to raise money for it, and it always made my parents proud with the memory of how many people had been affected by Daisy's death.

Bash knelt down and ran his hand across the shiny surface. "Elizabeth Daisy Prince," he read. "Beloved daughter, sister, and friend. And a heckuva ballplayer."

He let out a soft laugh and looked up at me. I shrugged. "What can I say? She was known for it. It's one of the things that helps me sleep at night. She died doing something she loved."

Bash closed his eyes for a few moments while the hot air moved past us in a gentle breeze. My sister wasn't there in that cemetery, but it was nice having a place to come to like this to remember and honor her.

When he opened his eyes, he still faced the stone. "You'd be so fucking proud of him, Daisy. His hard work and dedication is going to change the world. His idea is going to save lives. And... and I'm going to love him until the day he leaves this earth. I promise. If he'll let me..." His voice broke. The emotion was enough to bring me to my knees. "If he'll let me, I'll spend my life trying to make him happy."

I grabbed him and held him tightly, nearly knocking him into the freshly cut grass. His arms tightened around me. "I love you so much. I wish she was here so I could meet her. I hate that a part of you is missing."

I shook my head and pressed a kiss into the warm skin of his neck. "It's not. She's with me. She's been with me all along. And now I have you. I'm so fucking lucky. So thankful."

We stayed like that for several more moments before I decided it was time to go. Daisy wasn't here. And I could remember and honor her just as well on the beach in Southampton or at my favorite Indian place on West Fifty-Sixth Street.

"Time to meet Apple Butter," I said, wiping my face with shaking fingers. "Prepare thyself for an epic confrontation with evil."

Bash stood and laughed, grabbing my hand and squeezing. "I shall faithfully defend you from all the evil butters, apple or otherwise. I promise on my life."

We hopped back in the van and made a beeline to the ice cream shop for our second sugar snack of the afternoon. Once we were back in the van, I drove out past Luna Farm.

And saw a riot of daisies in full bloom all along the roadside for at least a mile. "What's this?" I murmured, slowing down and taking it all in. "There were never flowers here before."

Halfway down the long stream of flowers was a small wooden sign. I pulled over to get out and read it.

In glorious celebration of the memory of Daisy Prince and the life of Rowe Prince. ~ *The Brotherhood*

I looked back at Bash, who was ambling over more slowly, holding his phone up like he was taking a video. "The Brotherhood? *Your* brotherhood? That's the only broth—"

Bash nodded. "They're your brothers now, too. If you want. They wanted to make sure you knew that while they'll never take Daisy's place, they'd be honored to be your family now if you'll have them."

A tinny voice sounded from his phone. "Turn us around, dammit. We want to tell him ourselves."

I recognized the voice as Silas's. When Bash turned the phone around, five little windows appeared, each full of one of Bash's close friends.

"We love you, Rowe," they said in a jumble of voices. "Welcome to the family!"

I laughed through the tears that inevitably came roaring back at the incredibly kind and loving gesture. "Who says I want you assholes?" I asked with a watery sniff.

"Bash," Landry said. "Give the man a hankie. He's leaking all over."

Bash handed me the phone so he could pull something out of his pocket.

It was a green silk hankie. Connected to a yellow silk hankie. Connected to a red silk hankie...

And just like that, I knew I'd finally found my people. And especially, my very own prince.

———

What happens when Silas rushes to Vegas to stop his evil ex's wedding and accidentally ends up married to a (straight) stranger? Visit → https://readerlinks.com/l/4159323 to get your copy of Marrying Mr. Majestic...

And want to see what happens when Joey finally confronts the Sandwich Shark? Visit → https://www.subscribepage.com/polbonus for a bonus scene. It may or may not leave you with an ear worm. Don't say you weren't warned.

LETTER FROM LUCY

Dear Reader,

Thank you for reading ***Prince of Lies.***

I had so much fun writing Rowe and Bash's story! Some version of Bash has been living in my head since I started writing MM romance, and I've been so excited to bring him to life! Be sure to check out the bonus scene featuring Joey and the Sandwich Shark. It can be found here → https://readerlinks.com/l/4258162

You might have noticed I teased several other stories and characters in this book. I can't help myself. Up next is Silas' story, an accidentally-married-in-Vegas romance, and it's available now! You can grab it here → https://readerlinks.com/l/4159323

Be sure to follow me on your favorite retailer site to be notified of new releases, and look for me on Facebook for sneak peeks of upcoming stories. You can also join me on Patreon for exclusive content and behind the scenes glimpses.

Please take a moment to write a review of *Prince of Lies*. Reviews can make all the difference in helping a book show up in searches.

Feel free to stop by www.LucyLennox.com and drop me a line or visit me on social media. To see inspiration photographs for all of my novels, visit my Pinterest boards.

Finally, I have a fantastic reader group on Facebook. Come join us for exclusive content, early cover reveals, hot pics, and a whole lotta fun. Lucy's Lair can be found here → http://www.lucylennox.com/l/1437683

Happy reading!
Lucy

ABOUT LUCY LENNOX

Lucy Lennox is the USA Today bestselling author of over fifty gay romance titles including the GoodReads Hall of Fame winner Wilde Love. Born and raised in the southeast USA, she is finally putting good use to that English Lit degree she earned before the turn of the century.

Lucy enjoys naps, pizza, and procrastinating. She stays up way too late each night reading romance because it's simply the best.

For more information and to stay updated about future releases, sales and audio news and to grab some free and bonus reads, please sign up for Lucy's author newsletter on her website at LucyLennox.com or to stay in the know, join her exciting reader group, Lucy's Lair on Facebook.

facebook.com/lucylennoxmm

instagram.com/lucylennoxmm

amazon.com/Lucy-Lennox/e/Bo1NoIOYPT

bookbub.com/authors/lucy-lennox

patreon.com/lucylennox

pinterest.com/lucy_lennox

ALSO BY LUCY LENNOX

Find me online → https://linktr.ee/LucyLennox

Read my books:

Made Marian Series

Forever Wilde Series

Aster Valley Series

The Billionaire Brotherhood Series

After Oscar Series (with Molly Maddox)

Twist of Fate Series (with Sloane Kennedy)

Licking Thicket Series (with May Archer)

Champion Security Series (with May Archer)

Honeybridge Series (with May Archer)

Find a complete list of my stand alone romances and novellas at www.LucyLennox.com along with audio samples, freebies, suggested reading order, and more!

Made in United States
Orlando, FL
01 December 2024

54762237R00189